PRAETORIAN IV

***

Lions of Rome

by S. J. A. Turney

For Kate and her gladiator

Good friends and colleagues

Published in this format 2018 by Mulcahy Books

First Edition

Also by S. J. A. Turney:

The Praetorian Series

The Great Game (2015)
The Price of Treason (2015)
Eagles of Dacia (2017)

The Damned Emperors (as Simon Turney)

Caligula (2018)
Commodus (2019)

The Marius' Mules Series

Marius' Mules I: The Invasion of Gaul (2009)
Marius' Mules II: The Belgae (2010)
Marius' Mules III: Gallia Invicta (2011)
Marius' Mules IV: Conspiracy of Eagles (2012)
Marius' Mules V: Hades' Gate (2013)
Marius' Mules VI: Caesar's Vow (2014)
Marius' Mules: Prelude to War (2014)
Marius' Mules VII: The Great Revolt (2014)
Marius' Mules VIII: Sons of Taranis (2015)
Marius' Mules IX: Pax Gallica (2016)
Marius' Mules X: Fields of Mars (2017)
Marius' Mules XI: Tides of War (2018)

The Ottoman Cycle

The Thief's Tale (2013)
The Priest's Tale (2013)
The Assassin's Tale (2014)
The Pasha's Tale (2015)

Tales of the Empire

Interregnum (2009)

Ironroot (2010)
Dark Empress (2011)
Insurgency (2016)
Emperor's Bane (2016)
Invasion (2017)
Jade Empire (2018)

The Templar Series

Daughter of War (2018)
The Last Emir (2018)

Roman Adventures (for children)

Crocodile Legion (2016)
Pirate Legion (2017)

Short story compilations & contributions:

Tales of Ancient Rome vol. 1 - S.J.A. Turney (2011)
Tortured Hearts vol 1 - Various (2012)
Tortured Hearts vol 2 - Various (2012)
Temporal Tales - Various (2013)
A Year of Ravens - Various (2015)
A Song of War – Various (2016)

For more information visit http://www.sjaturney.co.uk/
or http://www.facebook.com/SJATurney
or follow Simon on Twitter @SJATurney

Simon is represented by Mulcahy Associates of London.

Maps

ROME
190 AD

1 Castra Praetoria
2 Vicus Longus bars
3 Private bathhouse
4 Dionysus' house
5 Curtius' house
6 Rufinus' house
7 Castrum Misenatum
8 Flavian amphitheatre
9 Forum
10 Tabularium
11 Soldiers' bars
12 Circus Maximus
13 Statio Annonae
14 Temple of Diana
15 Emporium
16 Horrea Galbana
17 Warehouse of Zela
18 Horrea Ummidiana
19 Porta Raudusculana
20 Porta Naevia

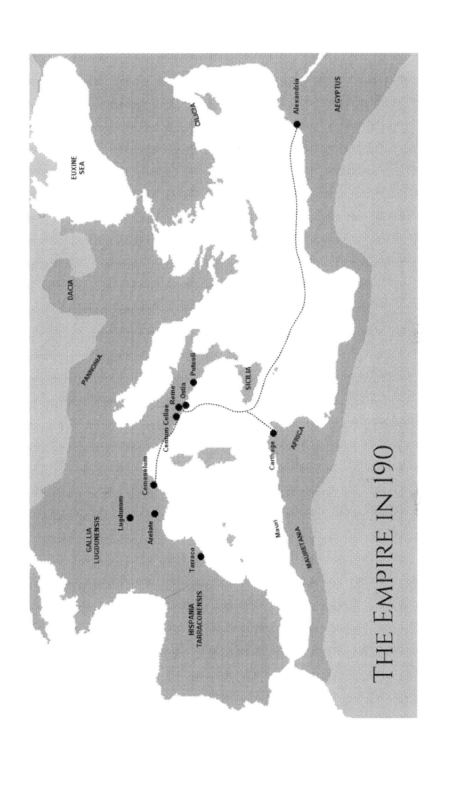

THE EMPIRE IN 190

PART ONE

THE LION'S PRIDE

"OMNIUM RERUM PRINCIPIA PARVA SUNT"

(THE BEGINNINGS OF ALL THINGS ARE SMALL.)

- MARCUS TULLIUS CICERO

CHAPTER ONE – NOVO HOMUS

Lugdunum, March 187 A.D.

Rufinus paused in the doorway and took a deep breath of the spring air which still contained a chill and was loaded with the scent of rain. He had spent the past three days in the townhouse of the governor with all its accoutrements of luxury and glory and had felt no real need to step outside into the real, and very dangerous, world. But things were beginning to move, and this morning's message had pushed them along a great deal.

He scratched his chin irritably and frowned. Rufinus had grown a beard three times in his life prior to this and each time had been a matter of simply being on campaign and not finding the time, energy and tools to shave. For sixty or seventy years now, since the days of Hadrian, who had only grown his own fuzz to hide his scars, beards had become steadily more popular. They were the growing trend for decades and had, by now, become the norm. Rufinus hated growing a beard, though. On the cheeks it was alright, but only until you could grip it between finger and thumb and then it had to go. On the chin was horrible and felt like some sort of animal was clinging on to your lower face. The moustache continually interfered with eating, drinking and any other mouth-centred habit. And as for the neck… he shivered.

And yet over the preceding months he had grown a beard almost to match that of Severus himself, bushy, curly, and thick enough to lose a squirrel in. It was irritating and itchy and awful, and he hated it, but it *was* fashionable. He had also grown out his hair into a short mane of shaggy locks that made him feel like he ought to be bouncing around the arena on all fours and trying to eat criminals. It was almost too much to bear, and it made him twitch almost as much as it made him itch...

But he would be the first to admit that he was unrecognisable.

And that was the point.

Because Gnaeus Marcius Rustius Rufinus was dead. He had died at the bottom of a cliff in the wilds of Dacia the previous year, and reports of his demise would have reached Rome within months, witnessed by Daizus, who would have reported to Clodius Albinus or Pescennius Niger. Either of those would have sent the dispatch to the capital, given that Cleander had sent him to Dacia, and no one could afford to fail to update the chamberlain. Cleander knew that Rufinus was dead, and with that came a strange freedom, albeit one that required a great deal of ongoing subterfuge.

Rufinus, still recovering from his wounds and accompanied by Senova and Acheron, had stayed with Septimius Severus after their meeting in Athens, travelling east to exotic Syria where the governor had become betrothed to the lady Julia Domna, a beguiling eastern aristocrat. They had dallied there until the end of winter when the marriage proposal was accepted by her father and then they had returned to Lugdunum, of which Severus was propraetorian governor.

The time in the east had given Rufinus the opportunity to heal fully and to recover his wits. At the behest of Severus he had begun to go by the name Aulus Triarius Rufinus, and Senova was now Julia Triaria, his wife. Acheron had been kept as far from the public eye as possible, for the sake of secrecy. Rufinus had questioned the use of his own name as part of his new guise, but Severus had been insistent that it was better to have a name that he would find it natural to answer to than some strange new moniker he would constantly forget. And it was not as though he had been the only Rufinus even in the capital, after all.

And so the old Rufinus began to be forgotten while Aulus Triarius Rufinus surfaced in the east as one of Severus' *comites* – his circle of trusted friends. He had begun to grow the beard and hair out there where such a fashion was very much the rage and somehow, through a network of contacts and via his own administration in Lugdunum, by the time the party returned from the east a few weeks ago, Aulus Rufinus was recognised by the Roman bureaucracy, owned land and estates in Italia and Gaul, had served in various lower administrative and military posts in Africa, Gaul and in the Fourth Scythica, all of which had at the time been under the direct control of Severus. Somehow, using his own records, his past and his contacts, Severus had created an entirely new Rufinus who even the fussiest clerk in the tabularium would recognise as authentic.

Senova had taken to the ruse with gusto, dyeing her hair with saffron and henna to a rich auburn, applying makeup for the first time Rufinus knew of, which somewhat changed her appearance, and not necessarily for the worse despite her natural good looks. Her mode of dress shifted up to that of a Roman noblewoman, with accoutrements to match. In fact, to Rufinus' mind she was enjoying the whole thing far too much, for when this was over, she would just be Senova once again, and her husband would be just a Praetorian soldier with a shaky record. But Acheron? Acheron was the only real hiccup in the plan.

Rufinus had not been without the big black hound now for more than half a decade, or at least not for any length of time. He was aware that the great beast was getting older now, but he was still a powerful dog and in rude health, and he was hopelessly attached to Rufinus, suspicious of most others. Yet he was also a talking point, and finding him in the company of the his owner would almost certainly crack or smash Rufinus' guise. Thus Acheron had, for now, become Severus' dog. At least the governor was one of the remarkably few people Acheron accepted, though the servants and slaves who were given the jobs of feeding, washing and walking him did so with great care and trepidation.

Rufinus' hand slipped down to the pouch at his belt that still held the message that had arrived by courier this morning. Sealed with the sign of the Castra Peregrina, Rufinus had opened it with a level of tense excitement, knowing the frumentarius Vibius Cestius to be its author. He felt assured it would be news of import, for Cestius was not a man given to inanities, but he still had not been prepared for its tidings.

His brother Publius had been released. After more than a year in the clutches of Cleander, a political prisoner in a gilded cage, Publius had been sent out into the world, free of interference and control. More than that, Rufinus' father had come to Rome, the two had spent a short while together, before Publius had taken ship for Tarraco in Hispania, the family's old estate, favoured for their timely exile.

The knowledge that Publius was free was an immense weight lifted from Rufinus' shoulders, though he knew his father for a meddling fool, and no good could come from the pair of them having been together. Still, it was better news than he could have anticipated. And for the first time since they had landed three weeks ago, dressed in noble finery and with a beard that looked like a well-pruned shrub, Rufinus had left the governor's mansion and emerged into the city. Somewhere in the low town called Condate across the river, the governor's major domo had told him, was a shop that sold the best wine to be found in all of Gaul. Despite his lofty role, Severus' tastes in wine were those of a soldier, and his favoured jar resembled poor vinegar to Rufinus' palate. He wanted to celebrate Publius' freedom, and so he would purchase the best jar of wine he could find and tonight he would drink it with Senova... *err, Julia...* while Severus quaffed his vinegar.

Patting the pouch containing the note, he set off with an unexpected spring in his step, nodding to the two soldiers on detached duty from the Eighth Augusta as the governor's guard. This being his first time out of the complex as Aulus, he had considered taking a bodyguard as was the norm with the well-to-do, but had decided against it. A man on his own raises fewer glances than a man with an escort in any circumstances.

Enjoying the freshness of the air and hoping that the promised drizzle would hold off until his return, Rufinus strode along the street, smiling at the various other folk he passed, crossed the grand façade of the theatre and turned, beginning the descent of the steep road that led down to the bridge and the more commercial old town. His senses alert, he was pleased to note that he was raising little more than passing interest from anyone, which was as good as he could hope. This was, after all, his first real test of his new identity, barring those days in the company of the governor in the east.

The street that cut down the steep hillside to the river and the grand stone bridge was vertiginous in places, and the rut in the centre that had been formed as a guide for the braking poles of carts was deep and well-used. For a strange moment, Rufinus was transported back to that day he had first signed on to guard the villa of the treacherous empress Lucilla, when the cart carrying the new recruits from Tibur had careered down a similar slope on the way to the country estate.

That had ended well. And badly, in a way.

As he strolled, casually with apparently not a care in the world, something nagged at him. Years of growing caution and intrigues that had honed his senses and reactions took control. He couldn't quite say what it was that had grabbed his attention, but he needed to find out. Something was prickling the hairs at his neck.

Very casually, he started to affect a light hobble, cursing and glaring down at his foot. With a heavy sigh, he crossed the pavement to where a heavy stone block sat, carved with an inscription naming the man who'd had the road paved. He sat on the stone heavily and reached down to his boot. As he did so, he subtly picked up a small stone from among the debris below the block, and held it tight as he unlaced and removed his boot. He then held the boot at head level and tipped it up, letting the pebble fall as though it had come from his footwear.

For just that moment his eyes scanned the entire roadway and landed on the source of his discomfort. He knew in an instant why he had felt the strange worry, even as he bent to his boot, slipping it back on and lacing it once more.

A man. A very ordinary man in an ordinary brown tunic with ordinary sandals and an ordinary beard and hair. He carried a basket with some sort of bread and provisions. He was no different from any of the other folk in this street, but for one thing.

He had been across the road, reading a sign on the wall, when Rufinus had emerged from the house. Logic told Rufinus that any ordinary man could easily be there and then here too. Rufinus had reason to be in both places, so why not this man? But logic could go hang. There was an answer to that. Rufinus was in no hurry and was enjoying his first walk out in Lugdunum. He had ambled slowly on his journey, with no timetable to keep to. This man, though, was carrying provisions. He was, therefore, a man with a purpose and times to keep. While he could easily stroll at Rufinus' pace, it was unlikely that a man in his position would be as slow as Rufinus and that very simple fact had set off the alarm in his head.

The man was following him.

He made sure to sit and be slow tying his lace so that the brown-clad man sauntered past him. He was good. Not once did he look directly at Rufinus as he passed. But again even there he had failed, given the years of training in intrigue Rufinus had undergone. Other folk in the street naturally glanced over at the wealthy fellow sitting on the stone and holding his boot as he cursed. It was normal to be interested in such things. But the man in brown had not even glanced as he passed, so intent was he on not being noticed.

Standing and ostensibly testing the boot to make sure the stone was gone, Rufinus set off once more. Now, just to add a little conspicuousness to himself, he began to whistle a tune that he had heard often in the court in Syria.

What to do about the man. First of all, of course, he had to be certain. He was, anyway, but even Severus, suspicious as he was, would worry that Rufinus was grasping at straws without any further proof. Well, the moment he was certain, he would have to confront the man. Somewhere private.

His gaze now began to scour his surroundings, logging anything and anywhere that might be of use. The man in brown was a little ahead. Rufinus was just beginning to doubt himself when the man slipped on the rut in the centre of the road and flailed, a round loaf of bread wrapped in cloth falling from the basket. The man cursed and stopped, rubbing his sore ankle and gathering his fallen provisions. Rufinus had to force himself not to smile as he once more passed the brown man and became quarry rather than hunter.

The man *was* good. Not as good as Rufinus, but better than most.

He was sure now. The man was watching him. But the question of why remained unresolved. He had been picked up at the governor's residence. While it was possible that the man had been waiting for him, it was at least equally possible he was watching the whole residence and had just selected Rufinus because of his mode of dress and interest value.

He had to know. Everything was just too damn dangerous at the moment to leave anything to chance. Eyes taking in everything, Rufinus reached the bottom of the hill and entered the small suburb by the river. He could smell the port off to his left with its refuse and endless fish deliveries, and he could smell the tanneries and fullers nearby. No wonder anyone with money lived on the hill. He could just see the top of the amphitheatre from here, above the roofs of Condate on the far bank, but he wouldn't cross the bridge. Condate was reputedly a thriving mercantile place and it would be more difficult to find anywhere appropriate over there. Rounding the bend in the street Rufinus could see the bridge ahead. The bulk of humanity on this street was passing across that bridge in one direction or another, most of the rest turning along the river front and making for the port.

Rufinus settled on a decision. There were four streets between here and the river. He began to slow at the first, making a show of squinting at the street name on the brick wall. Shaking his head, he moved on. He was looking for an address, as far as any observer would guess. He moved on to the next side street and peered at the sign though in truth he was paying much more attention to his peripheral vision. Perfect. This was the place.

With a smile, as though he had found the street name he sought, he turned down it, not once looking back to alert the man following him that he was aware of the presence. This side street had what he needed. It was all-but deserted, with only a few slaves bearing trolleys of goods. It was also noisy and busy in the background, with the sound of industry only overwhelmed by the smell of it. Despite that, there were a few small shops built into the street frontages, and here and there were alleys and entrances to yards.

He strode now down this new street, his gaze moving from shop to shop as he came to them. These were not really stores to serve the majority of the public, who would visit the tabernac in the heart of town. These were shops that served the local industries. Not well visited. Quiet. And he was, to the casual observer, looking for a specific one of them.

Taking a chance, just to be sure, he stopped at an alley and scratched his head, peering down it. Out of the corner of his eye, he saw the man in the brown tunic stop at a shop front and pick something up to examine it. Satisfied once more Rufinus moved on, looking into the next alley. None of the alleyways were large enough to be of use – if this came to a fight he would need space to do it right. He sighed. It would have to be somewhere more open, then.

The next gap on his left opened into a fuller's, as Rufinus' nostrils already told him. As he approached, he saw a man in a good blue tunic with nice boots emerge, a clerk with a tablet and stilus beside him, writing as they walked. The man, presumably some sort of overseer, wandered off down the street, and Rufinus made the decision there and then.

He turned into the fuller's and as he entered immediately stepped left behind the wall. His eyes once more took in the scene. A thug with a club stood across the other side, constituting the main security of the business. Two freedmen moved around the place, snapping orders at the workers. The rest of the population were poor slaves in one of the less favourable destinations slavery could take you: treading the wool in the vats of urine to remove the impurities.

The whole place smelled as bad as any latrine Rufinus had ever used, and his nose hairs were curling as he breathed. One of the freedmen gave an alarmed call, and the bruiser with the club started to move purposefully around the edge, heading towards Rufinus, waving.

It all happened before the man could do anything about it, though.

Brown-tunic ducked his head in through the entrance. He had been astute enough not to just walk in, but had not quite reckoned on Rufinus being right next to the entrance and ready for him. The Praetorian's big arm slipped around his pursuers neck and pulled him in. The basket of comestibles fell away, bounced and ended up in a vat of piss, being trodden in by a slave who complained and yelped at the obstruction.

The man struggled, taken by surprise, but Rufinus was not going to give him time to recover. Spinning him, he released his grip and as the man reeled, trying to regain his wits, Rufinus gave him a solid jab to the sternum, not hard enough to crack it but plenty strong enough to cause pain. He followed up with a punch to the gut that winded the man in the brown shirt, who staggered backwards, gasping. The man reached the edge of one of the urine vats, whose occupant scrambled out and ran away. He teetered there for a moment, about to fall into the murk, and Rufinus grabbed hold of his tunic, holding him up.

'Here, what's this?' snarled the security guard, approaching with a brandished club. He was undecided as to what to do with this interloper and his victim. His orders would largely be to keep the slaves in line, and smacking a noble on the head with a club without finding out why he was there first could be a terrible career move for any man.

'This is a private matter,' Rufinus replied, without taking his eyes off the man in his grip. 'Go about your business and forget that this happened and there will be enough denarii in it for you and your friends over there to keep you drunk for a week.'

Threats would have done nothing with a man like that, and demands would probably rile him, but bribery was a whole different matter. The club man narrowed his eyes for a moment, glanced across at the nearest freedman, who nodded, and then smiled.

'Didn't see a thing, mister.'

A moment later he had turned his back and was wandering over to his favourite spot.

Rufinus still hadn't taken his eyes off the stunned and winded man in his grip. A movement in his peripheral vision drew his attention as the teetering man reached down. Rufinus' free hand batted his questing fingers out of the way, felt around the man's hip, found the concealed knife and removed it. Holding it in a threatening fashion, he gently shook the man.

'Who sent you?'

'What? I don't... I don't know what you... mean. I work for Tiberius Meno. Shipping man.'

'Bollocks. Who were you watching. What's your brief?'

'Tiberius Meno. He owns...'

Rufinus dropped the knife tip towards the man's groin, drawing widened eyes. 'If you say Tiberius Meno again I'm going to change your religion.'

'I...'

'The chamberlain?'

'No. What chamberlain? No.'

'Who sent you. The truth.'

'Fuck you.'

Rufinus let go. The man yelped as he fell back, but Rufinus caught him again only a foot lower. 'I can get very nasty. I've had a lot of practise at it.' He lifted the knife so that the man could see the scarred hand gripping it, with the smooth, strange finger ends, devoid of nails. The man gulped.

'Tribune. Tribune sent me.'

'What sort of tribune. Give me a name.'

'Praetorian. Appius Fulvius.'

Praetorians. And whoever this tribune was, his ultimate master these days would be Cleander, whatever this man thought.

'And what are you to do?'

'Just watching the governor. Standard practise.'

Rufinus gave him a nasty grin. 'That's not standard practice for the Guard. I happen to know that.'

A weary sadness flowed over him. He was going to have to finish the man. Whatever his duties might have been, he had now seen Rufinus. It would not take long to place him, despite the beard, given his injuries. And then everything would start to unravel. But it was not in his nature to kill a man in cold blood. He tried not to think of Scopius in the aqueduct. That was different. It had been personal. But this would simply be expediency. Damn it.

He learned to his cost that he had dithered too long. The Praetorian in his grip had clearly recovered both wits and wind, and had moved his hand again unnoticed as Rufinus wrestled with his conscience. A second knife appeared from somewhere and sliced through the air. Rufinus let go and lurched backwards, his instant reaction the only thing that saved his life, else the sharp blade would have neatly sliced his throat from side to side. In the event all he suffered was a slight nick on the chin that began to bleed.

As he lurched, the Praetorian in brown hit the pool of urine with a cry, piss splashing up in a wave that slopped over all sides of the vat. The man's shout was cut off with a watery gurgle as the vat's contents washed over him, filling his mouth. He rose like some latrine demon, coughing and gaging, cursing and blinking away the stinking liquid, still brandishing the knife.

Rufinus punched him. It was not a carefully placed, planned boxing move. It didn't really need to be with the man half-blinded, choking and swaying. It was a simple right hook to the man's face that broke his nose and pulled the wits from him once more. He fell again with another splash and this time Rufinus cursed as the urine soaked his boot.

The man had to be finished, but at least now Rufinus felt a little better about it. This was far from an innocent man, and he embodied, to Rufinus, everything that was wrong with the Praetorian Guard these days. He glanced for a moment at the knife in his hand and decided against it, letting that go to fall into the vat along with its owner. The authorities would have to be notified of the body eventually, and knife wounds would demand a thorough investigation. But a man who had apparently fallen into a vat of piss, hit his head and drowned? That was nice and easily wrapped up for any Urban Cohort, and they could tick all the boxes and be in the tavern for drinks without having to go through any inconvenient real work.

Rufinus crouched, not wanting to kneel in what was all over the floor, and reached out with a strong hand, grabbing the tunic at the man's neck and pushing him back down into the vat. He squawked and then disappeared beneath the surface. For a few unpleasant moments he thrashed and kicked and then paused, jerked a few more times, and then finally fell still.

Rufinus held him there a minute longer, just in case, and then lifted him, committing his face to memory, just in case. As he did so, a chain fell out of the man's tunic neck, and Rufinus noted the bronze scorpion hanging on it. So they were taking to wearing the symbol like that now? With a jerk, he pulled the pendant, snapping the chain. The body fell back and splashed into the vat once more and Rufinus rose with his prize. He strode over towards the thug with the club, whose whole life was spent amid this horrible stuff and who had no qualms about taking a good sum of money from the stranger's urine soaked hand. Rufinus paid him handsomely.

'A little extra for the mess,' he explained.

He left the fuller's, smiling at the security man's face as he worked through how he was going to explain a drowned man with two knives in one of the vats. He would do it. For that amount of money, Rufinus was sure of it.

He took a different route home, all thoughts of wine purchase gone from his mind. Marching on to the end of the street, trailing the reek of the fuller's with him as he went, he turned a corner and made for the western end of the port, where a less imposing street ran up the slope to the high city, the almost sole province of workmen and teamsters. This he climbed, raising horrified faces from even the poor and the enslaved at the smell he emitted. At the top, he hurried back to the governor's palace.

The two soldiers from the Eighth on guard at the door stared at him as he approached. He was well enough known to them that they admitted him without incident, but as the door closed, Rufinus heard the brief explosion of laughter before the portal shut with a click.

He moved through the house, raising startled astonishment and gagging noises from everyone he encountered and finally found Severus in his office. The great leonine governor with the swarthy skin and dark eyes looked up from his desk as Rufinus entered, and his brow creased.

'Where did you acquire that smell?'

Rufinus cast the broken chain with the scorpion pendant onto the table, where it landed with a clink. 'You are being watched by Praetorians, probably on Cleander's orders. For now they have two eyes less on you, but I'll bet there are more in the city yet.'

Severus frowned and lifted the pendant with his stilus, unwilling to touch it, peering at the design.

'Cleander is casting his net ever wider. Did you clear up after yourself?'

'Some poor bastard tripped into a fuller's vat, banged his head and drowned in piss,' Rufinus replied. 'Or at least I believe that's the way it'll be recorded by the time the report reaches your desk.'

'Good. I have news and was planning on a working lunch with you and a few others. I whole-heartedly recommend you visit the bath house first, though. I suspect the wine will go off with just being near you.'

Rufinus gave him a sour look. 'I need to take some time off.'

'You've barely started,' noted Severus. 'But as it happens I have a new appointment for you anyway. You can squeeze in a visit to your brother before you begin.'

Rufinus frowned. He'd long since given up being surprised when Severus knew things before he had any right to. As long as he was on your side that was all to the good. 'New appointment?'

Severus nodded. 'Aulus Triarius Rufinus, you are hereby appointed Prefect of the Misenum fleet by order of the emperor, ratified by consent of the senate.'

Rufinus stared as Severus lifted a scroll case bearing the imperial seal, made to pass it over, then thought again and replaced it. 'Perhaps you can read it *after* your bath.'

'Prefect of the fleet?'

'The *Praetorian* fleet,' corrected Severus.

'But I'm... I'm nobody. I don't even really exist.'

'Oh, you have an *illustrious* family history, young prefect. In fact, your father and I served together years ago.'

'But he doesn't exist either.'

'Please don't go letting logic get in the way out our work, Rufinus. The fact is that there are very few positions of import that are not appointed or ratified by Cleander these days. Prefect of the fleet just happens to be one that he has not got his claws into yet. And I like the idea of having fast ships at our command should we need them. We are beginning our great task now, Rufinus. All must be put in place in preparation. So go visit your villa in Hispania and see your brother, but make sure he does not drop your continuing existence into conversation with anyone. And then, when you're done, don't come back here. I shall send your wife and your dog to the safe house in Cemenelum, and you must head from Hispania straight to Misenum, where you will need to present yourself to your subordinates. I will leave messages for you there. Good luck.'

Rufinus continued to stand for a long moment, slack-jawed, staring at the appointment orders, which was clearly what the scroll case contained. Prefect of the fleet?

Today was just full of surprises…

CHAPTER TWO – VILLA MARCIA

Tarraco, Hispania, April 187 A.D.

Rufinus paused at the twin lines of Cypress trees that marked the start of the white, chalky drive leading up to the villa. The tension he had felt throughout the trip from Massilia, combined with the strange excitement of seeing Publius again, was now building exponentially as he approached the journey's end. He felt a frisson across his skin, prickling the flesh and raising the hairs.

'Wait,' murmured one of the four escorts that had accompanied him all the way from Lugdunum, and made a few gestures to his companions. Rufinus' eyes narrowed with suspicion. Ostensibly they were four ordinary veteran legionaries from the Eighth Augusta, assigned by Severus. And they were definitely experienced fighting men. But they appeared brighter than your average legionary and a lot quieter, more agile and more subtle. There was no way to tell for sure, and the men had snorted derisively when he'd mentioned the subject, but he'd be willing to place a good wager that at least one of them was actually a member of the frumentarii – that secretive subsection of the army that moved about within the forces, acting as the eyes and the ears – *and sometimes the knife* – of the emperor. They certainly had that same inscrutable professionalism he'd come to expect based on his experience with Dis and Vibius Cestius. Still, if they *were* frumentarii, that only made them likely *more* trustworthy, for they would die for the emperor and owed no loyalty to Cleander whatsoever. Something that once upon a time could have been said for the Praetorians.

Rufinus held up a hand to object, but the soldier shook his head. 'There's no point in having a guard if we're not permitted to guard you. And you might not be one of the Eighth, sir, but you're Prefect of the Fleet now. It doesn't do for a gentleman of your rank to get down and dirty with bruised knuckles.'

Bruised knuckles? Did the man know Rufinus was a boxer, and if so how, given that he wasn't that man any more. They had *to be frumentarii.*

'I trust your judgement,' he replied, levelly, 'but I also know this villa and its estate like the back of my own hand. Two of you peel off left. There's a side path about three hundred paces down the drive that leads to a small industrial complex with a wine press. From there you can follow the vegetation at the edge of the vineyards and almost reach the house itself unnoticed. Don't go inside without me.' He turned to the others. 'You two come with me. When I pass through the gate, I'll be visible from almost all angles. That should draw anyone out. You can follow the perimeter wall and deal with them, alright? I promise I'll try not to get into a sword fight.'

The men looked neither convinced nor approving, but all nodded their consent anyway. The small five-man party moved on down the path between the lines of neat cypresses and their leader's gaze remained on the distant shape of the main structure. The villa. Rufinus hadn't been here since that day he and his father had argued and called one another unspeakable things that could never be unsaid.

He had left the villa a young man, still green and untried. He had been wealthy and privileged, well-educated and expected to climb the cursus honorum in appropriate stages, beginning his career with a lengthy sinecure as a tribune in one of the legions. He had the best clothes, the best wine, the best oratorical tone. All this was limited, of course, to the confines of Hispania. The governor there was sympathetic to the family's plight, and could still secure Rufinus such positions, but their influence in Rome had evaporated like a spring's morning mist. Still, for an unpopular family in self-imposed exile, he could still have risen to perhaps a quaestor's role, for they might be exiled, but they were still of good blood.

Instead, he had left under a cloud with nothing but his good clothes, a few days' worth of food, his sword and a large bag of coins, and had marched off and signed on as a recruit at the lowly rank of soldier in a legion where he could have been one of the six most senior officers.

And here he was coming back, very different and almost unrecognisable. Now he was a prefect, a rank usually gifted to the equestrian class and not his own patrician blood, yet with impressive power and influence. He was no young and naïve scion now; he was scarred and weary, and not a little bit wily along with it. He wore only a drab tunic and breeches beneath a waxed *caracalla* – a Gallic military-style cloak.

At the side path he'd spoken of the two soldiers separated, trotting off towards the collection of tile-roofed buildings where the estate workers processed the harvest and began the production of the villa's wine. Casting his mind back to the tent mates with whom had endured the wars against the Marcomanni in the snowy north, he could hardly imagine that lot of farting bruisers sneaking around like this and engaging in skullduggery and observation. They'd all been brave and good with a sword, but half of them wouldn't have noticed if Jove himself had trodden on them, unlike Rufinus' escort.

These four men *had* to be something different…

He moved on with the other two. As they approached the villa's own surrounding wall, just a three-foot defining barrier of brick with grey capstones, he nodded at the two riders and they dismounted, tethering their horses, and peeled off heading both left and right, disappearing among the rows of vines. The plants were only at the start of their annual cycle, budding and low, pruned and neat, and the two men moved low at a crouch, surprisingly quiet and barely visible half a field away.

Rufinus put his hand to his sword hilt. He wouldn't draw it, but it felt better to be ready, just in case. There was every possibility that the villa was clear, yet he felt oddly certain that eyes would be on it. Unfriendly eyes. Cleander was sharp, if nothing else, after all. He might have let Publius go, believing Rufinus to be dead at the base of a cliff at the edge of the empire, but he would not be so overconfident that he would not keep tabs on the youngest of the Marcii.

No, there would be watchers.

Playing the open, honest, above-board bait, Rufinus rode towards the decorative arch. The family might have been away for some time now, his father in Rome trying to rebuild their influence, but the slaves had maintained the place well in their absence.

The thought of slaves drew him back to a mental image of his captivating better half, Claudia Senova, who remained in Gaul in a villa owned by one of Septimius Severus' most trusted clients. Of course she was a slave no longer, but a freedwoman. More than that, since Rufinus had purchased a ring in Emesa and offered it to her, they were betrothed. It wasn't entirely official, of course. Both of them were under assumed names, and he felt also that he ought really to seek the permission of Pompeianus, being her benefactor and the man who had freed her, before it could be announced. But all of that would have to wait anyway. When Cleander was no more, and Rufinus could be himself once more, the whole thing would become official, and Senova would be his in the eyes of all of Rome.

More realistically, he thought with a wry smile, *he* would be *hers*.

He walked his steed in through the gate, making for the door at a sedate pace. His eyes were fixed on the building ahead, but he had long since learned the value of peripheral vision, and that was why he saw what he saw out of the corner of his eye. Just a shadow. A shape. An impression of a human figure near the wall by a small stand of fruit trees. And that figure vanished without a sound. One moment there was a hint of a person, the next it was gone.

Another figure replaced it, and Rufinus turned and nodded at the soldier from the Eighth who now stood at the wall, cracking his knuckles meaningfully.

Paying no further attention to the scene, he concentrated on the reason he was here. Walking his horse over to the low hitching post for visitors, he dismounted and tethered the beast. He then paused for a moment, breath caught in his throat as he looked at the door. This was his house – he had been brought up within its walls – yet oddly he had been away from it for so long, living a new life, that if felt like someone else's now in a strange way. His and yet not his. He wondered whether propriety allowed for him to simply stroll in through the door as though he owned the place.

Surrendering to his social removal from the old homestead, he strode over to the door and clanged the bronze, dolphin-adorned bell hanging outside. There was a brief pause and then the shuffle of footsteps behind the door. The portal opened with a well-oiled silence and Rufinus looked into his ancestral home with odd trepidation.

'What can I do for you, sir,' muttered the old, stooped man at the door.

Rufinus stared. Ildutas had been the doorman at the villa in Rufinus' youth. He had been a big bruiser of an Iberian, a slave who had been used as a boxer for entertainment – the reason Rufinus had first gained an interest in the sport. He had always been a figure of whom Rufinus lived in a little awe. While it was impossible to deny that this stooped old man was Ildutas, it was also hard to reconcile the two after all this time.

The words 'Ildutas? It's me,' died in his throat. He *wasn't* him. Couldn't afford to be with anyone he didn't trust entirely.

'Is your master home?' he said finally.

'Do you have an appointment? The master is very busy.'

'He will make time. Tell him an old friend is here.'

'I need a name. The master is very…'

'Just tell him, man.'

The old slave gave him a suspicious look but, recognising that the man at the door was both important and determined, he nodded his acceptance and opened the door. 'If you'd care to wait in the atrium, sir, I will advise the master of your presence.'

Rufinus nodded and followed him in. Gods, but nothing had changed. The same mosaics, the same wall paintings, carefully contrived to look like the family's age-old estates in Italia. Even the same drapes and cushions. He stood there for long moments, watching the small fountain in the impluvium as a triton vomited up fresh water into the air only for it to splash back down on his face and into the square pool. The noise reminded him that the last time he had relieved himself had been over the side of the ship as it made for Tarraco harbour some four hours ago.

By the time Ildutas returned with the villa's current master in his wake, Rufinus was consciously clenching his bladder and trying to avoid crossing his legs. The need evaporated in a moment at the sight of his brother.

'Master,' the doorman said as he stepped aside.

Publius looked well. Rufinus took a moment to work through how he felt about that. Of course, he *should* look well. He had not been kept as a prisoner chained in a cellar after all, for all his importance to Cleander. No, he had been treated as a guest and had lived a life of relative luxury, just one with limits under the ever-watchful eyes of the chamberlain's men. A cage, but a gilded one.

His brother stopped at the entrance to the atrium. His eyes ranged up and down, taking in the visitor to the villa, his brow furrowing as he tried to make sense of a nagging uncertainty about this bearded stranger. His eyes fell upon the left hand, hanging at his side, and his eyes agape.

'Gnaeus?'

Rufinus shifted his gaze pointedly to the doorman, hovering nearby.

'Ildutas,' Publius said, 'we shall be in the summer triclinium. Have the staff give us total privacy, please.'

The doorman cast another wary look at Rufinus but nodded, and Publius gestured onwards. 'This way.'

Rufinus followed politely, as though he did not know the way better than anyone. Moments later they were in the family's favoured dining room, its wide windows looking southeast over the headland and out to sea, the whole room warmed by the morning sun and early afternoon. The wall paintings here, too, had not changed in all those years.

'Sit,' Publius said quietly and stood at the door for a moment, making sure none of the staff were hovering insolently nearby before closing it. He then, as Rufinus sank to a couch, strode over to the windows, checking that none of the slaves were loitering on the balcony outside either. Satisfied that they were, indeed, alone, he strolled over to another couch and sat, staring at Rufinus, who waited. After some time Publius nodded.

'It *is* you. I wasn't quite sure at first. It's the beard, of course. You always said you'd rather be dead than bearded.'

'And now I'm both. And I can tell you that death is still more comfortable than beard.'

'I held a small ceremony, you know?' Rufinus resisted the urge to leap up and run across to his brother as tears welled up in Publius' eyes and he angrily brushed them away with the back of a hand. 'I couldn't do much, of course,' he sniffed, 'because I was in Cleander's care. But I made libations and prayed for your ease. They said you died in a fight with an officer out in Dacia. Some sort of personal feud we were told.'

'I nearly did,' Rufinus admitted. 'And it was a lot more than a personal feud, but that's for another time. Senova saved me. She bore me to safety and I recovered in the company of friends. But given what was waiting for me in Rome, we decided that it would be better if I was believed to be dead at the base of a cliff in the middle of nowhere.'

'Gnaeus…'

'Don't call me that. Gnaeus Marcius Rustius Rufinus is dead. He died in Dacia and until he no longer has enemies, he has to stay that way.'

'So who are you?'

'I am Aulus Triarius Rufinus, Prefect of the Misenum fleet and comitus of the Governor of Gaul, Septimius Severus.'

'Prefect of the fleet?'

'Yes. Listen, everything you learn here makes things more dangerous. The less you know about me the better for both of us, in case either of us falls into the wrong hands.'

'Then why did you come? Why put us both in danger? You know that Cleander has men watching me? I see them from time to time.'

'Those particular eyes are closed right now,' Rufinus said, glancing out of the window and half expecting to see one of the soldiers from the Eighth hanging around on the lawns and cleaning his fingernails with a dagger.

Publius' eyes narrowed and his forehead creased to a frown. 'If they disappear, Cleander will pay even more attention to me.'

'And that is why *you* are going to disappear too.'

'I can't disappear,' Publius grunted. 'There is too much to do.'

'Like what? I assumed Father sent you here to keep you out of the way.'

Publius shook his head. 'As though Father ever cared that much for us. No, I'm here to pack all our remaining belongings and oversee the sale of any superfluous slaves.'

'What?'

'Father finally sold the place. Took him ages to find a buyer. No one wanted anything to do with him, partially because of you, I think. Or possibly the memory of our bad name. Or maybe it's just that with the recent raids of the Mauri along the coast of Hispania no one is interested in buying property here. Did you know Mauri pirates came almost as far north as

Tarraco last time? The African fleet doesn't seem to be able to stop them.'

Rufinus was floored. He'd felt oddly like a stranger in his own family home, yet now, suddenly, being told that it would no longer be theirs, he felt more like its owner than ever.

'I didn't believe he'd actually do it,' he hissed. '*Lucius* is buried here!'

'I was planning to retrieve the urn and the inscription and bury him again. Possibly in Rome. Father has rented a town house there.'

'Who has he sold the villa to? Not Cleander, surely?'

'No, Cleander wanted nothing of it. I think he's irritated by Father, who hangs around him like a puppy begging for scraps. It's embarrassing, really. No, he sold it to some merchant or other. The man got it at a steal, too. Father had knocked the price down five times before it finally sold. He only got half what he thought it was worth in the end. But then I suppose it'll be worth nothing if the Mauri ships go unchecked and the place gets robbed and burned.'

'The stupid old man. And you know what he's sold it for?'

'To climb the patronage ladder in Rome.'

'Exactly. You don't need to bribe and inveigle to do that. All you need to do is be honourable and worthwhile. That's how I've ended up working with Severus. He's a good man, and he'd going places, Publius. *He's* the sort of man we should be hitching our cart to, not some fat senator in Rome.'

He spotted something in Publius' expression for a brief moment - a mix of embarrassment, worry... fear?

'What?'

'It's nothing.'

'Tell me.'

'Father's not dealing with the senators. He says they've had their day. Freedmen are the new aristocracy, he reckons – the ones we need to watch.'

Rufinus blinked. 'Don't tell me.'

27

A nod. 'What did you expect. Cleander had his only son captive.'

'The short-sighted, numb-headed arsehole.'

'He thinks he will get a suffect consulship soon.'

'Him and half the empire. Cleander sells them, or so it's said. So Father sells our home and gives the money to our darkest and most dangerous enemy. I'll flatten his damn face when I see him.'

'Don't be stupid, Gnaeus. You've just told me you need to stay dead. You can't see him.'

Rufinus fumed, but his brother was quite right, of course. He thought through what he'd learned. He'd half planned for this moment, so at least things were in place.

'Do you trust me, Publius?'

'You know I do.'

'I mean *really* trust me. Above even Father.'

'Yes. On my honour.'

'Then forget what you're doing here. Let Father struggle through it or send someone else to do it. I don't see why we should spend any of our valuable time helping him make Cleander a little bit more rich and powerful, do you?'

Publius shook his head. 'But what...?'

'I have two ships in the harbour. One is a provincial Liburnian I brought from Massilia. The other is a trireme from Misenum. I came on the first, but I'm leaving on the other, bound for Misenum and perhaps Rome after that. The Liburnian belongs to the governor, Septimius Severus, and it's returning to Gaul. I want you on it in the morning, with all your own gear and any valuables you can carry. I'll help you pack all that tonight, and you can come to the port with me in the morning.'

'Where am I going, though,' Publius asked doubtfully.

'A safe house in Cemenelum, not far from Massilia. It's owned by one of Severus' men and has a private guard of retired veterans from his former legions. It's about the safest place in the whole world from Cleander, and no one knows about it other than a few of us in the governor's familia. My fiancée and my dog are there already.'

'Fiancée?'

'Long story. You'll like her. But stay there and stay out of sight. Wheels are in motion, Publius. Sooner or later, Cleander is going to fall, and when he does he's going to fall further than anyone in the empire's history, right from the Tarpeian Rock. I don't know how long it's going to take, but I want you out of the way.'

'I could help?'

Rufinus shook your head. 'No, you can't. You are too well known and you lack any real influence. Besides, the moment anything starts to move and Cleander feels the pinch, he's going to put pressure on anyone he can to try and hold on, and that would include you. I want you safe. I've lost one brother... I'm not going to lose another.'

Publius looked unhappy, but he nodded nonetheless. 'Father will be furious. He'll be angry that I've vanished, and even more so if I take anything valuable with me.'

'And that, right there, is as good a reason as any to have nothing to do with the selfish old fool: putting monetary value above family. Now, have someone stoke the baths' furnace up, prepare us an evening meal and organise a cold breakfast to leave in the kitchen for the morning, then dismiss the whole lot of them.'

'What?'

'Father doesn't deserve their help, nor the money you'd raise from their sale. Dismiss the servants and free the slaves and send them on their way with whatever they can carry. I want the villa to be empty of anyone but us by nightfall.'

'Gnaeus...'

'Aulus,' reminded the bearded prefect. 'Just do it. You won't need them after breakfast. The governor's men will see you safely to Cemenelum, and I'll give you the address to find there. You'll be safe there, and you're half expected already.'

There was a drawn-out pause and finally Publius, still looking rather unsure, rose from his couch and opened the door, calling for the major domo.

'I'll be back shortly,' Rufinus told him, 'to eat and to help pack. Don't let the slaves take anything too valuable and portable. You'll need them.'

Without further ado, Rufinus rested a hand supportively on his brother's shoulder and smiled, then strode off, back through the atrium, and opened the front door, exiting into the late afternoon warmth. Oddly, it was not that much further south here than in Lugdunum – perhaps three hundred miles – and yet the climate was totally different already.

Stretching, he set himself ready. The old world was passing. His home was sold, his father estranged, his legion days far behind and even his time in the Guard now little more than a memory. Time to make a new world. A one without Cleander's poison in it. And perhaps then, when that monster's influence was lifted, the Guard would be a thing he could go back to.

Balling his hands into fists, he strode across the grass. A legionary bearing the signs of the Eighth Augusta sat on the boundary wall, sunning himself with a smile. He straightened and dropped to his feet as Rufinus approached.

'Sir.'

'The man you took out. He's still alive?'

'Yessir.'

Rufinus vaulted up onto the wall and looked down the far side. The figure on the ground was dressed as any vine-tending field-hand might be, curled up on his side in the dirt, his hands bound with a cord that connected them with clear discomfort with his similarly-tied ankles. Once more, looking at the expert work of the knots, Rufinus could not help but suspect that the calm man in mail standing so casually nearby was one of the agents of the Castra Peregrina.

He crouched next to the field-hand-who-wasn't. He might be appropriately dressed, and his skin was rough, his hands hard, calloused and leathery, but Rufinus was not fooled. The callouses were consistent with a swordsman, and with the hardened grip of a shield. Moreover, the man was too pale to work in the fields.

There was blood on the back of the man's head, and a few paces away sat a rock that glistened wetly. That was how he'd been downed so swiftly and silently, then. Rufinus turned him over. He was wounded, but conscious and angry, his eyes blazing, if a little dazed. He had something balled up and stuffed in his mouth. A piece of his own torn-off tunic, Rufinus realised.

'I am not going to remove your gag or your bonds, I'm afraid. I don't think there'll be the need for an interrogation.'

He reached down and pushed his hand under the man's chin, while the bound figure struggled and grunted trying to fight back in any way he could. With little difficulty, Rufinus located and exposed to the light the pendant of a scorpion on a chain.

'I must one day thank Cleander for making his loyal agents so easy to identify.'

The man did not seem fazed by the accusation. Nor, even through the gag, did he try to deny it.

'Your friends here will have been similarly dealt with, I'm afraid,' Rufinus said through an unpleasant smile, 'so if you're looking forward to some sort of heroic rescue, think again. Your life is forfeit. You have put loyalty to a serpent in the guise of a freedman above your sworn duty to the emperor. I was a Praetorian, you see.'

A flicker of surprise and uncertainty passed through the man's eyes.

'In fact, I still am, in a way. The *real* me, that is. I was a Praetorian, and by all the gods I was proud to be one. Lifted by the hand of the emperor himself to the ranks of the Guard, I was proud to be one of you, and I devoted myself to the emperor and his safety. It cost me brandings and burnings and woundings and all the nails of one hand, but I would give it all again because being Praetorian meant something to me.'

31

He rolled the man onto his back.

'But the Guard has changed. In putting Cleander above the emperor whose safety is the whole purpose of the unit, you have negated your own value. You have lost your honour and cannot regain it while you serve that man.'

Slowly, making sure to take his time and be very, very clear with the doomed man, he drew his gladius.

'There is a cleansing fire coming,' he said quietly. 'It is coming to Rome. It is coming to the Palatine, where it is needed most. And it is also coming to the Guard.'

He rose, brandishing the sword, and the stricken guardsman's eyes widened in panic, the muffled grunting behind the gag becoming urgent.

'Try to live better in your next world.'

He made the blow quick and clean – a soldier's death despite everything.

'Did you not want to ask him anything sir?' the legionary murmured.

Rufinus looked down at the shuddering body of the dying man as he withdrew his blade and wiped it on the nondescript tunic. 'I don't think so. Pretty sure I know everything I need to know already.'

'What would you like me to do with the body?'

'What do you normally do with the bodies?' Rufinus asked slyly, half hoping to trip a frumentarius into revealing his position.

The soldier gave him an earnest frown. '"Normally", sir?'

The two men looked at one another for a time, until Rufinus broke off his glance. 'Leave him,' he said. 'Sooner or later, his presence will be reported to the authorities, who will find the scorpion necklace, put two and two together and trace him back to Rome and the Castra Praetoria. It won't go anywhere, of course. Any investigation will be quickly quashed, but it might at least cause a little embarrassment and make Cleander a little more nervous about sending out Praetorians to do his dirty work.'

The legionary nodded and Rufinus rose, checked the cleanliness of his sword, and then sheathed it. 'Check the rest of the estate. Finish off his friends, since he won't have been alone, and make sure there are no others on the premises. Then get yourself into quarters for the night. You can stay in any of the villa's rooms but mine or Publius's. The staff will all have gone. Then in the morning, the four of you are escorting my brother on board the *Nicostrate*. You will see him to Cemenelum and then return to Lugdunum and the governor's house. Is that clear?'

'Crystal, sir.'

Rufinus nodded, with a last look down at the Praetorian in the dust, blood pooling beneath him. Killing Cleander's lackeys was getting easier with every new corpse.

CHAPTER THREE – A NEW COMMAND

Rome, June 187 A.D.

The *Nemesis*, a ship of the Misenum fleet, and without a doubt the largest and most impressive vessel upon which Rufinus had ever trod, plodded up the Tiber. She had been designated his flagship, and she was more about impressing those who saw her than comfort or manoeuvrability, as he'd come to understand since first boarding her. She slid past the emporium inside the city of Rome, where those merchants who were not already docked moved feverishly out of the way of the grand warship. She slid past the various riverfront markets and edifices and finally, as she reached the Campus Martius region, began to slow.

Rufinus stood next to the great ship's trierarch as the man bellowed orders to his crew, and tried to look as important and naval as possible. His uniform was impressive, but heavy and uncomfortable. He'd never had to wear a muscled cuirass before and it seemed that even this, which had been made specifically for him, was ill-fitting and uncomfortable. With the heavy, salt-water-logged cloak, the helmet with the ridiculous crimson plumes that hung down like wilted flowers in the wet air, and the extra few pounds of rust he was required to lug around, not to mention the constantly wet boots that threatened some kind of foot infection, he was beginning to wonder why Prefect of the Fleet was a position to which men aspired.

He had begun to grow into the role a little on the crossing from Tarraco, though. He'd seen Publius onto the sleek courier bound for Gaul, and the Nemesis had then put to sea and made for Insula Minor, crossing to Marianum on the southern tip of

Corsica, through the strait between there and Sardinia and on to Antium on the Italian coast, and from there to the enormous Port of Misenum, home of the fleet.

Rufinus had seen ports in his time, from the great complex of Ostia to the riverine docks of the Danuvius to the ancient port of Tarraco, but nothing had prepared him for the home of the Praetorian fleet. Rounding the great rocky headland, Nemesis spun around with grace and powered north and then back a little west, making for the narrow entrance in an enormous breakwater. They had passed inside, from the open sea into gentle glassy waters of the harbour with ease and consummate skill. With the official structures drifting by on the mole to their right they had passed the town of Misenum on the left and made for the military jetties ahead, each occupied by an impressive warship. Rufinus, a man with little experience of the sea, had found himself unexpectedly fascinated and dying to find out more about this whole new world he had inherited. He had imagined himself presenting his person at the command building, being introduced to his officers and clerks, being shown around the complex and then spending a few days exploring and learning everything there was to learn about his new role and his new home.

He had been sadly mistaken.

Rufinus had waited until the Nemesis docked, and then stepped confidently down the boarding ramp only to be met by a soldier who looked harassed, desperately shouting for his new prefect.

The man was a weird combination of deathly pale and sunburned florid pink, with a shock of bright red hair and freckles that made Rufinus stare in the unsolicited belief that they might somehow mark out a pattern or image. The man bowed his head, clutching a pile of wax tablets, and as he did so a neck-chain slipped out from his collar. Recent encounters with scorpion necklaces had left Rufinus particularly alert to such things. What he wasn't prepared for was the chi-rho symbol worn by the weird sect of Christian pacifists dangling from the chain. The soldier opened his mouth to further address his prefect and Rufinus was just wondering how to deal with this clearly delicate and anxious man from the weird love cult when one of the passing marines trod on the clerk's foot.

'What the fuck do you think you are doing?' demanded the red headed soldier, rounding on the burly marine. His demeanour shifted from nervous clerk to drill-centurion in a rage in the blink of an eye, and Rufinus reeled.

'Sorry, sir,' the marine trembled, stepping back.

'Fucking right you are. Sorriest piece of dog scrotum I ever saw.'

The soldier hurried off and Rufinus adjusted his viewpoint rapidly.

'Prefect Rufinus?' the redhaired soldier asked, his whole manner shifting back to servile underling. 'I'm Philip, your personal secretary.'

'I… yes. That soldier…'

'A clumsy oaf. And I never forget a face.'

Rufinus realised oddly that the man had a centurion's vitus cane under his arm, and he was forced to shift his ideas once more.

'*Centurion* Philip?'

'Quite so, prefect. And all things being equal, I would love nothing more than to get acquainted with you, but sadly, you have other things to do.'

'I do?' Rufinus felt oddly at the mercy of this strange man.

'You do. Two missives arrived three days ago, one for you and one for me. This is yours.' He handed a sealed scroll case over and Rufinus took it, noting with interest the seal of Severus, governor of Gaul. 'Mine informed me that you would be leaving for the capital as soon as you set foot in Misenum. I have had a fast ship prepared at the Nola Tertia wharf. There is still time to depart and make it to Antium by nightfall.'

Rufinus stared and then, remembering himself and aware of his marine guard queuing respectably behind him waiting for orders, cracked the seal on the scroll case and opened it. The parchment within contained a short and business-like note, telling Rufinus that his presence was required in the capital and that he should make for his headquarters there at haste. Nothing more.

He had journeyed for days from Tarraco and had spent less than a hundred heartbeats in his new port command before being escorted onto a second ship, this one narrow and sleek and named *Celeritas*. Then he put to sea once more. This new ship was built purely for speed and apart from the few crewmen and the burly oarsmen there was barely enough space to accommodate Rufinus, Philip and the dozen men of the navy who Rufinus couldn't help mentally calling his 'wet guard'. They looked, in fairness, like ordinary legionaries, apart from the blue tunics and the tendency towards extreme tattoos. The Celeritas tore up the coastline like a dolphin atop the waves, with such speed that even Rufinus, who was never seasick, started to feel a little wobbly.

And so this morning they had arrived at Ostia and forged on up the Tiber for Rome. Now, the Navalia approached, that complex of buildings and jetties that served as the military's anchorage in the city. Rufinus felt a new level of tension and uncertainty slip through him. He had been in Rome before, but not since Cleander had reached his apex. Not since Rufinus was officially dead. And not in such a position of authority.

It was not until he was descending the boarding ramp to the cobbled dockside that it occurred to him he had absolutely no idea where his headquarters in the city was. He stopped in the middle of the port, his guardsmen shuffling and clinking to a halt behind him, and waited until the strange and incongruous figure of Philip appeared beside him.

'Where is…?' he began.

'Close to the Flavian amphitheatre sir,' the secretary butted in, anticipating the question impressively. 'Just below the Trajanic baths and opposite the Ludus Magnus.'

Rufinus nodded with a frown. At least he knew where to go, though he'd expected the naval headquarters in the city to be near the Navalia, or at least within sight of the river.

'I shall have a litter brought,' the secretary said.

'No, thank you Philip. A horse will do if there is one available.'

He waited in the midst of the organised chaos of which he was nominally in command, while the secretary hurried off to some building on the edge of the open square and returned a few moments later followed by a slave who took a side trip to a stable and reappeared impressively quickly with two horses. Thanking them, Rufinus hauled himself into the saddle, the weird secretary doing likewise. Moments later they were making their way through the city, the marines of his personal guard jingling along rhythmically behind them, though in accordance with ancient law they had left their blades on board and carried only clubs. It occurred oddly to Rufinus that he never seemed to enter Rome in a normal fashion. He was always either in a grand triumph or sneaking along aqueducts or as part of some military column.

The small party left the Navalia along the Via Triumphalis and then turned left, passing the theatres of Pompey and Balbus, riding in the shadow of the Arx and the Capitol with their triad of ancient temples, and descending into the forum. As they moved through the ancient streets, two things insisted themselves upon Rufinus as his gaze took in this great city at the centre of the world.

Firstly was the plague. The dreadful disease was nothing new, of course. It had been around as long as Rufinus could remember, a parting gift of the Parthian empire after Verus hammered them into submission. In Rufinus' lifetime the plague had come in waves, often subsiding into a background worry for years at a time between outbreaks, but this was the first time he'd been in the city when one of the epidemics had become serious. Bodies were being collected on low carts and half the population of Rome – those who weren't wailing and clawing at lesions and boils, anyway – moved about like ghosts, trying to distance themselves from the world with garlands of pungent flowers slung at their throats to ward off the ill humors.

It was appalling, but Rufinus would have handled that stoically had it not been for the overlying sense of disaffection and misery. The whole of Rome seemed to fester like one of the plague's overripe boils, on the very verge of eruption. It was a startling realisation and not at all a pleasant sensation. Rufinus was, for the first time, glad of his marine escort, for though he had nothing against the populace he recoiled when the infected people came almost within reach.

By the time they passed from the eastern end of the forum and opened out into the space before the great Flavian amphitheatre, Rufinus had become thoroughly disheartened with the state of the city and its people. Though he couldn't precisely come up with any solution to the plague that once more stalked Rome, he felt certain that the emperor and his court, especially with great physicians like Galen who was reputedly in the city these days, could at least do *something* to alleviate the trouble. And if that was beyond their capability, at least they could solve the underlying discontent. Cleander had to be removed. It was bad enough the gods visiting misery on Rome, without Rome doing it to itself as well.

They swiftly arrived at the Castrum Misenatum, a grand arcaded building on the lower slopes of the Oppian hill below the great baths and in sight of the amphitheatre. Two men in blue tunics and full uniform guarded the entrance arch, but with only wooden batons at their belts in keeping with the age-old laws against being armed for war within the sacred boundary of the city. Rufinus did not know whether to feel irritated at a delay considering who he clearly was, or to be proud of the level of security his men afforded their base, but either way the guards would not admit them until the proper documentation had been produced. Fortunately, it seemed that despite the various oddities that surrounded Philip, he was blisteringly efficient at his job, and the papers were produced in the blink of an eye.

Rufinus' confusion at the thoroughly landlocked location of the naval base was cleared up as he strode through the entrance hall with its statues of the great naval minds of Rome – Brutus, Augustus, Pompey, Agrippa, Pliny and many more that Rufinus did not immediately recognise. His gaze passed over these great luminaries to fall upon the open courtyard ahead, surrounded by the three-storey square arcade. At the centre a score of men in blue tunics were practicing hauling ropes which ran through pulleys and raised great heavy weights into the air, purely to build up their strength.

That was why the base was here. The men of the Misenum fleet, of course, also serviced all the theatres odeons and amphitheatres in the city, manning the ropes and pulleys that drew the sunshades across the top of the great venues. They were the only men who served Rome with a sufficient knowledge of ropes and pulleys, and probably the strongest men available to do so. It seemed that Rufinus would be in charge of more than just the disposition of the fleet.

The men of his guard peeled off now, saluting him, and moved off to their barracks, while his secretary pottered along beside him. 'Now, sir, there will need to be a briefing this afternoon. I did not bother you on board ship with details, but you need to know a number of things and will need a tour of the complex. I presume you are familiar with the city?'

'Yes. Some parts of it more than others.'

'Good, good, good. I will call upon you at your office in an hour to go through everything once I have caught up with the correspondence awaiting me. Your rooms are directly opposite the gate. Though it is assumed that you will have your own house in the city, of course, former prefects have found it expedient to have a small apartment available in the headquarters, so you will find half a dozen rooms there set up for your use, as well as the office itself, which is the first chamber you will come to. There are two keys to the door. One

I keep for access to the office in your absence and the other is yours, of course.' He handed Rufinus a key. 'Please feel free to ignore any work that has built up on the office desk since the departure of Prefect Abullius. I will attend to it all in due course and then walk you through anything that you need to see. Naturally it will take some days before you are familiar enough with the work to handle it without my aid, but that is what I am here for. There will probably be a few missives addressed specifically to you, and needless to say these are for you, and you may pass onto me anything you wish me to deal with, but leave anything unaddressed and I will handle it. There is a large mess hall and we have our own kitchens and bakery, though it is unusual for the senior staff to eat on the premises apart from perhaps breaking their fast in their rooms, and usually they prefer to socialise in the city with acquaintances and members of the senate. Work in the castrum starts before dawn and rarely finishes before the end of the waking day, as the men will often be late back from servicing some event in the city. Each day you will receive a list of troop rotations from Ostia and Misenum to Rome and back, and each day you will receive a list of what ships are expected to arrive and depart each base, and the reason for their journeys. Again, I can deal with all of this for you, but if you are a man who requires silence and peace to sleep, then the rooms here probably will not suffice due to the noise and busyness. Prefect Abullius preferred to sleep in his house on the Caelian.'

Rufinus, holding his key and staring at his secretary, wondered how long a person could talk before drawing breath. Philip seemed to be going for some sort of record.

'Now, with regard to your officers,' the man said, still without new oxygen, and Rufinus held up a hand that miraculously silenced him.

'Thank you. Clearly you have everything under control. I imagine, knowing the senior ranks of the empire's military as I do, that former prefects have been largely content to give out a few awards, make sure they can afford to hold a few good parties, use their rank as a sinecure in political circles, and leave the actual running of the navy to men like yourself.'

Philip's eyes narrowed, but he nodded. 'A rather astute and undoubtedly unpopular appraisal, I might say, sir. Yes, in truth Prefects of the Fleet come and go with remarkable regularity and few seem interested in the workings of their command. Few indeed seem to know one end of a ship from the other,'

'In that respect, I may not be much better,' Rufinus admitted, 'but I am a man given to hard work and I do not approve of men reaping rewards without getting their hands dirty in the process. I intend to do my share of the work, Philip, though as you quite rightly say, it will be some time before I can do anything without constantly bothering you for explanations. For now, though, I would like to leave it all in your capable hands while I settle in. Forget about the meeting this afternoon and schedule one for the morning. I shall likely live in the castrum apartments much of the time. I campaigned in Pannonia for years, so I am more than capable of sleeping amid the shouts of soldiers.'

I was one of them, after all...

Philip bowed. 'As you command, Prefect. I shall have your officers leave you in peace until the morning, then. Do you need a guard of men on your door? Some prefects feel it is a necessity of rank, others prefer their seclusion when they withdraw.'

Rufinus shook his head. 'I can't imagine needing a bodyguard in a fortress of my own soldiers.'

Images of the many Roman officers who had met death at the hands of an underling drifted through his mind, and he shook them off as Philip nodded. 'Very well, sir. I shall be in my office, which is beside the entrance lobby, if you need me.'

With a brief salute, the man turned and marched off, leaving Rufinus feeling a little baffled. With a deep breath, he turned and strode over towards the door indicated. He had to weave between groups of marines and sailors practicing things with ropes, and felt an odd pride in his first real command. In Dacia, he'd been a sort of subsidiary officer, beholden to all the others and very much out of his depth. Here, though he knew nothing about his job or command, he could content himself with the knowledge that all his predecessors had been in the same boat, so to speak, and at least he had some solid military experience, while most of those men would have spent their early days in the military drinking wine and discussing Macedonian tactics in the works of Arrian. This felt true. This was a proper command, even if he held it under an assumed name.

The key turned in a well-oiled lock in a solid door with a plaque noting his rank, if not his name, beside the frame. He opened it to find a clean and well-ordered office. Tables and scroll racks, a desk with piles of writing tablets and scroll cases on it. A map of the sea on the wall, covering everywhere from Hispania to Syria and Britannia to Africa. Without being told, he was certain that this neatness was not the doing of his predecessor. This excessive order and cleanliness was, he already realised, a mark of Philip having a hand in things.

He strolled over to the table, noting the door that would lead to his private rooms. Three of the documents on the table bore his name as well as his rank, the rest addressed to whoever held the position at the time and therefore considerably less important right now.

The first case bore the seal of the Palace, and so Rufinus went to that first, cracking the wax and sliding out the parchment contents. He read it with interest, swiftly. An invitation to an imperial dinner to be held during the Ludi Apollinares next month. While it as a great honour to be asked, Rufinus' first instinct was to find a way to be legitimately and acceptably too busy to attend. The chance of bumping into men who knew him, even men who hated him, at such an event was extremely high, and even bearded and hairy, he felt it would be unwise to circulate in such crowds.

The second case bore a seal he did not recognise, so he snapped that and examined the contents. It was a short note from his predecessor, congratulating him on his appointment, none-too-subtly suggesting that he might be able to make ready cash from his position if he works it wisely, and advising him to sit back and reap his rewards without fuss since his secretary was more than capable of running the whole place anyway.

With a roll of the eyes, he dropped that message and examined the third one, which bore the seal of Septimius Severus. This one was a short note, very much to the point, typical of the governor's business-like manner.

> *Congratulations, Rufinus. No time to settle in. Once you have found this message, keep yourself to yourself for the rest of the day. Do not leave the castrum and do not engage in conversation with anyone you do not have to. Once darkness has truly fallen, leave wearing only a toga. Exit the castrum by the rear entrance that opens into an alley below the baths. Make your way to my townhouse. Do not leave before dark, do not leave in uniform, and do not leave by the main entrance. Come alone. Once you have committed these instructions to memory, destroy this note.*

Rufinus blinked. Was he somehow working for the frumentarii now, as this sounded very much like their sort of business and not the actions of a senior and well-respected commander of a Roman fleet. Still, if Severus needed him, he would go, and the African most certainly wouldn't make such demands as these without good reason.

Not long after he had eaten the note, not being able to think of a more thorough solution, a knock at his door heralded four marines carrying his chests and bags from the ship, containing all his worldly goods. As he thanked them and they left the gear in the office, Rufinus wondered if it was coincidence that the top item of the pile was his neatly folded toga. The men saluted and left him in peace once more, shutting the door as they departed.

He spent the rest of the afternoon tense and impatient, wondering why Severus was in the city, which clearly he was, what he had to say, and why Rufinus couldn't simply head that way and hear it without all this drama. He examined his new apartments, found them to be easily the match of anywhere he'd ever lived, and visited the small bath house of the castrum to wash away the pervading odour of brine. With several hours still to go before he could leave, he began, despite what Philip had said, going through the baffling collection of lists, orders and requests on the desk. Perhaps one in every dozen he felt he could handle without asking his secretary what in Hades they meant.

He signed a few and put them in a new pile with a great sense of satisfaction, then spent an interested half hour examining the map on the wall. He'd seen plenty of maps in his time, including grand-scale military ones, but he'd never come across one like this before. It noted the garrison of each of the empire's legions and the capital of every province, but other than that the land was largely bare, other than where navigable rivers cut through it. The sea, on the other hand, which was usually fairly blank on maps, was a riot of information from trade routes to currents and notable wind systems, ports, known trouble spots, fleet bases and so much more.

He noted the presence on the coast of Africa of the fleet based at Caesarea Mauretaniae, whose duties included supressing those same Mauri pirates of whom his brother had spoken raiding Hispania's coast. He wondered whether perhaps the Misenum fleet should be lending a hand to their lesser African brothers since they seemed not to be up to the task on their own. He would ask Philip in the morning. He also noted the grain routes, which were marked in dotted lines. He was interested to see, as well as the grain routes from Africa and Aegyptus, and other lesser yet still well known ones, a line from southern Gaul that led to Misenum. A supply for the fleet, clearly, but one that came from Gaul. Not from Gallia Lugdunensis, run by Severus, but Rufinus did remember hearing that the governor of southern Gaul, a man called Cilo, was also a very good friend of the African.

By dusk he had done just about everything he could do, including putting away all his gear and examining the map over and over again, committing it all to memory. As the last light slid from the sky, he donned the toga as requested, still having trouble settling the folds into place without a slave to help. He would ask Philip about a body slave. Barely had he made that decision before he thought guiltily of what Senova would say. Still, she was a slave no more, and *she* would have to have slaves of her own if they were to live properly.

Wistful memories of her began to drift into his mind, and he spent the remaining hour or so wishing she was here in Rome and not tucked away for safety in a villa in southern Gaul. Finally, satisfied that he was appropriately attired and that the light had gone from the sky, he left the chambers, locking the door behind him, and strolled along the courtyard edge until he reached the archway that led to the rear entrance. The marine on duty there was surprised to see him, but he now wore the seal ring of the fleet prefect and a brief flash of it was enough for the door to be opened without question.

The narrow street outside was empty, though far from quiet with the sounds of the sailors inside the complex and the light blaring out from the public baths above on the hill. Rufinus turned right and shuffled away from the place at the strange pace adopted by anyone who had to try and walk casually in a toga. It took him the better part of half an hour to reach Severus' townhouse, which stood on the Viminal hill.

He found the house, whose address and description both had been committed to memory long ago while in Syria, easily. The doorman opened the portal and without asking who he was or even uttering a word, stood aside for Rufinus to enter. He did so and was led to a triclinium with a wide window that somehow, though the careful placement of surrounding buildings, contrived to offer an unparalleled view of the city. Severus was standing looking out across the rooftops, hands clasped behind his back.

'Governor.'

'Rufinus. Good. Settling in?'

'I will be. Not really had time yet. Why the summons? Is something amiss?'

'No. But your arrival has taken a weight from my shoulders. We have a meeting. An assignation if you like. Two days from now. I had worried you might miss it, but no. You are here. There is a warehouse on the Aventine just south of the Horrea Galbana that belongs to one Publius Zela. It is easily identifiable and bears a sign of five barrels. The day after tomorrow, at the ninth hour, you need to be there. I will meet you at the warehouse, along with a number of others.'

'Might I ask the nature of the meeting?'

'No. You might not. Though you'll likely already have guessed. You will leave here now. Go somewhere for a bath or a massage, listen to some music, have some wine, and then return to the Castrum Misenatum and do not leave the place then until the time you come to the meeting. In between do not draw any attention to yourself, do not mention my name and do not speak of the meeting, the warehouse or even the Aventine to a single soul.'

'Why are we being so secretive?' Rufinus pressed. 'You have every right to be in the city, and so do I, and it is well known that I am your friend and we travelled together in the east.'

Severus nodded. 'But our enemy has eyes and ears everywhere and they spend all their time making connections and finding treachery even where there is none. We must remain careful and the less we are seen together the safer it will be for both of us. Only leave the castrum when you have good reason, and preferably when you know it is safe to do so. Cleander has eyes on your headquarters as he does almost every institution in the city. This is why you timed your departure carefully. I have an arrangement with friendly frumentarii who are contriving to keep those watchful eyes distracted at key times to allow us a degree of free movement. Now go. Do your work in the castrum, be completely nondescript and then meet me at Zela's warehouse at the ninth hour.'

Rufinus nodded, a mixture of discomfort and unhappiness in his expression as he was shown to the door. He did not like all this subterfuge. And clearly the meeting for which they were bound concerned Cleander. He wondered in what respect, and who else would be there.

Still, however irritating it might be, he was glad at least that things were beginning to move. Cleander's fall was imminent, and Rufinus was determined to play his part.

CHAPTER FOUR – CONSPIRATORIAL WHISPERS

Rome, June 187 A.D.

The mid-afternoon sun beat down upon the streets of Rome with merciless power. Rufinus, in his toga only though with a discrete knife at the belt beneath just in case, plodded along the lower slope of the Aventine, sweating buckets and wondering, if this was what mid-June was bringing the city, what it would be like in August. The great and the good of Rome would be abandoning the urban sprawl for their seaside villas early this year, especially with disease stalking the streets as it was.

The nobility tended to think themselves immune to such horrors, living as they did behind high walls in the more exclusive areas of the city, but Rufinus knew they were all as much at risk. More than once a patrician with a nervous disposition had kept his townhouse sealed tight, planted sweet fragranced flowers and refused to accept visitors only to have death come calling anyway. Every house had to eat and cook. Every house had to send its slaves to the markets to buy food and charcoal, and sometimes they came back with more than they bargained for.

One notable merchant had stocked up with all his goods for half a year, deigning to eat salted meat like a legionary on campaign just to keep his house sealed. He had filled his house and garden to the brim with flowers to ward off the bad airs from the city around. The gardener had brought the plague, and because of the owner's refusal to open his doors the whole household had been dead half a month before they were found. Such were the stories now abounding in Rome.

Rufinus was constantly struck by the sadness and horror of what he saw around him but, though he might flinch from contact, on the whole he walked freely as though there was nothing wrong with the city. There was no defence against the plague, no dodging or parrying its blows. If the gods were to be kind, he would walk untouched. If they were feeling wicked, he would die. Nothing he did would change that, and so he slogged on in his heavy white wool toga, making for the address he had memorized with Severus.

The area bounded by the Aventine hill, the river, and the huge mound of broken pottery that was already nicknamed the 'eighth hill of Rome' was a sprawl of warehouses, granaries, workshops and stores. Businesses operated from the district – perhaps up to half the large mercantile companies in the city, even – and traders had their main stores here. Private concerns owned more than half the great structures, and here and there were government-controlled units. The main one of those was the *Horrea Galbana*, a massive courtyarded complex of warehouses, granaries and offices, all centred on the tomb of the man who'd had it built centuries ago. The Horrea Galbana was the main government store for the gathering and distribution of the grain unloaded monthly on the waterfront emporium nearby.

But it was no government structure Rufinus was making for today. He turned off the main thoroughfare and moved into the warehouse district with relief, leaving behind the larger crowds. Partially, of course, because of the ever-present risk of plague, but there was also the knowledge that he was bound for some clandestine meeting and that despite his level of awareness and every precaution he had taken, crowds were easy places to follow a man.

Wary dark eyes watched him now as he moved along a side street, turned down forks and alleys, then made circuits and back to roads he'd already trod, trying to be certain he was not being followed. Every store house in this whole district, whether privately owned or controlled by the administration, had its guards. Privately owned armies of ex-soldiers, ex gladiators or simply thugs with a level of self-control patrolled these structures for their owners, making sure their precious commodities were safe. In some areas there were better dressed, higher class knights of Rome moving about offices and doing business deals, and teamsters, workmen and clerks were in plenty of evidence, but many of the buildings were devoid of offices, being simply large storerooms, and so the only life around them was its watchful guards. It was into these areas that Rufinus began to stray.

He found the warehouse of Publius Zela without too much difficulty, and knew immediately why it had been chosen as a meeting place. The building was in about the most secure location in the entire district. The slopes of the pottery mountain rose behind it, the steep sides treacherous for climbing, formed by broken shards of pot loosely held together by budding tufts of grass. To the north: a wide street that separated it from the massive complex of the Horrea Galbana, to the south: a sprawling, poorly-tended garden of some merchant's house and to the east: the solid wall of a huge granary. Best still, the only approach by road was either in public view outside the Galbana or a side alley that ended dead outside the warehouse door, surrounded by high walls. There was no easy place for an eavesdropper to lurk.

Rufinus noted the guards even before he turned into that side alley. Ostensibly they looked no different from the similar groups of private mercenaries protecting other people's buildings, but Rufinus could see a difference here. These men might be *dressed* the same as their counterparts elsewhere, but they were not. Few in the streets would have noticed it, but Rufinus was becoming adept at these things. The men watching over Zela's warehouse were arranged with the precision of Praetorians around the emperor. A military mind was behind their disposition. They were in two rings around the building, the inner ones close to the walls like all other groups, preventing easy approach or access, all within sight of one another. The outer ring was disguised as ordinary folk in the streets.

He could see them for what they were, though. The beggar on the main street side, opposite the alley turning. His arm looked dreadfully bent and twisted. It was dislocated, nothing more, but it made him look the perfect beggar, and he was good enough that even other mercenaries were tossing him the odd copper as they passed. Behind the warehouse, he could see two homeless wretches digging around the pottery on the hill, trying to find reusable pieces. But they were no poor denizens, for they moved about the treacherous slope with the sureness of a mountain goat. Two merchants stood at the corner opposite the Horrea Galbana, arguing and haggling. Both were far too muscular to be traders. No, this defence had been carefully prepared by a man who knew what he was doing. Once more the word *frumentarius* popped into his head.

He turned down the alley and was impressed that the men in the outer ring were just so good that they never even twitched as he passed them. The beggar coughed and spat something into his hand, wiping it on his tunic, and Rufinus smiled as two of the other men close to the warehouse moved closer together, directly ahead of Rufinus.

Arm hooked beneath the drape of the toga, his fingers danced lightly on the hilt of the small knife. Technically, he was not breaking the law. The knife was not a weapon of war, though if would as easily carve through neck as peach. Mind you, out here in the sub-urbs, they were outside the Pomerium anyway, and so that law did not count, as was evidenced by the blades hanging at the sides of many of the district's mercenary guards.

As he neared the warehouse, two of the men converged on him.

'Prefect, welcome to the auction. If you would like to find a seat, bidding will begin shortly.'

Rufinus smiled and nodded to the men, slipping between them and making for the door to the warehouse. He opened it with a certain level of trepidation. Everything in his life these days carried the threat of danger and intrigue, but he had rarely felt it as sharply as right now, especially as he still did not know what to expect, other than it would certainly be no auction.

The door opened without a sound, throwing a huge trapezium of light across the floor of the structure. His gaze took in everything at once, despite the change in light levels.

The warehouse had been largely cleared to create an open space at its heart, close to the door. Crates had been moved to the periphery and stacked high. Rufinus smiled. Not only would they be out of the way there, they would prevent anyone lurking in shadowy corners and help deaden any sound to the outside. Chairs had been arranged seemingly haphazardly, and single boxes stood around in careful positions, bearing lamps that lit the interior surprisingly well. Half a dozen figures were already here.

Off to his right sat Septimius Severus, a gaunt, tall figure with thinning hair and sharp eyes beside him, both men toga-clad. Off to the left, as though facing them in negotiation, were two more men, both with the aristocratic bearing of a senator, and another pair in military tunics milled about, pacing impatiently.

Rufinus entered and the door was closed behind him. Severus waved him over.

'Governor.'

'Rufinus. Good, you made good time. Allow me to introduce Papirius Dionysus, the *Praefectus Annonae*. Papirius, this is Aulus Triarius Rufinus, Prefect of the Misenum Fleet. I feel it would be extremely useful if the pair of you were better acquainted.'

Rufinus nodded a friendly greeting at the man, who smiled back, which changed his somewhat skeletal appearance and warmed his expression thoroughly. This man had not had to come far, then. The prefect in charge of grain distribution in the city, Dionysus would be based in the Horrea Galbana just across the main road. He must be under some pressure at the moment with the plague affecting farm production across the empire.

'Who are the others?'

Severus gestured to the two men pacing in military tunics. 'Don't know their names but one of them is the prefect of the Castrum Lecticariorum, and the other is a tribune from the Urban Cohort.'

Rufinus' brows rose to meet in a peak. The man in charge of the city's higher-level transport and litter bearers and a senior officer from the city's police cohort. Along with the grain commissioner, a Prefect of the Fleet and a governor, there was a lot of political weight in this room.

'The two over there: the fatter one on the left with the scowl is Arrius Antoninus, a former consul and until recently proconsular governor of Asia. You actually met him while we were in Syria, but you wouldn't remember him. The man with him is his nephew. Antoninus was always a bit of a hot-head. He almost started a war when he was a tribune in the Fourth Scythica. I worry about any endeavour involving him, and I cannot imagine his nephew is much different.'

Rufinus nodded, scrutinising the other figures. As he was about to ask what was going on, the door opened once more and two more men entered. One wandered over to a chair and sat drumming his fingers on his arm. The other moved towards Rufinus and his companions. The second man bowed his head and acknowledged them before seating himself tactically close enough to be considered part of their group, but far enough away to distance himself if he had to.

'Nicomedes,' Severus explained quietly, 'the Praefectus Vehiculorum.'

Rufinus blinked. Another very important man, Nicomedes in his position would control the entire courier system, including the way stations, all across the empire. The idea of the level of influence and power growing in this room set Rufinus' teeth on edge.

He sat tense as every now and then the door opened and another luminary entered to take a seat. Senators and soldiers, administrators and oligarchs, the occupants of this room could quite easily had built a new empire. He was beginning to worry about the strategic sense of gathering so many people in one place when the door opened once more and the most surprising figure of all entered.

The woman was young and extremely attractive, with dark lustrous hair and a perfect complexion of pale caramel, no make up needed to enhance her beauty. He felt immediately guilty just looking at her and promised himself to complement Senova as soon as he next saw her, for though this woman was definitely beautiful, he knew his Senova to be every bit her match. She was clearly rich from her dress, though she had covered it with a large cloak for journeying across the city.

'Our hostess,' Severus whispered.'

Rufinus turned a baffled look on him, and the governor leaned close. 'Marcia, freedwoman of Lucius Verus. They say she's been the emperor's lover since childhood.'

'But he's married,' insisted Rufinus, though his memory furnished him with an image of the pretty little alabaster woman he'd met those years ago in Pannonia when the old emperor died. She'd not looked to be particularly close to Commodus then. They had been married by the will of his father after all. Another look at the intoxicating figure of Marcia made it very easy to believe that she had attracted the attention of the emperor. Was she why Commodus had become so removed from the world these days?

'She's the one who seems to have drawn everyone together,' Severus hissed. 'I was aware of some of these men harbouring a personal hatred of Cleander, and Nicomedes and I have discussed matters before. But this is impressive. She has been casting her net wide and in the best of ponds.'

As Marcia moved into the centre of the room another figure opened the door and joined them, and Rufinus almost shot to his feet in panic. The man was wearing the tunic of a Praetorian prefect. Had they been discovered? But no, for the man moved across and stood close to Marcia, and the atmosphere in the warehouse began to shift. The presence of such a man clearly gave everyone heart. But then, not everyone knew how corrupt the Guard had now become.

A further three men who Rufinus either knew by sight or whose wealth and power was made clear by their mode of dress opened the door and came into the warehouse. Oddly, Rufinus noted that already two groups were coalescing in the dim light. One seemed to be gathering on Severus, the other on the chubby senator about whom the governor had already expressed his concern. Rufinus had seen enough debates go bad in his time to recognise already the direction in which this was going. Nicomedes, the courier prefect, moved chairs a little closer, forgoing his neutrality and visibly siding with Severus.

A few moments later a final figure entered: another senator, clearly. This one paused and locked the door behind him, indicating that he would be the last. Rufinus looked about once more. This room read like a list of the rich and powerful in the city, from almost every walk of life.

At the centre of the room, Marcia and the Praetorian prefect, now seated, shared an unseen look. The latter shrugged and the young woman rose to her feet.

'I see no reason to tread lightly around matters,' she said, her voice as intoxicating as her appearance. 'We all know why we are here, and we may as well now speak openly of it. If our enemy's spies are at work, then we are already doomed.'

Rufinus nodded his agreement. Given the level of guards outside they should be as safe as anything. He realised now, with the presence of the Praetorian prefect, that those figures would probably be men of the Guard. He hoped to Hades the prefect knew what he was doing. So many of the Praetorians would be collecting coin from Cleander now. There were other nods around the room, some encouraging, others more reticent, uncertain.

'Cleander has to be removed from power,' Marcia said in a matter-of-fact tone. Rufinus looked around the room. Fewer men were nodding now, more seeming unsure. He realised oddly that it was because of the speaker. No matter how much influence she might have on the Palatine, and no matter how involved she was, these senators and soldiers were unlikely to acquiesce to the power of a woman. Marcia sighed and nodded at the Praetorian prefect, who stood beside her.

'Friends,' he addressed the room, 'we cannot afford to tarry here longer than necessary. Any of us could be missed and cause concern. The reason we are here is to discern any way to bring about that which we all desire.'

'And *carefully*,' said Septimius Severus, sitting beside Rufinus with folded arms. The entire room turned to look at the governor, and Rufinus tried to look sure and calm, supporting the powerful man at his side.

'No one ever butchered an animal carefully,' snorted that heavy-set senator directly opposite.

'You have clearly never seen a butcher at work,' Severus replied. 'There are many ways to go about this, but we have to consider the results of everything we do. A knife in the dark has several disadvantages. Firstly, if it fails, it opens up all those involved to scrutiny, and I suspect none of us wants that. Secondly, it requires putting all our faith into the hand that wields the blade, and if the empress' conspiracy against her brother taught us anything, it should be that such a choice is foolish. Thirdly, if it succeeds, then it is simply a murder, and not justice. As such there would have to be an investigation and culprits found and dealt with.'

The Praetorian prefect shook his head. 'It is considerably more black and white than you suggest, Severus. You'd be surprised what the Guard has witnessed. How then would you go about this?'

Rufinus nodded. There was some sense to that. He could see Severus' point, and it was a good one, but the Praetorian commander probably wished to cut the rot out of his own force. That somewhat endeared him to Rufinus. It showed that there was still a glimmer of honour in the Guard.

'Carefully,' repeated Severus. 'Take note of Perennis' fall. He died by the emperor's own will, despite the fact that the emperor believed him innocent and counted him a friend. His power and respect were gradually whittled away beneath him by a cunning opponent, leaving him perilously balanced and awaiting a simple push to fall. This is how Cleander needs to be dealt with.'

'Severus,' muttered the younger senator – Arrius Antoninus' nephew – put in, 'every day Cleander gains more power and targets more enemies. If we do not act soon, it will be *us* under the sword and all will come to naught.'

'Act too precipitously, and you invite defeat,' Severus replied. 'I suspect I am the only one here who has fought a war.'

Rufinus shot the governor a sour look. Severus might have led armies in battle, but Rufinus had been at the sharp end of the war against the Marcomanni, up to his knees in mud, blood and shit. Still, he knew he was not supposed to be that person any more, and Severus was trying to make a point as strongly as he could.

'Believe me,' the governor went on, 'when I say everything needs to be carefully coordinated. Rushing off to find a knifeman is idiotic.'

Senator Antoninus was shaking his head in disagreement, which was already infecting that clique that had gathered around him. Rufinus felt his spirits sink a little as the Praetorian prefect gave Marcia an odd look and then drifted over to stand near the senators.

'I have no stomach for conspiracy and clandestine meetings,' the Praetorian said. 'I favour a simple fight. Looking down my blade at my enemy.' The senators nodded.

The polarising of the room was almost complete now. Half the occupants had moved closer and closer to Severus and his companions, while the rest, including the Praetorian commander, had gathered on the senator. Only the sultry figure of Marcia remained alone in the centre, the failure of this meeting clearly weighing heavily on her. Rufinus realised with some sadness that the emperor's freedwoman had probably risked everything to bring so many conspirators together, and far from colluding and forging a plan to bring down their mutual enemy, they had split into two distinct groups, one favouring a blade in the back, the other a subtle conspiracy to cause the public downfall of the man.

Rufinus swallowed noisily and fought the urge to rise and cross the room to stand with the others. He could not help but respect the Praetorian prefect's stance. A strike of blade to body and excise the rotting flesh. Cleanse Rome with a single blow. It was an attractive idea, and in truth was much more the way Rufinus liked it. But he owed Severus. And he trusted him. And Severus was insistent that care was the way forward.

The governor suddenly rose beside Rufinus to address the gathering.

'I have a number of ideas. The fleet play a part in it. Dionysus here has a role, I think. It will take good time to put things in place, but I can expound upon my plan as it forms, and include all of you who wish to play your part. Those who do not need to stay well clear, for the more voices in a conspiracy, the more chance of someone being overheard. Do I presume that you gentlemen wish to have no part?'

The Praetorian and the senators opposite rose and stood together. The prefect looked pointedly at another man in a military tunic to whom Rufinus had not been introduced, but who Rufinus had seen enough of to suspect he was a centurion, and the soldier simply shook his head sadly, and crossed the open space, to Rufinus' surprise to stand by Marcia. The Praetorian prefect grunted his disapproval. 'You may feel free to play what games you wish, Severus, but there shall be no acknowledgement of your value when we plant a blade in Cleander's neck.'

'Good,' the African replied, and Rufinus once more felt the power of his patron. 'Be certain, when you fail, to keep any name from your lips no matter how many fingernails they pull out.'

Rufinus felt his blood run cold, the memory of what had happened to him in the cellars of the empress' villa snapping into his mind's eye. He winced, driving the image away and shot an irritated look at Severus. The governor had not taken his eyes from Senator Antoninus. On a whim, realising that important choices were being made here, and knowing where he needed to stand, Rufinus rose beside Severus and folded his own arms. He glanced over at Nicomedes, the praefectus vehiculorum, who dithered, looking distinctly uncomfortable, but who finally rose to his feet and took two steps to stand at Severus' other shoulder, opposite Rufinus.

The Praetorian prefect seemed to take this as some sort of challenge, and his finger shot out towards Severus. 'The same goes for you. While you plot and plan like low criminals, remember to keep our names out of your workings.'

As though the meeting had been shattered by the words, the Praetorian prefect and the two senators with him strode away towards the door, pausing only long enough for a barely polite nod at the woman who had gathered this powerful group together, only to watch it fragment before her very eyes.

They slipped out, and the group of men at that side of the room who had been gathering around the three followed them out, exiting the building in a gaggle, and leaving only the men around Severus and Rufinus facing the emperor's favourite and the centurion beside her, who cleared his throat, his gaze locked on Severus as the door shut behind them.

'Do you think it can be done?'

Severus nodded. 'But I think the fewer people involved the better. You are daily among the Guard, which contain not only Cleander's men but also Rufus'. Bend all your own time to staying safe and out of matters. And the lady here? She is far too central to power to be personally involved. Cleander already hates her. Domina, you must, like Laetus, look to your own safety.'

The lady gave Severus a sad and troubled nod, and she and the centurion both left the warehouse. After them, others who had stood in support of Severus followed, bowing to the governor as they went. When the door finally clunked shut, Rufinus turned to see Papirius Dionysus and Nicomedes still with them.

'What now?' he asked.

Severus, cleared annoyed, drew a deep breath. 'Our friends out there are going to try something direct and visceral. I do not think they will be successful. If they are, then Cleander will become some poor victim and those of us opposed to him will be scrutinised for our part in it. If they are not, then if they are lucky, they will die in the attempt. If not, they will go through something similar to what happened to you years ago. And you know how easily a man can break under that. I pray they do not name our names when that time comes. So we must be extremely careful. In times past, men have died for the deeds of others for simply having no way to prove their innocence. We must needs be clearly nothing to do with those men. If we are ever named and dragged in, we must be clearly innocent of involvement.'

He sighed. 'Yet at the same time, we must begin to move slowly but surely ourselves. I fear we need a further meeting. Just us, though, and perhaps a friend or two I have in mind. I have the bones of a plan, but I would prefer to add to it a little muscle and flesh before I open it up to you. Keep a low profile for now, and I will be in touch with you all. And while our friends out there were short-sighted enough to leave in a group, I would prefer that we depart in a staggered manner, perhaps slowly over an hour. That way we are considerably less noticeable.'

Rufinus was surprised and a little disappointed when Severus indicated that he should be the first to leave. It felt a little as though the governor had got rid of him first to share a private moment with the other two prefects and Rufinus forced himself to accept the likelihood that Severus would leave last and was simply separating out a man with whom he was known to share a bond first.

Rufinus left the building and exited into the afternoon sunshine, blinking repeatedly. The men outside the warehouse did not acknowledge him as he passed, and closed in protectively once more. They would be counting the men leaving and would know when the building was empty. Now that he knew more, Rufinus realised that the men were mostly Praetorians in disguise. He resisted the urge to demand that they open their tunic necks. If only one of them were wearing a scorpion pendant then it would suggest that Cleander knew something of what had happened and their lives would all be forfeit. Still, all seemed quiet, and he could hardly do that, so he ignored the men and made his way by a roundabout route away from the warehouse and out of the commercial district. He strolled back between the Aventine and the Little Aventine, and around the end of the Circus Maximus.

As he walked tensely along the side of the Palatine hill towards the great Flavian amphitheatre and his headquarters beyond, he looked up at the great aqueduct that marched across the valley from the Caelian, remembering that dreadful night when they had crossed it, pursued by dangerous enemies. The night another Praetorian prefect had been doomed: Perennis.

He shuddered, remembering that night and their dangerous flight across the lofty bridge, and brought his eyes back down to ground level only to almost leap in shock. His old friends Mercator and Icarion were strolling towards him along the street, dressed in togas but with their swords showing as bulges beneath.

He felt a wave of panic. Of all the men in the Guard it was these two he would automatically trust, but right now he couldn't afford *anyone* to recognise him. In a panic he almost fled, running across the wide road to the other side to be out of their way, but such urgency would only draw extra unwanted attention.

Gritting his teeth and sweating like a roasting hog, he forced himself to maintain that same steady pace as he walked forward. The two soldiers, his oldest friends in the Guard, glanced at the man approaching them and angled to the side, talking quietly to one another.

They passed Rufinus right by at a distance of less than five feet and gave him not another glance.

Shivering at the close encounter, and wondering once more whether he was really cut out for this kind of subterfuge, Rufinus marched on, willing himself home where he would await Severus' next message and perhaps a clue as to what the future held.

CHAPTER FIVE – AN UNCONVENTIONAL PARTY

Rome, July 187 A.D.

Rufinus felt the litter tip to the side a little and grumbled. He still felt more comfortable moving about by horse, or better still by the feet the gods had gifted him, but he was a senior man in the empire's military now and certain standards were expected, especially when he was on official business. The interior of the shaky little vehicle was stuffy and very hot, and with the heavy wool toga he wore for appropriateness he was probably losing a pound of weight in sweat with every couple of paces the bearers took.

He twitched aside the curtain of the litter, partially to look at the bearers once more, and partially to see if he could stir a faint current of air, but there was no more breeze outside than in, and all it did was admit the dry-dung aroma of a city summer to the vehicle.

The litter bearers raised suspicion in him. He had rarely ever travelled by this mode of transport, but he'd seen plenty of litters before. The bearers were generally specially chosen for their matching size, their strength and their ability to keep the vehicle level and comfortable. The four men currently lifting Rufinus had apparently been selected for their inequality in height, their ham-fistedness and their inability to stop the bloody thing swaying sickeningly. But then he was fairly sure they were not normal litter bearers. They were probably soldiers by the look of them, and likely serving ones rather than retired veterans. In fact, once again he had the notion that perhaps they had come from the camp of the frumentarii. That the prefect of the Castrum Lecticariorum, who would have been the man who assigned the vehicle to Rufinus, had been in that warehouse did not go unnoticed. Perhaps he had been assigned extra protection by other conspirators. Perhaps they were keeping an eye on him for the prefect. Whatever the case, he would play his role perfectly, and if the worst happened, he had his guard of eight burly marines and a personal slave here anyway.

His destination, a large house on the Esquiline, lay ahead and the noise and bright lights from it were already overwhelming, even above the other wealthy estates of the region all celebrating the festival.

Tonight Rome celebrated Neptunalia in honour of the sea god, his main festival of the year. Papirius Dionysus, the grain commissioner, was hosting a grand gathering and a group offering to the god for his favour in the coming year in terms of the grain fleets and their voyages. Naturally, he had invited all the great and good of Rome but, being Neptunalia, he had also invited all those with a vested interest in the favour of the sea god.

Shipping magnates, priests of the god, the prefects in charge of water supply, drainage, river control and more, the Ordo of Ostia, to which Rome looked for almost all seaborne trade and, of course, the prefects of the two main fleets: the Misenum and Ravenna classis. Rufinus was here in his official capacity and had no need for subterfuge, which was nice even if it meant playing the pampered pillock.

He sat back as the vehicle slowed, listening to his men jingle to a halt and line up. With a sickening lurch, the litter was lowered to the ground, and Rufinus adjusted his toga carefully. While he generally disliked wearing a toga, he had to admit that it was the perfect garment when it came to maintaining a disguise. Gnaeus Marcius Rustius Rufinus was easily recognised by the simple absence of the fingernails on his left hand. It had not been noted among the majority that Aulus Triarius Rufinus favoured his right, his left hand often hidden or tucked into his belt, or gloved when aboard ship or riding. But with a toga, things were perfect, for it was standard practice to drape the heavy wool folds of the toga over the left forearm and use the right hand. Just a little adjustment allowed him to hide his maimed hand within the garment without looking at all out of place.

Satisfied that he was attired just right, he stepped out of the litter. His men were lined up like the soldiers they were, and he nodded to the officer among them. 'If you head around to the servants' entrance, I am led to believe there will be food and drink for you all while the festivity continues – cheese, hazel nuts and wine. I shall send for you when I am ready to leave.'

With that he stepped away, towards the door in the perimeter wall, which remained closed, lit by two lamps and with a huge, heavy knocker. The sounds of revelry arose from within, but the street was empty. He was approaching the door, hand rising towards the knocker, when he sensed something amiss. Pausing, he listened intently. There was the faintest susurration behind him, across the street where a small park stood with an ornate fountain at its centre. The sound could so easily have been a faint breeze brushing the leaves of the trees. But there *was* no breeze.

He turned, hand instinctively going to where a sword would normally sit. His guards had noticed nothing unusual, and were watching him with concerned interest. He tensed, and a moment later a figure stepped from the shadow of a tree. Rufinus almost exploded with relief at the sight of Vibius Cestius, the officer of the frumentarii he had met two years earlier while trying to save Perennis. Cestius was one of very few men in the city he would trust without question. His eyes widened in surprise as he noted Cestius sliding a knife back into his belt as he emerged. There was no visible evidence of violence, and by the time he was in the open street the frumentarius was perfectly relaxed, but now Rufinus knew what the susurration was. Poor bastard, whoever he'd been.

Cestius nodded. 'Prefect.'

Rufinus felt a momentary panic. Was he supposed to know openly who Cestius was? Should he reply as a polite stranger? He had no idea. Nor even whether Cestius was here with an invitation. The man was wearing a white toga which had somehow, miraculously, escaped blood spatter among the trees, and so Rufinus presumed the man was also bound for the door. Settling for something nondescript, he returned the greeting nod, but said nothing.

He rapped the knocker on the gate three times and the door was opened by a thick-set man with a face that looked like he'd been danced on by horses. There was a momentary flicker of recognition between the doorman and the frumentarius, and Rufinus congratulated himself on his ever-growing powers of observation. So, Dionysus' doorman was working for the frumentarius. Nothing was simple in Rome, even opening a door...

The man stepped aside and gestured for them to enter and as they did so, a slave hurried over with a tray of pastries and glasses of wine. The two visitors took a glass and a small delicacy and then followed the slave into the gardens.

Dionysus had outdone himself.

Neptunalia was one of those unusual festivals that was held outside in the open air rather than in the house. A rough shelter was often made of bent branches and foliage, but what had been constructed in Dionysus' garden must have taken days. Weeks, even. The entire garden, which was a huge and sprawling affair, was covered by a series of wicker structures, all interlinked by passages made of the same stuff. The wicker had all been interwoven with live flowers, specifically chosen for their night time scents. With the lamps burning all around it was like some sort of divine thicket. Figures milled about under the branches, chatting and laughing, wine in their hands, and slaves darted hither and thither, making sure that no glass ran dry for even a moment, and no hand was devoid of sweet pastries.

The slave led them to the centre of the garden, where they entered the largest of the wicker domes and Rufinus goggled, his breath stolen. Dionysus' garden had a large ornamental pond at its centre, and this huge dome covered that pond, while wooden walkways had been constructed and floated out onto the water, bound together to make a latticework of paths across the expanse. At the centre a fountain shaped with four tritons spewed water up into the air. Before it stood an altar to Neptune, at which guests had already begun laying their offerings.

He spotted Dionysus speaking to a togate man with dark hair and started to stride towards him. The prefect of the grain spotted him and smiled, waving him over and Rufinus returned the smile, his blood turning suddenly to ice as the man next to the prefect turned.

Cleander!

Rufinus felt his blood start to surge, his skin prickling into a shiver despite the overbearing heat. He felt panic rising. He had been invited here ostensibly, and quite reasonably, due to his position as Prefect of the Fleet, but the note from Severus that he had dutifully eaten as soon as he'd read it had told him to attend, for he would find it useful. Was this it? Had Severus somehow moved his plan towards fruition without even letting Rufinus know what was happening? Would the chamberlain die tonight? Here?

He chided himself for his panicky stupidity. Of course they wouldn't try anything here and now. It would be exactly the kind of precipitous move that Severus had argued against. Of course, those senators might have a different idea. He wondered if they were present, and his gaze swept around the garden with a new purpose, peering at the other attendees. Now, he realised that there were Praetorians all over the place, indistinguishable from the rest of the men in white togas but for the suspicious bulge of a concealed blade. It would be nice to think that they were loyal men placed here by that prefect who had been in the warehouse, but the presence of Cleander suggested that they were far more likely his own hand-picked men. Suddenly, Dionysus' glorious garden felt like the most dangerous place in Rome.

'Ah, Prefect,' the commissioner said warmly as Rufinus approached, and reached out to clasp his hand. Rufinus glanced momentarily down, making sure his maimed fingers were hidden within the folds of the toga. The last thing he wanted was suddenly to be horribly recognisable right here.

'Prefect,' Rufinus replied, bowing his head, neatly avoiding meeting Cleander's gaze. He realised with a start that he had automatically affected a faint Gallic accent, so prepared was he to hide his identity that very moment.

'Have you met the chamberlain?'

Rufinus felt his flesh pucker again in worry as he turned a horribly false smile to Cleander and nodded his head. 'I do not believe I have had the pleasure.'

Cleander looked at him carefully, clearly checking him out, sizing him up, and Rufinus wondered for a moment whether despite everything the chamberlain had seen straight through his hirsute disguise. 'Prefect Triarius Rufinus, I believe,' he said in a deep voice that made Rufinus squirm with panic and hatred in equal measures.

'Chamberlain,' Cestius said, leaning past Rufinus to shake Cleander's hand. The chamberlain gave him a blank look. Oh to be so anonymous, Rufinus thought.

'Vibius Tribulus,' Cestius introduced himself, 'commander of the Euxine fleet currently on detached duty in the camp of the foreigners.'

Cleander nodded and shook, having immediately written Cestius off as unimportant. Rufinus stared at his friend. Such a bare-faced lie that could easily be uncovered by checking out who *was* the Euxine prefect. Moreover, the camp of the foreigners was the Castra Peregrina, also home base of the frumentarii. So brazen. But then Cestius had once told him that the best lies were ninety per cent truth.

Rufinus was saved further panic and decision when a voice called to Cleander and the chamberlain excused himself and wandered off. Papirius Dionysus gave two newcomers an impudent smile and then spoke in low tones to Rufinus. 'Wait for a count of fifty and then walk away past the statue of Diana. At the end of the passage there you will find a door. It appears to be locked, but that is only because it sticks. Nudge the edge two feet below the handle and go in. Then you,' he turned to Cestius, 'count another fifty, get yourself another drink and do the same. I will join you shortly. Now laugh outrageously as though I have been telling you the crudest of jokes.'

Rufinus roared with laughter, and Cestius smirked and chuckled. Grinning mischievously, Dionysus walked away. Rufinus strolled over to the altar to Neptune and began to count to fifty as Cestius circulated. Reaching the end of his count, Rufinus strode off. The door was easy enough to find and, courtesy of the planning of the wattle domes and passages, out of sight of everyone. A quick shove in the appropriate place and the door groaned open, revealing a garden shed or outbuilding that had been re-plastered recently and was lit with three oil lamps, couches arrayed around the walls. There were no windows and the door was thick and solid. He took a seat and was just fidgeting with the folds of his toga when the door creaked open and Cestius entered.

'Greetings, Prefect of the Fleet,' the man grinned, and closed the door behind him.

'Who was that you killed in the park?'

'None of your concern, young man. But before anyone else arrives and we get down to the business of treason, I needed to speak to you privately.'

Rufinus frowned. He'd not seen the man since before he went to Dacia, and Cestius had immediately dropped back into conversation as though he'd never left for the edge of the empire, uncovered a conspiracy, and died there.

'I told you I would find you the names of your six horsemen.'

Rufinus felt a sudden thrill of grim hope, leaning forward hungrily. The six men had killed a frumentarius at the imperial villa half a decade ago, and Rufinus had vowed a just death for each of them.

'Tell me.'

'Well we know Glabrio, who you dispatched at the mansio during the Perennis trouble, and Pollius who you *accidentally* hit a little too hard in a boxing match.'

Rufinus nodded, nothing more. Both men had deserved what came to them, and Rufinus felt not a jot of remorse. He would do it exactly the same again. In fact, he would do similar to the others.

'And Vedius died of bite wounds in the Praetorian fortress, which I presume was your little pet.'

Rufinus nodded. He'd been a lucky find. The first of the six to die, the morning Rufinus saved the emperor's life. 'So I know about the dead. What about the others?'

Cestius sucked his lip as though trying to decide whether he should tell the eager Praetorian or not, but then he started to count them off on his fingers.

'Appius Fulvius has had a meteoric career change. From ordinary trooper to a tribune of the Praetorian cavalry, coinciding almost precisely with Cleander taking control of the Guard with the new title of *dagger bearer*. Fulvius seems to be one of Cleander's chosen in the Praetorians and can do no wrong. You'll not find anyone in the Guard who'll dare stand against him.'

'*I* will. Who else?'

'Decimus Curtius. He was the oldest of the six. He seems to have been given an honourable discharge from the Guard due to some minor injury, but his pension outweighs that of most tribunes. He lives a rich and easy life now in a house on the Quirinal hill, where he seems to remain one of Cleander's men, a hub of information and blackmail, I suspect. His nose is officially clean, but the man's working *something* for Cleander, for sure.'

'And the other?'

'Gaius Hostilius Arvina. He might be the toughest to get to. He's risen in the last few years to the position of centurion, but he's no ordinary Guard officer. His remit is the security of the imperial palace. He lives on the Palatine and every soldier there is under his direct command. I'd say it's somewhat telling the direction the Guard is heading that they concentrate so heavily on the security of the Palatine whether the emperor is there or not, for usually Cleander *is*.'

'Thank you. I will see to it that all three of them join their friends before this is over.'

Cestius shot him a warning look. 'Given what you're engaged in – *we're* engaged in, I suppose – your fellow conspirators would disapprove of you jeopardising the grand scheme for the sake of small revenge, no matter how justified it might be.'

Rufinus shook his head. 'When Cleander falls, those who took his coin will fall with him or soon after. These six men deserve worse than that. They need to die knowing that it's because they murdered an innocent man in cold blood, not because they later signed on with Cleander. It is a matter of simple principle.'

Cestius chuckled. 'A man of principle. A rare thing in the Guard these days. I respect your decision, but I will advise you to be careful and circumspect in your dealings with them. Do not allow this quest of yours to interfere with the grand plan. It is too important.'

There was a click just then as the door slipped open once more and two figures entered together.

Severus wore his toga like a cuirass. Never had a man looked more like a general even in civilian clothes. With him was Nicomedes, the head of the state courier service.

'Rufinus. Cestius.'

The governor and his companion strode over and took two more of the seats. No one spoke now, and Rufinus found himself swinging back and forth between nervous fretting about what was about to be discussed and impatient anger, wanting to leave and hunt down the first of those three doomed cavalrymen. Fortunately only a few moments passed before the door opened and Dionysus stepped in. The door shut behind, and the grain commissioner made for another chair.

'A redundant question, I know,' Severus muttered, 'but we *are* safe to talk here?'

Dionysus nodded. 'I have two ex gladiators on my staff, both of whom are mute and deaf, but are paid so handsomely that their loyalty is unquestioned. They guard the room close enough to stop any eavesdropper. Additionally, the wicker passage has been moved. Anyone who follows us will find that now the path leads them only back into the villa. I am very careful, Severus.'

'Careful enough to invite Cleander.'

'A stroke of genius,' put in Cestius. 'No one in their right mind would invite Cleander to somewhere they had something to hide. This is the last place his men will be looking for trouble. And if the two men Dionysus speaks of are the two I think they are, then they owe their muteness and deafness to the chamberlain too, so I cannot imagine a safer pair of guards. And I made sure that the man who followed Rufinus from his castrum disappeared before we came in.'

Rufinus blinked. He'd been followed? He had no idea. So *that* was who'd been on the receiving end of the man's knife beneath the trees.

'Very well,' Severus said. 'I realise that we all have our vested interest in this matter, but I also know that I am in the best position to take the lead. For sure Cleander will have men in the courier service, and among the grain stores. Neither of you gentlemen can move too freely. Cestius lives among a camp of spies. They may be very loyal, but no sane man plots within a camp of spies. And then there's the Prefect of the Fleet over there, who is nicely inconspicuous, but believe me, if Cleander spends any time close to him, or his agents pry too much, Rufinus will come unstitched remarkably fast. I, on the other, hand, have never put a foot wrong with Cleander, have spent much of my time away in the provinces and have occupied myself over much of the past decade with building a clientele and military network upon whom I can rely. So I trust no one will mind that I believe I have found the way to pull this plot together.'

A chorus of nods confirmed this, and so Severus leaned forward.

'As I suggested in the meeting with the others, I believe the trick to this is not to directly bring about the chamberlain's downfall. A blade in the dark or an open accusation will both fail. A knife in the back would cause a round of investigations and proscriptions that would see us all tortured to death. And no one can get enough on Cleander to accuse him without him wriggling out of it, which would then set him seeking revenge.'

Cestius nodded. 'Quite true. Believe me, I have spent the past year digging and putting together information. The problem is that the whole world can see what he's doing, but none of it breaks any specific law, and those that have been bent too far have been done so with the emperor's permission. No court case will bring him down.'

'Precisely,' Severus agreed. 'So what I propose is something akin to what happened to Perennis. We know that the accusations made against him were false, and time would have allowed us to prove the untruths of the evidence. But Cleander had been clever. He made sure to set the whole of Rome against Perennis, and the mob might have no say in the senate, but when they speak with one mouth even emperors are forced to listen. Perennis died simply because the Roman people demanded it. Only something similar will bring down Cleander. He needs to be universally despised, so that there is no man willing to stand for him. Only then will his defences be down and he stripped of his power.'

'But how do you plan to turn the whole of Rome against him?' Dionysus murmured.

'Simply. He needs to be seen to be at fault when Rome suffers. What was Juvenal's rule for the mob?'

'Panem et Circenses,' Rufinus put in. 'The people will always be satisfied with bread and circuses.'

Dionysus' eyes narrowed. 'Bread?'

'Exactly. How is your history? Who is aware of the revolt of Clodius Macer against the idiot Nero?'

Rufinus felt his heart lurch. He had an idea of where this was going. 'Macer was governor of Africa. He rebelled against the emperor, but he was supposedly urged into it by a woman. Calvia something-or-other.'

Severus smiled. 'You know your histories, Rufinus. Calvia Crispinilla. She formed a plan to interrupt the grain shipments from Africa and Aegyptus, to starve Rome into capitulation. Rome would see that Macer sat in Africa with more grain than he knew what to do with, claiming the throne, while Nero floundered in the capital, unable to do anything about his starving people. The mob is fickle. They would so easily turn on their emperor for such a thing. And if an emperor might be brought down in such a way, how much easier a freedman?'

Papirius Dionysus shook his head. 'The grain distribution is *my* responsibility. I am the man the people would tear apart.'

'Not if we work a way to displace the blame,' Severus argued. 'Cleander has his hand in every pie, and any dish free of his influence he covets. It should not be difficult to get him to take responsibility for the grain if he thinks it will make him popular or powerful. He is vain and ambitious enough to leap without considering the danger. And who better to do this? Rufinus commands the fleet that keeps the west coast clear and safe for grain shipments, Dionysus distributes them when they arrive in Rome. I control the access to the fleet's grain mills at Arelate, and can get close to Cleander, nudging matters as they require it, steering events. Nicomedes can control the flow of information, allowing us to proceed as we wish, and Cestius can make sure that this all remains quiet and unnoticed. I did not gather you four men by chance, you know. We can emulate the plan of Calvia Crispinilla, land the blame with Cleander, and watch the people of Rome bay for his head.'

'There is another problem with this,' Rufinus said quietly.

'Oh?'

'Your plan somewhat relies upon starving the people of Rome. I for one am not comfortable with that. Rome suffers enough already with the plague. Emptying the bellies of babes and old folk is not worth it to bring down one man, even if that man is Cleander.'

Severus fixed him with a look that brooked no argument. 'This is war, Rufinus. You've suffered war. You know that sometimes you must position your men in danger to draw out an enemy so you can cut them down. Sacrifices have to be made.'

'*This* sacrifice is too much.'

Severus looked around at the others, and Rufinus followed suit, but was disappointed to see only grim nods as the rest of the room reluctantly agreed with the governor, who then turned back to him.

'I cannot do this without you. I brought you into my house and had you appointed to power so that you could be part of this. We are committed to a path. And while the path I chose is strewn with thorny roses, it is still the best path for that we seek. I am not a vicious man by nature, Rufinus, but I *am* willing to sacrifice men to save the empire. Currently I believe I have all the pieces of this puzzle, though I have not yet quite worked out how they fit together. That might yet take some time, for I would far rather be slow and certain than fast and risky. While I work all of this out I grant you, Rufinus, time to come up with a viable alternative plan. If when we next meet you can persuade us of a better way then I will acquiesce. But if not, then you will submit and continue with our plan. Cleander must fall, and I will not falter in the task.'

'What use is the fleet anyway?' Dionysus put in.

'What?'

'The grain fleets are formed of private contractors paid for by the state. There is no imperial owned fleet, and they do not even have a military escort. Of what use, then, is the Misenum fleet?'

'As I said, not all the pieces are in place in this puzzle,' Severus reiterated, 'but the grain fleets are at the mercy of the usual perils of the sea, and of all the fleets in the empire the Misenum fleet is the strongest and most important, and above all it secures and maintains the coast upon which lie the ports where the grain arrives. We may not be able to exert control where the grain comes from out in the southern provinces, but Rufinus here controls the sea where it arrives.'

Dionysus nodded his acceptance of that.

'Then we are agreed?' Severus said, deliberately avoiding Rufinus' troubled face. 'I shall return to my planning. Each of you I suggest look to the security and loyalty of your own spheres of influence. Anyone you have reason to mistrust, post them far away in some unimportant role, and build a close support of men you know well. If one brick in this tower crumbles the whole thing could fall so easily.'

Dionysus rose. 'We have been absent for time enough. I will be missed before long. We should return to the party and enjoy ourselves for the rest of the night. I suggest we leave in a staggered manner at counts of one hundred, and do not meet for the rest of the night if we can avoid it.'

Their host went first, leaving the rest of them in the room together. Dionysus frowned deeply for the count of a hundred, clearly considering the extreme danger of his particular part in Severus' plan. When he departed, Nicomedes spent some time with an unreadable expression before he too rose and left. Severus and Cestius shared a nod a moment later, and the frumentarius was the next to depart, leaving Rufinus alone with the governor.

'You *know* that this is the only real option.'

Rufinus tried to find an argument, but he'd spent the count of three hundred so far already ruling out other possibilities.

Severus was simply, harshly, horribly right: the only way to bring about the chamberlain's downfall without repercussions was to turn the public against him, and however that was done it would cause hurt to the people. He didn't like it, but the chances of him coming up with a viable alternative were infinitesimally small. In the end, he nodded.

'And it will be difficult,' Severus added. 'Centuries of Roman administration and organisation have been put in place purely to make sure the grain dole is safe and uninterrupted. It will take time and ingenuity. But when it is done, we will have cut a cancer out of Rome. We do the work of the gods, Rufinus,' Severus said with a sigh, as he rose and made his own way to the door.

Rufinus sat with a heavy heart and watched him go.

Quite.

But which gods?

CHAPTER SIX – THE HORSEMAN

Rome, October 187 A.D.

The visitor was unexpected after three months.

Three months of wondering what Severus was planning. Three months of not seeing anyone else involved in the conspiracy. Three months of wondering what would be expected of him when the time came and the plan unfolded. Three months of tension and worry.

And then this.

'Show him in, Philip,' Rufinus said to the centurion with the red hair. He had not only become used to the strange foibles of this man, but had come to very much rely upon him. Clearly Philip had all-but run the Misenum fleet for almost a decade now, serving under three entirely useless, greedy, narcissistic and almost entirely absent prefects. Whether he was relieved to have a boss who actually took an interest in his role or was perhaps peeved at a boss who interfered Rufinus couldn't say, and the centurion was smart enough not to let anything on.

Philip bowed and stepped out and Septimius Severus, Governor of Gallia Lugdunensis and loyal servant of empire, strolled in as though out for a morning stroll and with nothing of import on his mind.

'Governor,' Rufinus acknowledged and rose from his seat to shake Severus' hand.

'Prefect.' Severus stood in place until the door shut behind him, and they heard the footsteps of Philip crossing the courtyard back to his own office. The governor took Rufinus' hand in his tight grasp and then sank into a seat. 'How secure is your office?'

'Perfectly,' Rufinus replied. 'I've tested everything thoroughly. Even when a man sings in here you have to be standing within ten feet of the door to hear it. And I have standing orders that all activity is kept twenty paces from my office so that I can get work done. The courtyard is open and square, so no one can lurk nearby unnoticed, and Philip's window looks out across the open to here, so he can see if anyone is breaking the rules.'

'And you're sure of Philip? You're sure of everyone upon whom you rely?'

Rufinus nodded. 'Philip is a Christian. I know. Strange. I never expected to find one in the army, but he seems perfectly happy to bow to the statue of the emperor and he's bloody good at his job, so I have no issue with him. But talking things through with him, it seems that one of the tenets of his faith is something about not lying and always seeking to do right. I'm not sure how that sits with the fact that I keep catching him belting seven shades of shit out of a soldier for a minor infraction, but he has vowed his loyalty, and I know he is personally disgusted with the chamberlain. Believe me, Governor, since the party I have been working through the fleet, putting everything in order. Anyone who has even the remotest connection with Cleander has been shifted to a position in Misenum, safely out of the way, and two men who I had particular reason to distrust have been cross-promoted to a more senior post in the Ravenna fleet across the other side of the peninsula. I've been very careful, and I've been quite thorough. I have, after all, had three months to do it. I had hoped we'd be moving by now.'

Severus nodded. 'Glad to hear you've got things under control. Similar surgeries have been undertaken by the other prefects and even in my own administration. So you believe we are safe to talk openly?'

'We are. Why the delay. What is the plan?'

'Slowly and carefully, Rufinus. Precipitous movement lands men in trouble. I have things being moved into place, and I have an extra notion which I have begun to act upon. But to leap feet first into something as dangerous as this would be disastrous. And that is why I am here.'

'Oh?'

It had been a surprise to see Severus here after the man had been so adamant that the conspirators not associate, but it hadn't occurred to him yet what had driven Severus to break his own rule. Now Rufinus could see something in the man's eyes. Something worrying. Something dangerous that was causing tension even to the Lion of Leptis sitting opposite him.

'Certain acquaintances of ours came into the hands of the Praetorians this morning.'

Rufinus' heart skipped a beat. Dionysus? Nicomedes? Surely not Vibius Cestius?

'Two senators, along with sundry accomplices. Antistius Burrus and Arrius Antoninus.'

Rufinus felt a moment's heady relief that it was not the men involved in their own circle of conspiracy, but that was swiftly swept aside as he realised that they had all been at the warehouse meeting together. Rufinus and Severus had attended along with all those men who sought Cleander's downfall.

'Shit'

'Succinctly put,' Severus replied. 'I warned them against such precipitous acts. They moved too fast and without sufficient care. It seems that both the senators and a nephew had been trying to expand the web of their conspiracy, drawing in men who had access to Cleander to prepare for an assassination. Someone said the wrong thing to the wrong person. Word of their plans reached a man called Decimus Curtius, who dropped the information into the lap of the prefect of the Urban Cohorts. He, Seius Fuscianus, conspired immediately with Cleander's favourite Praetorian prefect, and they had the senators arrested forthwith.'

'Will they name names?'

Severus shrugged. 'It is highly likely. All we can hope is that they are too busy under torture selling out those men who are actually involved in their plot to get to those of us who once just happened to be at a meeting with them. And if our names happen to crop up and we ourselves are brought in, we are in the best of positions as we have all been perfectly open and clean. None of us have met – until now – and none of us have moved against anyone. The chamberlain's spies will be able to confirm to him that we have had nothing to do with the senators or their ilk. Much is now down to either chance or the determination and strength of those men under interrogation. I suggest you expend all your spare coin on offerings to the gods, praying that our names go unspoken.'

Rufinus frowned. Something there had triggered a memory. He fretted at the information, replaying it in his head. What was it?

'Consequently,' Severus said, 'I am putting any further movement of ours on hold. I have a few things in place and one more plan underway, but we need to be absolutely clear of all trouble now until this latest nightmare blows over. If by some chance we get away without becoming involved in this failed plot, we must lie low for a few months before we dare move once more. Be careful and do not do anything other than your precise job until I give you the word. We will drop all threads of our web until at least Saturnalia. Be absolutely innocent of everything until then and pray that we ride this out. Seius Fuscianus and his informer have no connection to us, so with luck we…'

'The informer,' Rufinus spat, sitting forward, gripping the chair arms tight and interrupting Severus.

'What?'

'The man who passed the information on to the Urban Prefect. What was his name again?'

'Decimus Curtius.'

'Shit. I think that I might have to do one more thing before we lie low for a time.'

Severus narrowed his eyes. 'What is it?'

'I told you of the six cavalrymen and why I was hunting them?'

'Yes, but your personal vendettas have to take second place to the true goal at the moment, you understand that?'

'Quite, but one of the remaining three cavalrymen retired with Cleander's support. He became something of a hub of informers for the chamberlain. Decimus Curtius is Cleander's man, and he is one of the men I'm hunting.'

Severus sat back, sucking his teeth. 'Perhaps it would be better to let this man keep about his business. His death would be another suspicious event, and we don't want anything else that might point our way right now.'

Rufinus shook his head. 'Curtius is too dangerous to allow his freedom. He has already been responsible for the downfall of our senatorial friends. How long before his web of informants learns something of us.'

'Still…'

'And there is no known connection between he and us, official or not. As long as I'm careful, there should be no reason to trace anything back to us. In fact, it will likely be seen as revenge by one of the senators' co-conspirators.'

Severus nodded slowly. 'There is something in that, for sure. And I have to admit that having one of Cleander's principle sources of information silenced would be more than a relief. But you are too high profile. I think I should pass this on to Vibius Cestius. He and his ilk are experienced in dealing with problems like this.'

Rufinus shook his head. 'He might be the natural choice, and I have every confidence in Cestius, but this is my task. I vowed to Apollo and Nemesis both that I would kill those men, and I will hold true to that vow. Would that we could do something about Seius Fuscianus while we were about it. Not only does he now seem to be in bed with Cleander and part of this web of treachery, but he was also in the purse of Clodius Albinus. It was his name I found on bars of gold that were meant for the treasury. Do you think Albinus might be in league with Cleander?'

Severus shook his head. 'Cleander only has underlings, not equals, and Albinus is far too ambitious to tie himself to Cleander. Like every man of position, he knows that the emperor's succession is wide open and has his eyes set on the throne. No, likely the Urban Prefect is simply taking what he can get from two different masters. A lucrative game, but it will prove a dangerous one if either of them finds out.'

Rufinus sucked air in through his teeth, thoughtfully. 'It's a shame I came out of Dacia without the evidence. If I could have dropped that beautiful gold bar somehow with Cleander, he'd have killed Fuscianus himself. Little is more satisfying than watching your enemies remove each other.'

'Let's not get ahead of ourselves. I think we have spent long enough talking of such dangerous matters. It matters not how secure you believe this place, nowhere is safe for long. When I leave here, I shall be heading back to Lugdunum, where I shall quietly wait out the rest of this year in the hope that the torturers manage to wheedle out of our senatorial friends only their close conspirators. I need you to send orders for a few of your ships – preferably with very loyal, trustworthy trierarchs – to be assigned to the Rhodanus river between Lugdunum and the sea.'

Severus retrieved a scroll case from his belt and dropped it on the desk. 'Official request from the governor of Gallia Lugdunensis for the support of the Misenum fleet in securing the trade route of the Rhodanus in the wake of the deserters' uprising. Also to guard the Arelate grain mills and secure their supply of the fleet. In fact this did need doing anyway, and is somewhat overdue, but it is also a very good reason for my being here and explains away our meeting perfectly. I shall be in touch again in due course. Be very careful in everything you do, and I wait with bated breath for news of a certain informer's untimely demise.'

Without further ado Severus rose, shook Rufinus' hand once more and left. Rufinus saw him out and closed the door behind him, satisfying himself once more that no one had been within earshot during their conversation. He felt oddly panicky that Severus was returning to his posting in Gaul. He, Dionysus, Nicomedes and Cestius were all influential and clever men, he knew, but it was Severus who was the driving force behind what they were doing, and without him nothing would happen. That he would be absent from the city for months, especially when their names might appear on a proscription list at any moment, was not a comforting thought.

He took a deep breath and returned to his desk, sinking into his seat, deep in thought. He could do with speaking to Cestius but Severus had been quite definite that none of the five of them should meet now, while the danger of the failed senatorial plot hung over their heads. In some ways, Rufinus felt that what he should really be doing is packing up everything of importance and preparing to disappear into the provinces somewhere under an assumed moniker, before the senators revealed his name under the torturer's knife.

It was darkly humorous that being Gnaeus Marcius Rustius Rufinus had become so dangerous that he had faked his own death and lived under the assumed identity of Aulus Triarius Rufinus, who was now in danger of being even more sought-after and troubled than the *real* him. Might he now have to somehow kill off Triarius and become someone else? He'd grown a beard and shaggy hair to change last time. What was next? Shaved bald like an Aegyptian priest? How many hims would there be before he could walk free and safe once more?

He forced himself to calm down, knowing that he was becoming more and more agitated as he thought about the many dangers pressing in on him. He needed to be more relaxed and careful. He needed to be ready for anything, but not to *plan* for failure. Severus seemed content that there was a chance at least that their names would not be blurted out in some Praetorian cellar, and he was quite correct that the best thing they could do was seem to be absolutely normal and to avoid any suspicious activity.

How then to go about the murder of a prominent citizen, and friend of the man who effectively controlled Rome, without being suspicious?

He drummed his fingers on the chair arm. First thing's first, he would need to know exactly where Decimus Curtius lived. His eyes strayed to his gladius, hanging on the wall in an ornate scabbard that had been supplied by Severus, decorated with bronze fretwork leaping dolphins and all the imagery of the navy. That sword would be used soon enough.

The days passed as Rufinus worked at his job, doing nothing that might draw undue attention. He paid attention to all the news that came out of the forum and the Palatine, mostly related verbatim by Philip with ever increasing relief. It transpired that somewhere along the line between the senators and the Praetorian prefect, who had begun to plan their assassination, and the ears of Curtius who passed it on to Cleander, the details of the plot had become confused. By the time Cleander and the Urban Prefect sent out men to round up the conspirators, it was believed that the villains had been plotting to kill the emperor, and had nothing to do with his chamberlain. Consequently it became a trial of treason against the state under the *lex maiestatis*, and brutal execution awaited them all.

It seemed miraculous to many, and no doubt unacceptable to Cleander, that somehow word of the conspiracy's unmasking reached many of those destined for the knives of the torturers and they managed to open their own veins in their homes before the Guard came for them. It must have been staggeringly irritating for him that even Antistius Burrus and his nephew, the two most high profile arrests made, managed to hang themselves between being captured and being tortured. In the end only one man made it to the tables in the Praetorian cellars, and that was the other senator, Arrius Antoninus. It would all seem so miraculous to Cleander's web of villains, because unlike Rufinus they did not know that the Praetorian prefect Laetus, who was the leading figure in the arrests, was also one of the conspirators and one of the few who had gone unnamed. Laetus in the end received something of a dressing down for his shoddy handling of the whole affair, including assigning over-zealous men to the interrogation of Antoninus, men who accidentally killed the senator before he could say too much.

It appeared that, despite everything, Rufinus and his friends had come through the whole affair unscathed. Prefect Laetus, a guiding light behind the failed attempt, and a man who had managed to contain the damage, dropped out of sight after that for a while, keeping his nose clean. Rufinus silently thanked the man for his care and vowed to make his gratitude tangible when this was all over.

He wondered now how long Severus would wait before he returned to the city. But then he was a provincial governor and was naturally expected to spend most of his time in his province. The longer he stayed there, the more normal it would appear.

Rufinus waited ten days after the whole arrest and execution affair died down before beginning to move again. Firstly, he needed to find that house. To do so, he would need either to ask someone in the know or search official records. The first option was out, unless he wanted to make his actions too well known. So he had to find a reason that he could explain away readily to visit the tabularium – the city's central record office.

It was easy enough in the end, when he thought it through, and was quite pleased with his own subtlety, which he felt was approaching that of Severus and Cestius. He searched the records in his own offices until he located a former trierarch by the name of Sextus Curtius. Close enough. He then managed to make a few minor adjustments to the retirement records of said ship captain and, once he was satisfied that he had done it all well and nothing could be traced back to him, he announced to Philip that he had come across a captain who had retired some years ago, but due to an error in accounting made by some clerk or other he had been dismissed with only three quarters of a full pension. Philip was appropriately horrified, unleashing a tirade of blistering invective against the poor long-gone clerk, and had vowed to see it all put right immediately. Rufinus carefully and heartily assured his secretary that it was all the fault of the clerk and that Philip suffered no culpability, but that Rufinus felt it should be the senior officer who delivered the news and the back pension to the man.

And so all his reasons went down as a matter of record in official channels. He visited the tabularium at the base of the Capitol to find the address of his retired sailor, and it was a simple task while looking up the residence of trierarch Sextus Curtius to also check the location of one Decimus Curtius.

That evening he complained of a bad back, attained, he said, from leaning over a desk so much. He took a walk to straighten out the kinks. That walk took him up the Quirinal some way until he passed the small temple of Florus and entered a leafy lane where the warm and sultry night was alleviated a little by the lines of trees by the road. The low wall on his left reached neck height and afforded him a fine view of a sprawling villa set amid sculpted grounds with a large ornamental lake, arcaded walkways, a grand nymphaeum and more. Working for Cleander really was lucrative if this was now the house of a man who had been no more important than Rufinus in his time.

There would be private guards, of course. Any man of that kind of wealth had such a force of mercenaries, and a man who had served in the Praetorians would be more careful than most. But this estate was large, full of structures and flora, and the perimeter was low and easily accessible.

He returned to the Castrum Misenatum, claiming the walk had done his back the world of good and there spent the next two days doing nothing unusual, keeping his nose clean while he waited for the bean counters of the classis to produce a small chest full of coins that constituted the 'missing' pension for trierarch Curtius. That evening, at dusk, he left the camp with his honour guard of eight burly marines, and strolled up to the house of the trierarch, refusing a litter as the evenings were currently far too hot to travel in a curtained vehicle.

He reached the man's modest but pleasant house and was greeted with some surprise. His guard remained in the atrium as Rufinus explained how an accounting error had left the man short of pension money. The trierarch was baffled, clearly, since he knew he had received the correct figure, but no man turns down free money from his employer and so he gratefully, and with stolid forgiveness for the error, took the chest of money. Rufinus managed to steer the conversation to his own experiences with the fleet, and soon the trierarch was launching into stories of his days at sea. Predictably, and a relief to Rufinus, he insisted that Rufinus stay for the evening meal and entertainment, and much good wine. He offered to make room for the guards among his servants, but Rufinus declined, dismissing his marines and sending them back to barracks. He then stayed, and genuinely enjoyed the meal and some social time with a man full of wonderful tales. He made sure every now and then to be visible from windows, enjoying himself like a good Roman noble. Once he thought he saw a figure in the street opposite, watching him. His alibi was good. He carefully cut his wine with a lot of water. He had become used to not drinking in the past year or two, and while he trusted himself these days to stay within respectable limits, he also did not push it. Plus he had much to do.

He left the trierarch's house late in the evening. He kept his senses alert and his eyes open as he moved, heading back towards the castrum, but by the time he had gone six streets and turned several corners, he was convinced he was entirely alone up here in this open area. Content that anyone following him earlier had given up in the knowledge that he was busy socialising with a former sailor, he changed direction and headed for the Quirinal.

He met only five people on his journey, for much of Rome's elite were absent at their summer retreats, and the posher areas of the city were something of a ghost town in the hottest months. The poor, who couldn't afford to have a seaside villa, did not venture up to these empty spaces, staying near the Subura where the nightlife raged on.

For almost half an hour he stood in the street near the wall of Curtius' estate, watching from the shadows of a beech tree. There were, indeed, roving guards on the estate, but they had been assigned with the military precision of a career soldier. In half the time he stood there, Rufinus had worked out the routines and routes taken by each man on guard. Just the slightest observation had given him his best route.

He waited until the man with the white hair had passed to the left, where he would disappear into the hedged garden for a count of almost a hundred, and the tall man with the limp had passed to the right, where he would next investigate the bath house. As soon as the two men were out of sight, he moved, crossing the street and vaulting the wall with ease. He landed on soft grass and began to run, bent low, counting under his breath all the time as he went. At fifty, he had crossed the main lawns and was at the row of tapering poplars that lined the path from villa to bathhouse.

He waited there, hidden in the shadow of a tree, until those two same guards returned, met and departed again, and then began to count once more as he ran along the grass beside the path to cut down any noise.

He stopped at the edge of the nymphaeum. Here he could barely see the wall he had initially vaulted, which meant he was more or less invisible to those two guards. He listened carefully. Over the splash of water he could hear the voices of various folk, and footsteps on gravel and stone. He would still be visible, but any low noise he made now would go unnoticed. Rounding the nymphaeum, he moved to the wall of the villa proper. Along the wall he crept in the shadows, pausing at each window to rise momentarily and peer in. He found two occupied rooms swiftly, one of which was a triclinium, occupied by three men drinking. One had to be Curtius, for the master of the house would surely be there. A quick glance at the men and he was fairly sure which of them was his target, two appearing a little wet and soft, while the third was too rough for this rich life. Marking the room and the man he moved on, quietly, in the shadows. He found what he suspected was the room he sought three windows further on. Lit only by one dim lamp it was a bed chamber decorated and adorned to the highest quality. It had to belong to the master.

It was not difficult to reach up inside the half-closed shutter and lift the catch, allowing access. Moving the shutter slowly and carefully to avoid suspicious creaks, he opened sufficient space to climb into the room. Once inside, he paused to let his sight adjust and then checked out the room. The sword hanging on the wall, soldier-style, confirmed it for him. This was the room of a former Praetorian. Curtius himself.

Crossing the room, he carefully drew the sword. He had thought to use the small knife at his belt, but this was much better. Weighing the sword and deciding that it was a good example of the type, he breathed deeply. He didn't like killing. Oh, not in battle, mind. That was different, though. Killing a man deliberately in his home felt wrong, and it sat badly enough with Rufinus that he had to wind himself up the act, even though he knew even the gods themselves would demand this death, for he was thoroughly deserving of it.

As he waited, he peered around the room. His gaze settled with surprise on a small desk by the far wall, and he padded over to it. A pile of vellum notes and letters lay on the desk beside a stilus and a block of sealing wax. Surely the man was more careful that that? He lifted a list and peered at it. It seemed to be a timetable of someone's daily routine, though he couldn't identify whom. Gods, but this stuff was *gold!* The man clearly still had the mentality of an ordinary soldier, even if he'd risen to playing the great game with Cleander. He had not yet discovered that even his own home was not safe. Grinning nastily in the darkness, Rufinus gathered every sheet he could find, rolled them up and stuffed them into one of the scroll cases on the desk, which he then secured into his belt.

He was just congratulating himself when the door opened and he leapt behind it urgently, poised. He lifted the sword ready to strike as the door moved again.

It was a slave with an armful of bedlinen. The poor sod avoided death by a hair's breadth as Rufinus changed the grip on the falling blade and instead struck the slave with the pommel, driving all sense and consciousness from him. The slave went down like a sack of turnips, and Rufinus dragged him to one side, kicking the linens away.

There he waited in the silence and the gloom of the one dim lamp.

As he waited, now focused, he worked through his first moves time and again. He had to be quick. The slave had not seen him, so at least that was good. He began to feel the tension of the wait, counting to one hundred repeatedly.

Still, despite his preparedness, the opening of the door took him by surprise.

'Attalus?' called the voice, clearly expecting his slave to be within, perhaps making the bed. A figure stepped into the room, his shadow huge in the golden rectangle of light from the door. As he passed the door itself, Rufinus gently pushed it shut behind him.

Decimus Curtius turned in surprise at the movement and it was the last thing he ever did.

Rufinus' blade hit him in the ribs, entirely unprotected with just a tunic in the warm night, and slid in, piercing the heart even as the young attacker's other hand clamped itself over his victim's mouth just before he screamed, dampening the sound to a muffled gasp.

'This if for Dis. Dionysus of the frumentarii, who you and your tent mates murdered in an imperial villa on the orders of a traitor. There will be no coin for your passage, and the ferryman will not take you. Wander here forever if you must, knowing that justice still exists in Rome.'

He watched the light die in the man's eyes. For years he had not been able to do that, but so many things had changed since he had started playing the great game. As the body of Decimus Curtius went limp, he lowered it gently to the floor, trying avoid what seemed to be an ocean of blood. With care, he positioned the body facing the bed that was close by and bent the man's arms, wrapping his hands around the hilt of the sword through his chest.

After a few moments he rose and realised with irritation that he had trodden in the blood. Swiftly he removed his boots. Whoever found the body, and he prayed it was that poor slave, else he might somehow be blamed, would have to come to the inevitable conclusion that Curtius had fallen on his sword in the ancient manner. That might not pass if a bloody footprint were found at the scene, of course. Unarmed now and holding his boots in his hand, he padded back across the room and checked for anyone outside before slipping out of the window and into the night.

The return journey should be easy.

Another of the murderers had met a just end and Rufinus could hardly wait to reach safety and read these documents. What revelations they could hold...

CHAPTER SEVEN – UNEXPECTED ENCOUNTERS

Rome, December 187 A.D.

Rufinus trod wearily and angrily through the frost-coated glory of the forum, documents confirming the appointment of three trierarchs and ordering the construction of two new triremes clutched in his right hand, knuckles numb with the cold. The irritation flooding through him was nothing to do with the work, though, and unconnected to the seasonal drop in temperature. It was to do with the tense necessity of doing nothing.

Once more, months had passed since Severus had left for Gaul and Rufinus had hunted down the fourth cavalryman, and the danger of being arrested seemed to have abated fully. The "plot against the emperor's life" by two disaffected senators and their cadre of friends had been almost forgotten and the world crept quietly on. Rufinus had finally broken the silence, unable to take the immobility any more. He had found a reasonable work excuse to visit Nicomedes, the prefect of the courier service, and had discovered that his fellow conspirator was as tautly impotent as he. Nicomedes had now reorganised his service sufficiently that he could, he believed, safely convey messages between them all with no danger of the letters dropping onto the chamberlain's desk. Still they had been careful to hide any real discussion among a slew of droning daily work, for in the Rome of Cleander only a fool believed himself truly safe. And so the two of them and Dionysus had begun to discuss their next moves carefully, though none of them dared contact Severus or Cestius.

Sadly, as Rufinus could really have predicted, no one could really move without Severus detailing what had to happen next in his scheme, and so they meandered on, still impotent. At least the documents he had taken from the cavalryman's villa had been of use. Among the huge array of names that identified men and women working as Cleander's eyes and ears in the city, the conspirators had discovered a man in Nicomedes' courier service, two in Dionysus' employ and one among Severus' own personnel. After some discussion among the three of them, they had decided that the best way of dealing with those men was not to remove them for fear of alerting their master, but to make sure that nothing more important than a wage chitty passed their way, keeping them bored and with nothing to report. Rufinus had sent a very carefully worded note to Severus warning him about his man, carried by one of Nicomedes' own relations aboard one of Rufinus' personally-appointed ships. There had been no reply, and no one felt like nudging the governor, just in case.

And so despite everything life droned on. Rufinus had begun to get used to his new role and had been surprised, and a little disappointed, to discover that ninety five percent of the role of Rome's most senior officers seemed to be making dull decisions and accepting or declining requests on parchment. Moreover, much of the remaining five percent seemed to be telling other people to do the same.

With a curse of irritation, Rufinus righted himself as his soft calfskin boot slid across a frosty flag and he almost ended up in a heap on his back. That would not look appropriate for one of Rome's elite in a public place. Plus it would hurt.

Skittering a little, he made for the portico of the Basilica Aemilia, where the staff had dutifully swept the flags clear and scattered grit for safety. Once beneath the arcade, he made once more for the tabularium to lodge his documents.

He was humming an old tune and frowning to himself, trying to remember the words, when he saw them and stopped dead. A woman in a saffron-coloured stola almost walked into him as he halted, and called him something mean before she haughtily swept past him and away. Rufinus ignored her and stepped into the shade of one of the columns.

His father was at the far end of the arcade, speaking to a man in a pale blue tunic. He'd not seen his father in so long, and the old man looked more drawn and haggard than ever. He felt the bitterness and resentment rising at the very sight of the old man and realised oddly that he was shaking, standing hiding behind a column in a very public place. People were watching him with interest. Damn it. Taking a deep breath, he ducked inside the basilica's nearest door. Inside, the place was thronged with people, even at this time of the year and in the coldest of temperatures. While it was still a public place, it was much easier to lurk and go unnoticed here among the crowd and so, not entirely sure why he was doing it anyway, he shuffled along the archways inside until he came to another door to the portico closer to his father.

The man his father was with was unknown to Rufinus, and thoroughly nondescript. He was in ordinary, if well-made, clothes, clean shaven and with neat hair. He could have been anyone, really, but Rufinus had the distinct feeling, even if he couldn't say why, that the man was one of the lackeys from the Palatine. His father seemed to be demanding something from the man, who was clearly telling him that it was not possible. He watched his father becoming quite irate and seriously began to think he might hit the fellow, but finally the man in blue shook his head a final time, turned and walked away.

As his father spun in irritation, Rufinus ducked back out of sight. The old man probably wouldn't recognise him anyway – might not even have recognised him *without* the disguise, frankly – but he couldn't risk it. In fact, he was unlikely to learn anything of value here, and there was nothing he could do. His father was already clutching at Cleander's tunic hem, desperate for a scrap of power, and yet somehow, having found the old man, Rufinus knew he had to watch, had to learn more.

Carefully, he stepped to the side, pretending to examine of the tablets in his hand but truly looking over the top of them. His father was still there, almost vibrating with anger. Just as Rufinus wondered what the miserable old fool would say if he thought his older son was still alive, his father stomped off across the square, threading between the few stalls who could be bothered setting up on a morning like this.

Without reasoning why, Rufinus followed.

His father passed the great Basilica Iulia and left the forum along the Vicus Tuscus, heading into the busy streets.. Rufinus, practiced enough now at such things and having sufficiently recovered from his initial shock, moved with speed along the street some fifty paces behind, keeping to the far side and pausing every now and then to make sure he didn't catch up. His father was moving with purpose.

They entered an area Rufinus knew well. In this part of the Velabrum were shops and taverns galore, but the drinking establishments here tended to cater for the better class of soldier from the Palatine. Rufinus had been here a few times, and he knew several of the Guard spent much of their free time in one of the half dozen establishments that had set themselves up as a largely 'soldier's bar'. What his father was doing here, he could not imagine.

The old man paused outside a tavern by the name of *Thirty Elephants* – a reference to Rome's first great victory overseas, playing to the vanity of the military. He stood for a few long moments, peering in through the door, and then pushed his way inside, much to Rufinus' increasing surprise. His father was lowering himself to many things that he would have berated Rufinus for doing in the old days.

The young prefect in the street with the armful of documents dithered. In a way, he felt there was little to be gained from taking any further interest, and yet still he could not stop himself. Nibbling his cheek in tension, he paused outside the door for the count of fifty, a habit he'd picked up at

Dionysus' party and a good one to acquire, and then made his own way inside.

The tavern was half full, which was good business this early in the day at this time of year. A quick sweep of the interior with his gaze told Rufinus everything he needed to know. The majority of the bar's patrons were Praetorians who had come off night duty and were having a few drinks before heading back to the fortress. He half expected to see people he knew, but the gaggle of toga-clad soldiers were all strangers. He found his father easily enough, standing at a table in the far corner, another white-toga-clad man seated before him.

Rufinus, confident that he appeared military enough to be here without raising comment, wandered across to the bar and ordered a small jar of wine and a cup. The jug of water was placed beside them, and he paid the paltry sum, repeatedly flicking his gaze towards his father. The man was having a discussion in low tones with the man at the table and as Rufinus turned, at this new angle near the bar, he saw something that surprised him.

On the bench behind the table, next to the toga-clad soldier, was a vitus – the vine stick of office of a centurion. Sure that somehow this was important, Rufinus took a few sips of wine, each time taking the opportunity to look over the cup's rim at the man, committing to memory ever detail he could. The man had a long face and was clean shaven with pronounced lines from his nose down to the ends of his mouth, and prominent cheekbones, giving him something of an equine look. His hair was a spray of black and grey curls, cropped reasonably short in a somewhat archaic fashion – the one favoured by Rufinus, truth be told. One of his eyes had a slight film of blue, suggesting that his sight was slowly going on the left hand side. He was perhaps forty years old, and the blotchy red of his nose and cheeks spoke of a long-time drinker. This last was confirmed when the man poured himself another cup of wine and did not bother adding water before taking a large swig.

His father seemed to still be angry, and the centurion was handling it with the blasé attitude of a man who knew it made no difference to him at all. If only the bar were a little quieter, Rufinus would be able to get hints at least of what they were saying.

He returned his attention to his own drink, adding yet more water, stung by the sight of the centurion's habit and the memory of his own dark time with that demon on his shoulder. Every now and then he glanced across at them, and could see that his father was arguing fruitlessly about something. The Praetorian centurion was not about to agree to whatever it was, and was happily sitting and taking the tirade, waiting for the old man to finish and simply go away. Rufinus tensed. He knew men like that. Happy to sit and let it wash over them, but prone to snapping. He could see it building now in the man. If his father didn't stop and leave soon, the man would turn on him, and a Praetorian centurion was not a man to anger.

Fortunately, it seemed that his father was aware of the building tension, too, and finally subsided, sagging with angry disappointment, and turned away. Rufinus took another sip of his own wine and found himself torn. His father was now heading for the door once more, but the centurion remained at the table in the corner, brow folded in thought as he watched the old man go. Should Rufinus follow his father or now keep his eyes on the centurion? He wasn't sure. He felt oddly certain that both had a tale to tell.

Another toga-clad man entered the tavern, grunting for Rufinus' father to move out of the way, and the new arrival jolted Rufinus into a realisation. He had been side-tracked from what had been a normal and unsuspicious activity and had begun to lurk and pursue his father. But numerous times now he had learned that he himself had been followed. What if one of Cleander's men was on him even now? He would certainly be giving the man something to report, wouldn't he.

The old man left the tavern, turning left, and Rufinus fretted. The centurion could wait. He had a good image of the man committed to memory now. He would follow his father, but if he did so and he *was* being followed himself, then he could be heading for trouble.

He paused for the count of fifty, sipping wine and taking in the rest of the occupants carefully. If anyone had been following him, he was content that they were not in the bar. Everyone in here was a soldier and committed to their drinking. Only two men had come in after him, and neither was anything but a Praetorian with a thirst, he was sure.

He thanked the barman, finished his cup and left. As he emerged into the cold light, he blinked repeatedly and held up the documents he carried to shade his eyes from the glare. As he did so, his gaze took in every face in the street. No. He was sure none of them had been there when he entered. Off to his left he could just make out his father's shape in time to see him turn left again towards the slopes of the Palatine.

Hurrying, he lowered the documents and followed his father. As he reached the corner where the old man had turned, he carelessly dropped one of the wooden tablet cases and crouched to retrieve it, his gaze darting momentarily between all those around him. No one seemed suspicious.

He turned down the alley, which ran between ancient crumbling brick walls, up the gentle slope. A little higher the alley wound around the rear of a small bath house and then a side passage connected it to the Scalae Caci, the ancient staircase from the end of the circus up to the plateau. Rufinus knew the place. He had spent enough time as a guard here to have used the alleys as a cut through between work and drinking pit. Few people of quality used it – only soldiers and slaves and beggars – for there was simply too much danger of one of the city's many muggers lurking in a dark corner.

He could not see his father, but there were few places he could go. He was either headed for the baths or the stairs. Hurrying now, he padded up the slope until he reached the corner, where he slowed. He turned to look back. No one had entered the alley behind him, and no one was watching from the entrance. He hadn't been followed today.

Gritting his teeth, he turned the corner slowly to see his father standing in the next alley, learning on the wall and catching his breath. The climb was not especially steep or gruelling, but then his father was not a young man.

'Who are you and what do you want?' his father snapped suddenly, turning to face him.

Rufinus felt a shock of worry flood him. They were alone in the place together, and he'd made no attempt to silence his own footfall, being concerned more now with who might be following him. His father had become aware of his own pursuer.

Somehow, suddenly, in the presence of his father, Rufinus felt an odd and overwhelming sadness that his family had come to this. His mother long dead, his older brother buried in a tomb on an estate that had now been sold out of their hands. His younger brother in danger and hidden in a safe house in Gaul, his father clutching at the heels of the empire's greatest villain just for a taste of the good life once more. And Rufinus: dead, yet walking.

Before he had truly decided what to do, he stepped forward, arms low, unthreateningly.

'Do you not know me?'

The old man frowned. 'If you're one of Curtius' men...'

'I'm not. And don't let the beard and the hair fool you. Look deep.'

Why was he doing this? He shivered. This went against absolutely everything he and Severus had decided. The governor would be furious if he knew that Rufinus was even in contact with his father. He was supposed to be dead. He was involved in a plot against Cleander. And the old man was one of Cleander's flunkies now. But the sudden hollowness he felt when he looked at his father robbed him of alternatives. His family was falling apart, and now, just here, once and briefly, he might have the chance to stop it.

'I don't know you,' his father spat, 'and if I don't already know you, then I don't *want* to know you.'

Still time to walk away. Rufinus felt torn, the inner debate raging. He clamped down on common sense and rode on instinct instead.

'Publius is safe.'

That got the old man's attention. His father pulled his hand from the wall and straightened. 'What?'

'You might be playing the world's most dangerous game, but you won't bring Publius down with you. I sent him off somewhere safe. Neither you nor your new friends will ever find him without me. I lost one brother, and I accept my part in that, but I will not lose the other. Publius is safe.'

His father's face moved through a wide array of expressions, not one of which were pleasant, and he took an involuntary step forward.

'Gnaeus?'

'Yes. I know. The hair and beard. I don't like it, I truth.'

'You died. In Dacia. I had a letter.'

'I *am* dead. *Gnaeus* is dead, anyway. I'm not me anymore. I'm not the son you watched leave the villa and seek a new path. I *found* that path and by all the gods it was a dangerous and winding one to bring me here. And I should not have followed you, and probably no good will come from it, but family is family and I would not rest peacefully if I knew I'd had the chance to do something but had done nothing with it.'

'What are you blathering about, boy?' snapped his father and for a moment Rufinus was years younger in their old atrium, listening to a barrage from his father and vowing to leave and never turn back. He fought down his anger. This was too important.

'You are on a path to ruin, Father, but you have been out of the game too long. Those years in Hispanic exile have left you rusty. We may never have been friends, but I used to think you were at least clever enough in your own way. You certainly should be bright enough to see the trouble you're headed for.'

'Speak your piece, Gnaeus. I'm a busy man.'

'The chamberlain. He's evil. In every way, he's an evil man. And when he falls, which will happen soon enough, he will end very badly and everyone who's tied to his purse-strings will fall with him. Do not hitch the family cart to that horse, Father, I implore you.'

'Don't be a fool, Gnaeus. He's the most powerful man in Rome. *You* may have given up on your name and the legacy of our once great family, but *I* would see it ascendant once more. You can live in your poverty under an assumed name, but if a man hopes to rise in this Rome, then he needs a patron like Cleander to help him.'

Rufinus' eyes darted back and forth as though speaking the name might summon the chamberlain.

'Father, you are betting on the strongest horse, but the race is far from over. I'm warning you…'

'No, Gnaeus, *I* am warning *you*. The Marcii are now clients of Cleander. The villa is gone, sold and done with. We have a townhouse here now, and a few small clients of our own. The last stock of the estate wine has come to Rome and I have a man setting up a business with it. We shall have all the wealth of the mercantile classes and the culture of the patricians. That is what Cleander has done for Rome – his very presence in power has torn down so many barriers.'

'Father, you will get yourself killed.'

'No. You just cannot accept that I am right; you never could, and that is partially why you threw away everything I gave you to wallow in the mud with barbarians. And now I go to seek an audience, for I have urgent business to attend to. While I recognise that I cannot drag Publius' location from you by force, I tell you here and now that if you do not let me know where he is or summon him back to Rome, I will be forced to take steps. For now, though, I will keep your secret, for your very existence like this undermines everything I have worked for with the chamberlain. But you must disappear and give your brother back to me, or I shall use my contacts among the Praetorians to force you to do so.'

'Don't threaten me, old man.'

'My son is dead. He died in Dacia, and I am content that this is so. Go away and think upon my words'

His father turned and stumped on up the alley, leaving Rufinus standing at the corner, frustrated and angry. He was horribly aware just how much danger he'd just put himself in and, worse still, everyone else he was involved with. Severus would probably gut him in an instant as a liability. He would have to keep this little encounter entirely secret.

He turned back, cold and angry, and stomped down the alley, slipping only once, until he emerged onto that main street once more. Without really intending to, he found himself slipping back into that tavern and ordering another wine. The centurion had gone, and Rufinus took his table. He conscientiously picked up the water jug to mix with his wine, and then banged it back down on the table in irritation, swigging the rich, strong, unwatered wine. He sighed as the old familiar comfort of the heady liquid swilled down his throat, and felt just one thread of the tension within him loosen.

It was noon when he left the tavern, and he knew as he emerged into the cold light, shivering, that he had consumed a lot more wine than was good for anyone, let alone for him. He had broken a vow he had made to himself and to Senova years ago, never again to succumb to the vine as he had just done. Cursing, he told himself that it was just the once. After all, who could blame him with what had just happened? Tottering only a little, he headed back towards the forum and decided that the tabularium could wait. He felt that trying to deal with the minutiae of administration with a slight blurring around the edges of his mind was a bad idea. He would take the documents tomorrow. Now, he would return to his rooms at the Castrum Misenatum and have a lie down until he felt a little more human.

With the speed and warmth of a man wearing a wine coat, he pushed his way through the chilled busy streets and past the great Flavian amphitheatre. He wondered what had happened to the world since he had won his fame there, saving the emperor. He had hoped, assumed even, that things would be golden after that, and yet he seemed to have slipped down a slope into Tartarus gradually over the ensuing years.

He reached the castrum, and the guards, now fully familiar with their prefect, stepped aside. He moved into the archway and emerged from the shade once more into the bright cold light of the square where sailors practiced their moves. Making his way between the groups, he closed on his office. Reaching the door, he pulled it open, for he had left that unlocked, securing only the door between the office and his personal apartments. He stepped inside, shivering, and stamped his feet, closing the door behind him.

'Hello, my love.'

He turned in shock to see Senova sitting behind his desk, dressed in elegant finery and with auburn hair and pale, beautiful face. By the wall stood three chests and several bags.

'Senova?'

'No, dear. I am Julia Triaria, of course. Your wife. Has it been that long?'

Rufinus blinked. He was suddenly acutely aware that he probably stank of wine and looked rough. On the other hand, the fuzz had all gone, this sudden shock sobering him up in an instant.

'But what are you doing here?'

'The governor sent me, dear. Everyone has a part to play, even the wife of the fleet prefect.'

Rufinus felt a momentary flash of anger. Severus had no right to drag Senova into this mess. 'He shouldn't have…'

'I insisted, dear. What use was I sitting in a house in the middle of nowhere, listening to your brother fret over what was happening elsewhere. Like a good Roman matron I am here to see to the management of your household. And the first thing we have to establish is that this is not your household. You have a townhouse in the city, according to the governor. We need to move you there so that you are more appropriate. And there we can work together.'

'Doing what?'

'Why ruling the seas, of course, dear. You have your fleet to deal with. I have the considerable finances of our family to invest and, on the advice of the governor, I am thinking of investing it in mercantile vessels. Particularly ones from Africa, Aegyptus, Ostia and Puteoli.'

'Where the grain fleets operate.'

'Oh? Do they? Well that would be very inconvenient for someone, if I were to outbid government contracts and retain the services of the larger vessels for our own little empire, eh?'

Rufinus felt a chill run through him. He had been silently urging Severus to move with his plans, but he'd not expected it to start with Senova. He tried to find a reason to refuse, but every excuse evaporated as he grasped it. It was the norm of a Roman wife to invest the household's money and to control all the finances. And some of the women of the equites in Rome were well known for their business acumen, controlling numerous cartels and organisations that kept the family coffers overflowing. There would be nothing unusual in what Senova was planning. And Severus had clearly managed to secure plenty of money to support it. His eyes strayed to the chests, which he'd assumed were full of clothes, but he now began to suspect contained coins. She was in danger, yes, but probably no more than where she had been before. His disguise was complete with a wife, and moving out to their own house would be nice and secure. And he knew her to be clever and headstrong. He couldn't imagine her ventures going bad. No, ridiculously he could find no solid reason to argue.

'It will be nice to work with you,' she smiled.

Rufinus chuckled, despite everything. He could not deny that it would be nice to have her home.

'And,' she said, rummaging in a bag and fishing out a scroll case, 'here is a letter from the governor for you.'

Rufinus, still reeling from today's events, broke the seal and let the vellum sheet slide out. Unfurling it, he ran his eyes down it. Oddly, he'd half expected something like this for months.

'What is it?' Senova asked.

'Severus thinks it is time the purge began. I'm to excise the rotten flesh from it all.'

A list of four names, all of whom he had found in the cavalryman's paperwork.

It had started.

Chapter Eight – Purgo

Ostia, mid-January 188 A.D.

Neratius Onirus leaned on the rail of the barge and relaxed, watching the river slide by like a cold, grey-green dream. He had been tense all his time in the city. Working in the Horrea Galbana was easy enough, when you were at a sufficiently important level to lift nothing heavier than a wax tablet and stilus, but it was not the work that was nibbling at the edges of his nerves.

He was starting to think that his boss, the Praefectus Annonae Dionysus, was onto him. There had been small hints over the last month. Onirus, and his companion Silvius, had been given more and more mundane and distant tasks. Having been at the heart of the work in the capital, they had gradually found themselves being sent further afield to perform unimportant and menial tasks that kept them out of the city for extended periods. Ten days ago Silvius had been sent to Centum Cellae to negotiate priority docking for grain ships there, as though more than half a dozen ever put in at that small northern port each year. And Onirus had been dispatched to Puteoli to oversee the rebuilding of a granary there. The two men had quite by chance returned to Rome at the same time, two days ago, hoping to spend a little informative and lucrative time in the capital, but Dionysus had immediately given them orders that carried them out of the city once more.

It was going to be extraordinarily hard to make any money like this.

And money was all of it for Onirus.

He glanced to his left, where Quintus Silvius similarly leaned on the rail, looking either relaxed or bored. It was hard to tell with Silvius. The man had been recruited by the chamberlain's men almost a year ago. Onirus didn't know the precise details, though suffice it to say the deal must have been tempting to lure the dour Silvius in. But then the man was an idealist, and idealists were always easy to hook if you knew what bait to use.

Silvius was a freedman who had climbed the ladder swiftly following his manumission. His master had been fond of him and had willed him his freedom when he passed away, and Silvius had taken his savings and put his administrative talents to use. Eight years later, he was one of the more important men on the grain commissioner's staff. But despite his master's generosity, Silvius had continued to harbour that background disgruntlement that all freedmen seemed to have towards the ruling classes. He had hated all the old blood of Rome. He'd spent years pulling them to pieces over lunch with Onirus, so it came as no surprise when he began to work for Rome's most prominent freedman. Silvius believed in a new Rome built upon talent and hard work and not the family into which one was born. He had a vision of a Rome where the poor and the disenfranchised had as much say as the old families. It was ridiculous, of course, but Onirus could see why it had happened.

That was Silvius. A man of principle who worked for Cleander because he thought Cleander would bring about his utopian world. And over the last year, Silvius had gradually and very carefully introduced to Onirus the idea that he too might work for the chamberlain.

Onirus was *not* a man of principle. He was a pragmatist. He too was a freedman, though his manumission had come about entirely by chance. His master had set his price of freedom at a fairly high sum, which Onirus was unlikely ever to amass through his meagre earnings. And then one day while out on a chore, the poor slave had happened across a pouch of coins resting on the edge of a fountain. He'd taken it, of course, and had been astonished at the small fortune it contained. He suddenly had quite sufficient funds to buy his freedom. He'd approached his master that night at a party the dominus had held, and his master had been angry, demanding to know where he had found enough money, and raising the price by more than double. But his noble friends at the party had been scathing and persuaded him that he should just take the money and smile, for he could easily buy another slave cheap, while money was always useful. So Onirus had become free. And he had worked half a dozen minor jobs before landing his position on the grain commissioner's staff.

But Onirus did not care about Cleander or the plight of the slave or freedman. Silvius' perfect world was unimportant to him. Money, on the other hand, opened doors. And occasionally underwear when he was feeling flush enough. And Cleander's network offered money in return for information.

They had had a good year for a while, sending weekly reports of every aspect of the grain commissioner's work, listening to the talk of the other men and sending on details of anything that sounded dubious, dangerous or important.

Three men had disappeared in direct response to their reports. Men who had voiced dislike of the chamberlain or concerns over his actions. Three men had gone to the torturer's cellars on the say of Silvius and Onirus. Silvius had been proud to do it, happy that he was helping create his new world. Onirus had been happy, too. The recompense had kept him drunk and in a whore's bed for days.

But now there was no chance to earn money like that. Things had changed.

This morning, in response to the latest orders of Papirius Dionysus, the two men had reported to the dockside on the emporium and boarded the barge for Ostia Portus. As part of the prefect's drive to improve the grain flow, given the ever increasing need and the tightening supply during such a time of plague, Dionysus had put in a bid for a plot of land close to the waterfront at the port, where he intended to construct a new granary complex that would store the overflow from the African shipments that could not be immediately transferred to Rome via barges. Silvius and Onirus were to examine the site, confirm its condition and sign the purchase documents. Then they were to retain the services of a building firm and begin work, only returning to Rome when the granary was under construction. It would keep them away from the city and out of money-making circles for a month at least.

Damn it.

He turned away from Silvius now, looking ahead past the prow of the ship. They were approaching Portus. Ostia itself had once been the prime dock for Rome at the mouth of the Tiber, but the sheer volume of sea traffic had proved to be far too great for that city to handle, and Claudius had constructed a new port a mile or so up the coast, attached to the river by a canal, effectively bypassing Ostia entirely. Even this new complex had proved inadequate for the volume of shipping, though, and consequently Trajan had enlarged the place immensely with a whole new enormous harbour and surrounding complexes, even including an imperial residence.

They drifted past the marble yard with its perpetual noise of hammering and clouds of white dust, and a small region of workshops and storehouses, past a small but pretty temple to Mercury. Ahead, the small channel – if a waterway fifty paces across could be called small – continued on to the coast, but before that the entrance to the great Trajanic harbour cut off to the right. Onirus heaved a sigh as the barge turned laboriously with all the handling ease of a dead ox, and made for the narrower canal that led into the harbour.

This perfectly straight and angular channel cut between a grand colonnaded market on one side and a series of high private granaries on the other. Ahead he could now see the priority wharf, where ships that carried important persons or loads that were destined to make a quick drop and then depart within the hour were moored. He noted with interest a quinquireme secured there. The great vessel was of a rare and huge design, not often seen in civilian harbours. His interest deepened as he noted not only the colours of the Misenum fleet, but also the pennant at the rear that announced the presence of an admiral. The Prefect of the Fleet was in Portus for some reason.

He kept his gaze on that magnificent vessel as their own barge began to slow once more ready to make the right hand turn into the main hexagonal harbour. He could see a company of marines lined up on the deck in gleaming finery, looking like seaborne Praetorians. There was a standard there and a small group of officers at the rail, looking out over the water. Possibly even the prefect, though uniforms were a mystery to Onirus. Still, it might be worth putting in a report to pass on to the chamberlain. Might be enough to earn him a few coins and keep him in wine.

What happened next came understandably as something of a shock. A crewman bellowed out in alarm, drawing looks from both Onirus and his dour companion. Neither of them knew much about ships, but the note of urgency in the man's voice suggested that something awful had happened. Onirus turned, thinking of making his way to the captain to enquire, when the entire ship suddenly tipped to an alarming angle. Gripping the rail, Onirus felt his feet slipping out from under him as the barge listed more and more.

Someone was shouting something about a hole. The ship was sinking. Right here, in the middle of the channel of one of the world's busiest ports, the barge was apparently sinking! And it seemed to be doing so with alarming speed.

All along the ship men were staggering and falling about, shouting in panic. Onirus watched sailors leaping overboard into the channel. He turned to Silvius, whose face was a picture of disgust.

'The documents,' his friend said. In their cabin, which was a sectioned-off part of the hold, they had important documents from the prefect, but also two unfinished reports to their contact in the chamberlain's employ.

'Fuck the documents... the *money!*' Onirus replied. He had brought all his remaining money with him, planning to find a nice brothel where he could spend his evenings.

The two men lurched away from the rail, skittering along the dangerously slanting deck, heading for the stairs down. Sailors were leaping to safety all around, and only the captain and his steersman remained at their post, bellowing orders fruitlessly, since no one was listening. Twice on the rush across the deck as men screamed and timbers groaned, Onirus slid and almost fell across the boards into the water, but they managed to reach the stairs, and there he paused.

'Can you get my money?' He didn't like the idea of going below while the ship was clearly sinking.

'Get your own damn money,' snapped Silvius, as he started down the stairs. 'We've got plenty of time.'

Onirus was not so sure. The deck below was still dry at this end, though he could hear the roar and slosh of water off in the dark somewhere, as it slowly filled the barge. Still, they only had to grab two things from their cabin. He slid down the stairs and followed Silvius across to their door, where the miserable looking man produced their key, unlocking the cabin door and slipping inside. Onirus followed, wishing they had a lamp. It was dark in here, darker even than the gloom in the hold itself. Still, he knew where his purse was, under his pillow on the bunk, and he could find it by feel.

He ran across to the bed while Silvius crossed to the other side and began to gather up their documents.

There was a bang and a scraping noise behind them, and Onirus turned in the darkness, panic rising, wondering what the noise had been for only a moment before he realised. The door to the cabin had shut. Forgetting his money now amid his rising fear, he ran back to the door and hauled at it.

It was locked.

Silvius had left the key in the lock when they opened it, but how in Hades had it slammed shut and locked? Panic filling his world now, he wrenched at the door desperately. It was a solid timber construction, though. Nothing short of an axe was getting through it without the key.

Panic. Pure, unadulterated panic. There was no other way out.

'Open the door,' Silvius snapped, crossing to him.

'I can't. It's locked.'

'What did you do that for?'

'I *didn't*,' Onirus wailed.

The roar of water was becoming deafening beyond the door. The hole in the ship must have widened somehow and the speed with which they were sinking increased dramatically. Water began to swish into the room through the crack beneath the door, soaking Onirus' boots.

'Oh shit.'

The report of the sinking of the grain barge Demeter was lodged with the port officials that cold January afternoon. It was generally considered to be lucky, as it could have been so much worse. The barge had been empty, destined to load up in the port, and the entire crew escaped with their lives, the water claiming only two passengers who had been foolish enough, according to witnesses, to disappear to their room below deck while it sank.

Tusculum, late January 188 A.D.

Curtius Primus smiled to himself. His last missive to his contact about the movements of the praefectus vehiculorum had been so well received that he'd been given a fat purse of coins. Better even than that, the prefect, Nicomedes, seemed to think that Primus was his best, most trusted man. So much so that even as Primus betrayed his master, Nicomedes sent him to Tusculum undercover with a remit to check the mansio there, as it was rumoured that the man was creaming off much more than the anticipated ten percent of all takings before sending it to Rome.

A week in the pretty little hill town with his expenses paid and a remit to lounge about in the mansio there, making use of the baths, the restaurant and the rooms, and to go along with it, he had a small fortune from Cleander's own hand to spend while he was there. He was going to have a rich old time. That arse Nicomedes was such a fool. Primus wondered idly whether he should save half his money in case the prefect assigned him to some boring task in the city the next week, but he decided against it. He would undoubtedly be able to find something of use for the chamberlain and make more cash.

He glanced across at his companion. The second rider, the only other person within sight, had cost him above the odds, but he had been worth it. Nicomedes had told him not to take guards, since he was undercover and not visiting in an official capacity, but still the roads of Latium were dangerous, and so Primus had hired a man for the trip. In his role as inspector of installations – southern Latium, he had come across the dangers of travel more than once through the years.

The guard was an ex-soldier with some weird, eastern name that matched his swarthy skin and dark eyes. But he seemed both confident and competent, and the bureau from which Primus had hired him had assured him of a good reputation.

His eyes slid back to the road. Twin lines of trees bordered it as it bent gently to the left. At the next farm drive it would angle right again. Primus knew the road well, had travelled it on plenty of occasions in his time with the service. He could see the hills above Tusculum now between the trees, just two and a half miles further on. He would be there before dark, settling in to a warm bath before the evening meal. The mercenary could do as he liked then, staying in the city or returning to Rome, as long as he was at the mansio's door in a week's time ready to escort Primus back to the capital.

Danger came without warning.

An arrow hissed from some unseen source, slithering through the air entirely unanticipated until it thudded with finality into the neck of Primus' horse. The animal gave an unearthly shriek and bucked. Primus could ride, but he knew he was far from the best horseman in the empire, and he felt a moment of indecisive panic. Should he try and control the beast or leap free?

Being on foot with some unseen attacker nearby sounded like a bad idea, but the animal was clearly doomed, and he knew he would not be riding the poor thing away from here, so he let go of the reins and tried to jump. The good, secure, four-horned saddle was designed well to keep a rider in his seat, and it took Primus three goes to lever himself out of it as the beast bucked and thrashed, dying on its feet.

He hit the ground hard, winded, and barely managed to scramble away before the horse landed in the same spot, thrashing wildly. Staring in horror at the animal's flailing hooves, he backed away further. His eyes swept this way and that, now. His guard's horse had similarly been hit, and the easterner had leapt from his saddle with considerably more success than Primus, not that it had done him much good.

The ex-soldier had clearly landed on his feet and ripped his sword from its sheath, but he would never get to use it. Already he had an arrow jutting from his left shoulder and another from his right thigh. He staggered and turned pleading eyes on Primus.

'Help me,' he begged.

'Piss off,' snapped Primus, his retort punctuated by two more arrows that thudded into the guard, one into his chest and the other his face. The man toppled backwards, howling, to land on the road, shaking in his death throes.

'Oh, bollocks,' Primus managed. He knew bandits were not unknown in the region, but usually they would think twice about attacking an armed man, and they seemed to have had no fear of this easterner.

Desperately, Primus scrambled further away from the scene until he reached the line of trees beside the road. There, he ducked behind a trunk and sheltered in its lee, shaking like a leaf. If he got out of this he was going to refuse this sort of job in future. Let Nicomedes do his own dirty work. Primus would find something juicy on him and report it to his contact, try and make lots of money. Then he could retire, perhaps.

Voices emerged over the fading noises of dying man and beasts. He could hear at least four men shouting.

'Which way did he go?'

'I thought you had him?'

'I lost him behind the horse.'

'Why didn't you shoot him first, not his horse?'

'Fuck off, Tiberius, I'm not an archer, am I?'

'He went that way. Across the road.'

'Behind the trees.'

Primus felt the panic return in a massive wave, then, as booted footsteps clomped across the road, becoming louder as they grew closer.

Bandits. But maybe they could be reasoned with? Certainly if he just sat here he was doomed, and he'd never outrun four or more men. But he was a negotiator born and bred. Taking a deep breath, he rose and stepped slowly out from the tree, hands raised.

'Wait.'

'There he is.'

There were five of them, in fact, two with bows still strung and in hand, three with swords out, and they were now angling his way, converging on him.

'Listen,' he said, 'I have money, which you are welcome to. Take it and leave me, and it'll be worth your while. But bear in mind that I have the ear of Marcus Aurelius Cleander, Chamberlain of the Imperial household and Commander of the Praetorian Guard. Doing me harm would be a terrible mistake with probably fatal consequences. Take the money and go. Easy pickings and no trouble.'

There was a hiss and a thud, and he turned wide eyes down to the arrow shaft his leg had sprouted suddenly. For just a moment all he felt of it was a strange pressure and a warm numbness. Then the pain flourished. He shrieked as his leg gave way and he toppled to the ground. He'd never experienced agony like this. Was this what soldiers expected? Why would anyone sign up for the army?

The pain failed to dim at all, but breathlessness ended his screaming as he heaved in air, rolling about on the grass, eyes screwed tight and shaking.

'Oh dear. Had an accident have we?' taunted a gruff voice.

'Listen,' Primus said desperately between gasps, 'you can still walk away… from this. Cleander…'

'Cleander is a treacherous piece of shit, and his days are numbered,' snapped a bandit as he reached Primus and stood over him, sword brandished.

'He's powerful,' wailed Primus.

'Does he feel powerful right now?' said one of the bandits nastily, a young bearded fellow with a network of scars and a glove on his left hand. The man crouched, as did one of the other bandits opposite him. Primus noted with passing surprise that the second man had a tattoo of a stylised trireme on his arm, along with the name *Celeritas*. The gloved man did not have any tattoo, but burns and scars marked his arm as he positioned his sword above Primus' chest.

'I have money,' he pleaded.

'It's not money I want.'

The blade plunged down hard, robbing Primus of his life quickly and efficiently.

Rome, February 188 A.D.

Marcus Calatorius looked up irritably from his desk. The noise in the emporium was too much some days. He would have liked to close the folding, concertinaed doors to help keep the office quiet, but it was common practice to have them open here. Closed doors suggested that the business was closed, while open ones invited customers.

On his desk sat three different deals all waiting to be confirmed and signed off or refused and discarded. He would have to have them finished with by the ides. Severus was not a forgiving boss, and his business interests were important to him.

But despite their clear importance, they would have to wait until he had finished this. Ideally, he would be writing this letter at home, in the seclusion of his room, rather than here in public. But time was of the essence, and if he was not in his office during working hours, it might get back to Severus, who was a suspicious enough man as it was.

He trembled slightly as he wrote. He might be sealing his employer's doom with this letter, and that was no small thing, but Calatorius' true master needed to know. It had taken him several weeks to confirm what he suspected, but for a man who knew what to look for in figures and reports it was all there if you cared to dig deep enough. The connections to Dionysus were dubious, but he felt that they were tangible enough to mention, and the links to Prefect Rufinus were clear. What Severus was up to he had no idea, but the feeling that the governor was building some kind of web to rival Cleander's was strong, and he felt the chamberlain would reward him well for the information. Possibly this latest letter would buy him a way into the palace in the chamberlain's legitimate service. Almost certainly it would buy Severus a one way trip to the Palatine's cellars, and Calatorius would be out of a job.

His stylus slipped on the wax and he looked up angrily. The din out there was unacceptable. The emporium was always a noisy place, of course, filled with offices and warehouses, quays and ships, merchants and sailors, but today it was noisier even than usual.

He glanced out of his door. His office was one of fifty identical ones lining both sides of a wide hallway in a building set back a little way from the dock. From here he ran five different business concerns for the Severan family, though not today, given the import of his troubling current task.

Outside, in the wide hall, there was a lot of activity and raised voices.

He rose from his seat and plodded across to the doorway, keeping glancing back at the incriminating document on his desk for reassurance. A quick peek out into the hallway told him all he needed to know. A dozen or so sailors were engaged in some friendly competition of athletic prowess in the wide marble hall, cheered on by the bystanders both mercantile and nautical and a few stray children. Shouts of encouragement and the odd insult were hurled. Many other offices had disgorged their occupants to the doorway to watch the fun. Not so Calatorius. He had more important matters to attend to, although he wished they would hurry up and win or lose so that they could take their din elsewhere.

With a cantankerous grunt, he dismissed them out of hand and turned back to his work, crossing the office and sitting at the desk. He picked up the stilus once more and paused, trying to recapture his train of thought. The wording was important in any missive like this, especially one destined for the subtle and careful chamberlain, selling out a propraetorian governor.

The noise outside was so loud now with cheering and screaming and chanting names that he was having real trouble thinking straight, and so loud, indeed, that he didn't hear the man approach his office until the footsteps were inside. With a start, realising he was not alone, Calatorius snapped his wax tablet shut, fingers edging close to the scraper on his desk, with which he could erase the writing in just a couple of short strokes, freeing him of any incriminating evidence.

He looked up sharply.

'What can I…'

His words died in his throat as he saw the bearded sailor closing his office door.

'You can't do that. I am open for business.'

'I think your business here is done,' said the sailor in a threatening voice, turning, his non-gloved hand going to his belt. Calatorius' eyes widened as it came back up gripping a small, sharp knife of the kind used to peel fruit.

'Who are you?'

But he realised in that moment who it had to be. After all, had he not just written this very man's name in the tablet beneath his fingers.

'Our mutual friend, your employer, is a trifle unhappy that you seem to be serving two masters.'

Calatorius' fingers closed protectively on the wooden tablet case, although Rufinus couldn't possibly know what was in it.

'I serve only the propraetor, Prefect. No one else.'

The way you grip that tablet suggests otherwise,' Rufinus said with an unpleasant smile. 'Shall we read it together and prove me wrong?'

Calatorius moved in a flash, one hand flipping open the tablet, the other whipping across and scraping the page clear. A malicious smile crossed his face as he looked up.

'There seems to be a lack of evidence to…'

His words tailed off as the fruit knife cut through his windpipe. Rufinus had moved fast too, stepping to Calatorius' right hand side where he was out of the path of the jet of crimson that washed across the desk.

Thank you for erasing whatever you were telling the chamberlain,' Rufinus hissed. 'Saved me one tedious chore.'

Calatorius could say nothing, indeed could make no sound other than the gravelly, bubbly hissing noise of air and blood escaping through his neck. He stared in horror. He was dead. He'd been killed, even if he wasn't quite there yet.

He tried to stand but discovered that all strength had left his body and he couldn't quite lever himself out of the chair. Prefect Rufinus had moved away from him again now, edging around the periphery of the room, staying out of the way of the impressive spray of blood. Calatorius gaped in fascinated terror at the lake of red across the desk and floor, covering those three important documents he hadn't dealt with and now never would.

Oddly, he thought he could feel himself dying from the ground up. His legs that couldn't support him had now lost all feeling, numb and cold. His stomach seemed to contain a frozen stone and his arms were chilling rapidly. His throat still felt fiery, and his face felt flushed, but he suspected they would chill soon now. As he marvelled at his own death, he saw Rufinus reach the door, open it and slip out into the hallway and to the emporium once more. The noise lasted only for a few moments longer and then ended with a huge cheer. Calatorius wondered idly whether the competition had simply been convenient or whether the prefect had set it all up to mask his murderous activities.

It was the last thing he ever thought.

Rufinus returned to his town house in a sombre mood, where, despite the glares he received from Senova, he drank an entire jar of Chian without water.

The purge was over.

PART TWO

CAPRICIOUS NEPTUNE

"EXITUS ACTA PROBAT"

(THE RESULT JUSTIFIES THE DEED)

- OVID

CHAPTER NINE – ON MERCANTILISM

Rome, April 188 A.D.

Senova turned from the desk in the tablinum of their townhouse, stacking a small pile of wooden tablet cases that she had spent a laborious quarter of an our scraping clear. Rufinus stood in the doorway, a frown of mixed confusion and suspicion plastered across his face.

'I don't understand what you're doing,' he said in a disapproving tone.

She gave him a sweet smile. 'That's why it's me doing it and not you, dear. In the same way, I doubt I would be much good at setting the deployment of a fleet on a monthly basis.'

He harrumphed and continued to frown. 'But you need to go out, yes?'

'Yes, dear. I need to go out. I shall be perfectly safe. I have my servant...'

'*Slave.*'

'Servant... and four of your rough sailors for protection, and the praefectus lactorum...'

'Praefectus Lecticariorum...'

'Yes, him, has made sure I have a litter with four of the burliest Aegyptian carriers you ever did see. I will be fine. You cannot spend all your time worrying about me stepping outside the house. I am aware that Rome is a dangerous place, but I have lived in more dangerous. You have enough things to worry about without me.'

His frown stayed in place, but he nodded reluctantly and wished her a good day before turning and bellowing for the officer of his personal guard. Senova smiled indulgently and let him go, turning her back on the door. She then leaned over the desk once more.

Three piles of documents awaited her attention, though only one was urgent enough to need dealing with before she went out.

She shifted the small wooden marker with the word PARTI – *acquisitions* – etched into it. She was fluent these days in the Roman tongue, but while she was fast with speech she still had to concentrate to read the words, for her native language had not had such a thing as writing. They had never needed it the way the Romans seemed to.

She moved the marker to one side, lifted the four invoices and ran her eyes over them. Each one took much concentration and translation, for while the language itself was simple enough and logical in its way, and while public inscriptions and high Roman text were neatly chiselled in perfect lines, no matter how good that looked personal writings by individuals always looked to her like a spider had walked through ink and then meandered across the page.

Still, she refused to submit and bent the words to her will. She knew she had people who could read it faster than her, but she was the one in control of all this, and she was determined to be the only person who had the details of it all – in the household, at least.

Replacement rigging for three ships, including a full set of wooden brail rings for each main sail.

She smiled to herself at the ingenuity of her system even as she signed and sealed the document ready to send to the vault for payment. In addition to the four men assigned to protect her, Rufinus had given her an entire contubernium of eight of his most trusted marines to escort any and all payments she made, which she had approved of as an entirely sensible choice.

The rigging was bound for the three damaged ships she had purchased from a merchant in Antium at a ridiculously low price. She had visited with an expert she'd hired and had managed to knock the owner down to a pittance given the amount of work the ships needed to become viable once more. Of course, they never would. They languished in Antium and would get a few bits of the rigging to work on, maintaining the appearance of refurbishment, while the bulk went into a private storehouse in Portus where it would be made available for the other business interests.

A similar thing would happen to the next invoice for three new steering oars, only one of which would make it to Antium, the other two entering the dark world of her private storehouse. Thus she had managed over the past month to stockpile a surprising amount of equipment for ships without it ever being noted in official channels.

The third invoice was for her legitimate shipping operation: a double-masted merchant vessel called *Helios*, which she had already decided to rename *Isurium* after her home town back in Britannia. Rufinus would be horrified, since she was supposed to be in disguise and hiding her true origin, but she couldn't imagine something that small giving the game away, and it would be something of a homage to her homeland. The *Helios/Isurium* had been impounded in Centum Cellae by the authorities when its owner had been discovered to be illegally importing all sorts of things that had not been marked on his manifest. Senova's factotum had swept in like a vulture and bought the ship, once again at a massively low price. It was her prime ship now. Of course, she had already bought two others, and had purchased an interest in consortiums that owned four more, but this would be her first large, prime vessel entirely her own that needed no work.

Already, she was surprised at how easy it was to acquire work for her new enterprise. As soon as her ships came available and her man put out word in the appropriate quarters that a new mercantile venture had ships ready for the transport of goods, merchants from all over Rome, and from more distant parts of the empire who happened to be in the capital or its ports, soon descended seeking the best price she would give to transport their wares.

In the first week, she was astonished at how much her collection of ships netted in cold cash for the family coffers. Of course such lucrative ventures were beyond the capabilities of most folk. She had needed to sink a good fund of coin into the business before she could even think of making any money – thank you governor Severus for your generosity – but she had always been shrewd at things like this. It was just a game. If you learned the rules, you could play to win and be confident in the result. Soon, her fledgling little business would become a major enough concern that she would rival that cow Claudia Catilina who had stared down her nose at Senova when she had first registered with the tabularium.

The fourth invoice was the one she needed to confirm: a private warehouse with its own jetty at Portus. There was nothing flash about it, and it was small and unimpressive compared to others she could have bought in the port, but this private dock had one unmatchable advantage. It lay directly beside the existing warehouses that belonged to her other interests, allowing for goods to be subtly moved back and forth between legitimate business and private concern without once meeting the eye of the public, *or* the port authorities.

When you knew the rules…

She smiled to herself and signed, sealed and closed the fourth invoice. She would get to the rest of the work later on, but for now she had other fish to fry. Standing, she gathered up the four invoices and carried them from the room.

'Atticus?'

The short, bald man with a face like a pale half-moon and bulging blue eyes appeared from a side door as though he had been waiting there for just this call. She would have been suspicious of the man had it not been for the fact that she had personally selected him. Rufinus had wanted her to have a clerk from the vast pool of ex-military that hung around in the city seeking just such opportunities, but she had been distrusting of them. Her experiences with the soldiers of Rome had not always been positive, after all. Instead, she had gone to the slave market, found a man who had recently been the tutor to a rich house's children until those children had outgrown the need for a teacher, and bought him.

She had spoken to Atticus at the market for only moments before she realised just how bright he was, and how good with numbers. She had bought him and, with Rufinus' disapproval but grudging acceptance, manumitted him the same day, re-hiring him as a freedman. Consequently, of course, Atticus was about as loyal as a man could be in this seething cesspit of a city.

'Domina?'

'These four all need paying. The top one has priority. Take my keys and arrange the delivery of appropriate funds. All information is on each invoice. And don't forget to take the guard with you. The last thing I want is you dying in some alley because you forgot to take an escort.'

And the huge sum of money he was with in the pockets of a Roman thief.

'Of course, Domina. I shall see to it immediately.'

Without further ado, Atticus took the tablets and turned, stalking off towards the atrium. Senova hurried over to her chamber – she had her own bedroom as well as the one she shared with Rufinus. Partially it was a nice nod to the hidden truth that they were not really yet man and wife, but mainly it was a relief when Rufinus' snoring became too much.

Her servant – she was damned if she'd call her a slave despite the fact that Rufinus remained stubborn in his refusal to free her – was busy carefully folding her clean clothes and placing them in the cupboard.

'Pera?'

The girl looked round and bowed her head respectfully. 'Domina?'

'We are for the baths. I have business there. Could you gather everything I'll need. And tell Optio Laevinus that he and his men need to be ready to go presently.'

The slave, a plain but pleasant Thracian girl, nodded her head and placed the rest of the folded clothes down on the side, now dashing around and gathering her mistress' garments and accoutrements for the bath house.

Senova spent the time as she waited running through everything she needed to do this week, smiling at the list. Back in Lugdunum and then in Cemenellum as the guest of the governor Severus, she had wanted for nothing. She had had books and visits to the theatre and music recitals, she had been brought almost anything she could ask for. But it had been boring, nonetheless. This, though, was something entirely different. Not only was she working for the cause now, doing her part, but in doing so she was playing a mercantile game and learning new things every day. It was entrancing and heady and thoroughly fascinating. She could understand why the matrons of Roman houses ran their husbands' business interests. It was a lot more interesting than loafing about in the house and complaining about slaves. And while most matrons played only at the highest level, pulling the strings of merchant puppets, Senova was far more involved. She had discarded those strings and was down among the puppets, positioning their limbs herself.

Shortly thereafter she was out of the house in the comfortable litter, with Pera trotting alongside, the four Aegytpians grunting under the weight of the vehicle and four jingling marines trudging along on either side, the front men clearing the populace out of their way. This was what it was like to be a wealthy Roman, and Senova knew with a guilty pang that in principle she utterly disapproved of this sort of extravagance and behaviour. Yet it was rather nice to treat herself at the moment, while she had to play the part anyway. And there was the added fact that it kept her a little further away from the plague-ridden poor in the alleyways of the city.

Her timing was perfect as always, as the litter came to a wobbling halt before her destination and she pulled back the curtain to reveal the grand façade of Trajan's bath complex. The first time she'd come, it had been in the middle of the afternoon and she had had to feign forgetfulness when a lackey explained to her that it was after noon, so the baths were closed to women. She had come back the next morning and spent an irritating fruitless time among other women in the discovery that during the morning men were not allowed. She'd assumed that men and women bathed together. They did back in Isurium and the baths of Britannia, but then they had considerably fewer amenities out there and probably had to cohabit to make good use.

Here in a city with a thousand bath houses, some of which could hold the population of Isurium twice over without cramping, the old law of Hadrian's separating out the sexes in the baths still held sway. The men had the baths after noon, when they had got their morning business done and the heat of the day drove them to cooling leisure. The women had the baths before then. It had taken a little investigation only to discover that though this was law, the lines were in truth a lot more blurred than Hadrian might have liked.

Women had the baths in the morning and men in the afternoon, but women were only *told* their time was up just before noon, rather than being actively ejected, while men would in practice begin to drift into the baths a good hour before their allotted time. This blurring allowed for an hour or two each day of mixed bathing, which permitted the city's whores to ply a very lucrative trade, and everyone in this decadent pit to enjoy themselves that little bit more while still feeling self-righteous that they supported the morality laws.

And so Senova made it her practice now to reach the baths two hours before noon, so that she could make good use of the facilities and then still have her meeting. Leaving her guards and litter bearers at the door, where they would cross the road to one of the many eating and drinking establishments that catered for those who were left outside to wait, Senova took Pera and strode in through the great entrance.

Initially the grandeur of this, the largest and best-appointed baths in the city, had quite taken her breath away. Now, after months of it, she had become somewhat blasé about the whole thing. As was her wont, the moment she was out of the company of her male escorts, she and Pera become more sisters than mistress and slave. The two women passed into the *apodyterium* – the changing room – found an unoccupied alcove and there began to undress, the other female bathers still visible through the arch, most in their own alcoves but a few in the open room. Here and there a little Sapphic indulgence occurred, which did not bother Senova in principle though she would prefer that they indulged such lusts in a more private place. She couldn't imagine *men and women* copulating in the changing room being permitted, after all. Still, she accepted the wooden clogs and the towel and white tunic from the bath slave, as did Pera, and left her possessions in one of the many alcoves under the staff's watchful eye, taking her chitty to mark which niche was hers. With a sigh of relaxation the two women moved into the baths. The noise and activity around and in the huge open cold swimming pool was inviting, but it was poor practise to enter the communal pools before cleaning.

Consequently they hurried along the arcade and approached the radiating warmth of the heated area of the baths. At the corner of the structure stood the room for which they were bound. Outside, dozens of hopefuls hung about with the tools of their trade, waiting to be hired for a session of oiling, scraping and massage, for not every visitor to the baths brought their own people, obviously. Senova and Pera ignored the line of hopefuls, since they had their own strigils and oil.

They entered the laconium, gasping for breath in the plume of steam that billowed out into the open air of the bath complex. Inside, it took some time for them to acclimatise enough to find their way. The entire room was thick with hot steam, and half a dozen women stood around or sat at the periphery, sweating out their impurities. At the room's centre a large labrum sat – a giant marble dish of water, sitting atop a tile column filled with heat billowing up from the furnaces below, turning that water into the vapour that filled the room.

Senova and Pera sat close together and picked up the conversation as of equals that they only shared in the baths where no one knew Pera was a slave and all impropriety evaporated in the natural equality of nakedness. She was learning much of Pera's history and homeland in these small snippets – a region she and Rufinus had come close to but bypassed as they fled Dacia to the sea.

A quarter of an hour there was enough and they emerged from the steam, glistening and breathing deeply, into the warm room beyond where they took careful turns to use the strigils they had brought, scraping away the oil and the dirt with the sweat in every pass of the smooth, curved bronze. Shortly thereafter, they took a dip in the warm baths, then the cold baths, and then made their way back out to the great communal pool where they spent a contented half hour floundering about.

Finally, men began to drift into the complex and consequently Senova and Pera dried off and donned the tunic and clogs to move about in more modesty. They exited the main bathing structures of the great bath complex and wandered west along the arcade, watching other bathers make use of the gardens and lawns for strolls and even impromptu foot races. At the western edge of the great square of Trajan's baths the perimeter wall was bounded by small tabernae, where the bather could buy everything from jewellery to sweetmeats, to wine, to books and much, much more. Senova and Pera paused at their favourite regular haunt and purchased a cup each of warmed mulsum and a handful of spicy pastries.

Thus equipped, they made their way to the nearby nymphaeum with is booths of comfortable curved seating and small tables. Senova was nothing if not prepared. Since their third visit, when they had not been able to sit in the booth as it had been occupied by a horrible red-faced woman and her cowering daughter, Senova had paid two of the bath staff a monthly stipend to occupy that one booth until they came along. They reached the secluded seating area and the two attendants bowed their heads and left the bathers to slide into the seats and eat and drink their wares.

Of all the many lounging areas in the baths, these booths by the two grand nymphaea were the ones favoured by those who preferred their conversations private. For one thing it was near impossible to get close enough to hear without being visible to those upon who you were eavesdropping, but secondly, the constant jet and cascade of water down the fountains and around the statuary into the numerous basins made it difficult even to hear each other, let alone anyone else.

The two women chatted amiably over nothings for a while, until at some time just after noon a shadow fell across their table and they looked up.

'Good afternoon, ladies,' said a man with a worrying grin. His jaws numbered half as many replacement metal teeth as they did natural ones, giving him a weird appearance, though despite this, he was actually not unhandsome. Pera offered to leave, as she always did, but Senova trusted her and motioned for her to stay, turning to look up at the man standing at the booth's edge.

'Master Titinius, how pleasant to see you again. Do join us.'

Secundus Titinius grinned his troubling grin and slid into the seat indicated, opposite Senova, brandishing his own mug of wine, which he placed on the table before him.

'How goes your business, Domina?' the man smiled.

'Fine and lucrative, thank you, Secundus. Now let us get down to business. I need an update on matters. I had hoped by now to be in a more commanding position. I am not sure to what timescale I am working, in truth, since there are numerous other factors outside my control, but I would like to have everything set and confirmed long in advance of any need. So tell me of your achievements.'

Titinius raised his brows.

'One would think from your mode of speech, mistress, that you were engaged in some underhand and devious criminal enterprise. How thankful am I that I know you so well these days and can say with my hand on my heart that the lady Triaria is merely engaged in healthy business practices that will result in her undercutting her unpleasant competitors.'

'Well quite,' Senova smiled. 'Do tell.'

Titinius took a pull of his wine. 'We now have three companies running. One in Ostia, which is an import and export business with a number of suppliers in the ports and cities of Gaul thanks to your unnamed contacts. That company is already managing to turn its own profit, about which its owner is naturally very pleased. He will be forwarding on to you your cut of the profit in due course.'

Senova nodded. Severus had been more than helpful in supplying the names of a few merchants who would be willing to become part of this new company's supply chain. Sales in the city here had been excellent so far.

'Within the month,' Titinius continued, 'we should be in a position to use those same ships to transport our goods back to Gaul rather than acting as transport for other traders, and our profits should rise appropriately.'

Again, Senova nodded. A private trade company that linked Severus' province and her household in Rome and granted them freedom to move goods about without Senova or Rufinus' name entering the equation. A solid start, that.

'The second company is doing well, too. They have branched out from pottery into copperware, which can be lucrative, given its Gallic source. The prices are just right so that we make money while not drawing anyone's undue attention.'

Good, since it was through the trade of this company that Severus' money was invested in goods, traded, sold on to other investors, used to purchase further goods, and then finally employed to pay that first company, where the money finally came into Senova's possession, its source untraceable to all but the shrewdest and most suspicious of eyes. Perhaps one of the oddest results of the securing of mercantile shipments was that although he didn't know it, Rufinus' father was now reliant upon his daughter-in-law's ships for his own budding wine trade. She'd not told Rufinus that, mind. She wasn't sure he'd find it as ironically humorous as she did.

'Excellent. But this is all by the way. It is our third and newest endeavour that I really wish to hear about.'

Titinius suddenly looked a touch nervous.

'This is the only part of your business that makes me a little uncomfortable, Domina. I know there is no law against it, but we are edging close to something that might get us investigated and closed down.'

'Of that I am aware. And that is why upon the advice of some very trusted and clever men,' *Vibius Cestius and his frumentarii, in fact*, 'I retained your services, for there is, I understand, no better man in all of Italia, or perhaps even the empire, for the task.'

He was good enough in fact that he acknowledged the complement as simple fact and not flattery.

'I have agents working under assumed names for three non-existent companies, the details of which will evaporate under the lightest scrutiny. In actual fact they work, of course, for your third face company, though through so many levels of separation that connecting them to the company would be the work of months even for a dedicated investigator, before even attempting to connect that company to myself or you. I am confident that we are working completely unnoticed, and that it will take so long for anyone to trace our actions back that we will have plenty of warning and time to drop all connections and clear our books before any trouble strikes.'

'But with what *results* have your men been working?'

Titinius shrugged. 'The results one might expect. We are meeting with moderate success, but not as fast or as thorough as one might hope. We have secured the services of two traders in Carthage, one in Sicilia and two in Alexandria. They are prominent traders, and their own fleets constitute some of the best vessels used in grain shipment, but even with those five we have cornered only the smallest percentage of the entire grain fleet. Not enough to make much of a dent in shipping.'

Senova nodded. 'What is making the other traders reticent? Why do they cling so to their state contracts? Are we not offering enough? Money is not the stumbling point for us that it might be for others.'

Titinius shook his head. 'Money is not the issue. In fact I would only agree to sweeten the pot by the tiniest fraction. Right now we look like entrepreneurs trying to secure the best transport available, which we know to be part of the monthly grain fleets. If we start to offer too much, though, it will look increasingly suspicious, and even greedy traders will be less inclined to deal with us, worrying that we are up to something… well, probably something that we *are* up to, in fact.'

'So what is the problem, and how to we solve it?'

'Simply there is not the need. Those we have tempted over to our private service away from the grain fleet are those who know that with the plague and the famine building, the competition for grain shipments is going to become ever tighter. They are fleeing the nest now before they find themselves struggling to secure a cargo and losing money. Unless the number of ships available increases dramatically or the quantity of grain available at source plummets much faster, the rest have no real need to look to us. After all, we are a new and unknown quantity, while the imperial contracts are constant and reliable.'

Senova nodded again. 'And an increase in ships fighting for contracts and shipments would be working against our end goal anyway, so that is of no interest.'

She pondered the problem for a long moment and gradually, with light dawning, a broad smile crossed her face.

'I do believe I have the answer, Titinius. You are aware that I have a legitimate mercantile concern under my name?'

The man nodded. 'Very much a requirement if one is to play this game. I might say that word in the marketplace is that your company is fated to fail, for you have few vessels and half of those are in port in Antium and barely seaworthy. I recognise that you are not relying upon them for anything more than a public face for your money, but you could do with expanding a little or getting those three vessels afloat.'

Senova chuckled. 'We'll do more than that, Titinius, my friend. I think it is time that the house of Triarius began to invest in grain shipments. Put the foreign acquisitions on hold for now. What I want you to do is take every sestertius of profit we make, from legitimate and hidden business alike, and invest in it getting good ships up and running for the family business. I will add my own skills to the mix and we will swiftly build a large fleet up. At the same time, I will secure a contract with the imperial grain administration. It so happens I have a way in with the prefect in charge.'

Titinius' eyebrow rose at that.

'We shall take over a large share of the grain trade,' she grinned. 'And we shall undercut the other merchants so we can guarantee that we land the shipments. Simultaneously, as other traders inevitably turn to different avenues from the grain to make ends meet, our face companies will buy up their contracts and use them on lucrative routes with Gaul. The money they make us there will surely offset the losses from the cheap grain contracts?'

Titanius laughed. 'Gods, but remind me never to play you at a game with wagers. That is cunning and unexpected. If it plays the correct way, those ships in Africa, Sicilia and Aegyptus will bite off our hands when we offer them contracts, while you will secure the lion's share of the grain shipments.' He sat back. 'Very well. I will begin to put these things in motion. Secure your contracts and deal with your own company. If you are planning to expand the way you say, you will need to hire new men to work for you. Good men, too. And a number of new captains and crews for your ships. If this is to become a legitimate concern then you must do things properly.'

Senova grinned and took another sip of her sweet mulsum. 'It so happens that I am married to a man who knows the best retired trierarchs in the empire.'

CHAPTER TEN – THE PRICE OF TENSION

Rome, June 188 A.D.

Rufinus bounced this way and that in the litter, becoming increasingly irritable with every bone-jarring jolt. It had not escaped his attention that even now, months down the line, Senova had the perfect litter and bearers, while Rufinus' still seemed to be mismatched and clumsy. He wondered if at some social event he had offended the prefect of the litter bearers. It was possible. He had been to several such events and had never been the most easy and graceful of socialites.

Such musings brought him back to Senova and to why he was here. He'd been against her being involved in this horribly dangerous enterprise, despite the comfort of having her with him. He'd have preferred to keep her safe, but Severus had had other ideas. It turned out that she was extremely adept at commercial enterprises, involving herself at a close level in matters that utterly baffled Rufinus. In the end he had just left her alone to get on with it and trusted that she knew not to get herself in any trouble. Still, he wished she had stayed in Gaul.

But she was definitely doing something. She now had quite a fleet of ships and had one day, without even consulting Rufinus and checking how it might impact upon their grand plans, visited Papirius Dionysus and secured for her growing fleet of merchant ships a solid contract for grain shipment from all the major sources: Africa, Aegyptus and Sicilia. She certainly seemed to be making money, though she probably wasn't making any friends among those traders who had been knocked out of the grain fleet, unable to compete with her low prices for the contracts. That wasn't all she was doing, though. There was something else moving in her mercantile web, though she steadfastly refused to discuss it, citing Severus placing her in control of this aspect of his plan as her reasoning.

That had rankled more than it probably should.

The fact remained that Rufinus was impatiently awaiting the next phase in the governor's plan, and once more nothing seemed to be happening. He'd removed the traitors from within their various organisations early in the year on Severus' instructions, and had then expected things to accelerate. Instead they had once more sunk into inactivity. Despite his concerns over Senova, she seemed to be free of suspicion and investigation and happy to work on her project while Rufinus suffered impotent impatience. Her dealings all appeared to be above-board anyway, but since the news from the Palatine had leaked out, Rufinus could see why the chamberlain and his people were probably too busy to deal with small fry. It seemed the empress had been caught in a web of adultery and had been shipped off to some island in exile. The palace would be in an uproar, and everyone would be shifting their allegiances and vying for position. Rufinus had found himself wondering whether their would-be patroness, the lady Marcia might come out rather well from this, given the rumours that she had already been the emperor's mistress anyway. Perhaps *that* was what Severus was waiting for?

Anyway, the fact remained that the grain shipments continued unchanged, which concerned Rufinus, given that their failure seemed to be what Severus' plan hinged upon. Oh the shipments were coming up short, of course, but that was nothing new. In this time of plague, farms were being left untended, and grain from all sources was becoming scarcer. But with the reserve always held in the Roman granaries, the supplies being brought in from the south by sea would still be adequate and would cause little issue.

That in itself caused conflict in Rufinus. He still was not entirely comfortable with the idea of starving the Roman poor just to bring down one man, but he was in the minority, apparently.

But what was Senova up to helping bring in the grain like she was?

The litter lurched to a halt and Rufinus twitched aside the curtain, checked where they were and, satisfied, climbed out. The Horrea Galbana stood beside him, his guards lining a short walk to the entrance. Inside, Papirius Dionysus would be in his office at this time of day, for the man had recently moved his base of operations from the office complex of the Statio Annonae to the hub of Roman grain distribution, here at the horrea. If there was one man in Rome who had the answers to any grain import questions, it would be him.

Accompanied by his marines, Rufinus marched in through the high archway of the central of three gates. Clerks hurried out of the side offices to intercept the new arrival and attempt to 'direct his enquiries' appropriately, but his rich toga and the presence of eight armoured marines made them think twice and pause at the doorways. He stomped out into the long, wide courtyard, heading for the offices at the far end. To each side every doorway had a sign above it, labelling its contents and owner, if that was not the state, and each door had additional tags, dating the arrival of the goods and their destination if in only short term storage here. The far end of the courtyard held five offices, and the central one belonged to the prefect.

Leaving his guards in the courtyard, Rufinus marched into the office, rapping on the open door as he entered. In his experience a trader or administrator with an open door was available to visitors anyway.

Dionysus looked up from his desk and blinked in surprise.

'Prefect Rufinus? What can the office of the grain administration do for you?'

Rufinus closed the door behind him.

'We are safe here?'

'As safe as anywhere, and safer than most. Why?'

Rufinus leaned on the desk opposite him. 'Nothing seems to be happening, other than my wife supplementing my income by helping bring in the grain. I'm just seeking some reassurance that things *are* happening. I'm getting sick of sitting in my office listening to sailors fart and tell mermaid jokes while nothing really advances.'

Dionysus shrugged. 'The governor's plans are not entirely ours to know, Prefect, and that is probably for the best. Each of us plays the part we are given and does not interfere with the others. That way there is precious little chance of any of us causing trouble for one another. All I will say is that, though I do not have the details of your wife's activities, if she is doing what I *suspect* she's doing, then she is doing it very well and with a great deal of subtlety. She is a perfectly acceptable Roman matron doing exactly what every other matron is doing to keep their households in coin, and she is above suspicion. Her business is perfectly open.'

'But?'

'But something she is doing *is* having an effect, Prefect, even if you don't see it. Like most of the uninitiated, you simply see large grain shipments coming in each month. What you don't see is the truth hidden in the figures. Those shipments *are* falling off, they're just doing it so slowly and subtly that it is not immediately visible. The decrease in arrivals is also a little too large to simply be laid at the feet of impoverished and unmanned farms. No, your wife is slowly, *very slowly*, squeezing the grain flow. Like me, you would do best to leave her to her task, for she is doing it very well, and the more we contact and interfere, the more danger we bring upon one another, in relation to which I would say *this* visit was unnecessary and dangerous.'

Rufinus dropped two wax tablets on the table.

'Orders from myself to assign two triremes to the coast between Alsium and Lavinium, as there have been a few small incidents with locals thieving from ships at anchor off the coast. I wanted to officially warn you about it, and make sure you knew not to have any unprotected barges until the authorities in Ostia haver sorted it out. Also a request for grain – and yes, I know that's ironic – for the fleet. Despite the production of the mills at Arelate, the current wide distribution of the fleet is making supply troublesome. I want to create a few small granary bases in coastal towns where the fleet often operates, to save large scale transport becoming a necessity.'

Dionysus frowned, then nodded. 'It makes sense, I suppose. Yes, I will sign that order and pass on your warnings to the liaisons with the grain fleet owners.'

'So,' Rufinus said, returning to his private reasons for attendance, 'the supply is falling, then. How much grain can Rome survive on before it begins to feel the pinch?'

Dionysus shook his head. 'How long is a piece of rope, Prefect? It depends on the fluctuations in population, the mood of the poor, the effects of the plague, and small hiccups like fleet prefects requesting extra grain for their ships.'

Rufinus huffed. 'So we have no idea of a timescale for any of this?' he grumbled.

'Of course we haven't. We must just keep carefully squeezing and nudging and tweaking until things finally happen. This was never going to be a job that was over in a month. The idea, Prefect, is that we're moving so slowly with the entire thing that no one is noticing anything happening at all, even the suspicious chamberlain and his network of men. The only thing that would make a sudden difference would be the failure of the grain fleet to arrive at all for a month. *That* would put us in trouble and strain the reserves. But short of war, pirates, disastrous storms or sea gods jumping up and down amid the ships, the notion of the entire fleet failing is preposterous. Too many safeguards are in place.'

'There *are* pirates,' Rufinus mused. 'Whatever the great Pompey did in Cilicia did not entirely remove their taint from the seas.'

'But the Cilician pirates are far from the grain routes, as are the Euxine pirates. The only known haven of piracy anywhere near us is the Mauri to the south of Hispania, and they are kept in check by the Africa fleet.'

'Not very well,' Rufinus snorted. 'They continue to raid the Hispanic coast. But yes, they pose no real danger to the grain fleets. And my own ships keep the coasts of Italia safe. Only two possibilities to change that lie open. If the African fleet could be drawn away, perhaps the Mauri might cut off our supplies. Or if we could somehow seal off the channel between Africa and Sicilia, the fleet would be forced to use the Strait of Messana, and we all know how perilous that can be. Even Odysseus knew about Scylla and Charibdis. No one uses those straits if they can be avoided.'

Dionysus shook his head. 'Stop trying to push this cart, Prefect. It is rolling slowly downhill of its own accord. It is moving slowly enough that no one cares. If you give it a shove someone will try and stop it. Don't you have your own orders from Severus to deal with?'

Rufinus shook his head. 'Not yet. I'm just twiddling my thumbs and watching nothing happening.'

'Then what you need is a hobby. But stop trying to push things. The governor knows what he's doing. We'll know what we need to when the time is right.'

The visitor hovered, impatient, irritated, while Dionysus signed and sealed the orders for the grain release, and then held it out.

'Good day, Prefect.'

Rufinus pursed his lips, wishing there was something he could say to change things, but clear in the knowledge that there wasn't.

'Good day.'

He left the office feeling no less tense and impatient than when he'd entered, and stormed back to his litter with the marines in tow. During the uncomfortable journey back to the house, he decided to try and persuade Senova to let him get involved with whatever she was doing. Right now, it seemed that she was the only one of them actively making a difference, and perhaps in offering to help, she might explain precisely what it was she was doing.

The litter lurched to a sudden halt and Rufinus slid off his cushion, clacking his teeth together painfully as his head hit the side.

'Can you lot not manage to walk straight for one damn day?' he snapped, pulling open the curtain.

His brow creased as he realised they had stopped because the road was blocked. Praetorians stood in lines, keeping the crowd at bay, and Rufinus slipped from the litter and strode across to an optio who was dressing the lines.

Rufinus' eyes shifted from the ranks of Praetorians the moment he had confirmed with relief that he did not know any of them personally, and to the street beyond.

A small heap lay at the centre of the street, two Praetorians standing close by. The body was someone important, for it lay wrapped in a toga that had been white before it became soaked in blood. This was no robbery or street murder, though, for the two Praetorians were busy cleaning their blades. Rufinus felt a cold stone of worry settle in his belly. Once, years ago, he had bloodied his own weapon as a guardsman, killing a young toga-clad man and saving his beats. But this? The emperor was nowhere to be seen. A suspicion formed in his mind and he felt his lip twitch sourly.

'What happened?' he asked the optio.

The junior officer turned angrily, ready to berate this civilian for interfering, but the sight of a small force of marines backing Rufinus up spoke eloquently of his military rank. The optio cleared his throat.

'Praetorian business, sir.'

'I am the prefect of the Praetorian fleet, soldier. What happened.'

The optio dithered. Despite the name that gave them a connection, he would be well aware that Rufinus had no authority in the actual guard, but he was still an important officer in the Roman military and might have the ear of the emperor or his chamberlain. Caution won out.

'We have apprehended a traitor to the empire, sir. Marcius Quartus.'

Rufinus remembered the man from social engagements. An ex-prefect of the Urban Cohorts who hadn't lasted long, probably because he was too outspoken against Cleander. Actually a very distant cousin, though at a distance even Jupiter himself couldn't cover with a thrown bolt. He'd seemed a nice enough fellow. A little too serious for his own good, like most of the distant branches of the family. Certainly didn't seem the sort to plot against the throne. But then did Rufinus and his companions have the air of conspirators? Yet here they were...

'Take the body away and clear the road,' came a commanding voice with a faint slur, and Rufinus turned to see a centurion marching towards the optio. 'We're causing a hold up for everyone.'

Rufinus' eyes narrowed. The long, drawn face. The blotchy nose. It was the same centurion he had seen in the tavern, talking to his father.

'Yes Centurion,' the optio answered, and immediately began to move everything, four men collecting the body and carrying it, dripping, from the street. Rufinus was just about to return to his litter and move on, when a man in a Praetorian tribune's uniform appeared on the scene from some side street, gesturing at the centurion.

'Arvina, this should have been kept off the streets,' he admonished angrily.

'He ran, sir. We had to chase him down.'

Rufinus heard nothing more. He turned his back and hurried to his litter, clambering in, his guard forming around him once more. As they moved again, his marines and litter bearers taking a wide arc around all the blood, he peeked out between the litter's curtains. The centurion was still there, defending his actions to his superior. The tribune Rufinus didn't know, but that horse-faced centurions name had fired off connections in his memory.

Arvina.

Gaius Hostilius Arvina.

The centurion in charge of security on the Palatine. One of the two remaining murderous cavalrymen on Rufinus' list. To think he'd been right next to him in the tavern. He began to fret and think and plan. Arvina would be hard to get to, Cestius had said. He spent most of his time on the Palatine, where he was based, and the rest of the time he would be in the Castra Praetoria. In both places he would be untouchable. So he had to be caught somewhere in between.

He was a drunk.

Rufinus remembered his red nose and cheeks from both occasions he had met the man. The first time he had been drinking neat wine as though it were water. The second, just now, he had a noticeable slur to his voice. *That* was his weakness. *That* was where he would be found.

'Stop.'

The litter lurched once more and Rufinus banged his head again. He peered through the curtain. They were quite some way down the street now with the populace in between, but he could still just make out the scene. The tribune had vanished and Arvina was directing his men in the cleaning up of the scene.

Rufinus slipped from the litter. 'Go home,' he told them. 'All of you.'

The optio of his guard gave him a frown of disapproval, but saluted. He was a soldier, given an order by his commander, and no matter how much he might not like it, he would follow the order. As soon as the litter and its guard were on the way, Rufinus turned and made his way back up the street. The Praetorians were still at it, and the small crowd of grimly-fascinated onlookers had not yet dispersed. It was a simple matter for Rufinus to join the small gaggle of people, at least half a dozen of whom wore togas.

He watched Arvina. The man might have been drinking, but he was compos mentis and clearly in charge. By the time he'd had six buckets of water thrown across the blood to wash it into the sewers, only half a dozen soldiers remained on the scene with him. Rufinus watched, tense. He would get few opportunities at Arvina.

'You,' the centurion said, jabbing a finger at two of the guardsmen. 'You two come with me. I'll have to report this to the prefect at the fortress before we can head back to the palace. Bloody reports. I'll have half a dozen to write up tonight, now.'

A third soldier brought across a horse for the prefect. Rufinus fretted still. He was going to have to follow Arvina, and see if the opportunity arose to move on him. But the man was going to be on horseback and with two or three guardsmen as escort. And Rufinus stood out a bit in his white toga, too. As soon as they moved away from the centre into the poorer areas towards the Praetorian fortress he would be horribly visible. His gaze zipped this way and that, and then settled on an old man in a drab cloak with a wide-brimmed straw hat keeping the summer sun from his brow. Rufinus hurried over to him.

'How much for your cloak and hat?'

'Ain't fer sale,' the old man drawled.

'Come on, man,' Rufinus hissed, grabbing his purse and lifting it, opening the string. The old man's eyes lit up. 'How much?'

'Oi's got a pale 'ead, see. Burns easy.'

Irritably, Rufinus tipped out enough coins to buy the man five brand new hats.

'An' it's an hair-loom, y'know.'

'Handed down through the generations, was it?' grunted Rufinus sarcastically, adding two more coins to his palm.

'Oi loiks that one,' the man grinned, pointing at a shiny coin still in the bag. Rufinus gritted his teeth and added the coin to the payment. The man nodded and took the coins, removing his hat and passing it over. Rufinus took it, noting with distaste that half the heirloom generations seemed to have had almost critical dandruff and must have left half their heads in the lining. Shuddering, he plonked it on his head.

'Now 'bout moi cloak...' the old man said.

'That was for the hat *and* the cloak,' Rufinus snapped.

'No, that was fer moi 'at. Cloak's a good 'un.'

Rufinus unwound his toga with some difficulty and threw it into the man's wooden trolley. 'That's worth a fortune.'

'Not ter me. Not loik money.'

Rufinus glanced around. Arvina was already moving off down the street with his men. The prefect turned back to the old farmer. 'Here.' He dropped five coins into the man's hand.

'It were an hair-l...'

'No it bloody wasn't and you've already made a month's money from me in a dozen heartbeats, now give me the cloak and sod off.'

The old man seemed to weigh up his options for a moment, but finally shrugged and passed over his cloak. 'Noice doin' buzzy-niss with yer.'

Rufinus gave the man the blackest look he could muster and then, donning the smelly cloak, scurried off in the wake of the Praetorians. Before long they were in the wide thoroughfare of the Vicus Patricius, the street that ascended the Viminal hill to the vast fortress of the Praetorians. As they moved, Rufinus kept to the edges of the pavement while the centurion and his men trotted along the centre of the road with an air of ownership. Rufinus became steadily less enchanted with his disguise as he went, his head itching from the acres of scalp previous owners had left in the hat, and smelling unpleasant thanks to the cloak and its distinctive odour of bovine urine.

He was starting to wonder what he would do when they got to the fortress. He would have to wait somewhere, quietly, for Arvina to finish his report and emerge once more. And what then? Would he just go straight back to the Palatine? Rufinus chewed on his lip, wishing for an answer, praying in fits and starts to Fortuna and Nemesis, the goddesses of luck and vengeance.

The divine pair must have heard his entreaty, for the centurion suddenly thrust out a finger and he and his three men crossed the street to a tavern called *Nero's Torch*. Rufinus shivered at the reference, and wondered how the city's seemingly growing Christian community felt about such reminders of their darkest hour.

At the door, Arvina dismounted and handed his reins to one of the men, who stayed outside with a bored, resigned expression while the centurion and his other two men entered. Rufinus sniffed and looked down at himself. He doubted he would be welcome in there looking and smelling as he did, but as luck would have it – thank you again, ladies – he happened to be standing outside a store that had tunics and cloaks for sale.

Discarding his in one of the refuse piles at an alley's entrance, he entered the shop, ignored the sniffs and pulled faces of the staff, and bought a new tunic and cloak. At a temporary stall nearby he purchased some rosewater perfume and a comb, and with just moments in that alley raked his hair clear, doused himself enough to hide the cow piss stench, and dressed like a normal citizen.

Flapping the cloak to clear some of the excess perfume, he made for the tavern.

Arvina was already at a table with his men. He was the only one with a cup, Rufinus noted, and there was no water in evidence. He bought himself a small, well-watered wine and a bowl of nuts and sat down at a table not far away, where he could watch.

Had he had any qualms about what he had planned, they would have easily been put aside as he watched the centurion tripping young serving girls as they walked past and making lewd comments about them at which his men dutifully laughed. When a man brought him his second drink and began to water it, Arvina gave him such a back-handed slap that the fellow collapsed to the floor, then hurried away, shaking.

Rufinus watched him carefully. This was one of the men who had murdered Dis in the villa grounds, mutilating him and hanging him in the trees. This was a cold-hearted killer who had betrayed his vows and signed on with Cleander, gaining influence and power by supporting Rome's most wicked man. No, there was no doubt that Arvina had to go.

He continued to watch for almost an hour. Clearly the centurion's love of the vine had overcome the urgency of reporting to his prefect. So as well as being a murderous arsehole, he was also a poor officer and a bad soldier. Finally, the man began to drain his cup without waving for a replacement, and Rufinus realised they were going to leave soon. Irritably he tried to come up with something, and it was only when he accidentally dropped a nut from the bowl on the table and bent to pick it up that he saw that which decided him.

Arvina's leg was shaking. It was not a spasmic thing, he was sure. He'd seen the man enough now to know there was nothing like that wrong with his leg. That was simply a symptom of a full bladder. The centurion picked up his almost empty cup, lifting it to finish, but Rufinus was already moving.

Private latrines were not common in Rome. Few taverns had them, relying instead on either public ones or the expensive and lucrative privately owned variant. But the better taverns sometimes had them, and Rufinus had already spotted the doorway out back with the sign showing a figure of a man with an unrealistically high arc of urine painted on the wall beside it. Hurrying in order to be ahead of Arvina, he dashed through the door, gripping his crotch as though on the verge of desperation.

The latrine was cunningly placed around three corners, each with a window into one alley or another which created a through draft that kept the stench of the latrine from filling the tavern. Rufinus hurried past them, aware that Arvina would be close behind. He found the latrine around the last corner and dashed inside. There was no door, and it was a small room, no more than eight feet across. Very cosy. A three seat latrine lay along the wall, the air above the holes wavering with the heated smell. He forced his lunch back down into his throat from where it threatened to burst free at the stench. On the other walls sat a bucket of water with sponges in it and a bowl of clean water with a jug for the washing of hands. Rufinus paused. There was nowhere to hide. He'd planned to make himself hidden and leap out, but this room and the approaching corridor made that impossible. As he dithered he became aware of the sound of hobnailed boots closing on him.

He was trapped. There was nowhere to hide.

Taking a deep breath, he waited in the open, at the centre of the room. He would have to be quick, and keep it silent, for a blood-curdling scream would certainly bring others, and there was no way back out of here except through the bar. He mused, for just a moment, whether a man might fit down the latrine pipe, but decided it would be impossible, even if he considered it.

He flexed his fingers and biceps. He was still fit and fast, and Arvina would be slowed by the wine.

Silence first. Then speed.

The centurion turned the corner, entering the room with his hands already at his belt, ready to free himself for relief. He frowned at the sight of a figure standing in the centre of the room.

Rufinus hit him just once. His knuckles crunched into Arvina's throat, breaking bone and cartilage, crushing the windpipe and silencing him instantly. The centurion gasped, eyes going wide. He was dead already. Rufinus knew the blow he'd delivered would choke the man and there was no repairing it. But that wasn't enough. Arvina needed to be prevented from flight, and he needed to know why this was happening to him.

Rufinus moved in a slow arc around the stricken man, until he was between Arvina and the exit. The centurion staggered around to face him, eyes bulging, fingers clawing at his throat.

160

'Seven years ago you were a cavalry trooper serving in the Castra Praetoria,' he said quietly. 'On the orders of the prefect Paternus, who proved to be a traitor in the end, you murdered a loyal frumentarius – a servant of the emperor, at the villa of the lady Lucilla. And now you serve Cleander as though he were the man to whom you took your vow, and not the emperor. But it is for Dis, the frumentarius, and your crime that day in the villa grounds, that this has happened to you. You are the fifth. Only one remains. I shall place no coin in your mouth. If you are lucky and the fates are kind, your men will find you and do just that before the ferryman turns his back on you and condemns you to an eternity among the ghosts. Either way, you are paying for your crime and your time among men is done.'

Arvina gasped something pleadingly, and as an oddly peaceful look descended on the man's rosy face Rufinus had a strange moment's epiphany. Though there was no way to be sure, he felt certain that Arvina's drinking had begun that day after the murder of Dis. The man had been haunted by his deed ever since and now, as the centurion collapsed to the ground, twitching, his breathing halted for the last time, he looked content, as though he'd been waiting for this moment for years.

Rufinus felt an odd wrench of pity.

He couldn't forgive Arvina for what he'd done, but a show of remorse went a long way. With a new resolve, Rufinus crouched, removed a coin from his purse and, despite what he'd said, slipped it beneath the centurion's tongue, closing his mouth and sliding his eyelids shut.

Rising, he turned his back on the latrine and its sad occupant and made his way back along the winding corridor with its open windows and its welcome breeze, and into the bar. The two soldiers at the table looked up and, realising it was not Arvina, returned to their conversation. Rufinus hurried past them and out into the street. Back to the nearby alley, he turned and ran, taking the most complex and obscure route he could find back into the city's centre.

Five down, one to go.

Chapter Eleven – Traders and Watchmen

Rome, September 188 A.D.

'Will you stop pacing?' snapped Senova, counting the figures on her list for the third time in a row, and with a different total each time. It was bad enough that she still had to concentrate to work in the Romans' written language without having her 'husband' stomping back and forth across the room and harrumphing impatiently like a goat, constantly distracting her.

'I've got nothing else to do. The fleet is at rest, the seas are calm and safe, and unless I want to watch sailors hauling canvas this way and that, I've nothing to do.'

'Go and read or something. Go to the games. There's always games on these days.'

Rufinus nodded. It was true. The emperor, periodically closeted away with his mistress and then suddenly in the public eye being his golden self at times, seemed to have races and games on every week now, such was his love of them, or so it was said. Rufinus had a private suspicion that the constant flow of gladiatorial fights, animal hunts and chariot contests was as much about keeping the public happy and their mind off the plague-ridden misery of the streets as anything. Panem et circenses, as the saying went.

'I wish we could move on the plan.'

'What plan?'

Rufinus harrumphed again. 'The plan I don't know, that Severus seems to be shuffling along at snail's pace.'

'Darling, everything is in order. Every day things change just a little. And perhaps Severus will approve your scheme today. Just be patient.'

But Rufinus was past patience now. Every day he waited for a letter from Severus, agreeing to his request. Dionysus had said that the only thing that would push the plan forward in a leap would be if the grain fleet failed to arrive at all in a month. Rufinus had latched onto that. And since he could not control the weather and no matter how much wine he poured into the altar of Neptune the seas failed to swallow the grain ships, the only chance was piracy.

There would be no feasible way to get pirates to intercept the grain fleets from their hideouts in the Euxine sea, past Dacia, and similarly the infamous pirates of Cilicia were out of the picture. That left the Mauri, that race of people who lived along the African coast from Sicilia all the way to the pillars of Hercules in the south of Hispania. The Mauri had always spawned raiders, from desert horsemen who ambushed caravans to bandits who ravaged undefended villages, and in more recent decades, the plague that made much of their land non-viable had driven them to sea to hunt. Mauri corsairs had caused endless trouble for the governors of Hispania, especially in the south, but they were broadening their horizons all the time, perhaps driven by boldness, and perhaps by the fleet that had moved to pen them in and suppress their piracy.

The African fleet, run by a prefect out of Caesarea Mauretania, had been given carte blanche to stop the raids, but had managed only to *minimise* the trouble, rather than ending it. The people of that land were insular and protective of their own and the forces there, including the Third Legion, had failed to root out the sources of the pirates. The fleet had managed to contain the worst of it, and had caught a few vessels at sea, sinking them, but the pirates were managing to get across the water to Hispania. It was Rufinus' suspicion that the prefect of that fleet, given a difficult task and inadequate ships to take care of it, had concentrated on keeping the pirates away from the eastern end of their region, where the important provinces of Africa and Sicilia lay, and the critical passage of trade routes between those two. The prefect had almost certainly placed most of his fleet there and left the west poorly covered, enabling the pirates to operate towards Hispania. In fairness, it was what Rufinus would do.

He had initially been surprised on learning all of this that the prefect of the African fleet had not come to him and asked for support, but then that would be tantamount to admitting his failure in dealing with the matter himself, which would be a poor career move.

Rufinus had reasoned that the grain shipments from Africa and Aegyptus, which between them constituted perhaps eighty percent of all grain doled out in Rome, were perfectly safe from harm while the African fleet was concentrated in that area. The only thing that would put them at risk was if the African fleet were re-deployed. Rufinus had no authority to arrange that. In fact, only the emperor or the senate – or Cleander – could really order the prefect to move his fleet, though a powerful governor might have enough clout. And so, having no other ideas and nowhere else to turn, he had sent to Severus, asking the governor to see if he could somehow have the African fleet ordered west, to concentrate on Hispania. That way, the east would be easier pickings for pirates.

But for now, he would simply have to wait.

'Perhaps we should go out. Both of us. To the races maybe?'

Senova shot him an irritated look, and then began again, pointedly. 'Twelve. Twenty one. Forty seven...'

'I'll leave you alone.'

He turned, feeling as frustrated and impotent as ever, and found himself face to face with one of the house's slaves. The man's face was ashen, the sight of which formed a lump in Rufinus' throat.

'What is it?'

'Visitors, Domine. It's... er...'

'Spit it out, man.'

'It's the imperial chamberlain, master.'

Rufinus felt terror settle upon him, his feet rooted to the floor. Cleander? Here in his house? But he'd done nothing. He was so damned innocent right now that it ached. Had the man somehow caught wind of one of the communiques with Severus?'

'Tell the chamberlain I'll see him in the summer dining room.'

The slave, still terrified, added embarrassed to the looks on his face. 'I'm afraid it's not you he's here to see, Domine. It's the mistress.'

Rufinus' brow creased in confusion. 'My *wife?*'

'Yes, Domine.'

Senova turned and Rufinus was astonished to see a calm and collected face, if stung with a little irritation that her accounting had been interrupted once again.

'Show him in, Albius.'

'Listen…' began Rufinus.

'Be polite,' she interrupted. 'Be calm, and try to wipe that expression off your face. You look as though someone put a knife to your manhood.'

Rufinus was just considering disappearing entirely, hiding in the back rooms somewhere, when the sound of approaching footsteps made escape impossible. He attempted to brush away the panic that he would be recognised, despite the beard and hair, and tried to pull on an easy smile that felt incredibly fake and embarrassing. He also felt a small nervous fart sneak out and prayed that it didn't smell.

As the footsteps grew closer and louder, he snatched up a tablet and concentrated on it, trying to be so boring as to be entirely invisible. At the very last moment as the visitor arrived, he remembered to shuffle the folds of his toga over his nail-less left hand.

Cleander strode into the room with a confidence that Rufinus wished he himself could count upon. A slave followed at his heel and Rufinus heard the distinctive clatter of half a dozen pairs of Praetorian boos as the man's escort settled in the atrium.

Cleander looked a little older than Rufinus remembered, even since that evening of the party at the grain commissioner's house. Was the strain of power getting to him? The chamberlain had such an easy, pleasant smile that Rufinus almost had to shake himself to remind himself how dangerous and unpleasant this man really was.

'Lady Julia Triaria, it is my profound pleasure to finally make your acquaintance, and it is somewhat remiss of me having left it so long.'

Cleander bowed politely to Senova, who flashed him a winning smile. He turned to Rufinus.

'Prefect, when we met at the party you never told me you'd had the fortune to marry a goddess.'

Rufinus tried to jack up his fake smile, though in his mind's eye he had grabbed the seal-knife from the table and slammed it repeatedly into the bastard's face until the whole room swam in Cleander's blood. For a moment, he wondered whether he could do it. Could he manage to kill Cleander before the Praetorians outside ran to stop him? He would die for it, of course, but that didn't matter.

But Senova would die for it too. And all his contacts would be unpicked. Severus would die. Publius would die. Gods, but the aftermath would be appalling. He drove the idea from his mind and tried to look welcoming.

'Can I offer you wine, Chamberlain?' he asked, wondering if only he could hear the shakiness in his voice.

'Thank you, but no,' Cleander replied. 'To my eternal regret I am here on business and in something of a hurry.' He turned back to Senova. 'The emperor continues to request games be held. I'm sure this will come as no surprise. And while supplies of gladiators continue to be a concern between the plague and the drafting of such men into the armies of the former emperor, we continue to source men for the arena. What we are finding trouble with is exotic beasts.'

Senova nodded sagely. 'I would imagine the hunters must range far and wide for them.'

'Quite, but it is not the capture and containment of such beasts that concerns me. It is the *transport* of the creatures.'

Rufinus felt a lurch of worry. What had she been up to?

'They are troublesome?' she asked.

'Indubitably. I assume you have seen the beasts we supply for the public's edification in the arena? Cameleopards, one-horn beasts, elephants and the like.' He smiled oddly. 'Even mongoose. I'm sure with your business concerns you can appreciate the impressive requirements of a vessel to carry elephants across the water. We can hardly divert a trireme with little or no hold space, and the vast majority of merchant ships are inadequate. Obviously some beasts are brought in by merchants and we simply buy them in Rome for the games, but the increased quantities we require these days has required a certain level of state involvement. We usually arrange temporary contracts with certain merchants in the African ports or in Ostia or Puteoli. We pay well, after all.'

Senova nodded, and Rufinus tried not to quake. This sounded as though it were leading somewhere dangerous.

'The issue I am coming across is that the people we usually use are currently contracted to others in what appears to be lucrative and, sadly, entirely legal business. The ships simply are not available for the task. Very little enquiry was needed to learn that one mercantile venture in particular seems to have the vast majority of large traders. The house of Triarius seems to have something of a monopoly currently, supplying much of the grain fleet's vessels. Only those large ships are of real use to us. You are contracted to the grain shipments, but I must assume that you have other vessels that are engaged in more private ventures?'

Rufinus felt the edge of panic again, but Senova simply nodded. 'Yes, there are a number of vessels that I use in private enterprise outside state contracts. Do I presume you wish to bid for their use?'

Rufinus blanched. What was she doing? *He wants ships! Give him the bloody ships so he'll go away.*

Cleander gave an indulgent smile. 'I would like to charter three large vessels on a semi-permanent contract if you have the ships available. They would be required to be available at any time for the transport of beasts, supplies, and men for the arena.'

Rufinus saw a flicker of distaste and defiance in Senova's eyes, and he realised with horror that she might be about to refuse. It was the damn gladiators. She had such a thing against slavery that she could conceivably ruin everything right now by refusing to ship gladiators to their deaths. He shook his head as subtly as he could manage behind Cleander's back and felt a flood of relief as Senova noticed and that defiant flame ebbed.

'You will understand, I hope,' she said, 'that my ships are our house's livelihood, and are engaged in very lucrative trade. To take them out of that and sign them over for a long period will not only impact on our finances, but also might impinge on my reputation, if I can no longer supply my merchants?'

Rufinus' eyes widened. She was *haggling*. With the most powerful man in the empire, who could snap his fingers and have them both peeled of skin. He began to shake his head again.

'I will, of course, assure you of adequate recompense,' Cleander said smoothly.

Senova's mouth curved into an odd half-smile. 'I have been in business long enough to know that one man's "adequate" is another man's "poor", Chamberlain. Might we discuss specific terms before I agree?'

Cleander laughed, a chilling sound. 'Gods, but it's no wonder your commercial empire is growing in a world where everyone else's is shrinking. I've half a mind to second you to the treasury.' His face became very serious so suddenly that

Rufinus started to panic all over again. 'You are aware of the power I wield? I could, of course, simply impound your ships.'

'But that would damage your reputation, of course, Chamberlain. Rome is still reeling from the many deaths of that last conspiracy. The emperor and the court can scarce afford bad feeling among the people right now.' She smiled sweetly. 'Besides, you know I'm in the right.'

Again, Cleander laughed. 'Gods above and below, but you drive a hard bargain, lady Julia. And yet I find myself feeling more and more indulgent as we talk. You are, of course, correct in all you say. And I would be pleased to contribute to your growing empire. The emperor and I always try to support the equestrian class in their endeavours, for this is the age of the common man, and the old guard of patricians are reaching the end of their days. Name your price.'

Senova smiled again, while Rufinus privately filed away that little dig at the patrician class to which he belonged when he used his real name.

'Forty denarii for every hundredweight of cargo hauled, plus fifty denarii a day per ship when idle.'

Cleander straightened suddenly. 'Domina, you are either joking or deluded. No trader would ever consider such a price.'

'It is, as you might note, Chamberlain, a seller's market.'

Rufinus shook his head as hard as he could and Senova chewed her lip, thinking it over. She smiled. 'I must remain competitive. Just as you have your reputation to maintain, Chamberlain, so do I, and I cannot afford for my competition to see me as a pushover. I am willing to accept thirty two denarii per hundredweight and forty a day when idle. Per ship, of course. And please bear in mind that twelve denarii of that is the port fee I have to pay. Though for stooping so low, perhaps you will sweeten the deal?'

Rufinus' eyes bulged at her insolence, but Cleander appeared to be chuckling.

'Thirty a hundredweight. Thirty five per idle day. And access to the senatorial seating with reserved place for all events in every theatre, amphitheatre and circus in the city for the duration of your contract.'

Senova frowned for a moment, and then sat back. 'Agreed. You drive a hard bargain, Chamberlain.'

Cleander snorted. 'And between your trade fleet and your husband's command of the strongest classis on the sea, the Triarii have become a family to watch. I appreciate your time, Domina. I will send the appropriate documentation and an instalment with one of my secretaries later today.'

Senova simply bowed her head, and Cleander turned, his clerk scribbling notes at his side.

'Your wife is a commercial lion, Prefect. If she continues as she is, soon the state will be coming to her for a loan.'

He smiled at his own humour and then strode out, gathering his guard, and departed.

Once he heard the outer door close and the military footsteps were no longer audible, Rufinus exploded as all tension drained from him.

'What in Hades were you doing?'

'Bartering, dear. It's what pays the bills.'

'*Severus* pays the bills,' he grumped.

'Don't be foolish, dear. I have repaid the governor his investment. As of a month ago we are working purely on our own profit.'

Rufinus boggled. 'But you undercut everyone for the grain contracts. How can you be making so much money?'

'Come, dear. You do not surely believe the grain ships are our only investment. But best not to pry too deeply into other areas. I doubt you'll like what you find.'

Rufinus sighed and retreated from the room, defeated.

October 188 A.D.

Rufinus stepped out of his door and nodded his head in greeting to the three men on the front step. Flanked by two marines, so fresh off the ship that they still smelled of brine and fish, stood a man in the tunic and with the satchel of the imperial courier service.

'From Lugdunum?'

The courier nodded and fished in his bag, producing a scroll case bearing the seal of the governor, Septimius Severus. Rufinus breathed lightly. Word at last. He smiled at the three men.

'Thank you.'

As they turned to depart, he left his doorman to close up and strolled back into the atrium, peering at the unopened scroll case. Senova stood there, for once devoid of reports and letters.

'From him?'

'Yes.'

'Open it.'

Rufinus nodded and strode over into his office. Senova followed and closed the door behind them. He leaned back against his desk and snapped the seal, opening the case. A single vellum sheet was rolled up within.

Aulus,

I write to inform you with great joy and jubilation that Julia has given me a son. Lucius Septimius Bassianus was born in the spring, and already Julia's belly swells with a sibling. Upon my return to Rome, I shall be hosting a grand celebration in our town house and I extend a happy invitation you yourself and your wife.

Rufinus sagged. All that wait, and it was a letter filled with family matters.

'What is it?'

'Severus has had a son.'

'How wonderful.'

'And unimportant.'

He drifted back down to the letter and skipped over other mundanities involving his province and family matters, and was so bored with the inanity of it all that he almost missed it.

I have heard, by the way, from an old friend, Pollienus Auspex, the governor of Hispania Tarraconensis. He is so perturbed by the ongoing Mauri raids on his coastline that he has arranged for the African fleet to concentrate on saving his lands. Would that he had your ear, eh, with your powerful fleet. Still, perhaps the move will finally end the Mauri problem for him.

He then went on to drone about trade routes in the Rhodanus and price fixing in Gaul, but Rufinus lost interest. He had what he wanted.

'I take it from that beaming smile that you got what you were waiting for?'

'Yes.'

'So I can look forward to your new pirate friends moving east to the rich pickings of the Carthage straits and sinking all my ships?'

Rufinus huffed. 'Don't get so involved in your little trade game that you forget our true purpose. Every one of those ships that fails tightens the grain rations and puts pressure on Rome. *That* is what we're about.'

He looked up, but realised that Senova was grinning. He chuckled. 'Sorry. Strain has been making me tetchy.'

'I hadn't noticed, dear. And as you yourself pointed out recently, the grain ships are not where we're making our money anyway. We can stand to lose the entire fleet and still turn a healthy profit. Indeed, that is the very situation towards which I have been working.'

Rufinus laughed. 'You're a damn marvel. When Cleander came calling I thought you'd slipped up, you know? I thought something you'd done had us all for the chop.'

She smiled. 'Will it ease your fears, dear, if I assure you that absolutely everything I have done from the outset is actually legal, in the strictest sense. Some of it may not be ethical, and it was certainly bending the rules at times, but there is nothing for which we could be prosecuted.'

The humour slid from Rufinus. 'In the Rome of Cleander, innocence is no defence. If he has reason to believe you're doing something against him, he'll have us picked up and taken to the Palatine cellars regardless.'

'Then I had best continue to be careful,' Senova said. 'I assume you are confident that the Mauri will try their luck with the grain fleet?'

'They would be foolish not to. They've never had a chance like this before, and they might never again. Just one of those ships, if they can capture and divert it, will pay more than half a year of raiding coastal villages.'

'Will the emperor expect you to do something about it?'

Rufinus nodded. 'A month, maybe two, after the first time they hit the fleet, I will be told to secure the sea lanes. I will have to start providing trireme escorts from the African coast to Portus. Of course, before then I shall have had to send more ships to Gaul to help secure the grain from Arelate, and probably more to Hispania to aid the African fleet. Given the number of men the emperor needs me to provide for the awnings and suchlike of his amphitheatres and the need to keep the Italian ports secure, I will not have enough ships to provide escort for every vessel. I would estimate that each month up to a third of the grain fleet will be at risk, and yet I will appear to be doing everything I can to prevent it. And with luck I will be able to sink a few Mauri pirates and make a good show of it all. Yes, I think we can safely say the grain shipments are about to dwindle a little faster.

Senova smiled. 'Only you could be so enthusiastic about sinking our own people and starving Romans.'

Rufinus felt his smile slip. Damn it.

He spent the rest of the day at the castrum, finding cunning ways to second his best ships to other duties around the western empire, gradually depleting the pool of vessels from which he would be able to draw when the time came to protect the grain ships. By the time he'd finished, satisfied that every posting was both realistic and justifiable, it was already dark and he knew that Senova would be getting twitchy waiting to eat. Locking up, he found Philip in his office, bade the strange man good night, and left for home.

It was a cold night, and he was for once grateful to climb into the litter and let his mismatched bearers lurch him home, surrounded by loyal marines. He wondered idly if this was what it was like to be a consul or suchlike, always having transport and an entourage. One day perhaps even Rufinus might be preceded by a column of lictors announcing his importance. He grinned at the thought. His father would kill to have that, and yet despite everything, Rufinus felt certain he was closer to that than his father. He wondered momentarily what his father was doing. Time had worn on, and Rufinus had not seen the old man again. Probably his father was expecting Publius to appear at any time. Soon he would become impatient and make some demand on Rufinus.

That was a worry he would deal with another time.

Slowly and uncomfortably, but with a new and unusual sense of progress and determination, he bounced his way back home. Outside his house he dismounted from the litter as his marines rapped on the knocker and had the domus door opened. He dismissed the litter back to its yard and his men back to the castrum, telling them he would need them at dawn the next day, and stood, shivering in the night air for a moment as they all departed, his doorman waiting patiently for him to enter.

A movement caught his eye for just a moment, and he turned to peer across the road. A public fountain with a grotesque head spouting fresh water stood in a small triangular park of stone chippings with three lovely flower beds, all overlooked by three beech trees that were now shedding the last of their leaves, which lay as a damp carpet on the stone below.

There was no one there. Perhaps it had just been the trees in the breeze?

He turned back and entered his house, the doorman closing up behind him, but as he did so he felt that strange tingle and the hairs on his neck stood proud. He could feel someone watching him. He paused for a moment in his entrance hall, his eyes on the small altar to the household gods. It made him smile a little to see that Senova had added her own statue of Minerva she'd bought in the forum and scratched the letters BRIG into, to make it her own foreign goddess.

His smile faded once more. There was only one window on the side of the house where the front door was. He was wealthy enough not to have shops occupying either side of the door, but still his house presented a plain façade to the street as was normal, all openings and windows generally looking inwards to the atrium and the garden. There was one, though. Nodding to the confused doorman, he moved past to the man's little cubbyhole beside the door. It was dark in here, as the man had been dozing when the door went, and Rufinus carefully approached the small window, just a hand-span across and barred with iron. There he paused and let his eyes adjust.

The small triangular park remained empty. He wondered if there was someone in one of the trees, but decided it was unlikely. There were not really enough leaves to conceal someone. Then he saw it. Just a tiny movement. Someone was crouched behind the fountain, and he kept seeing just the crown of their head. He dismissed out of hand the possibility it was a plague-ridden beggar. There was something just too suspicious about the figure.

What to do about it? He fretted again. He'd been watched since the beginning – that had been clear – but he'd not seen signs of it recently and had assumed that Cleander's men had decided he was unimportant and had lifted their surveillance.

Certainly for well over a month or two he'd seen nothing, and he'd been looking, too. Why now? Why had he attracted new watchers?

He tried not to connect it to Senova's work with civilian shipping or his own deployment of his fleet, or even his subtle shifting of the African ships to the west. He failed. He could see no reason for fresh surveillance unless it was as a result of Cleander's recent visit. And if they were on to him...

The chamberlain had certainly seemed uncharacteristically friendly. Was that him trying to catch them off-guard? Was this whole thing with hiring ships for the emperor's beasts just a way to probe their businesses? Push hard and see if something springs out of place?

Damn it. Whatever the case, he couldn't afford to be watched right now, just as he'd finally started to do something after months of inactivity.

Taking a deep breath, he left the little room, passed the still-baffled doorman, and pulled open his door. He was wrapped in his toga and unarmed, like any Roman gentleman. For a moment, he considered taking the doorman's club, but reasoned in the end that his own fists were far more dangerous. As he crossed the street towards the small park, he sized up the situation as he'd always done, as though he were about to meet someone in the ring.

The man had to be lithe and probably small to be so well concealed behind the low fountain. He might be strong, but probably not too much. He was a watcher. He'd been chosen for speed, subtlety and observational qualities, not the ability to kill, probably at least. That being the case, he would probably try to run rather than fight. Back would lead him into a narrow alley that ended in a small square between houses. The man would know that and know that it was a dead end. To the north he would be moving further out of town and into areas in which he'd be more visible. So he would go to his left, Rufinus' right, heading back into town, where he could get lost among the crowds. He would probably be fast enough to get away, but not if Rufinus got the jump on him.

He crossed to the fountain, clearing his throat.

'Come on out,' he said in a threatening tone.

Readying himself, he took a pace to his left, as though rounding the fountain, but shifted his weight in the process. Predictably, the man burst out the other side, but Rufinus was ready for him. With his weight thus shifted to brace, he launched himself at the man. He was fast, this fellow, but not fast enough. Rufinus' arms wrapped round his thighs and brought him down with a bang to the ground.

'Who are you working for?' he grunted, already knowing the answer but needing to start the questions somewhere. There was no reply and he pushed himself up, allowing room to turn the watcher over. His heart fell as he did so. The lady Fortuna was clearly not with him tonight. He had tackled the man safely enough, but when they fell, the watcher's head had struck a boulder protruding from the leafy carpet. His head was a mess, and blood was pooling in the fallen foliage.

'Vesta's knockers!'

He reached down and felt the man's neck. There was a pulse, but it was slower than it should be, and faltering. Even as he worried, he felt the throb slow further. He pulled an eyelid open in the smashed face, and could see the pupil shaking. The man's brain was broken anyway. He would be dead in a few heartbeats.

Cursing, Rufinus rose. He'd only meant to question the man. He needed to know why he was being watched, that was all. He hadn't wanted to kill the man. He was within his rights to confront someone spying on his house, and nothing untoward might come of it. But having accidentally killed one of Cleander's spies watching him was unlikely to make the problem go away. In fact, it was likely to become a lot worse.

Perfect timing, now that he was actually planning to *do* something at last.

CHAPTER TWELVE – SAILORS AND SOLDIERS

Off the coast of Sicilia, June 189 A.D.

Herennius Buco leaned on the rail of his ship, the *Korinthos*, his steersman heaving slowly on the great oar, turning the heavy, laden vessel slightly more northerly in line with the other ships. They had departed Carthage yesterday morning and made the nail-biting run across to Sicilia, overnighting at Lilybaeum, in the usual manner. Despite the increased threat of pirates, who had been ravaging these seas all-but unchecked for the past half year and had claimed several vessels, the master and crew of the Korinthos had spotted nothing yesterday. The Misenum fleet had managed to assign a trireme to this little flotilla, which perhaps accounted for the peace of the journey, but still one trireme might not be enough. There were a lot of ships to protect, and the rumour was that the pirates were also numerous.

This morning the six grain ships had put to sea once more from Lilybaeum, hugging the coast of Sicilia until they were in a position to make the jaunt across open water to the Italian coast. There they would be relatively safe. The Misenum fleet had that coast secured, and the pirates went no further than Sicilia at the moment. This small fleet had been several days late departing due to staffing issues in Africa's farms and trade stations, but they hoped to rendezvous with the rest of the Africa and Sicilia fleet on the Italian coast south of Puteoli.

Hoped...

Buco sighed. He'd *leapt* at the chance to sign a contract with the Triarii. His business had been more than a little uncertain of late, what with the plague and endless troubles in the provinces, and he'd faced ruin a couple of times, barely scraping by. Then he'd been offered a permanent contract for the grain fleet by the factotum of the Triarii. Grain shipping was almost always safe and a guaranteed earner, and he'd leapt at the chance. Then the African fleet had been called west, the Mauri pirates had made the most of the freedom, and suddenly being a grain ship was horribly dangerous.

Why was he pondering so on the perils of his life?

Some preternatural sense made him turn, shivering, his hair standing on end, almost crackling with static. Sure enough, he saw them just as the lookout bellowed his warning. Four triangular sails, and from the angle bearing down on the Korinthos and its companions.

'Enemy sighted.'

The steersman cast Buco a look leaded with questions.

'How far to Lipara?' Buco bellowed to his navigator.

'Two hours at current speed, sir.'

Buco fumed. The Korinthos was built for capacity and stability, not speed. She could carry more than most and stood a better chance in the occasional storms, but she would ever be in danger from faster ships.

'We'll not make it.'

Lipara might only be a small island, but it had the benefit of being occupied, including a small military installation armed with several pieces of artillery. The pirates would not get too close to the place, and it would provide a haven for the beleaguered grain ships.

Not for the Korinthos, though.

He looked ahead. The warning had gone up among the other ships, too, and they were putting every effort into forging east, towards Lipari. Each of them would be faster than this sow, and the Korinthos, slow as she was, was already bringing up the rear.

He could perhaps coax extra speed from her is they tipped the cargo over the side. But even before he made quick calculations in his head he knew that it would make no difference. By the time they had lost enough grain to pick up adequate speed, the pirates would be on them anyway. The Korinthos was doomed. The best they could be was a decoy to save the other ships.

'What do we do?' the steersman asked in a tight breath.

'We prepare for trouble. We can't outrun them and the rest of the ships are leaving us behind.'

'But the trireme?'

Buco looked ahead once more. The military vessel had dropped back from its vanguard position, but was making no sign of turning to come to the defence of Korinthos, simply falling back to the position of the other ships where it could protect them.

'The trireme knows we're done for, but he can still see the other ships to Lipari and they'll be safe from there.'

Buco marvelled at how calm he sounded. He didn't feel it, but it was important to keep a controlled, level head at times like this. They were doomed. He had a potential way out, or so he understood, but it would only be useful for a few of them. It was only supposed to be for *him* in reality. There were sixteen men on board. The Korinthos was at least blessed with a lifeboat, but it would take only ten men. Probably twelve would fit uncomfortably for a short distance. That might work.

'Alright. Everyone except Gallio, Vetus and Papus get that lifeboat in the water. Get inside and row as though Hades himself were nipping your arse. I don't know whether you'll make landfall, but with luck once this is over the trireme will make a sweep back and find you.'

The crewmen, relieved beyond measure despite the unknown peril they still faced, went about their task, hurrying to get their means of escape into the water. Buco turned to the steersman. 'I'll take over there. You and the other two help the rest get that boat in the water.'

As the crew worked feverishly to save themselves, Buco heaved the steering oar once more, turning the ship. The Korinthos might be doomed, but at least he could buy the rest some time. His hand went to the canvas bag at his belt, waterproof and the most valuable thing on the ship right now.

The ship began to turn, cutting to the left, beginning a wide, slow arc. As it did so the lifeboat hit the water with a splash, its ejection hidden from the approaching pirates by the ship's hull. With luck they would get away unnoticed. The men began to leap from the ship into the water, swimming over to the lifeboat and climbing aboard.

He watched in irritation as the navigator, Vetus, also threw himself in, desperate to escape and ignoring Buco's orders. Oh well. The lifeboat was already overloaded anyway, and the fewer left on board the more likely his way out would bear fruit.

With the bulk of the crew gone, rowing like mad towards the diminishing shapes of the fleet, Buco continued to circle. The four small, fast pirate ships were closing on him now. He had contemplated denying them their prize. He could probably have holed the ship and sunk it before they got here, or even thrown much of the grain over the side. But the ship being full was a much better bargain for the enemy. Denying them their prize would not be likely to put them in a good mood.

As they approached and slowed, Buco and his two companions furled the sail and let the Korinthos drift to a halt. A quick glance showed the lifeboat to be already some distance away, little more than a black blot on the horizon. They would be safe. From the pirates, anyway. Who knew what else they might face.

Buco stood proud at the rail of his now lifeless ship, just Gallio and Papus beside him. One of the four pirate ships had moved out ahead of the others. Buco could see men with grapples and lines, and half a dozen figures stood with bows nocked and drawn. The men aboard wore brightly-woven tunics, and their dark skin was made all the more so by the black curly hair and beards that had grown out to be plaited and knotted.

'Surrender your ship,' shouted the leader in a thick Mauritanian accent.

Buco nodded. 'You have her: the Korinthos, loaded with grain bound for Portus.'

'Where are your crew.'

'Gone.'

The man nodded. The crew would have fetched them a few coins at the slave markets, but herding a captured crew usually meant trouble, and the real prize was the grain. 'You will come onto my ship. Kneel and be bound. My men will crew your ship back to land.'

Buco watched as the other ship came now close enough that the men threw out their grapples and pulled the two together. With a deep breath and a prayer, Buco reached into his pouch.

'No, no,' admonished the pirate leader, wagging a finger, but Buco continued anyway, fishing out the wax tablet from within.

'Do you read Latin?'

The man gestured to another beside him. 'Jora does. Give.'

Buco handed over the wooden tablet case and the second man snapped the seal of the Triarii and opened it. He read the contents, frowning as he tried to make sense of the words. Finally, through the impatient huffs of his master, Jora finished reading and began to explain in their own weird Mauri tongue what it said.

Buco felt the faintest tinge of irritation. He had no idea what the tablet contained, and it seemed unlikely he was going to be told, since they had switched to their own language. Whatever it was, it certainly seemed to take the pirate leader by surprise. He pondered something for a moment, and then there was a brief exchange between the two of them. Buco held his breath. Whatever the tablet was, it seemed to be working. He had been given it by the Triarii's man when he signed the contract, with instructions to hand it over if ever he found himself in this situation.

'You are lucky man,' the Mauri pirate said, turning to him.

'I believe so.'

'We accept your master's offer. Your ship and your grain are ours. You will be put ashore at the next opportunity and may go your own way.'

Buco felt the relief almost buckle his knees. He would lose his livelihood, but a business could always be rebuilt. Being alive to do so was the hard part. He was almost tempted to ask what the tablet said, but it had bought him his life and freedom, and he had no interest in jeopardising that. He would take the freedom and run. Rome would miss the grain, but at least it looked like Buco and his men would live to sail another day.

The pirate leader chewed his lip for only a moment, then gestured to his ship.

'Come aboard.'

Rome, August 189 A.D.

Rufinus waited impatiently as the clerks from the tabularium worked, hanging their burden on the designated hooks on the side wall of the rostrum in the most central part of the forum. Two soldiers stood close by, urging the watching public to keep back while the clerks worked. Rufinus did not feel the crowd pressing, of course, for his marines kept them safely at bay. He watched with interest, waiting for the news.

The *acta diurna* were posted in this place, and all across the empire copies would be distributed at staggered times. They comprised the official records of important government news, imperial edicts, social and political notices and everything of import right down to the planning of upcoming games and races. It was a marvel really that every single day men worked to compile and sanction this list of public news, had it hammered into large bronze sheets and distributed to inform the Roman people of the daily affairs around them. And as the day's acta was hung in place, the previous day's was taken down and carried to the tabularium, where they would be stored for posterity as the city's records. Even the quickest calculation suggested that in the two and a half centuries since the great Caesar had initiated this practice, more than ninety thousand of these sheets must have been produced. So much bronze. And surely they could not all still be kept at the tabularium, for there could not possibly be adequate room.

His musings were pushed aside as the clerks took the old acta away, accompanied by the two men of the Urban Cohort. The guards watched the crowd closely. It was not unknown for the acta to be stolen by the brazenly enterprising, for a large sheet of bronze melted down was worth quite a few coins.

Rufinus turned his attention to the acta. He received the naval news before it reached the clerks, of course, but he so often only heard anything else important when it was relayed to him by Philip, who made a habit of being present when the acta were posted. Today, Philip was in Ostia, overseeing the commissioning of seven new ships, and so Rufinus had dropped in to the forum to look at the news for himself for a change.

His eyes ran down the list, taking in all details of interest. As he read, he tried to ignore the feeling of being watched. He was getting used to it now. Since that night when he'd accidentally killed the watcher outside his house he had been very careful to do nothing untoward. New watchers had been set, and while the death of one such must have been suspicious, the nature of his injuries made it at least possible to explain as an accident. But now, even here, he knew he was under scrutiny. As such he had played the roles of "Prefect of the Fleet" and "master of the Roman Domus" to perfection, showing no sign that he worked to undermine the position of Rome's most powerful man, halt the flow of grain to the city, and seek the death of one remaining murderer within the Praetorian cavalry.

Damn it.

And damn it even *more*. Two of the items of news near the top of the list were clearly linked, and both affected him. A new proconsular governor had been appointed to Africa: Publius Helvius Pertinax. Rufinus remembered the man well – a good man and loyal to the empire, with no love of Cleander, but also not part of their secret group and therefore entirely unaware of what was currently happening. Pertinax might well get in the way entirely unintentionally, and with only well meaning. Indeed, the second piece of news was almost certainly direct from Pertinax in his new role. The senate had vowed to curb pirate activity in the western seas and secure the shipping lanes.

Undoubtedly that would involve drawing the Africa fleet back from Hispania to where it could protect the grain fleets. And very likely a directive from the senate would hit Rufinus' desk in the next few days demanding that he put his fleet at the service of Pertinax and Dionysus to secure the seas. So long working at moving the naval power of Rome around unnoticed to put the grain ships in danger, and Pertinax had, in one fell swoop, come in and undone it all. If only they'd included Pertinax in their plotting.

No. Pertinax was just too law-abiding. He might sympathise with their cause, but he would never be an active part in it. Rufinus suddenly felt a tingle of distaste in his mouth. He had once been an idealist. When had flouting the rules become so acceptable to him?

His gaze drifted down the news. The emperor had announced the appointment of a new suffect consul, though that in itself was a joke. The emperor was off in some seaside villa, shacked up with his mistress and having fun away from the plague-ridden streets of Rome. It would have been Cleander who had appointed the suffect consul, as he seemed to be doing with alarming regularity.

Someone in the crowd behind Rufinus snorted. 'Another pigging consul. We're getting one a month now.'

'They can't stay in office long enough to get anything done,' grumbled another.

'But Cleander's purse must be getting heavy,' barked a third, raising a raucous laugh.

Rufinus winced. It was common assumption that the chamberlain was selling titles to anyone who fancied themselves in a position of power. Of course they would owe the man even after appointment, and their power would be subject to his sanction. But still, the number of ex consuls in the city must have doubled in the last few years. That was not why he winced, though. The wince was in sympathy for the poor wag who'd made the comment. Rufinus would wager a ton of gold that there were at least a dozen pairs of eyes and ears in the crowd that belonged to Cleander. The speaker would be nabbed before he could leave the forum, and would quickly learn to regret speaking so about the chamberlain.

Rufinus' heart sank as he read on. The new consul was none other than Pescennius Niger.

He had last seen Niger in Dacia two years ago, when the man had sold him out. Admittedly, Niger had then secretly helped him escape, but the new consul was so tightly tied up in webs of conspiracy that it was impossible to say where his loyalties might lie.

Two new appointments, then. A man wo would accidentally work against them on simple principle governing a province critical to their plan, and a man whose motives he couldn't trust in one of the most powerful roles in the empire.

He sourly devoured the rest of the tidings and was at least grateful that nothing else in there impacted upon him. One more piece of news remained, though, for just as two men in the crowd nearby were moaning about the state of the city, being hungry and sick, someone else interrupted them with a barked shout.

'Well you won't be hungry for long, man. Didn't you hear? The grain fleet's been sighted on the Tiber.'

Rufinus felt his spirits sink that little bit further. They said that bad news came in threes, and that certainly seemed to have been borne out today. He had been planning to return to the castrum after this and make a few last efforts to send his ships to distant regions before he was ordered to put them all in place to protect the grain. Instead, he suddenly decided to change plans and visit the river to see for himself. It would hardly be noteworthy for the chamberlain's spies tailing him. Plenty of others in the current situation would be rushing to see the grain arrive, and as the Prefect of the Fleet, especially given the news in the acta, he very much had a vested interest in it.

Escorted by his marines, he crossed the forum and clambered up into his litter, bracing himself for the lurching, bouncing journey across the city. He directed them as they travelled, along the Vicus Tuscus, in the shadow of the Palatine and past the tavern where he'd encountered his father and the Praetorian centurion. Then around the end of the Circus Maximus for, though the river was visible nearby, the *forum boarium* around it was filled with masses of folk and the stench of meat and animals, and the best place to view the Tiber downstream of the city would be from the heights of the Aventine, above the smell and the packed streets.

They climbed that hill, and crossed to the point where the slope dipped to the south, where the ancient city walls still stood, crumbling amid the buildings that had long outgrown them. Here, at the gap in the walls that had once been the Porta Navalis, they stopped and Rufinus alighted from his litter to stand on one of the few sections of hillside that was not so crowded with buildings as to obscure the view.

Out of habit his gaze first fell upon the huge structure of the Horrea Galbana across the way, and he was struck once more by the seeming lack of activity in the area. Rome might not yet quite be in a grain crisis, but surely there should be more going on at the granaries than that?

His gaze slid from that enormous warehouse system, down over the vast roof of the Porticus Aemilia and to the complex of the Emporium by the river. Busier than the granaries above, but still not as thriving as it was at the height of its usage.

His paused, eyes widening.

The grain fleet was indeed arriving.

Every month the grain ships arrived at Portus, usually staggered over anything up to ten days depending upon the distance of the journey, the season, and the conditions of the seas. There it was unloaded, gathered and stored, until it was all accounted for, when it was moved onto the huge barges that would then ply their way up the Tiber, delivering it to the city. In recent months, with the increased need for the precious foodstuff and the decrease in its availability, it had been moved upstream by barges in several stages, as and when it arrived, but even at their smallest, the flotillas of barges that reached the emporium to unload usually numbered more than twenty vessels.

Rufinus double checked, but there was no mistaking it. There were just two barges making for the dock. They had been overdue, and by now usually the city had its full grain ration unloaded. Two ships would not feed one single region of hungry mouths, let alone the whole city.

His pulse drummed at the sight. Had they done it? Had the pirates sunk Senova's ships and crippled the grain ration? Was this what they had been waiting for ever since Severus began to plot his scheme?

Suddenly overcome with hope, he hurried back to his litter and gestured to them to move off, heading down the hill to the emporium. All the way, bouncing down the slope of the Aventine, he found himself desperate to speak to others. To Philip, to see what news had come from the fleet's escort vessels if any. To Senova to find out if she had had news of her grain ships. To Dionysus to confirm that the situation was truly becoming as dire as it appeared. To Severus to find out how close they were to his goal.

They had barely stopped moving at the heart of the emporium before Rufinus leapt from the litter and scurried over to the office of Dionysus' man there. The *Aedile Cereales*, the man in charge of the unloading and recording of arriving grain shipments, was in his office, haranguing a man in the tunic of a sailor. Rufinus strode in through the open door, and the shouting stopped instantly as the aedile dismissed the sailor angrily and turned his attention to the new visitor.

'Prefect?'

'Two ships?' Rufinus barked, trying his best to sound indignant, horrified and angry, rather than elated and relieved.

'Yes, Prefect. It would appear that two ships is all.'

'Are the others on the way? What of my escort triremes?' That at least sounded good. Sounded as though he was worried about his fleet.

'It would appear that two ships is all we are likely to get at least this month, Prefect.' Rufinus stood still, heart racing, glare still riveted in place, urging the man to continue. The aedile sighed and leaned back wearily in his chair. 'It would appear, I'm afraid, that despite the dangers posed by piracy, it is Neptune himself who is angry with Rome. The lion's share of the grain fleet was swallowed up by a storm off the coast of Lucania. Four ships made it to Portus, and one of those is too far gone for refit, two thirds of its grain lost to water-logging. Apparently five more limped in to Paestum, though we cannot expect their loads for another week. The vast bulk of ships went down with all hands and cargo. As for the fate of your triremes I cannot say, Prefect, but that I would normally expect you to know before me.'

Rufinus nodded. He didn't quite trust himself to speak without sounding happy about it all. Finally, marshalling his grumpiest tone, he took a deep breath. 'Do what you can to bring those loads from Paestum, and drain any granaries in Ostia and Portus.'

The aedile gave him the withering look of a man who had just been told to do the blindingly obvious and feigning irritability Rufinus turned on his heel and strode from the room. He had the distinct feeling that had Philip not been in

Ostia today, the moment Rufinus crossed the threshold of the castrum, the centurion would have hurried over with almost the same tidings, though he would begin with the fate of the escort ships, and then be unable to give sufficient detail of the grain fleet.

Clambering into his litter, he decided that he would make a stop before he returned to the castrum. Consequently a quarter of an hour later he alighted at the far end of the Circus Flaminius, passing on foot between the portico of Octavius and the temple complex of Hercules, accompanied by his marines. Here, tucked away and almost hidden by the grand surrounding structures, stood the ancient temple of Neptune.

Rufinus strode calmly towards the temple. Outside stood one of the ever-present, ever-hopeful traders in livestock, close to the tables of the other 'offerings merchants' This one was *particularly* hopeful. In his little pen at the roadside, surrounded by piles of dung, stood an ageing and ill-looking bull, tethered to a ring in the paving. Half a dozen chickens clucked disconsolately round in a large wooden cage, and a ram stood in the corner, still looking belligerent even with the fate clearly awaiting it.

Rufinus paused. He'd been intending only to libate to the god with wine and incense, but for a moment wondered whether his prayers might be borne aloft better in the blood of a bull or a ram. In the end he shook his head, declining even a chicken, and bought some very expensive Arabian olibanum and a jar of the very best Falernian wine from one of the other merchants. Walking reverentially into the place of worship, he nodded his head in respect to the attendant and to two men who were kneeling on the floor, praying to the sea god for something. He crossed to the altar, proclaimed Neptune to be 'great' in the traditional formal manner, and then began to pour wine into one of the purple-stained dishes on the central altar. The stone figures of two Nereids watched him as he leaned across the frieze of Ahenobarbus and placed the incense in among the detritus of used frankincense, and used a taper to light it.

Thus honouring the god, he made his prayer silently, his lips barely moving. For while the public, and Cleander's spy who would be lurking somewhere close by, would imagine the Prefect of the Fleet to be beseeching Neptune to spare his vessels, or praying for their safety in coming days, only Rufinus truly knew that he was actually thanking the god for swallowing the grain fleet.

He left the temple feeling rather more upbeat than he had done in some time, which lasted all the way to the Castrum Misenatum, though not beyond for there a new message awaited him. Thanking the clerk, he sat at his office desk and peered at the scroll case. It bore Severus' seal, and Rufinus had to fight hard to dismiss the notion that the governor had somehow already known about the fleet. How could he have? But then the timing was incredibly coincidental if not.

He cracked the seal and began to read.

Rufinus,

Forgive my brevity and directness. I do believe that your time serving the fleets of Rome is almost at an end. You have filled that role admirably, but the time is almost upon us when there are better places for you to be.

If you remember the story you told me when we met in Athens about your friend with the Midas touch, then you will remember who the man with three initials was. It is time he was confronted with his past and made to step down. His position will shortly need to be vacant, for his successor already waits.

I trust you will deal with this matter with your own 'Midas touch', swiftly and efficiently.

Yours,

Lucius Septimius Severus

Rufinus stared. Did Severus know what had happened to the grain fleet even before word had reached Rome? It certainly looked that way. He considered Rufinus' time as Prefect of the Fleet to be up. He had done all he could. Well, that was certainly the truth. He *had* done all he could, and no man in the role would be able to repair the damage now done. He would, in truth, be glad to give up the role, especially if it meant a return to his real life.

But no. Not that just yet. He could not be himself as long as Cleander lived.

What next then?

His heart lurched as the suspicion fell upon him. P S F were the three initials – those of Publius Seius Fuscianus, the prefect of the Urban Cohorts. The man had been accepting bribes in the form of gold from the Dacian mines controlled by Clodius Albinus, and had been a willing client and co-conspirator there. Rufinus was to persuade him to step down as Urban Prefect? How? He knew what the man had been up to, of course, but he had no proof, since the gold had been taken back by Niger in Dacia. But if P S F was to be removed from office, what did Severus intend? Surely Rufinus could not move into that position? It would be too close to Cleander. He would so easily be recognised and undone.

But whatever the case, one thing was certain: his days with the fleet were almost over and as the plot moved on, accelerating now towards its climax, Severus had new tasks for him.

Chapter Thirteen – Trouble

Rome, July 189 A.D.

Rufinus alighted from his litter and looked around in surprise. The last time he'd seen the Horrea Galbana, from the hill opposite, there had been little life and activity about the place. Now, only nine days later, the street was thronged with people.

It took only moments to realise that these were not teamsters and warehouse labourers or the everyday folk of the region. These were the hungry people of Rome. There was an air of discontent that was almost palpable. His marines closed in a little, creating a better protective cordon about him, leaving the litter bearers to fend for themselves if there was trouble.

And there could very well be trouble.

Along with numerous other government-owned horrea across Rome, this, the main such institution, was one of the locations where the people could come to collect their ration of the grain dole. The whole system had been something of a mystery to Rufinus to begin with, since he had belonged to a wealthy exiled family out in the provinces, and the grain dole had been something that happened to other people.

When he had first learned of it, he had assumed that it was a measure of charity, that the emperor and the senate imposed a system to feed the poor and hungry of the city. In actual fact the whole system was a lot more subtle and jaded than it appeared. Near a third of a million people received free grain in the city on a monthly basis, which constituted perhaps a third of the city. Those recipients were kept on a list and were thus privileged. But the fact was that those third were the male citizen-only population over the age of manhood. Only an adult male citizen received the free grain. More or less the voting population of the city, unsurprisingly.

That being said, the poor and the disenfranchised gained from the grain dole anyway. Those who received the grain were at least partially those who could easily afford to feed themselves, and their ration was accordingly passed on to their clients, slaves, servants and those who owed them loyalty. Thus did the state buy the loyalty of voters and the voters buy the loyalty and support of their lessers.

Moreover, the bulk free supply of grain in the city kept the grain prices with the private merchants at an acceptably low level, so that the poor who had no one to rely upon for charity might be able to afford to buy bread anyway.

It seemed so charitable while in reality being so political, yet the result was unarguably beneficial regardless.

His gaze took in those in the street. They represented a specific stratum of society. They were, to Rufinus' eye, the 'citizen mob', those who had the right to vote and played a part in the functioning of the great city, but who belonged solidly to the plebeian class with no one below them to shout on their behalf. They were gathered for their grain hand out. The rich would send their slaves to do it for them and the truly poor were ineligible anyway.

Rufinus straightened. He was well-coiffured, dressed in an immaculate toga and with expensive boots. He had arrived in a litter with a guard. He was clearly not one of them.

Taking a deep breath he nodded to the optio, and his guard began to move towards the door of the Horrea Galbana, keeping him surrounded, urging the crowd back. The mob watched him with barely concealed anger, and Rufinus realised now just how dangerous Rome was becoming. On normal days, if a pleb cast at his betters the kind of looks Rufinus was getting, the guards of that better would teach him a lesson. The ire of the city was rising.

He was more grateful than he'd expected to be when they reached the door and he marched inside, past the two men of the Urban Cohorts on guard there. The situation really was becoming bleak, as was silently evidenced by the open doors to the majority of the granaries and store rooms, awaiting delivery of something to store. Very few doors were closed and those that were seemed largely to contain olive oil or other such items. Grain was hard to find.

He approached the office of the Praefectus Annonae, and nodded to his marines to wait outside.

Papirius Dionysus was sitting at his desk rubbing his head in exasperation. His desk was covered in reports and two clerks were busy at work on a huge trestle at one side, compiling lists.

'Prefect,' Rufinus greeted Dionysus with a weary tone.

Dionysus looked up, saw Rufinus and turned to his clerks. 'Out. Close the door.'

They did so and Rufinus, content that they were alone and only his marines stood even the faintest chance of hearing them, approached the table.

'Every time you come here, it represents a danger to us all,' Dionysus muttered.

Rufinus shook his head. 'I have been ordered to liaise with you among others over the protection of the grain fleet. I am here quite legitimately. And you won't have to put up with me for much longer anyway. I am standing down before Saturnalia. The senate already have my replacement lined up, though I pity the poor bastard stepping into the mess we've left him.'

Dionysus nodded gruffly. 'Fair enough. To what do I owe this visit then, or have you *actually* come to coordinate with me over the safety of my grain?'

Rufinus shook his head. 'Things are moving. Things are changing. With Severus still out in Gaul and keeping his full plan largely to himself, I want to keep myself abreast of the situation. There are angry people outside, so tell me where *we* are right now?'

Dionysus shrugged. 'You first.'

'Alright. My ships have been largely pulled back in from diverse assignments and are now patrolling the Italian and Sicilian coasts and the sea lanes around there. We have secured the strait between Sicilia and Africa and I have ships in Carthage, Syracuse and Puteoli with orders to escort any grain shipments that depart from there. The African fleet has been pulled back from Hispania and with the aid of my ships are containing the Mauri once more. Indeed, with the help of the Third Legion and the governors of the southern provinces, it is believed that we have rooted out two of the pirates' strongholds and flattened them. Piracy has all but collapsed. I am six ships down after that storm last month, but we have new vessels in production. I am actually being lauded in high circles for my part in the solution of the crisis, but the one who has come off best is Pertinax. He took over governing Africa, promised to end piracy and has more or less done so within a month. He is a golden figure now. I suspect he could have his pick of positions if he but asked. All of this is moot, though. We've got safe and secure seas, but there is still no grain, since the majority of the fleet was ravaged in one grand storm. The senate has voted money to replacing them from an emergency fund, and already new ships are being retained, but finding and constructing vessels large enough takes time and there will be no adequate grain fleet until the spring, I am told. So what I want to know is where that leaves us here, Dionysus.'

'Well, Rufinus, it leaves us deep in the cess pit, up to the neck, as you are no doubt aware. We have less than half the grain we need to fulfil the dole, and I am holding out on distribution until the very last moment in the hope that extra can be found. We have cleared out the state granaries and warehouses in Ostia, Portus, Puteoli and any other main local source. We've put in for extra from those provinces who have their own stores set against a bad year such as Achaea, Hispania and Gaul, but it will take time for them to arrive.'

'And that all means?'

'Essentially, it is unlikely that anyone will receive their full ration this month. I foresee distributing a half ration of two and a half modii per recipient. That will be insufficient for the bulk of the populace and ill feeling will only rise. If we do not have some kind of breakthrough within the next month, then the following month we will be lucky to distribute a single modius of grain to each recipient, which is a fifth of what they are due. And the public can hardly afford to buy from private sources. With the available quantity so restricted, prices have risen high. A modius of grain that would normally cost a man perhaps thirty sestertii is currently nearing two hundred. I think you can imagine what's going to happen soon.'

'Riots?'

'Very likely. And I and my department and all our installations will be the prime target of disaffection. That is why the men of the Urban Cohorts now guard my door, and that is why I've had another missive from our mutual friend. He has instructed me to begin working on Cleander, urging him to stockpile the grain we have in private guarded storehouses. I just need to work out the way to persuade him that it's the perfect solution, and that instead of making us villains it will make us heroes. Not an easy task, but I'll do it. I only hope I can shift the blame to him before everything explodes and I end up with my head bouncing around on a spear tip.'

Rufinus nodded. Something else had occurred to him as Dionysus spoke. The Urban Cohorts... Severus had instructed them *both* to move on with the plan now. Dionysus' part in it would be to increase misery and tension in the city and then lay it firmly with Cleander. Rufinus' was to effect a change in command of the Urban Cohorts, the very force that would be required to deal with the city's rising tensions. He had a sinking feeling about his ongoing role in that respect.

'Right. Well I have to carry out my own instructions for now, so I had better leave.'

Dionysus frowned. 'And they are?'

'Let's just say don't call on the Urban Cohorts for help just yet.'

The grain commissioner's eyes narrowed, but he said nothing. Rufinus gave him a weary nod and then turned, leaving the office and collecting his marines. As they strode across the huge open courtyard of the horrea, he ran through it all again in his head. Rome was building to an eruption. He could feel it. And if Severus had got his timing right then just as it finally exploded, the blame would all lie with Cleander and Rufinus would be part of the military that needed to impose control and limit the damage to the city and its people. He had yet to see how Severus expected him to command the Urban Cohort without Cleander realising. It would be impossible to take on such a role without the chamberlain seeing him regularly, and that would just raise alarms for the man.

Moreover, he was starting to harbour another suspicion. Severus had been directing everything thus far from his provincial palace in Lugdunum, out of Cleander's eye and ostensibly uninvolved in anything in the city. To an extent Rufinus could see the sense in that, but he was also beginning to suspect that Severus intended nothing more than to direct all matters from a distance, while men like Dionysus and Rufinus did the actual dangerous work. Still, there was little he could do about it all now. He had nailed his colours to Severus' mast and there was no taking them down.

As they approached the exit to the complex, Rufinus could already feel the disaffection, anger and resentment boiling in the air. He suddenly found himself worrying for Dionysus, and for himself too. The grain commissioner was a good man, and clever, and seemed to be content that he could pull off this shifting of the blame. But Rome was close to the edge, and riots were dangerous and unpredictable. If the city exploded before they were ready, or in an unexpected direction, then he and Dionysus would be the Pompeii and Herculaneum to Rome's Vesuvius. He shivered.

His marines surged ahead of him as they passed beneath that great arch. Two of the men of the Urban Cohort stood in the archway still, preventing unauthorised entry. They looked nervous as they stepped aside to allow Rufinus past.

There was a surge of noise from the crowd as Rufinus and his men emerged, and he could pick out the threads in the rise and fall. Hope, to start with: hope that this heralded someone coming to inform the crowd that the dole was ready to be distributed and they could go home and make bread. At the realisation that it was just some rich man with his private escort, the hope sank into misery and despair that the grain was still not forthcoming, and hunger would continue to assail them.

Finally, as the small unit of marines and the toga-clad man at their centre began to move through the crowd, shoving angry citizens out of the way, the despair turned into something else...

Anger. Hate. Disgust.

This man in white with his soldiers represented the regime that was withholding the grain, and all in Rome knew there *was* grain, even if it wasn't enough for all. Rufinus could almost hear the words going through their minds. Distribute what you have. Feed who you can. And truly, that would probably be the humane thing to do. But it was not what they *needed* to do.

The morality of what they were attempting once more sank into Rufinus' heavy heart. He and his friends and companions had *caused* this misery. There had already been hunger and illness and misery in ever increasing amounts, due to the plague and its effects on food production across the empire, but this was different. Rufinus and the other conspirators had deliberately made it far, far worse, and were continuing to do so, all in order to bring down one man. Yes, the storm had done most of the work, but perhaps had he not have played with the fleet and beseeched the god, that might not have happened. Certainly this was what he had wished for.

He hardened his heart. It was almost done, and when it was they could try and heal the damage. But for now the most critical thing was to continue with their plan to bring down Rome's most dangerous man.

And that meant moving on to Severus' next step. Oddly, this little display might just give him the opportunity he required. He needed to visit Publius Seius Fuscianus, the Urban Prefect, and had been planning to do so ever since the directive had arrived from Severus. But though Severus had not mentioned it, it had occurred to Rufinus that the Prefect of the Fleet visiting the Urban Prefect might raise questions, and he knew perfectly well that he had been shadowed by Cleander's creatures for months now. He'd spent days trying to work out how to visit the man without being followed. And he'd known there were eyes on him all the way from his home to the horrea this morning. Somewhere in this crowd those eyes were still watching.

He took a deep breath. All he needed was an excuse. A surge of this crowd could perhaps cover his departure? His marines were forming an ever tighter circle around him as they moved, the crowd thrumming with angry noises and refusing more and more often to step back willingly. He was now halfway to the litter.

It came out of the blue. Some angry citizen in the crowd found it too much and threw a small jar. A cheap earthenware thing about the size of a hand, it hurtled across the crowd just above their heads, seemingly aimed at Rufinus, but instead it smashed into the back of one of the marine's heads, sending him lurching forward with a cry of pain. His mates hauled him back upright, but Rufinus knew what would happen next. According to law and tradition, being within the Pomerium boundary much of the time, his men were not armed for war but they did carry a stout ash stick for protection. Half a dozen such weapons were immediately produced and brandished. The optio yelled at his men to hold their position. All it would take was one soldier to hit a citizen and what was already ugly and dangerous could turn into a bloodbath.

'To the litter. Quickly,' Rufinus commanded, and his men surged through the crowd, now giving no care to the health and safety of the throng, pushing and shoving and barging and elbowing. The wounded marine, blood matting the hair on the back of his head, was being helped along. Rufinus kept his head down. That would look natural, given what had just happened, but it also made him very difficult to spot. With the crowd thrumming and roaring, his men pushing hard, brandishing their stout cudgels but restrained from actually using them as anything more than a deterrent, they heaved through the crowd. It seemed like hours, though could not have been more than a hundred heartbeats, and Rufinus expected more thrown missiles at any moment, but to his immense relief they reached the litter without incident. The anger all around them was reaching a critical level. If they stayed, they would certainly be in trouble. He hauled himself up into the litter and shouted loudly down to his bearers.

'Back home!'

Even as the litter began to move at the periphery of the huge mob, Rufinus was busy inside disentangling himself from the heavy white wool folds of his toga. He twitched aside the curtain on the far side, away from the mass and the horrea, and looked out. They were almost at the edge, ready to move into a different street. The marine optio looked up at him.

'Straight home and inside, with the litter and all. Got it?'

The marine nodded, brow furrowed.

Rufinus waited only a moment until they were in the shadow of a tall warehouse, and lithely dropped from that side of the litter, opposite to that which he'd entered, ducking between his own guards and, staying low, slipping in among the crowd. Those who'd been closest to the litter had shouted in surprise, but he was fast and strong and in mere moments he was far enough into the crowd that those around him had no idea that he was the man who'd been in the litter, and he could only see the roof of his vehicle as it bounced away home.

He simply had to trust that he'd got away from his watchers, who would, with any luck, follow the litter back to Rufinus' townhouse and lurk there as usual, observing. Steadying himself, he pushed and threaded his way between the figures in the crowd until he reached a side street, where he emerged into open ground, breathing heavily.

In just a tunic, though he was relatively well-dressed, he was entirely unremarkable and would blend in unless anyone looked too closely. Everything now was a matter of luck and of brazen nerve. As he hurried through the streets, in his head he vowed an altar to Fortuna if she would just look after him for the next hour or so. He meant it, too.

And he would need every bit of luck the goddess could spare to visit the Urban Prefect. The man had two offices in Rome, and his own town house of course. That last was the easiest place to visit, but would most certainly be under Cleander's scrutiny every bit as much as his own, and so he would put that last on his list. Moreover, at this time of day, Fuscianus would almost certainly be in one of his offices. One of those was located, rather inconveniently, on the Palatine. And despite that, this location was still the second easiest to visit. Yet Cleander's eyes and ears would be everywhere there, and so he had to try and avoid that, too.

That left only the man's *other* office. This had two benefits as a visit. Firstly, Fuscianus would spend the vast majority of his time there, so it was most likely he would be found in that place. Secondly, it was in one location where Cleander could not simply have men lurking on a corner watching it.

There *was* a downside, of course. The Urban Prefect's main office was in the fortress of the Praetorian Guard. The Urban Cohorts had no fortress of their own in the city, and occupied a set of barracks in one corner of the Praetorian camp, their number being only a quarter that of the Praetorians. And because of the almost permanent low-lying distrust and animosity between the two units who shared a base, they kept almost entirely to themselves. That was the one redeeming feature in this plan. The Urban Cohorts were not directly under Cleander's control, and his Praetorians would be prevented from keeping them under too close scrutiny, even though they shared a fortress.

Still, this was going to take balls.

Rufinus crossed the city on foot, pausing only briefly to buy a cloak despite the heat of the Roman summer. By the time he had descended the Aventine, crossed the valley of the Flavian amphitheatre and then climbed the Oppian and Viminal hills, his feet hurt and he was feeling parched. He decided that perhaps he had spent far too much time being ferried around in a litter and not enough time exercising. Still, perhaps with Severus' next stage of the plan he might not require a litter.

He angled his direction of approach so as to arrive at the Castra Praetoria at its southern gate – the *porta principalis dexter*, rather than the most common *porta praetoria* to the west, which admitted ninety percent of all traffic. With a last exhortation to Fortuna, he approached the gate.

'Halt,' called a voice from atop the wall as he neared, and he came to a stop, looking up, praying over and over that those men in the Guard who would remember him were elsewhere on other duties. The last thing he needed right now was to bump into Icarion or Mercator.

'State your business.'

Rufinus shrugged back his cloak, largely to show that he wasn't armed, and stood proud. 'I am here to see the Urban Prefect, Seius Fuscianus.'

'Do you have an appointment?'

Rufinus swallowed. *Brazen. Luck. Balls.* 'No, but he will want to see me.'

'Oh? Why?'

'Because Albinus sent me.'

The man shrugged, clearly disbelieving him. Rufinus took a deep breath.

'Escort me to the prefect and he will see me.'

There was some deliberation at the wall top and Rufinus stood still below, praying over and over to Fortuna. He was almost ready to turn around and leave when he heard the thuds and clunks of the gate being opened and finally the inset wooden portal within the huge main gate swung outwards.

'You'd better not be wasting our time, fella, else I'll put my foot up your big arsehole to the ankle.'

Rufinus bowed his head. 'Please, trust me.'

Two Praetorians inside were waiting to escort him. They were at the gate closest to the Urban Cohort's barracks yet the walls, gates and all patrols were carried out by the Praetorians, for this was still their fortress as far as they were concerned, and the Cohort were just rabble that had been foisted upon them. Once more it came as a great relief that neither of the guards were men Rufinus recognised.

He tried not to look too familiar with the place, though in truth he could have found his way to the office of the Urban Prefect with his eyes closed. No normal civilian knew the layout of the fortress, after all. He followed quietly and carefully as the two Praetorians led him to the Urban Cohorts' barracks, where another couple of men, this time in the madder red of ordinary soldiers rather than the white of Praetorians, moved to intercept.

'Where are you lot going?'

'Visitor for your commander,' one of Rufinus' escorts replied in an aloof tone.

'We'll take it from here.'

'Gladly. Just try and remember to deliver him back to the porta principalis and not just leave him wandering the fortress.'

The two men of the Urban Cohort gave the Praetorian withering looks and, as the guardsmen marched off, turned to Rufinus.

'Name and business?'

'Aulus Triarius. Business is private, but you can tell the prefect that Albinus sent me.'

The two soldiers paused for a moment, then shrugged and set off towards their commander's headquarters with Rufinus in tow. In his time serving in the fortress, Rufinus had never been in this quarter. The Cohort and the Guard had always had a professional rivalry. One saw themselves as proper soldiers rather than gilded pretty-boys, the other as superior to ordinary soldiers like the Cohort. Still, the atmosphere Rufinus had encountered thus far had been more tense and spiteful than he remembered from his own time here. Perhaps Cleander's control of the Guard had driven an even deeper wedge between the two. If so, it was a good sign, for that meant the Cohort might be trusted to do the right thing.

Within moments they were outside the prefect's office. Rufinus waited with one soldier while the other went inside. He returned swiftly. 'Surprise, surprise. The prefect will see you.'

Rufinus thanked the goddess under his breath. Despite what he still had to do, simply getting away from Cleander's agents and gaining access to the prefect was always going to be the most troublesome part. Now all he could do was hope. He had to rely on a few things being just how he imagined, and if they were, then this should be possible. He followed the soldier to the prefect's office. Outside the door he was checked for weapons. The soldier was quickly satisfied that Rufinus was unarmed, though he had noted with some surprise the network of scars and wounds. He was then ushered inside and the door was closed behind him. As Rufinus looked across the office at the Urban Prefect, one of perhaps the top six most important men in Rome, he heard the retreating footsteps of the soldier leaving. They were alone. Naturally, given who Fuscianus must think he was.

'Albinus can demand of me anything he wants, I'm not playing his game any more,' the prefect spat with no preamble. 'I only let you in so I could tell you that myself and you can pass it on to your prick of a master.'

Rufinus felt his nerves twang. He hadn't banked on that dubious relationship having crumbled. Still, his plan remained the same.

'In actual fact, I haven't come from Albinus at all,' Rufinus said in flat tones.

'Then who are you?' Suspicion ranged across the prefect's face and Rufinus could see the notion forming that he might be part of Cleander's web.

'No, I'm not the chamberlain's man either. In fact, I'm something entirely different. I'm a blackmailer.'

'What?'

'Interested parties would like to see you resign the office of prefect before the year's end. You will be permitted time to enact any last rules and regulations should you wish, and to get your affairs in order. You need to be very clearly resigning of your own free will. I would suggest that perhaps you are doing so before the chamberlain gets his claws into the Cohort as he has the Guard. I care not, but you need to step down before Saturnalia.'

The man stared at him in disbelief.

'I'm quite serious, Prefect,' Rufinus added.

'You are a comedian, clearly,' snorted Fuscianus.

'Far from it. My sense of humour is somewhat distant these days. But you will comply with this request, and in return your reputation will continue unsullied and you can move on to fulfil whatever military or political position you like from here.'

'I don't know what you think you have on me, man, but…'

Rufinus took a step forward. This was his gamble. This was what he was relying upon.

'You remember that shipment from Dacia that never arrived?'

His gamble paid off. He watched shock and then dismay sink into the prefect's face. He'd bet on the fact that the gold bar he had found in the mines in Dacia that was bound for Fuscianus in Rome had never turned up. He'd taken it, and

Pescennius Niger had taken it off him. But he had been fairly sure that Niger was the sort of man to keep the gold, as potential evidence or blackmail stock should he ever need it. Rufinus had apparently read the man right. That case of gold had never been sent to the prefect in Rome after all.

'Yes,' smiled Rufinus. 'A bar of gold from the Dacian mines controlled by Clodius Albinus, all nicely boxed up and meant for Rome, right down to having your initials on it. Imagine the deep shit you could find yourself swimming in if that little piece of evidence turns up in Cleander's hands? Or perhaps even the emperor's?'

Fuscianus had gone pale. 'I am not working for Albinus. In fact, I quickly regretted ever becoming involved with the man. What gold he sent has been moved, melted, recast and given as gifts to the emperor and his court. I am a loyal officer of Rome.'

'Nevertheless, there is still evidence to the contrary. I watched Paternus die. I watched Perennis die. I have no wish to watch another prefect executed. I give you my word that the moment you step down that evidence will disappear and there will be no danger of it falling into the wrong hands.'

'You bastard.'

'I am very sorry about this. And I am but the messenger,' Rufinus sighed. 'But be assured that the reasons for this are the very best and Rome will benefit in the end. Would you not rather face a career change than ruin?'

'You *bastard*,' Fuscianus repeated, his tongue dripping with spite.

'I shall leave you to contemplate your options. I trust we shall not see each other again. Good day.'

CHAPTER FOURTEEN – CHANGES

Rome, September 189 A.D.

The announcement from the doorman came as something of a surprise.

'The proprietor Lucius Septimius Severus to see you, Domine.'

Rufinus looked up from his breakfast, meeting the eyes of Senova, who seemed equally surprised.

'Show him in.'

Severus strode into the room at the doorman's heel, impressive and tall, a clear warrior even in a toga and soft sandals. He inclined his head in greeting to the pair of them and then gestured to the doorman. Rufinus nodded and the slave left the room, closing the door behind him.

'I presume your house is safe and you trust those within it?'

Rufinus nodded.

'Good. And while I must apologise for my general absence during most of the recent months, I am also going to be largely absent for the near future. I have laid down my imperium in Gaul at the request of the senate, only to be appointed to another province.'

Rufinus sagged. He'd hoped that when Severus finally put in another appearance their plans would suddenly leap forward. It seemed now that was not to be the case.

'Another province?'

'Yes. It would appear that I did such a sterling job of Gallia Lugdunensis that I am required to turn my hand to Sicilia. It seems that the current grain crisis has put extra pressure on Sicilia to fill the granaries in place of lost cargo from Africa and Aegyptus. I am not unaware of the irony of me being sent to solve the grain crisis, either. But no matter what the senate hope I will do, everyone is aware that *whatever* extra I can squeeze out of Sicilia will make precious little difference in Rome. I foresee my tenure on that island not lasting past winter. A short appointment. And in fact I intend to make it so, for I have been put forward for a suffect consulship next year, and I intend to see that I have it, whether it comes from the hand of Cleander or his successor. It would open many doors.'

Rufinus felt a lurch there, and hope trickled back into him. 'Successor? You see Cleander's end coming soon?'

'Conditions are almost right. The grain of our plot is almost ripe for harvest. Rome simmers and seethes. It is visible in every street as one passes through, and soon it will explode. I have set Dionysus to work already with the next step.'

Rufinus nodded. 'He is already persuading the chamberlain that stockpiling the grain is the answer. Cleander will be the man to sign the deed and it will be into his granaries it goes.'

'Better still, while Dionysus can fall back upon a defence for as yet withholding the grain dole, we shall see to it that Cleander has no such cushion. No matter how angry the public get, at the moment they know that there is not enough grain in storage anyway. Dionysus cannot be held accountable for starving the people.'

'But Cleander can?'

'He can, once the lovely lady Julia Triaria here makes her last business deal for me.'

'Last?' put in Senova, and Rufinus was frowning but not about her cessation of business. 'What can she do?' he asked. 'The ships of ours in the grain fleet are almost all gone thanks to the storm. The few that are left sit in Carthage waiting for grain that probably isn't coming.'

Severus gave him an infuriatingly knowing smile. 'How are your *other* ships faring, mistress Julia?'

'Very lucrative, thank you Governor.'

Rufinus turned narrowed eyes upon his wife. He knew she had some other business going, for the grain fleet was not making them rich, but *other* ships? He'd not heard about this. Where *were* these other ships?

'I am afraid,' Severus said, 'that it will be time shortly to abandon your guise and your businesses, my dear. But for that last deal I mentioned, I would like you to send every ship you have to Arelate on the Rhodanus in Gaul. As soon as Cleander has given the order and our paltry grain supplies are moved into his granaries, your ships will carry the extra supplies governor Cilo and I have been hoarding in secret in southern Gaul, and add them to Cleander's stockpile. It will all be done according to his orders, but he will not know that the *quantity* being secured in his buildings is a great deal more than is currently in Rome's horrea. In fact, it would be enough to alleviate all Rome's hunger for a time. I expect you can imagine where things will go from there?'

Rufinus, wide-eyed, nodded vigorously. 'If word gets out that while Rome starves Cleander has stockpiled enough grain for all and is not distributing it, the whole city will turn on him.'

'Quite. And therein lies our goal. Our game is approaching its last move. This is all a matter of delicate timing. The grain must be shipped in secret into Cleander's stores once he has given the order and before the city erupts, but we want it there the shortest time possible in case the unexpected high quantity is discovered and all comes undone. Fortunately for you both, I will take on that responsibility myself. Once the lady Julia sends her ships to Arelate, my factotum there will deal with matters under my regular instruction. The sad truth is that the lady Julia Triaria and her husband the prefect will be leaving the city.'

'We will?'

'The Prefect of the Misenum fleet will stand down his command in three days' time and retire into private life. I would urge the lady Julia to consider one of two safe estates, either close to myself in Sicilia or perhaps the one in southern Gaul, in the lands of my friend and ally Governor Cilo of Gallia Narbonensis. Either should be safe enough to sit out the rest of this affair without stepping into danger.'

Rufinus could see Senova winding up to one of her indignant explosions at the notion of being put away somewhere safe instead of in the thick of it, and he cleared his throat to override her before she began.

'It will need to be Sicilia,' he said. 'I should be close when you need me.'

'My dear Rufinus, I was speaking of your lovely wife. *You* will not be leaving.'

'But you said…'

'I said the Prefect of the Fleet will be leaving. He will disappear into provincial obscurity. You, on the other hand, will have a new role to play here.'

Rufinus was baffled, but still his suspicions had already taken root.

'I cannot be the Urban Prefect, if that's your plan. Cleander would uncover my identity in days.'

'Quite so. And you will not be. Publius Helvius Pertinax returns from Africa in three days. In gratitude for his part in the securing of the sea lanes, he has been appointed prefect of the Urban Cohorts. I'm sure you'll agree that he will do a fine job. He is a man of principle and though he is not party to our schemes, I believe we can rely upon him to oppose Cleander appropriately at all turns. And if not, Gaius Valerius Maximus will be there to guide him onto such a course.'

'I am totally lost. Who is this Maximus?'

'You are, you fool.'

Rufinus blinked. 'What?'

'We have no further use for the Prefect of the Fleet or his enterprising wife. Their part in the plan is now done. And to see that side of it through to fruition is now the role of myself and Dionysus. Nicomedes will continue to keep us all informed with letters that stay safely out of the hands of the chamberlain's men. Vibius Cestius will continue to make sure that any eyes or ears that pick up anything they shouldn't never live long enough to reach Cleander.'

That came as something of a surprise to Rufinus. He'd not seen the frumentarius for months and had almost forgotten about the man in the stress of his work. And he knew he'd been watched, but it had not occurred to him that Cleander's men had picked up anything over that time.

'Has Cestius had to cover our tracks, then?'

'Dear boy, you have no idea. That man and his fellows have killed half a century's worth of spies over the last year, many of whom had reports of meetings or connections between us. One, I am informed, had even uncovered your identity. Fortunately he was found bobbing in the waters of the Tiber before he could tell anyone. Cestius has done what he does best. He has operated in silence behind the scenae and done so with the utmost efficiency, protecting us all.'

Rufinus exhaled loudly.

'Anyway, as I was saying,' Severus picked up, 'myself, Nicomedes, Dionysus and Cestius are accounted for. That leaves you. In support of Pertinax, and guiding him if you have to, your task henceforth is to redirect against Cleander any and all trouble reported to the Cohort or to somehow lay the blame for everything at his feet. And while doing such, I trust you will live up to your own moral code and prevent this turning into a city-wide bloodbath that kills thousands. You must direct blame and limit trouble. You understand?'

'And I am now this Maximus fellow?'

Severus smiled. 'Gaius Valerius Maximus is being appointed as the senior centurion of the Second Urban Cohort on the same day Pertinax takes command.'

'And I presume you have created this fictitious Maximus already as you did my current persona?'

'Hardly. Maximus is a real man. Or rather he was. He sadly passed away last year while serving as one of my guard in the Eighth Augusta. In fact you met him several times while you

215

were in Lugdunum. Helpfully, Maximus bore a passing resemblance to you even if he were a little more blond, and some ten years ago he served as a centurion in the First Adiutrix under Pertinax no less. The new prefect will probably remember the name at least, so you should find it easy to gain his trust.'

Rufinus sighed. 'Nothing is simple with you, Governor.'

'Few things worth having are simple. But think on this: the various Urban Cohorts are critical to keeping order in the city, and some provincial places, too, and are also responsible for overseeing the grain dole is protected. Friends have already been put in command of the other cohorts in Carthage, Puteoli, Ostia and Lugdunum. We are securing out grip, but also preparing to save Rome from Cleander when he falls. Now, the day after Rufinus stands down as prefect, Maximus will report to the Castra Praetoria and take up his centurion's stick with the Cohort.'

'I'm no centurion, Governor.'

Severus shrugged. 'You'd never been an admiral until recently. And I seem to remember you telling me that in your time in Dacia you took on the duties of a centurion. Gods, man, if you can run a fleet you can command a century of men. But while performing the duties of a centurion, it is imperative that you remember your role and steer Pertinax where necessary. Oh, and it's time to lose the hair and beard. You need to change your appearance. I would suggest a stubbled chin and a close-shorn head, in the manner of the Pannonian soldiers. That way you should look like neither your true self, nor the prefect you have been.'

He turned to Senova. 'I trust you will manage to do as I asked with your ships?'

Senova smiled sweetly, though Rufinus could see beneath it her mind working at how to deny her exile to a safe house. 'I shall have quite a fleet in Arelate for you by the kalends.'

'Thank you. Now I must prepare to move on once more into the south. I shall return when I am able, and look for messages from me whenever anything of import occurs. Once again, thank you for all you have done and continue to do. Our scheme approaches its end, and everyone thus far has played their part excellently.'

Severus bowed to them both and then turned, opening the door and walking out into the atrium.

'What's that?' Rufinus said in surprise, pointing to a pile of kit bags on the marble floor, close to the impluvium.

Severus turned. 'That is the equipment and effects of Gaius Valerius Maximus. Keep them secured for the next few days, and on the morning after your commission ends, you can step into them and make your way to the castrum. At the same time, your good lady should have all her effects ferried to the emporium and taken aboard the bireme Celestia, which will ferry her to either Syracuse or Cemenelum, as she chooses. Either way, a friend will meet you at your destination, good lady.'

And with that he took his leave and departed.

Rufinus stared at the kit as the slave hurried off to close the door behind the governor, whose retinue had remained in the street. Rufinus hadn't asked how he was supposed to leave the house of the Prefect Rufinus dressed as a centurion without arousing suspicion, though he was fairly sure it had been dealt with. Likely Cestius had a hand in things again. Rufinus could quite imagine whoever was currently watching his house being led away temporarily by some frumentarii scheme.

Gaius Valerius Maximus.

A centurion. He'd been an ordinary soldier in a legion, and a Praetorian guardsman. He'd even played at being a centurion briefly in Dacia, though not with the best of results. He'd been the prefect of Rome's senior fleet, even if it was under an assumed name. Now he was going to be a centurion for real, and one of the force that protected the city, no less. He stared at the kit bags, and Senova appeared unexpectedly at his shoulder.

'The governor missed something.'

'Oh yes?'

'Just stubble and cropped hair is not going to be enough. You won't look like the prefect Triarius any more, but you might look quite a lot like a certain young Praetorian who disappeared in Dacia.'

He huffed. 'What do you suggest? Hack off an arm or wear a bag over my head?'

She shook her head. 'You are a man, and a soldier. I, on the other hand, know a few tricks. You'd be surprised at what the ladies of Rome will do to match the current fashion. The governor said this Maximus was a little blonder. I can attend to that with little difficulty. Let me get my makeup.'

Rufinus felt his heart sink. Makeup, now. Still, she was almost certainly right as to how he would look when he cut his hair, and if a little dye could make him look more like Maximus and less like Rufinus, that had to be a good thing.

Especially where he was going: the Praetorian fortress, where he had spent the first year of his service with the Guard, and where at least half a dozen men would remember the real him well.

There followed three of the strangest days of Rufinus' life. After spending so long in the role of the prefect he had grown used to it, even, he might add with regret, to its little luxuries. To clamber into the mail shirt and harness of what was more or less a legionary centurion felt very strange now. In fact, during the three days between Severus' visit and the morning in which Aulus Triarius Rufinus laid down his prefecture and retired into obscurity, he spent every free moment he had in the seclusion of the more private areas of their town house wearing his new kit and breaking it in, getting used to it such that his every movement seemed to be those of a man almost born into the uniform.

It was not enough to dress as Maximus. If his time in the navy had taught him anything it was that he now had to *become* Maximus the centurion. There must be no hint of suspicion that he was anything else. And that meant taking on the persona of a man considerably older than him, though Rufinus did look somewhat aged these days, he had to admit. But it also meant taking on that personality. He could not afford to be unsure. Nervous. Clumsy. Indecisive. Passive. Centurions were none of those things. If they were they did not stay centurions – or even upright – for long. And Maximus was a real person, or had been. He had been a long-standing veteran. Rufinus had to be a veteran centurion.

On the bright side, either Severus had been truly spot on when he noted how alike Maximus and Rufinus had been, or since the man's death the governor had had the uniform and armour re-worked and tailored to fit Rufinus perfectly. A simple glance in Senova's impressively flat floor-length bronze mirror had told him that at the least he did *look* like a veteran centurion. He even thought he was managing that world-owning swagger they all achieved.

Oddly, having spent so long scratching at his itchy beard and unruly mop, wishing he could get back to his short hair and clean chin, now that he had he was already missing it. The weather had turned cold recently and he'd been unprepared for just what a difference a full head of hair made in this weather.

Mind you, Senova had had the slave cut it far shorter than he'd ever had it. He was sure that if someone saw him from above his head would look pink, like an egg. Might as well have shaved it at this point. Then at least she needn't have lightened it with her saffron and yellow-petal mix. It would take Rufinus quite a long time to get used to the startling difference a brighter, lighter colour made to his hair. She had shown him how to apply it, to face fuzz and eyebrows as well, and had given him a whole jar of it to keep for re-application, telling him he would need to do so at least twice a month if not more.

How he was going to achieve the privacy to do such a thing in the world's biggest and busiest military fortress he had no idea, but at least centurions were afforded the luxury of their own accommodation, so perhaps he might manage it after all.

Then this morning had finally come around and Rufinus had prepared once more to say a temporary farewell to Senova. She did not appear blissfully happy to be leaving, but she had the good sense not to argue about it. The coming days and months could contain who knows what dangers, and she would be far safer elsewhere. Besides, she could no longer live with Rufinus. Centurions did not marry any more than ordinary soldiers, and their women certainly weren't permitted in the camps.

He had looked out of the townhouse that morning, most of the slaves already gone ahead to prepare Senova's new place in Syracuse, and had been struck by the emptiness. Oddly he could feel the lack of eyes on the place. He had known the watchers were there now for so long that it was actually noticeable – palpable, even – when they were absent. Clearly Cestius and his friends had done their job and, for a short time, their house was unobserved.

He had said goodbye to Senova, kissed her with the awkward mix of tenderness and embarrassment that was his norm, and watched her and the last of the house's staff trot away down the street, litter barely shaking unlike the crappy ones he always got. He'd felt a lot more of a wrench at the sight than he'd expected to, in all honesty.

Still, he had watched her go and somehow the house became dead without her. It no longer felt like home. Rufinus the prefect was gone. Senova would be observed at the emporium getting onto the ship for Sicilia and in the blur of Roman life, especially with no one watching the house, it would generally be assumed that her husband followed on. Rufinus the prefect had effectively left the moment Senova turned the first corner. All he was now was a grizzled veteran centurion of the Urban Cohorts rattling around in some rich man's empty house.

Hardening himself, preparing for his new role, he opened the door and left the townhouse, once more oddly aware of the different feeling when the place wasn't being watched.

He took his time in the city, for it was worth getting used to his kit and new persona before trying it anywhere more dangerous than the Subura – a comparison he'd never have thought to utter in the old days. At least he hadn't had to learn anything odd to fill in the background of his assumed name. Maximus had served in the First Adiutrix in Pannonia, in areas Rufinus knew well from the wars. Then he had transferred to the Eighth Augusta in Gaul, where he had been stationed as a commander in Severus' bodyguard at Lugdunum, with which Rufinus now had at least a passing familiarity. The man was originally from Narbo, which was close enough to Tarraco to allow for faint traces of a regional accent he'd never quite lost. All in all he and Maximus were close enough in many ways to have been brothers.

He bought in the markets a few things that he decided he might need in the coming days in the camp and finally, as prepared as he could be, he marched off up the hill to the Castra Praetoria, once again oddly missing the luxury of a litter, even as uncomfortable a one as he'd had.

His feet ached as he approached the fortress. He would have to get in slightly better shape, for certain. He adjusted his grip on his kit bag, his fingers a little numb in the leather gloves he'd bought from a dubious merchant on a poor market stall. It seemed that the wearing of gloves in cold weather had boomed in Rome these days, perhaps due to everyone wanting to keep skin contact minimal with the plague so rife, perhaps due to the influence of the troops returning from Pannonia and Germania, where gloves were common. Either way, he would wear them as an affectation through the winter, and worry about the summer when it happened. Though he was starting to regret not shopping around for better gloves. These ones itched like a flea party.

'Name and business,' called out the man on the wall above the gate as he arrived. Rufinus had to think for just a moment, so disguised the slowness of his response as a coughing fit.

'You'd better not be bringing the fucking plague,' grunted another man up there.

Rufinus bridled, recognising a chance to plant his standard in the ground from the start.

'One more word like that from you, soldier, and I shall see to it that you get latrine duty for a month and the only tool you'll have is your foul tongue. Now get down here and open the bloody gate. Centurion Gaius Valerius Maximus, Second Urban Cohort, assigned fresh today and reporting for duty.'

There was a pause and a brief confab on the wall before the thunder of descending feet and the gate creaking open. Rufinus knew exactly why: the two men would have been deliberating how much crap to take from the visitor. As a centurion, and a senior one, he outranked them as Vesuvius outranked a mole hill, but as a member of the Urban Cohorts, while they were Praetorians, they would doubt he had the power to exert any influence over them. Caution had won out in the end, though, and the two men stood contrite and respectful as Rufinus passed through the gate, proffering his orders in the form of a scroll case sealed with Severus' seal – possibly the man's last ever official duty as governor of Lugdunensis and therefore de facto commander of the Eighth.

The soldiers snapped the seal and checked the document and, content that he was exactly what he'd said, they saluted and gestured off to the right. 'Urban Cohort barracks are that way, Centurion. The prefect's office is...'

'I *know* where it is, soldier,' snapped Rufinus and marched off in that direction before he realised that that would seem odd. Why should a newly-arrived centurion from the north on his first posting here know that? Still, the common man had a tendency to write off things like that as unimportant and before he was out of earshot they were already gossiping about a friend and striding away.

Rufinus stumped off towards his new barracks, his mind going over and over everything he needed to remember. His hand was itching badly now, and he wondered whether these 'new' gloves he'd bought from the market stall had actually been recently filched from a plague corpse in the street. Shuddering at the thought, he ripped the glove from his hand and peered inside, making sure nothing in there was moving.

'Why don't you watch where you're going, Centurion,' snarled a hoarse voice and Rufinus halted, startled, at the sight of a figure in the Praetorian white uniform of a senior officer. He'd almost walked into the man, so absorbed was he in his own contemplations.

He straightened, remembering at the last moment to add a sort of hint of regrettable disobedience into his stance. After all, he was Urban Cohort and this man was Praetorian. If he was going to play the role, he was going to play it right.

The officer glared at him and, though he was actually slightly shorter than Rufinus, contrived somehow to manage to look down his nose at the centurion.

'Have you no nowhere important to be?' the Praetorian snapped.

'Just arrived, sir. Reporting to the prefect.'

'Then kindly stop staring into your apparel and blocking the street for *real* soldiers.'

Rufinus bridled again, but realised with a shock of panic that his nail-less, mutilated left hand was open to view, and the officer was looking directly at it. Instinct made him thrust it back into the glove sharply, as though by hiding it once more he could somehow make the man unsee his deformity.

There was an odd, uncomfortable silence and the officer walked on, casting one curious, disapproving backwards glance at him. Only now did Rufinus realise that the officer had had a soldier following him, carrying his things. With another thrill of worry, he noticed the hexagonal shield with its scorpion-and-stars design. A cavalryman. And an officer. Almost certainly a tribune, looking at him. Rufinus had not had a lot of interaction with the cavalry during his time with the Guard, for the division between horse and foot was almost as pronounced as that between both of them and the Urban Cohorts. But unless things had changed drastically in the last year or two he was fairly sure there was only one tribune in the Guard in command of the cavalry.

And that would make the man he'd just seen Appius Fulvius, the last of the six guilty murderers he hunted. His blood froze. *And Fulvius had seen him.* Seen his nail-less scarred hand. And Fulvius worked for Cleander.

He picked up the pace, hurrying on for the prefect's office. With luck the man would forget about him and he could blend into the fortress quickly. One thing was certain: he was going to have to be a damn sight more careful in the coming days.

Part Three

A Gathering of Crows

"Omnes Una Manet Nox"

(One night awaits everyone)

- Vergil

CHAPTER FIFTEEN – OF MEMORIES PAINFUL

Rome, Februarius 190 A.D.

It amazed Rufinus in some ways how easy it was to sink into the ways of a centurion.

'Maximus? In my office.'

He nodded respectfully at Pertinax and dismissed his men back to their barracks before turning from the Cohort's parade ground in the centre of their section of the castrum and marching into the headquarters.

It had been at once very familiar and similar to the routine he had adopted during his temporary commission before the campaign in Dacia, and yet so much easier. He was doing all the same things: weapons training, assigning duties, dealing with complaints and sick lists and the like, but unlike that awful month in Dacia, he was working with loyal and willing soldiers this time, with no men determined to make him fail. His century seemed not to be perturbed by his youth. But then the past decade had left more than ten years of wear on him, for sure, and Maximus was not a young man, even if Rufinus still might be considered so. The century treated him with the respect due a veteran senior centurion with a record of wartime success.

It made it so much easier.

And in the Cohort he felt relatively safe. It was something of a boon that the Praetorian Guard and the Cohort endured that divide, since it meant that Rufinus could spend all his time among his own men and avoiding almost all contact with the Guard without looking the slightest bit strange.

The only potential hiccup was the Prefect. He had met Pertinax a few times. Admittedly it had been years earlier, and he had only been a passing figure during meetings with the man, but Pertinax was shrewd and certainly no fool. Though the prefect dealt with Maximus in a perfectly expected and acceptable manner, Rufinus kept spotting an odd look pass across the man's face as though he thought there was something odd about the centurion, but he couldn't quite place what it was. Or, worse still, perhaps he already remembered Rufinus and was simply playing along with the ruse until he decided what to do about it. After all, the man had served with the *real* Maximus. Either way there was an odd hint of suspicion hanging over their relationship.

Rufinus' century had spent the winter engaged in largely camp-based activity. Like the new prefect, Rufinus was being eased into the role. And he was still learning. He knew the duties of a centurion, of course. As well as having been one briefly, he had served under a good one since the day he joined up. But it was more a matter of getting used to the routine of the Urban Cohorts and the vast differences in their duties from the legions. Thus he and his men had taken the lightest duties on the roster for the first few months at the insistence of Pertinax.

When they did go into the city, split up into patrols or guard units for various official institutions or routines, Rufinus was struck over and over by the changes wrought by the latest outbreak of the disease. It was not just the sickness itself, though that was appalling – bodies hugging the gutters of any alleyways and carts collecting disfigured corpses for disposal in the pits beyond the Esquiline – it was the atmosphere.

Between the fear of the ever-present pestilence and the growing hunger of the city's populace in a world where grain was in shorter supply by the month, the sense of simmering discontent was thick enough to cut with a knife. Even Rufinus felt it, but he heard his men talking about it, and that truly brought it home. These men lived and worked in the streets of

Rome. They saw the ordinary people of the city every day with their joys and woes, their troubles and triumphs. Those men now openly declared this to be the worst they had ever seen the city. Strong, veteran soldiers were beginning to live in fear of performing their duties in the city, for the threat of mob violence was becoming more pronounced all the time.

There were now angry demonstrations on an almost daily basis, complaining about food and the imperial administration's unwillingness to help. The emperor seemed to be out of the city all the time, huddled away in his seaside villa with his mistress, and Cleander might be becoming unpopular, but he was still strong and still untouchable, locked in the Palatine with his men. And the mob simmered, close to the boil. Angry crowds gathered, shouting, outside the horrea or in the forum, or even outside the Castra Praetoria. And on every occasion the Urban Cohorts were deployed in their least belligerent manner. The last thing Pertinax wanted to do was goad such demonstrations into full-blown conflict. So the men kept their weapons sheathed and their hands away from the hilts while their officers talked down the crowd, urging them to disperse. And though there were occasional thrown bricks or jugs or suchlike, the men were prepared, keeping their shields ready to ward off such missiles. The soldiers were actually serving with a level of calm and level-headed distinction that Rufinus had been impressed with.

As yet he and his century had not been deployed on riot duty. Though his men would be perfectly able to deal with it, he had not served in this capacity before and was still learning how to deal with civil disturbance by watching his peers at work.

With a deep breath, Rufinus walked into the prefect's office, chin high, vine stick tucked beneath his arm and helmet clutched in the other. He stood straight as a board, eyes locked on a point in the wall just above the prefect's left shoulder.

'Centurion Maximus. Good.'

There it was again. That flicker of suspicious recognition. Rufinus tried not to flinch.

'I understand you have put in for this afternoon as leave?'

Rufinus nodded. 'Yes, sir. Family business.'

Pertinax huffed. 'I was planning on shifting you and your men to the full active duty roster now. Vitulus and his men have been dispatched to deal with an incident in Ostia, and Lurco's century have been deployed around Pompey's theatre. There's an African troupe playing there at the moment and just the very fact that they're from one of the grain provinces seems to be drawing angry crowds. I'm expecting to have to disperse the mob there more than once in the coming days. So I'm short of men to send out on standard patrols. I realise that you have had no leave thus far, and you *are* due, but I wondered if I might prevail upon you to rearrange your business and take a full patrol today?'

Rufinus squirmed. The very last thing he wanted to do was refuse. Not only did he need to put forth an exemplary impression for the sake of his guise, but Pertinax was a good man, and Rufinus did not want to disappoint him. But some things could not be rearranged.

'It is the anniversary of my brother's death, sir,' Rufinus said, praying silently that this simple truth would not unravel his identity.

'My commiserations.'

'If I cannot be at his tomb this day, I have always found a way to visit a temple of Diana and make offerings. I owe him...'

Diana. The huntress. Goddess of the woodlands where Lucius had died.

Pertinax frowned. 'I would never stand between a man and the spirit of a departed sibling. But perhaps I can make a suggestion? If I redeploy the Sixth Century, who were due to patrol the region of the Horrea Galbana and the emporium, then you could take your century there. The Temple of Diana is on the Aventine and should be on your route. I'm certain you could combine the two?'

Rufinus paused. It seemed a trifle odd. His annual pilgrimage to the goddess was a very personal and very private thing. To go there at the head of a century of men would be strange. But in truth there was no real reason why he could not. He nodded finally.

'My men are just retiring for their noon meal, Prefect. I shall give them the orders and we shall leave at the next shift.'

Pertinax smiled. 'Thank you, Centurion.'

Rufinus saluted and left the office, marching off towards his barracks. As he did so, his mind churned. Finally they were being deployed. Thus far Severus' worries, and the reason for his placement here had seemed unfounded. Pertinax had been content to command and administrate from his office, had done an excellent job, there had been no grand issues, and neither the prefect nor Rufinus had needed to deal with anything untoward.

But that would change soon, no matter how it looked right now. The mood of the city was spiralling into chaos. At this point it was still building, and the Cohort were managing to contain it. One day, though, and soon, there would be trouble. The crowd would not back down at the sight of the Cohort. Rufinus and his men would have to defend themselves and put down a riot. They would have to do it as calmly as possible and with the minimum of violence. And when all this happened, and the cracks began to appear in the mortar of Roman security, Cleander would be increasingly tempted to step in and become involved.

He delivered the news to his men, who received his tidings with mixed feelings. While they were clearly grateful to be moving back into their standard routine, that would also mean more regular contact with the plague-ridden, starving mob that threatened violence with every breath.

A little over an hour later he and his men marched out of the castrum beneath the aloof gaze of the Praetorians on gate guard, and descended the hills of the northern side of the city, passing the great amphitheatre and the Palatine, circling the end of the circus and climbing the lower slopes of the Aventine. Opposite the barracks of the local vigiles, he called his optio, a competent man by the name of Sura, forward.

'I have a brief duty to attend to. Take the men on to the Galbana and circle around the streets nearby. If there's a gathering, keep them under observation and make your presence felt but without threat if you can, and I will catch up shortly.'

Sura saluted and continued to march on along the street with his men while Rufinus turned and headed west, along the slope of the hill. The Aventine was a region filled with housing both wealthy and poor, baths and temples and more, like a microcosm of the city as a whole. An urbs within the urbs. The temple of Diana, though, was one of the oldest structures on the hill, and one of the largest and most impressive. Though it had been rebuilt once, it still retained some work that dated back to the days of the kings in the earliest years of the city.

He approached the massive, grand structure with its double colonnade with a growing sense of sadness. It had been so long since he had performed his libations and offerings at Lucius' actual tomb. In fact, half a lifetime ago now. And unless he could get back to the villa and retrieve the remains from the tomb there, he might never do so again.

He nodded his silent greeting at a boy with a broom sweeping the colonnade's marble floor and passed through the open bronze doors into the dim interior. He paused in the trapezium of light from the doorway and blinked a few times. He could see the ancient altar there, so old that the images on it had worn down to indistinct shapes, the marble and wooden statues of the goddess watching over it from both sides. It seemed to be empty, and he strode over to the altar, fishing into the pouch at his belt for his small jar of wine and the incense he had brought along with a few gold coins and an arrow with a silver head he had bought at great expense.

'I suspected you would come here,' murmured a familiar voice.

Rufinus closed his eyes and took a deep breath. Damn it, but the man must have been lurking in the dark corner as he entered. 'Father.' Cold. No emotion. Not a son addressing his sire, but a meeting of strangers.

'Publius once told me you did this. It was the only place I might be able to find you.'

'And now you've found me. This is important to me, so say your piece and begone.'

There was a bitter silence and when the old man spoke again there was a quality of strained anger to the voice.

'You are chaos, child. Where you move in the world you create disaster. I should have known you were still alive when Rome began to descend into misery and trouble.'

'You are too kind.'

'I'm quite serious. You will be the ruination of our family. You began that task many years ago when you took Lucius from me. It was a relief when you left, and I began to concentrate upon rebuilding our ruined family with my hopes pinned to Publius as an heir.'

Rufinus felt his lip twitch. He and his father had never been close, but he'd not realised that the old man had even cut him from the inheritance.

'I managed to sell the villa,' the old man said. 'Despite everything, I managed to offload it and sink the funds it gave me into tying our family to the one man in Rome who has the power and influence to make us great again. I put everything in order and I send Publius to finish up, and then the ghost of my deceased offspring Gnaeus appears and stirs the pot. You took Publius from me too, now, despite my threat. And you are making trouble for the one man upon whom I am relying for our family's future.'

'I warned you not to hitch your *cisium* carriage to Cleander's mare. I told you it would end in disaster. I will not let Publius be part of the explosion that is coming.'

'I was livid for a while that you had kept my last son from me. That you had him hidden away. But now I am finally grateful. And when this is all over, if we are still alive, I will discover where you hid him and I shall retrieve him once the danger has passed.'

Rufinus felt a lurch then. What danger in particular? His eyes must have narrowed in suspicion, for his father nodded as if answering a question.

'Yes, there is true danger now for our family because of you. The last time I met with the chamberlain he rather expertly steered me into conversation about my sons. He asked after Publius, since he has not been around recently. I had to brush him off with an explanation that Publius was still in Hispania seeing to our old property. I am not sure he believed me. And then he asked me about you. He asked me how keenly I felt your passing, and in an almost kindly manner asked whether it would please me if he had your remains located and returned to me.'

Rufinus flinched. Cleander knew. How, he had no idea, but there was no other explanation. Cleander either knew, or at least strongly suspected, that Rufinus was still alive. Was it the fault of one of the Praetorians he had faced? He remembered with a sinking feeling the cavalry tribune he met on his first day in the Cohort. He had seen the scars. Had he put two and two together and told Cleander?

No. Not that. If he had, someone would have come for Rufinus before now. But still, it sounded as though Cleander knew.

'I understand that the chamberlain sent someone to accompany the Prefect of the Fleet and his wife to Sicilia, but miraculously, the man he sent never managed to board the ship. He was waylaid by thieves in the Subura and had his throat cut. Even *I* find that suspicious, so imagine how the chamberlain feels?'

Rufinus shivered. Cleander must have suspected that Rufinus the prefect and Rufinus the Praetorian were the same man. Gods bless Vibius Cestius, since it had to have been he or his companions who had stopped the spy. At least Senova was in the care of Severus. She would be as safe there as anywhere. But things were becoming difficult. If Cleander now suspected he was still alive and had been playing Prefect of the Fleet for so many months, then he was closing in. How long before he made connections with Papirius Dionysus and Septimius Severus, or had he already done so?

He realised with another plummet of the spirits that if his father was being probed for information, then almost certainly the old man was being watched, too. And his father wasn't shrewd enough to notice and throw off anyone following him. There were probably eyes that belonged to Cleander outside watching this very temple. And they would have seen a centurion of the Urban Cohorts entering.

'Whatever you are doing, stop doing it,' the old man said. 'You are causing new trouble now. Stop playing your little games and disappear. I fear that Cleander is starting to suspect that I am working against him, when nothing could be further from the truth. And I will not see our last hope for a return to prominence disappear because of you. I will not suffer for your stupidity, boy. If I find myself up against a cliff I will sacrifice you. Believe me on this. If Cleander demands it of me, I will give you to him. To save our name and my one remaining loyal son, I will give you to him, and I will do so gladly. And so I give you once again my one demand. Go away. Stop interfering in matters in Rome and go away. If you do so, perhaps there is still a chance that all this will disappear with you. If not, you will fall and badly.'

Rufinus growled. 'I took an oath to Rome and her emperor. I am loyal to that oath to the very end. I will serve Rome, and I will serve Commodus with my dying breath. I do *not* serve Cleander, no matter how much he aspires to rule. Cleander is anathema to everything I took an oath to protect. He winds like a serpent, sowing seeds of discord in the city and poisoning all about him, and he is dangerous for the emperor himself.

Cleander will fall because if he does not, he will ruin Rome. And I will be a part of that as I vowed from the start. I cannot disappear, but those I love are safe and secure. Only one real danger remains for me right now, and that is you. I put myself at risk in a foolish attempt to dissuade you from this awful path and as a reward for the act of a dutiful son you threaten to hand me to my enemies. No. I will not divert from my path. And you will not sell me to your evil master.'

'I will…'

'No you will not. Because if you do, I shall make sure he knows that you were complicit in everything I have done. I shall endure torture, for I've done it before. And in doing so, I shall protect my friends, but I shall mollify my interrogators by blaming you for it all. Remember that when you are tempted to sell me out. In doing so, you will nail yourself and the family name to that cross.'

His father recoiled as though struck.

'And so my advice to you, old man – for how can I ever think of you as a father now? – is the same as your advice to me. Forget your power games. Ignore your web of money and flattery in Rome and run away. Take what you can carry and hide until this is over. Then, perhaps, you can rebuild your name. Mine will be renowned and untainted for my loyalty to the emperor and my choice of patron. Now before you bluster and threaten any more, know that we are done here, and forever more. I have no wish to ever set eyes upon you again. And because you are a vain, greedy, stupid old man who blindly clings to a viper, you will not realise that he will have had you followed.'

He saw a flicker of shock in his father's eyes then. The old man really hadn't considered the possibility.

'When you depart, take an empty vial and some burned incense containers with you, so that at least it looks like you came here for a legitimate reason. And go north somewhere. I don't care where, but lead your watcher away from me. I shall wait a short while before I leave to give you plenty of room.'

The old man stood for a moment, silent and full of impotent, empty anger, mouth flapping like a fish.

'Go.'

Ignoring the old man further, he turned and strode across to the altar.

'Dear Lucius, I am so sorry to have brought such discord to you on this important day.'

He spent half an hour there, lighting the incense, pouring the wine, giving the gold over and praying to Diana that his brother 'live' on in happiness and peace in Elysium. Finally, feeling that somehow this year's visit had been irretrievably marred, he cast his brother the latest in a long line of farewells and left the temple. As he emerged into the cold February sunlight he paused, blinking and shading his eyes – a perfectly natural reaction to adjusting to the change in light level and conveniently a good way to surreptitiously examine the surroundings and pick out anything that looked out of place. If one of Cleander's watchers was still there, then he was very, very good. There were only two figures in the street outside. One was sitting by the roadside, moaning and praying, a bowl held out for money to help him survive with only one leg. An ex-soldier. And a one legged man would not be much use in tailing someone around the city. The other was an old woman in ragged clothes carrying a basket that contained what appeared to be rather limp looking vegetables. The open sores on her flesh and the blood she coughed up make it unlikely she worked for the chamberlain.

As satisfied as he could be that he was not being followed and could therefore not be connected with his father today, he marched away, heading for the Aventine plain and the Horrea Galbana.

The day was not shaping up to be one of his better ones, and as he rounded the corner into the street outside the city's largest storage complex, he decided that it may well be one of the worst.

A crowd had gathered in the street outside the horrea and though he couldn't hear the individual grumbles of the mass, the general murmur of discontent was clear. In the privacy of his head, Rufinus wondered what Dionysus was doing. Wasn't he supposed to have been persuading Cleander to move the grain into private storage? If so why were crowds still gathering outside the imperial granaries? Once more he cursed the fact that everything that was happening behind the scenes seemed to be happening so slowly.

Taking a deep breath he concentrated on the scene before him. This was his duty, after all.

His century had taken up positions in two double lines, one at each end of the street, containing the crowd, but far enough back not to appear to be moving against them. Sura, the optio, was at the far side, his gaze locked on the mob until he noticed Rufinus and waved an indication that he was uncertain how best to proceed.

Rufinus chewed his lip. On this occasion at least his duty was clear. Had this crowd been demonstrating outside one of Cleander's structures and not the public granary, he might have been forced to play things carefully, trying, in fact, to exacerbate the crowd's dissatisfaction with the chamberlain. Dionysus, though, did not need this demonstration. Rufinus had to somehow disperse this lot. He'd watched the other centurions doing it with professionalism and aplomb, but it seemed a monumental task now that it was his, and once again he appreciated just how different the role of the Urban Cohorts and their officers was to that of the standard army.

He cleared his throat.

'People of Rome…'

Perhaps half the crowd turned their attention to him, as did the two men from someone else's century who were guarding the one open doorway into the horrea

'People of Rome, we understand your unhappiness.'

'No you fucking don't,' shouted someone from the crowd. 'The *army* still gets fed.'

Rufinus forced himself to breathe calmly. Stirring this up would do no good for anyone.

'My men will be the first to tell you that they are now on quarter rations, and yet they stand their ground, loyal to the core. We know that you are hungry.'

'Then give us bread,' bellowed someone unseen.

'Yeah, what use are circuses without the bread.'

So there were some well-read wags in the crowd. This was your higher class sort of mob.

'Let reason and logic be your guide,' Rufinus called out. 'You know that no new grain has been put into this granary in months. And you know that there was already too little in there to feed even one region of the city. If we threw open the doors and doled out what there was, you would be back here in a matter of days shouting again, but over an *empty* granary, now.'

'But at least some would eat,' pleaded someone else.

Rufinus sighed.

'We are saving what little there is.'

'Why? Why save it when it's needed so badly?' called someone desperate – weren't they all?

He'd reasoned through this argument himself in preparation. 'Because what we have is earmarked for the vital services. If we cannot feed the vigiles, for example, who will put out the fires that burn down your houses? If we cannot feed the men who crew the barges and drive the carts, then when grain *does* arrive, how will you get it? And what little can be spared for the public is being directed to those of you who labour to provide other foods in an attempt to ward off the worst of the famine. Fishermen and farmers, butchers and bakers are getting grain, for without those men, who would provide you with the rest of the produce that is at least keeping you alive? Reason. Think about this.'

'It's hard to think with such an empty belly,' moaned an old woman, and Rufinus nodded his sympathy.

'I really do understand your plight and your anger. And I share it. I do. But everything that can be done is being done. Ships are being built and bought to replace those lost. I understand that subsidies are being given in the grain provinces to any man who will take on a ruined farm lost to the plague and make it thrive once more. Soldiers are being seconded out as farm labourers. What can be done is being done, and this will end. *Soon*, this will end. But casting first blame and then rocks solves nothing.'

'My dad died yesterday,' someone shouted. 'Not of the plague. He died of hunger.'

There was a murmur of agreement, but Rufinus could feel a thrum of something different in the crowd. Their misery and their need to vocalise was still there, but the anger had gone out of the mob. What had felt like a throng on the edge of violence mere moments ago now felt plaintive and sad.

'Please,' Rufinus called out. 'Disperse and return to your homes and businesses. When grain is available it will be handed out, but here and like this you are just putting yourself at increased risk of contracting disease from those around you.'

That was a gamble. It could easily have made the crowd twitchy, but it seemed to do the trick. A sudden nervous desire to be anywhere that wasn't within arm's reach of one another rose among the people. Rufinus gestured to his optio, who nodded. The men of his century stood at ease, and then split off, moving to the edges of the street to make room. Thankfully, there was no sudden change in attitude, and the crowd broke up like ice in a warming pool. In a matter of heartbeats there were few men left, and those were standing close to the granary entrance. Rufinus hurried over and his spirits fell once more.

The body of a boy, not more than seven or eight years old, lay crumpled on the horrea's threshold.

'What happened.'

'He tried to come in, sir,' one of the two guards on the door said, his voice dripping with regret. 'Tried to push past us. I didn't mean to hurt him bad. I just sort of whacked him to stop him.'

Rufinus nodded. It wasn't the guard's fault. He'd had to stop the boy, and it was probably a fairly gentle knock. But the boy was stick thin and frail, weak with hunger and possibly sick. A slight knock had been enough to finish him.

He was suddenly aware of Sura standing beside him.

'What was well handled, sir.'

'Thank you. Still one casualty, though.'

'One beats a thousand any day, sir.'

Rufinus nodded, grateful for the man's words, but he couldn't take his eyes off the boy. How long must this go on? This hunger was his fault. He and his colleagues had done this to the city. The horrible guilt began to gnaw at him once more.

This had to end soon.

CHAPTER SIXTEEN – NEW CHALLENGES

Rome, April 190 A.D.

R ufinus pulled the hood of his cloak lower over his brow in an attempt to ward off the worst of the rain, though all that really did was create a funnel down which all the collected water ran, tipping out in a waterfall directly in front of his nose, and no amount of re-jigging it seemed to make it any better. He nodded to the optio and instantly regretted the motion, since it somehow caused a rivulet of cold water to trickle through some unseen fold onto his neck. The optio saluted, apparently unconcerned by the torrential spring rain that has started at the end of their shift and seemed set in for the day, and gave the order for the men to fall out.

They had just returned from their latest civic duty, patrolling the Velabrum from the Capitol to the great Circus Maximus and imposing the rule of law upon the increasingly unstable city. During their time out there, Rufinus had rather hoped to catch sight of Severus, though he had been sadly disappointed. Septimius Severus, successful pacifier of troublesome Gaul during the Maternus war and then lauded governor of Sicilia for his achievements in doubling grain import from that island, was back in Rome. In actual fact, doubling the grain from Sicilia made very little difference and still accounted for only a fragment of that actually needed in the city, but it had still made the man popular with both the emperor and the senate and people of Rome. Now he had been granted a suffect consulship and lorded it over the city, along with his colleague the emperor, who remained locked away in some seaside estate with his mistress.

Though it shouldn't really, it somewhat smarted that Rufinus had recently taken a career plummet from the grandeur of Prefect of the Fleet to an ordinary centurion in the Cohort, while Severus seemed to be rising to ever loftier positions, now arm in arm with Commodus himself. In truth, Rufinus suspected that this was all part of Severus' plan, that now he was in a position to supplant Cleander in the emperor's circle when the time came.

Still, it was irritating. Severus was busy cycling through all the gatherings of the rich and influential, making laws and being praised, while Rufinus got to break up fights, threaten hungry civilians, and stand about in the cold rain.

This morning's patrol had been particularly vexing.

Rufinus had adopted a circuit of the Velabrum region that covered the entire area from the river to the edge of the forum and threaded snake-like back and forth across the land in between. Their duty was, as Pertinax had made clear, much a case of reminding the Roman people that there was a force of strong men in the city whose very job was to make sure that peace reigned through Rome.

Not long ago, even since Rufinus had taken on the role of centurion here, the populace had usually been as cowed in the presence of the Urban Cohorts as they were before the Praetorians. Now, with the rising tide of anger and discontent, things had changed. Now, the people glowered threateningly at the soldiers of the Cohort, as though they no longer saw them as figures of imperial law and authority, but as an oppressive gang of thugs, starving the poor.

Then this morning, Rufinus had been forced to impose control in new and unpleasant ways, narrowly avoiding an escalation into full-scale riot. Even then, the result had almost been disastrous. His century had been split into three units of twenty four men, led by he, Optio Sura, and the tesserarius, and the three groups had patrolled for some time without trouble. Then, with only an hour to go before the end of shift, Rufinus had rounded the ruined stones of the old Porta Trigemina to see a demonstration in progress. Heart rising into his throat even as his spirits sank, Rufinus had immediately deployed his men into three lines of eight, wishing the rest of his century were here too. The men brandished their stout ash nightsticks and braced into their shields every bit as professionally as the legions in the field.

A chant began to arise among the people, and Rufinus sighed as he heard the familiar refrain.

Grain for Rome. Grain for Rome. Grain for Rome.

As if anyone was likely to respond positively. There *was* no grain. In fact, Rufinus now knew that there was grain, hidden in provincial granaries by Severus and waiting for the right moment to be deployed. But *officially* there was no grain. The orders from Pertinax, supported by direct imperial command, were to mete out the absolute minimum of violence, yet to do what needed to be done in order to keep control in the city. Civilians had left such gatherings over the last month with cuts and bruises and even broken bones. As yet no further fatalities had been reported as a result of the Urban Cohorts' actions, though it was somewhat hard to judge, given the number of people now dying each day through hunger or the ever-present disease.

Rufinus had moved his men forward, stopping them fifteen paces from the edge of the crowd, where he had delivered once more his speech on pacification and the necessity of preserving what grain Rome had. He'd had plenty of opportunities to hone the oration over the months, and it was often successful without the need of a show of force – a tribute to Rufinus' rhetoric teachers as a boy, he felt. Somehow this morning, though, he'd known straight away that words would not be enough. Still, he trotted it out. Not only was it going to calm at least some of the crowd, but just as importantly it carried a subtle message of culpability.

'...the storage of what little grain comes in, against the possibility of shortage for the most important groups in the city.'

As usual, he noted the small group of men from the local vigiles unit who stood looking tense and troubled near a fountain. To give the vigiles their due, they were deploying without fail anywhere a gathering of people occurred. It was important that they did so for civic safety, but it also helped make Rufinus' point. He gestured to the men by the fountain, whose job was to arrest small-time criminals and prevent the outbreak of fires.

'Imagine if the pitiful grain that's been hoarded was distributed among those listed, many of whom may well be dead within the month anyway from the plague, and then these vital men here went hungry. One careless tip of an oil lamp and the city becomes a fireball. These men need to be fed before all others, even my own. This is imperial edict as sanctioned by the chamberlain, Marcus Aurelius Cleander.'

And it was. Of course, Cleander's entire role in matters had been to nod sagely and seal the document, confirming that the emperor had agreed to Papirius Dionysus' plan for the grain. Still it was undeniably the truth, and in the minds of those who walked away from these streets it would be Cleander's name they remembered in connection with their hunger, and the blame would land with him. Sooner or later the chamberlain would discover what was being done and would take umbrage, though, so Rufinus sincerely hoped that Severus' plan came to fruition before that happened.

The crowd had not reacted well to Rufinus speech that morning. Rotten fruit and veg began to pelt the line of shields and spatter the men holding them. Then, somewhere at the back there had been the sound of groaning, tearing and snapping wood. Rufinus had just caught sight, above the heads of the crowd, of a damaged shutter detaching from the wall of the building beyond and falling away unseen. He saw figures slipping through the window into the dark interior.

His pulse sped up. The building, nestled here between the old ruined gate and the temple of Ceres, goddess of the fields and the harvest, was the *statio annonae*. Here, until the recent grain troubles, had been the office of Papirius Dionysus and his grain men. They had moved to the horrea on the Aventine to assume direct control over the situation, and now their offices lay unused and dark.

And now someone among that crowd had broken in.

'Disperse now, in the name of the emperor and the chamberlain,' he bellowed. 'If this crowd does not disperse, I shall give the command to advance and all miscreants, agitators and trespassers will be arrested and dealt with. Go home, people.'

Some had. In fairness, perhaps half the crowd melted away. Others slipped into the grain offices, and the rest bristled, preparing to face the Cohort. Damn it.

Rufinus had been forced then to give a command he had hoped not to have to issue.

His soldiers had advanced along the street, clubs up, shields forth. The crowd had continued to pelt them with missiles, though they now included cobbles, pieces of torn timber and anything else that came to hand. Two of Rufinus' men were struck and disappeared with a cry, dropping out of the line and falling back to nurse horrible injuries while their compatriots closed up the gaps and marched on against the civilians before them.

He'd continued to hope that the public would see sense, but no such luck was to come his way. He watched in dismay as the crowd met the advancing soldiers with gritted teeth and desperate, hopeless bravery. The Urban Cohorts, grim-faced, went to work with their stout clubs, swiping and smashing, breaking bones and forcing men back with their shields..

Even at that critical juncture Rufinus thought perhaps the crowd might break, but then everything had descended to Tarterus in a heartbeat. Even as he drew breath to demand once more that they disperse, other noises erupted. Black smoke began to pour from the broken window of the grain office, leaking out from another half dozen apertures, too. Some men cried out in panic at the realisation that the building beside which they had gathered was alight. Others shouted in triumph that the symbol of that which had caused their anger was burning. Added to the roar of flames and the shouts of the crowd, above the struggle between civilian and soldier, came the desperate bellowed commands of the vigiles as they gathered water from the fountain around which they stood, bucket loads ready to tackle a building they couldn't yet get to for the crowd. And finally came a further set of calls as another unit of Rufinus' men, led by his tesserarius and presumably drawn by the commotion, suddenly appeared at the other side, near the circus, and began to wade into the far edge of the gathered crowd.

Rufinus watched as the mob was squeezed between two groups of soldiers, pressured and beaten with sticks until those remaining surrendered, throwing up their hands. The men of the Urban Cohorts gathered them up and began to rope their wrists until Rufinus told them not to.

'Go home and nurse your wounds,' he bellowed at the gathered crowd above the din. 'There will be no arrests today.'

A show of such magnanimity might go some way to preventing similar riots in the coming days, and the population in the street had immediately dispersed, clutching at injuries and limping away, casting hateful, suspicious looks at the soldiers who stepped out of their way.

Thus had the patrol finished. With the end of the demonstration the vigiles had got to work with their buckets. Fortunately, the grain offices had been empty and there was little inside to burn, so it did not take long for the vigiles to get it all under control, and there was little danger of any spread of the flames with the damp morning air.

Rufinus' mood had not improved as the units gathered once more and began to make their way back towards the Castra Praetoria, particularly given that it chose that moment to start raining.

And so here Rufinus was in the fortress once more, his men dispersing to their barracks, rain running down his neck and gushing from the tip of his hood, heart heavy with the morning's events and an appointment now to visit the prefect and report the near disaster. Pertinax would not be pleased, though he would at least realise that the blame was not Rufinus' so he would not suffer for it.

With a sigh – the latest in a series – he turned and strode off towards the headquarters.

He was busy formulating his speech to the commander when he suddenly became aware that he was not alone. Startled, he glanced left and right and took in the two white-garbed Praetorians. He knew neither of them by face, both of which were ugly and scarred. They were not dressed in the toga required for duty in the city centre, but in full armour and bearing their swords at their sides, comfortably so this far from the Pomerium that forbade weapons of war.

'Can I help you, soldiers?' he said, trying to keep his voice level. Given his superior rank, but the Praetorians' innate sense of superiority, it was a careful balance between maintaining the commanding tone of a centurion and yet not provoking trouble with the Guard, whose fortress they shared.

'Come with us, Centurion,' one of the soldiers replied, his tone equally carefully nestled between the respect due an officer and the disdain reserved for the Urban Cohorts.

'Impossible, I'm afraid, soldier,' he replied. 'I have to visit the prefect.'

'*After* this,' the man said, now on the border of insolence. His hand dropped to the pommel of his sword, Rufinus noted. A threat, and not a particularly subtle one at that.

'I do not bow to your authority,' Rufinus said in measured, careful tones. 'My prefect will be waiting for my debrief.'

'I'm afraid we must insist,' hissed the other soldier, his own hand now hovering close to his weapon.

For a moment, Rufinus considered testing out the theory that they might back down if pressed. Despite the permanent tension between the two units, few incidents had ever been reported. Those that did happen were usually at the lowest levels and kept between those in the know, unreported to the officers. Rufinus, though, was a centurion. A tussle between him and two Praetorians would not go unnoticed and would inevitably be reported. And the outcome of any fight would be far from certain anyway. On a level field, Rufinus was content that he could best them both. But here they were armoured and bore sharp swords, while he carried only his vine stick and a small utility knife. Far from even.

'This is most irregular and will be reported to Prefect Pertinax,' he said in warning, then nodded. 'Lead on.'

The two Praetorians took him by the shortest route out of the orbit of the Cohort's barracks and into the heart of the Praetorian areas of the fortress. A suspicion began to settle on Rufinus and seemed clear to be borne out as they angled towards the elegant, individual houses that belonged to the tribunes.

A sense of foreboding washed over him. They reached a door and stopped there.

'Your vitis,' one of the guardsmen said, pointing to Rufinus' vine stick of office. He shook his head. 'This stays with me.'

'You cannot enter the presence of the tribune armed.'

'Piss off,' snapped Rufinus, and turned to leave. He was surprised, though not unprepared, when the soldier reached for his shoulder. He spun, vitis still firmly jammed under his arm, and his right hand, already bunched into a fist, smashed into the man's face.

As the guardsman fell against the wall, crying out in pain at his broken nose, so Rufinus also yelped at the twin cuts he received on his knuckles from the cheek guards of the man's helmet. The punch had been well-placed, but Rufinus' fist had been larger than the gap between the bronze plates.

The other guardsman's hand went to his sword, but Rufinus levelled a blood-smeared warning finger at him.

'That would not be a clever move, soldier. Your friend got what he deserved for manhandling an officer, and my prefect will stand by me on it. Draw that thing and I'll have to sheathe it again for you. And you won't like where I sheathe it, neither.'

The soldier faltered, stepping back. His friend was still clutching his face and howling, blood flowing out between his fingers as he leaned against the wall. They were drawing attention now from every figure in view. Though he initially wondered about the wisdom of that, he now thought that perhaps it was a good thing. Witnesses to his arrival at the place might not be bad to have.

'Now step away and I shall visit your tribune, with my vitus where it should be: under my arm. You might want to help your friend to a medicus. I can find my own way back.'

Ignoring the man any further, he rapped smartly on the door and pushed it open, not bothering to wait for an instruction from within.

A tribune was a man of senior rank, of course, and with a house of his own within the fortress he was attended by a good level of staff as he would be at home in private life. Consequently, as Rufinus pushed open the door, he almost broke another nose – that of the doorman coming to answer the knock. As the man reeled back from the door and Rufinus strode in, he recovered himself and hurried to intercept, but the centurion was already marching on. Rufinus had been in enough houses like this in his time to know where he was going.

He ignored the two slaves who hurried out to intercept the visitor, marched through the atrium into the courtyard and looked left and right, working out which side contained the tribune's private office. It was not hard to spot, for the door was open and the tribune himself was visible behind a small desk, eating fresh bread and butter and drinking from a pewter goblet. Something nagged at Rufinus' senses, though he couldn't work out what, particularly with all the rain pounding down.

'Ah, good,' the man said, rising at the sight of the bedraggled centurion in the courtyard. Appius Fulvius looked just as sneeringly superior as he had the day Rufinus had first entered this fortress as a centurion a few months ago and bumped into him. Rufinus steadied himself. He was on Fulvius' turf right now. He had to be careful.

The tribune beckoned for him to enter the office and Rufinus did so, standing just close enough to attention not to be disobedient, but still with a fair level of insolence. Fulvius' lip twitched a little.

'How odd,' the man said in his hoarse voice. 'Here you are, just an ordinary Praetorian infantryman. Little more, really, than a legionary dragged out of place. And yet you seem to have acquired a centurionate in the Urban Cohorts, along with your perfectly fictitious name.'

Rufinus felt a pit open beneath him. He'd already panicked long ago that the tribune had identified him when they first met but somehow, since plenty of time had passed and nothing had happened, that worry had been consigned to his rather heavy bag labelled 'things to worry about when I have time'. He'd all-but forgotten about it, but now that worry came flooding back in and it was all Rufinus could do to keep a stoic expression and try not to show weakness. He remained silent. Some people were all about showing off, and he was comfortable that Appius Fulvius was just such a man. If he'd been a man of action and purpose he'd have already struck, and would likely have had him dragged here in chains in the first place anyway. Instead he clearly wanted Rufinus to see how clever he'd been in uncovering it all.

'Gnaeus Marcius Rustius Rufinus,' the man said, steepling his fingers as he sank back into his seat. 'Decorated hero of the Marcomannic wars. A man who saved the emperor's life, so I am told. A friend and supporter of the traitor Perennis, though. A man sent to Dacia to stop causing trouble and who supposedly died there. I wonder who in Dacia might be fascinated to hear that the reports were so wrong.'

'Very clever,' Rufinus nodded. 'You must be pleased with yourself.'

'I am impressed, upon making certain enquiries and digging deep, to discover that you rose to the rank of Prefect of the Misenum fleet recently.'

That, he hadn't expected. How could he have known that? Again that unknown something nagged at him. A feeling like being watched.

'A close ally of the consul Septimius Severus,' Fulvius went on, 'and with a beautiful wife by all accounts, now living somewhere in Sicilia.'

Rufinus shivered. Senova, at least, was a distinct weak spot for him. He would not let anything happen to her. Yes, she supposedly had Severus' protection, but if Fulvius knew this much, then how much more did he know? Still, Rufinus stood silent.

'I have asked myself time and again why such a man should feel the need to create fictional personalities and follow such a peculiar career path. Something underhanded clearly lay at the root of it all. I know that you hate the chamberlain. That much is clear from your dealings with him before Dacia. For a time, I actually thought you were moving against him, despite your ties to consul Severus, who remains steadfast and loyal.'

Rufinus felt a strange wash of panic and hope intertwined. Fulvius had sailed so close to the truth there, and yet seemed to have discarded it, oddly.

'But I learned something from my sources, which led me in new and very unexpected directions, guardsman Rufinus. I learned that you served undercover at the empress' villa a decade ago. The same year, in fact, that I and my tent mates went to that very same place on a mission for our prefect.'

Rufinus shivered again. *That*, then, was why Fulvius had discarded the truth: because he had latched onto *another* truth.

'I looked back over the records of my former companions, though I have to admit that we were never all that close. I'd lost touch with most, and so had been completely aware of how death seems to have followed my unit around, claiming us with alarming regularity.'

Rufinus managed to fight down his panic and hate, and settled into an unpleasantly predatory smile. Fulvius seemed startled for a moment, and then straightened.

'Vedius, killed by your hound. Pollius, victim of a sporting "accident". Glabrio, disappeared one night, never to be seen again. Curtius suicided recently, rather out of character too. Hostilius killed in a tavern latrine by an unknown thug. And then there is me. Very much alive and hearty.'

'And every bit as out of place as me,' Rufinus said quietly. 'I may be a Praetorian infantryman in a centurion's kit, but you are just a Praetorian cavalry trooper who's wheedled his way into command through selling out his oath and throwing in his lot with the chamberlain.'

For a moment, Fulvius shook, and Rufinus could see he was struggling to remain calm. Good. Keep him off-balance.

'You and your friends murdered one of the emperor's frumentarii,' Rufinus went on. 'That sort of thing comes back to haunt you.

'We performed an execution for our commander''

'A corrupt and base commander.'

Fulvius suddenly shot to his feet. 'Do not try me, Rufinus. The only reason you go on as you do is because I have been undecided as to what to do with you.'

And that was when it struck Rufinus, and he smiled wide. 'Of course you are. Because you'd love nothing more than to kill me. But you also know that I'm friends with Severus, and Severus is consul with the emperor, in a prime position to make like difficult for both you and Cleander.'

Gods, but that was a tenuous line to rely upon.

Fulvius nodded, though. He'd hit the nail upon the head. The tribune dare not deal with him without being certain there would be no comeback.

'And so, guardsman Rufinus, I have come to a decision. While your very existence vexes me, we shall have status quo. You shall go about your tedious, dirty little life, and I shall go about mine.'

Rufinus frowned.

'I see you are unsure,' the tribune said. 'Very well. Let me lay it out for you like a military map. I shall not arrest you or unveil your secret, for I would rather not answer to the chamberlain for any difficulty it might bring in terms of the consul and his friends. But equally, you will remove yourself from my life. You shall put in for a transfer if you wish, or simply disappear as you have before. And in return I shall not seek to identify the location of your woman, and I shall let your father blunder on in Rome as though he were some sort of nobleman. Yes, I know of your father, and his disappearance would raise no alarms in the city. So be a good boy. Go away.'

Rufinus felt slightly sick. Not over his father, who had signed his life over to a villain and deserved everything he got. But Senova? He could not risk pushing Fulvius into going after her. That undetermined something troubled him once more, and he felt the hairs on his neck rise. What was it? But Fulvius was watching him, and he had no time to ponder. He nodded.

'Agreed. Though I cannot simply disappear right now. Pertinax appointed me personally because he needs me to keep the city under control. It does none of us any good if the population riots.'

There was a long pause as Fulvius' eyes narrowed, but he also nodded.

'Get out of my sight.'

Rufinus did so, marching away through the house, feeling like a goat that had just walked into a lion's den, circled the beast a few times and left without a scratch. It was not quite feeling good about it all, though. The background worry of Senova remained. As the slaves let him out, he pondered whether he could get a message to her to move. Perhaps back to Cemenelum to hide. But now, with Fulvius having uncovered this much, he would have to be exceedingly careful about everything he did. One wrong move and he could undo everything they'd worked towards.

Senova… but not his father. That uncertain something he'd felt now returned, and finally he knew what it was, and it made some sort of sense. That presence he'd felt like a lurking watcher. It had been his father. His father had been there. And his father was one of few men who knew all those things about Rufinus that Fulvius had uncovered. The sour old man had threatened to reveal him more than once, and he'd finally done it. At least for some reason the information had only reached Fulvius and not Cleander. Thank the gods for small mercies.

Just for now, Fulvius was content to let him go, as he thought he was Rufinus' only target.

There were two option, then. Either he prayed for luck and went after Fulvius anyway, hoping to put the man down before he could do anything, or he let the man go and foreswore his vengeance for the time being, at least until the mess with Cleander was over. He would have to be careful if he did make a move. There was always the possibility that Fulvius had put something into place, such that if he died, Cleander would hear about Rufinus. That would unravel all of it.

But the very idea that Fulvius had threatened Senova cut deep. Cleander had done the same with his brother, and he would not allow someone to threaten his loved ones again.

He realised with a start that not once had Fulvius said he would not move against Rufinus. His terms had been very specific. He had said they would have status quo, but that just meant things going on as they were now. He had said he would not arrest Rufinus, that he would not reveal his secrets. Not once had he said he would not have him killed.

Rufinus was going to have to watch his back. Neither he nor Fulvius would be a ready target within the fortress, but then neither of them could avoid duties in the big, open, dangerous city.

Damn it. Why hadn't he dealt with Fulvius first?

CHAPTER SEVENTEEN – PROPOSAL

Rome, April 190 A.D.

R ufinus looked down at the note.

Visit me. Bacchus

It had been mysterious when it had arrived at his room, delivered by one of the empire's couriers, though Rufinus had spent only a short time puzzling over it. It had not taken him long to unravel *Bacchus*, being the Latin name of the god Dionysus.

It had also not been difficult to rearrange duties so that his century pulled the Aventine shift that afternoon. Pertinax had been happy so long as every shift was adequately covered, and the centurion whose duty it was had been more than happy to swap the troublesome region of the grain warehouses for the *Transtiberim,* which had been Rufinus' assigned region for the day.

They arrived at the horrea in damp air that promised another downpour, and the previous shift gratefully greeted them as they gathered and set off for home.

'Sura? Deploy sixteen men in the streets around the Horrea Galbana. Split the rest into two patrols. I want this place watched as a potential trouble spot.'

The optio saluted and gestured to two tent parties to detach from the unit and guard the horrea.

'I shall be inside, conferring with the Praefectus Annonae.'

Sura nodded and moved away, for there was nothing strange in Rufinus meeting the prefect. Grain was a contentious subject now, and the horrea was a target for public ire. Graffiti and damage were a daily occurrence here now, and every other angry demonstration that arose did so here. Every century that pulled this duty appointed a guard to the horrea, such that the place was under twenty four hour a day surveillance and protection, and yet still the damage occurred.

As the sixteen men moved into position, four at each side of the huge complex, Rufinus strode in through the doorway and made straight for the prefect's office at the far end. Two men stood outside brandishing clubs, both scarred and dangerous looking, almost certainly ex-legionaries.

'Urban Cohort. I need to see the prefect.'

The two men shared a look, but nodded and opened the door for him. The Urban Cohort were trustworthy. They did, after all, provide the main protection for the place at the moment. Rufinus walked in between them and closed the door before wandering over to the desk, where Papirius Dionysus sat, looking tired and drawn.

'I take it all is not well. You're hiring your own guards here now?'

Dionysus looked up with watery eyes. 'It's all well and good having your men here at the horrea and my own guards at home, but given the mood at the moment, I prefer to have a small entourage when travelling between the two. In fact you're lucky to catch me here. I'm not at the horrea often now. There's little that can be done here anyway.'

'Can we talk?'

'As long as you do it quietly.'

'You wanted to see me.'

Dionysus nodded. 'I am having some difficulty. Our mutual enemy is resisting my suggestions. Everything is ready to move, but there is nowhere yet to move it to. He is steadfastly refusing to take on the grain. He insists that it remain in public storage. I think that the worry over becoming a target of public anger is stronger than the desire to be seen to be in control. The worrying thing is that he seems to be drawing away from me somewhat. I think my pressure on him is making him suspicious.'

Rufinus chewed his lip. He had wondered what was the delay in moving the grain.

'And the longer it stays in this situation,' Dionysus went on, 'the more chance there is of me taking a knife in the dark from some disaffected citizen, and the more people starve. We cannot keep this up much longer.'

Rufinus nodded. 'I agree. I have been itching for things to move. But what can I do?'

'Our opposition has called a meeting. The emperor is blissfully unaware of the level of trouble in the city – he has been cloistered away in his seaside villa for long enough that he has missed the rising danger. I think the chamberlain is desperate to resolve Rome's issues before they are drawn to the emperor's attention. The meeting is at the Palatine tomorrow morning, and has been called with a view to sorting the situation finally. I will be present, as will the Praetorian prefects, two or three aediles, and Pertinax, as head of the Urban Cohorts. I need you to find a way to be there too.'

'I fail to see what use I can be,' Rufinus sighed. 'I'm only a centurion.'

'You are Pertinax's eyes on the streets. You see what is happening. You can marshal a persuasive argument. I need the support. Cleander must be persuaded to open his granary.'

Rufinus nodded. 'I think you're right. I also think there needs to be added impetus. Let me think on things. I will be there, though.'

With that he nodded, turned, and strode from the room, back past the two mercenaries and out into the Horrea Galbana. He stopped in the centre of the huge courtyard, usually filled with the bustle of working men and the smells of grain and goods and sweat and horses. Now it was deserted and silent.

How to persuade Cleander to move what paltry grain remained in official sites like this to his own private stores? There had to be a way.

He frowned as he turned a slow circle. What if the grain were endangered? Would that be enough of a spur? If what little existed was imperilled.

Ideas began to filter into his mind. There were half a dozen places like this across Rome. The others were easier targets than the Horrea Galbana, but that would only urge authorities to rely all the more on this central store, which would defeat the purpose.

No. This very place had to be put in danger. But the horrea was under twenty four hour guard by his own Urban Cohorts. His memory helpfully supplied him with an image of the grain offices, a window shutter torn away and black smoke rising into the sky from the windows. Could he dare? He shivered. It was horribly risky. He'd not worried so much about the attempted arson at the statio annonae, for the building had been almost empty, made largely of brick and concrete and with good spaces around it. But the Horrea Galbana was a different matter. It was huge and complex, formed of hundreds of tightly-packed offices and storerooms, some of which contained combustible items such as oil and grain. A fire at the horrea could easily and quickly get out of control, and Rome had a disturbing habit of catching fire, the flames rippling over whole districts and wiping out block after block. It was a very dangerous gamble to even consider a fire.

The only redeeming factor was that with the increased unrest in the city, the vigiles were more attentive than ever. Their stations were on permanent manned alert, and their squads could be spotted around the city, particularly in areas of high risk... such as this.

Was it possible? Was it wise? It would have to happen tonight if it were to be of use in tomorrow's meeting. He shivered again. It *had* to be done, and in his unique position, he was the only man who could do it. And he thought he knew how it should be done, but it would require a little help.

Moments later he was back in Dionysus' office.

'I heartily recommend that you do not work late tonight. And in the meantime can I borrow vellum, ink, wax and a scroll case?'

Rufinus sat at the window of one of the soldiers' bars on the Vicus Longus, the great sloping road that ran from the heart of the city up to the Via Nomentana and the Praetorian fortress. He smiled bleakly. Nine years ago, he had slid and fallen in the road just outside here, on his desperate, drug-addled rush to save the emperor from his sister's blades. Now he was here waiting to betray his own unit, attempt arson and lie to the imperial authorities, all in an attempt to bring down one man.

Had he fallen so far? Still, not as a far as the Guard who served that man, he consoled himself.

He had hoped to gods that the roster hadn't changed when he quickly penned his note in Dionysus' office. It had not been difficult to find a street urchin who would deliver it to the Castra Peregrina for the promise of coin. Whether it had actually reached Cestius and whether the frumentarius could, or indeed would, do as Rufinus asked remained to be seen.

He would find out soon enough. He peered up at the sky. It was just about true dark now, though it was hard to tell with so many torches and lamps in the busy Vicus Longus. He'd heard the blasts announcing the second watch not long before, and had waited at the window, expectant. He had until the end of the second watch. He'd been granted leave in the city for the first two watches of the night and had spent the three hours of the first one firmly establishing his presence in the soldiers' bars along the road, buying drinks for people indulgently and taking part in small inter-century competitions, even goading a bunch of off-duty Praetorians into an almost fist-fight over their honour. He would be remembered as being here. His name would be linked with excess and good humour. Now he had three hours to play with before he needed to be back in the camp, ostensibly sleeping off his hangover.

In actual fact, while raising a cup many times and buying numerous beverages, he'd hardly touched a drop himself. He tensed at the sound of nailed boots crunching along in perfect time and then deflated as a patrol of Praetorians marched past in white togas, on their way to some duty or other.

It was only fifty heartbeats later that the men of the Urban Cohort put in an appearance, another set of crunching boots on stone. Rufinus watched, heart pounding, as they closed on his position. It was Mamertinus's century, as he'd expected, and he let out his first exhaled sigh of relief. It had been the third century under Mamertinus that he'd labelled in his missive to the frumentarii. He'd got the first part right. The second part depended upon Cestius.

Rufinus waited until the unit had moved past, marching on down the street, and had paused until there was a cheer at the bar and the entire occupancy looked away, then slipped from the door and out into the cold air of a Roman spring evening.

He was wearing a nondescript military tunic and belt, with no weapons to hand and neither armour nor badges of office. He could be anyone, at any rank and from any unit, on a night out in the city. Taking a deep breath, he began to follow the men of Mamertinus' unit, slipping in and out of crowds, pausing here and there. He had followed enough people – and been followed by enough – these days to know precisely what he was doing.

The unit took the left hand fork in the road at the grand Avidian nymphaeum. Rufinus wondered where Cestius would strike, if he did, and how. Even prepared as he was, it came as a shock when it happened. The unit of eighty men were marching past a colonnade that sheltered a number of shops closed for the night and now the traditional night time home of beggars and homeless waifs and strays. As they passed there was a sudden strangled shriek and one of the marching men was pulled out of line between the columns. How it had happened was beyond Rufinus, for it was so quick.

Chaos broke out immediately. The entire column bellowed in rage and men ducked between the columns. What had happened to the man was clearly a mystery for though it had happened only heartbeats ago, the rest of the century immediately spread out into the colonnade and side streets, bellowing the name of their missing compatriot in anger and astonishment.

Rufinus shook his head in wonder. How in Hades had Cestius managed that? What he *did* know was that Mamertinus, like all the centurions of the Urban Cohort, was devoted to his men. He would no more abandon his soldier to an uncertain fate and let the unknown abductors get away with it than he would fall on his sword. That century of soldiers would turn the whole district upside down and inside out looking for their missing man. And that would take time.

Bless you, Cestius.

Happy that the second shift were now preoccupied he moved at speed, down the Vicus and across the valley of the amphitheatre, past the Palatine and beneath that aqueduct that still harboured unpleasant memories, up onto the Aventine.

Less than half an hour later he rounded a corner and stopped in the shadows, peering out at the Horrea Galbana. The men of the previous shift were still in position. Chewing his cheek, Rufinus moved back a block and circled the entire complex, which took more than a quarter of an hour. His expectations were met. The men of the century on guard were laid out the same as usual, with four men to each side. A unit of vigiles lounged in a small bar beside a fountain that overlooked the complex, their equipment close to hand. The rest of the century on duty were patrolling, but even now they were angling back towards the horrea. Rufinus moved around until he could see the optio commanding the horrea's guards. There he lurked in the shadows and waited.

The rest of the unit arrived and there was a short, heated debate between the centurion and his optio. They had expected relief in the form of the next shift by now. By rights they should already be marching off back to the Castra Praetoria. But Mamertinus and the next shift had not shown up.

The frustration among the men built over the next quarter of an hour, and Rufinus could imagine how irritated the centurion would be. Finally, the officer called out to his men and offered extra pay and wine rations for four volunteers who would stay to watch the place until the relief arrived. There were sufficient takers and in short order the four volunteers were positioned one to each side of the horrea while the rest of the unit stomped off back towards home.

Rufinus huffed. Stupidly, he had assumed that the centurion would just take his unit home and that for a brief window the horrea would be unguarded. It was an obstacle he would have to overcome.

Content that the rest of the unit had gone, he moved back a block again and circled until he was at his chosen position. During their patrols earlier he had selected his entry point with ease. Like all the exterior walls of this structure the only windows were small and high, making entrance almost impossible. An enterprising thief – or arsonist – though, could still find a way. Like all granaries, the storehouses that held the grain in the Horrea Galbana were constructed on raised floors to allow air circulation that stopped rats nesting beneath the supplies and prevented rot at the base. Most of the apertures for air circulation were too small to admit a human comfortably, of course, but Rufinus had noted one in passing where the brickwork between the gaps had fallen away and was in desperate need to repair work. It would just about admit a man if he struggled.

What he hadn't counted on was doing it under the watchful gaze of a soldier.

With a sigh of regret he admitted to himself that he was going to have to put that man out of commission first and hope that the alarm wasn't raised. Arriving at his chosen spot, he peered from the gloom.

The soldier was leaning against the wall of another warehouse nearby, watching the horrea, his position sufficient to display the entire length of this side wall at once. Even as Rufinus moved closer, he heard the man yawn and grumble. He would not be at his best. He'd already have done a full shift and would be tired and cold and bored. Rufinus moved on the balls of his feet now, the soft leather of his shoes making barely any noise. No one in the bars among the commotion had noticed that he was wearing soft civilian boots, not hobnailed military ones.

He approached the corner, preparing to silence the guard non-lethally, but as he reached the edge of the shadow, Lady Fortuna turned her back on him. He'd always had a tendency to clumsiness and, while it had ebbed somewhat with maturity, it still came back to haunt him from time to time. His foot slipped on a wet flag and he almost went down into the splits, his groin straining at the sudden pain. He yelped, and the guard around the corner was suddenly alert to hear.

Rufinus tried to recover, but the strained groin was painful and he was only just stopping himself from collapsing in a heap. The soldier, nightstick out now, had turned and spotted the man in the uncomfortable position at the corner, gasping with the pain.

Rufinus prepared himself to defend against the man, but instead frowned as the man slid his nightstick back into his belt and reached out sympathetic hands.

'Gods, man but that was impressive,' the soldier said with a grin. 'Can you walk?'

His helping hands reached Rufinus who, with help, pulled himself back upright.

'Thank you so much,' he said to the soldier, with feeling. 'Thank you, and I'm so sorry.'

'Sorry?' the man said, befuddled. 'What for?'

'This,' said Rufinus as his uppercut connected with the man's jaw and sent him sprawling back onto the ground. Rufinus braced himself for another round just in case, but the man simply lay still on the street. Rufinus bent over him, worrying momentarily that he'd done some proper harm, but the man was breathing. He manipulated the jaw a little and was relieved that it didn't appear to be broken. The soldier had been doing his duty and had gone above and beyond that duty to help a citizen in trouble. He'd not deserved this.

Regretfully, Rufinus dragged him back into the shadows and then began to move across the street. Ordinarily he would have loped like a gazelle or slunk like a cat. With the tearing pain in his groin, what he in fact did was lurch like a nauseous stork until he reached the wall of the horrea. It occurred to him unpleasantly that he would have to do everything he could until this injury healed to hide the fact that it had happened, for tomorrow, when the repercussions of tonight were being felt, there would be blame attached to a sneaky citizen with an injured groin.

Grumbling to himself at his luck, Rufinus dropped to the air hole at ground level. He was starting to worry whether he had overestimated the size of the opening, but there was little for it now but to try. He had such little time. Eventually Mamertinus would arrive with his men. Soon, mister helpful would wake up. And even if neither of those occurred, one of the other soldiers might just stroll round to say hello to his mate and find him unconscious in the shadows with a bruised chin.

Time was short.

Hissing with discomfort and pain, Rufinus wriggled into the gap, which was dark and cold, admitting a breeze, stank of rats and animal urine and far worse, and was filthy and damp. He wriggled further in until he was happy he was out of view from the street and then stopped, facing upwards. Above him, the stone flags of the granary were not identifiable in the dark, and he had to run his hands across them to find an edge.

He reached into the pouch at his belt that held three things and removed the first of them: a chisel. Moments later he was using it to scrape and tap and crack the mortar between stones. He knew he was succeeding by the simple evidence of mortar powder falling directly into his face. Once he had loosened it enough that he could feel the flag moving as he pushed, he replaced the chisel and pressed both palms against the stone, pushing until it lifted.

He was in. As the stone fell back, he rose like some sewer demon from the rancid air duct and climbed into the room, blinking away mortar dust. The extent of the grain shortage was never more clear than here and now. On any normal day, this room would be almost bursting with swollen sacks of grain, stamped with their provincial logo of origin. This room, large and echoing, held nine sacks, barely enough to feed the vigiles for a few days, let alone any ordinary citizens.

He shook himself. No time to worry and wonder. His groin ached like Hades, but he lurched around, at least knowing that no one would see him here. Once more the chisel came out and this time he moved around those nine sacks, ripping and tearing so that the whole room filled with dust and chaff, a choking cloud. He lugged the sacks into a pile and scattered handfuls of grain around. Then, with a deep breath, praying that he was doing the right thing and that the local vigiles were truly on their game, he reached into the pouch and retrieved his second item.

The fire-orb was an old soldier's trick. A roughly spherical object wrapped in linen, he unravelled it and peered at the fungus within. Found growing on the side of ash trees, the fungus burned slowly and held an ember for many hours with very little air. Soldiers would ignite the heart of one and then close it, wrap it up and carry it with them. Then, at the end of a long day of marching, they might have to gather fire wood, but at least they would have a ready source of fire to ignite them.

He pulled apart the two halves of the fungus he had lit in his room a few hours ago and, sure enough, there at the heart was a deep orange ember. He blew gently on it a few times to coax it back into life – a trick he had learned in those cold Pannonian winters during the war a decade ago – and once it was properly alight once more he prepared himself. He piled up the linen in which it had been wrapped on the top of the loose grain above the sacks, and then carefully placed the fungus atop it.

With a prayer to both Fortuna and Vulcan, he adjusted the positioning of the glowing fungus and then lurched back over to the hole in the floor, cursing his crotch all the way. At the hole in the floor once more, he dropped and slid himself down into the air duct, pulling the stone flag back over with a grunt.

Moments later he was shuffling along the channel and then pulling himself back up into the empty night time street. He angled for a different side road this time, not wanting to be next to the soldier he'd punched when the man woke up. There, lurking in the shadows, he waited and watched.

Had something gone wrong? Had his fungus simply gone out? His heart fell as he heard the rhythmic tramp of nailed boots announcing that Mamertinus and his century had finally arrived. Rufinus pulled back a little and stood silent, waiting, hoping.

He could hear shouts, and now they rose in consternation. Whistles were blown and feet began to run. The unconscious soldier had been found. Damn it. He couldn't stay. They'd be searching the entire area any moment.

He watched the ominously silent and dark horrea for only a moment more, and then turned and ran with the pained gait of a three legged gazelle. He was three blocks away and huffing when the horrea went up. There was an initial crack, almost like an explosive, and then a sudden commotion of cries a few streets back and the whistles of officers.

Rufinus ran.

Not far from the temple of Diana, he stopped at the small privately owned bath house he had visited after the morning shift. There he found the third and final item in his pouch: a chit from the bath house, and handed it to the attendant, whose nose wrinkled at Rufinus' stench. Still, word of him being here would never reach the Castra Praetoria at the far side of the city.

He bathed and cleaned as fast as he could, and then changed into the clean clothes he had left in the changing room, including proper soldier's boots. Gathering up his stinking, grotty clothes, he bade the attendant a good evening and went on his way, dumping his used clothes on a refuse pile in an alley he passed and then walking steadily up the street biting down on the pain and trying not to show evidence of his aching crotch. By the end of the second watch he was in his bed, lying on his back, which seemed to be the only option with his groin strain, and smiling to himself, hoping silently that the vigiles had managed to control the blaze and that the horrea, and indeed the whole Aventine, remained standing.

The next morning brought news. Among the stories sweeping across the fortress was a gem about some soldier in Mamertinus' century who had somehow disappeared as they marched through the city. He had been found half an hour later, after a thorough search, sprawled naked in a fountain, wearing a donkey mask and with a lump the size of an egg on his head, with no recollection of what had happened.

Other news included an arson attempt at the Horrea Galbana. The professional vigiles had managed to contain the blaze well, but it had burned four warehouses in the complex, including olive oil, grain and a stack of expensive cloth from Judea. There was talk that the Cohort would have to start pulling double shifts and concentrating more on guard duties than preventative patrols.

All this whirled around Rufinus' head as he accompanied Pertinax with his century of men, heading for the Palatine. Securing the duty of accompanying detail had been simple. Pertinax had been happy to accept Rufinus' request, though he had given the centurion a thoughtful look as he did so, as though trying to remember where he knew him from. That look was starting to worry Rufinus.

Still, here he was accompanying the prefect up the palace steps. Praetorian guardsmen were in evidence all across the

Palatine, as strong a presence as if the emperor himself were in residence, which he was not, taking the sea air as he was. Another sign of Cleander's ever-growing power, that, but not the worst, nor the most shocking. That came as they were ushered into the aula regia. Cleander was seated in the emperor's own chair, upon the dais and facing the room, as though he ruled Rome himself. Rufinus ruminated sourly on how that was almost the case, now.

He had kept his gaze on the Praetorians as they passed, having left the unit of the Urban Cohort at the door. He'd half expected to see Mercator or Icarion, but they were not in evidence. Part of him wondered at how he'd passed so long now around and among the Guard without seeing either of his old friends. Perhaps they had retired or sought provincial duties to keep out of Cleander's way, for he couldn't imagine either of them falling in with the chamberlain's lot. The alternative, that they had refused and had met a grisly end, was another worrying possibility.

He tore his thoughts away from Merc and Icarion and instead concentrated on the state audience hall. Praetorians stood at every door, and two beside Cleander's 'throne'. The man was always well-protected these days. At least Appius Fulvius was not one of them. The two Praetorian prefects who served beneath Cleander were there, as was Papirius Dionysus and a number of fellows Rufinus did not know. Septimius Severus was notable to Rufinus through his absence. He tried to assign to the consul the honourable notion that he was keeping himself detached in order to drive a wedge between Cleander and the emperor, and not that he was just trying to keep his hands clean for plausible deniability.

'Tell me what must be done,' Cleander said sharply as the doors to the chamber clicked shut and left them alone.

'The food must go to the people,' said one of the aediles present flatly.

'What food?' snorted another.

'Quite,' Dionysus put in. 'There is little more than a trickle reaching Rome now and although the grain fleet grows once more, it will be months or even years before the dole reaches its full flow. We are barely managing to feed the emergency services, let alone the people.'

'We must increase the tribute and taxation on the grain provinces,' the first aedile said. 'And promote new grain farms in the others. I hear Dacia has prime grain land, and yet all we get from there is gold and trouble, and neither of them fill bellies.'

Pertinax shook his head. 'You can impose whatever taxes you like, gentlemen, but they will not increase the grain flow. The plague has depopulated whole regions. Farms wilt and die untended. I saw it in Africa as its governor. There is no swift solution to this. Many more Romans will starve before the problem goes away. Your first step must be the plague. Have all the physicians you can find bend to seeing this latest outbreak gone. Sacrifice to the gods and pray like a childless couple. For when the plague declines, so will the population in the provinces rise once more, and the farmlands will begin to recover. Then you will get all the grain you need. And by that time, the fleets will have been reassembled. Sadly, that is all there is to it. Time. We must bear out our current discomfort with stoic patience and attempt to keep the city from tearing itself apart while we wait.'

Cleander rapped his finger-ring rhythmically on the emperor's throne arm.

'You are telling me that nothing can be done. We can but wait.'

'I am.'

'And so, Prefect, what do we do with Rome in the meantime, for the city seethes.'

'You must hoard the grain,' Dionysus said harshly.

'I have told you my thoughts on this time and again, man,' Cleander snapped. 'I will not be responsible for the grain. That is your job, and yours alone. Keep it in the public warehouses. It's not as if you're short of room.'

Rufinus looked across at Pertinax, a question in his expression. The prefect, who seemed to have forgotten the centurion was with him, nodded, and cleared his throat.

'Sometimes, gentlemen, we might be accused of seeing things from too lofty a position. Might we benefit from an eye at street level? One of my senior centurions: Maximus.'

Rufinus cleared his throat, desperately hoping Cleander didn't see through his thin disguise as Fulvius had.

'Sirs, all I can say is that the unrest in the city threatens what supplies we do have. There are almost daily demonstrations outside the public horrea. Someone vandalised and attempted to destroy the empty grain offices. Last night someone tried to set fire to even the great Horrea Galbana, which is under constant surveillance. Matters are only getting worse daily and the Cohort is becoming stretched in its need to keep control, even with Praetorian support. If this is what we face now, what might we see a month from now, or two?'

He gestured over at Dionysus.

'I fear the Praefectus Annonae has the right of it, and the only feasible solution for now. The people know there is grain in the public warehouses and as long as they do, those places will remain targets for them. The grain must be moved to secure locations out of the public domain, where they can be safeguarded and rationed out to those to whom it does the most good. Then when the public horrea are empty, the public outcry at such places will dissipate. Think on it, sirs. Grand public edifices known to be withholding grain and guarded by soldiers of Rome, or small private warehouses out of the public eye that can be more than adequately guarded by private forces which do not draw public attention.'

He'd gone on longer than he intended, and had somewhat hammered the point. He could see the worry in Dionysus' eyes, for the man also thought Rufinus had gone too far. There was a long, uncomfortable silence. Finally, just when Rufinus was starting to tremble, Cleander nodded.

'Claudius,' he gestured to one of the aediles, 'we recently took control of several granaries, did we not?'

'We did, sir.'

'Details?'

'The Horrea Ummidiana were the most recent, sir. They've been floating around in a state of chaos for years, ever since the emperor's sister failed in her plot. They were impounded with much of the family estate and have stood empty. Only recently did we look at reinstating them or selling off the land to developers.'

'So these granaries are currently unused and all-but unknown?'

'They are, sir. I have the documents for exchange of ownership and change of purpose on my desk.'

'Then move the grain to there. Keep it secret and do not advertise the fact. The grain's new location must be hidden from public view.'

Rufinus tried not to smile. Tried not to let his elation show. He could see in Papirius Dionysus' flat face the fact that the man was also holding in his jubilation. There were many nods around, and Rufinus settled back now into silence, feeling the approving gaze of Pertinax upon him. He'd done well, as far as everyone in the room was concerned, no matter what their goal.

He allowed himself a small covert smile as the discussion moved on to what to do to increase the grain flow once this current crisis was over.

As the discussion ebbed and flowed, Rufinus let it all wash over him. In his private silence, he was wondering at what must happen next. The whole point of this was to make Cleander responsible. Having the grain held in hidden granaries under the name of dead traitors would be of little use.

He looked up briefly and caught the expression of Dionysus as the man looked back at him. There it was. Determination and contentment. Rufinus had no idea how he was going to do it, but Dionysus clearly had a plan for the next step. In the meantime, Rufinus would have to keep the peace, preserve the grain and try not to fall foul of a blade in the dark sent by a certain Praetorian tribune.

At least life in Rome was never dull.

CHAPTER EIGHTEEN – THE AVENTINE

Rome, late April 190 A.D.

The century of men of the Urban Cohort waited patiently at the second mile marker of the Via Aurelia. Rufinus shuffled from foot to foot. After so long here he was, facing the calends of May and finally beginning the push that would end this drawn-out nightmare.

True to his knowing smile, Papirius Dionysus had somehow contrived to get the impounded warehouses of the Horrea Ummidiana signed over into Cleander's name. The confirmation had arrived two days ago in another cryptic message that had come courtesy of one of Nicomedes' trusted couriers.

All was in place. They had the flames roaring and they had the pot of water. Now they needed to put the pot on the fire and watch it boil. The granaries belonged to Cleander, and he had given the order to fill them with the meagre grain from the public warehouses to keep it safe, on the condition that the move remained secret.

Dionysus had been very conscientious over that last part. Complying with Cleander's instructions, he had begun shipping out oil and all manner of goods stored in the Horrea Galbana on the pretext of ordering repairs to the burned parts of the complex. The movements had initially drawn a crowd who had been interested in the moving of goods out of Rome's main public granary, but they had dispersed and lost interest when it was revealed that it was other, non-critical goods that were actually being shipped out.

Dionysus received the approval of Cleander for his care. And both knew that the grain could now be slipped out amid the other goods without raising a public outcry.

What remained now was for Rufinus to ruin all that.

He had waited patiently as the timing unfolded. Dionysus continued to ship out nonessential and uninteresting loads right until the next coded message came. Senova's fleet had docked at Centum Cellae in secret some forty-five miles north, along the coast and out of the main focus of trade and officialdom. There, sufficient grain to feed Rome for a month or more had been unloaded in secret at night and transferred to very nondescript wagons. The next morning the huge caravan had begun to travel the Via Aurelia to Rome.

Rufinus had made sure some time ago that Pertinax assigned him to the grain project, which the prefect was happy to do given the centurion's close involvement thus far. Rufinus and his men had been taken off regular duties and assigned full-time to liaise with Dionysus and the grain office. Consequently here they were, outside Rome to the west of the city, watching the long grain caravan rumbling towards them.

This was it. It was all about to explode, and he knew that as soon as word reached Cleander the man would be furious. Blame would have to be carefully spread around so that no one man took the chamberlain's ire, else there would be executions.

The wagons began to roll past him and up towards the rise. Alongside the road the great arches of the Aqua Traiana carried the least palatable of Rome's long-distance water supply into the city, where it spilled into decorative fountains and sporting facilities, eventually flushing out latrines and baths before pouring into the Tiber having never once been drunk from. The aqueduct gradually converged with the rising ground until it became little more than a low wall with a flagged top that continually rumbled and gurgled alongside the road. Rufinus tried to neither look at it nor think about it. He'd had enough of aqueducts in his short and eventful life. Rarely had they been a good thing.

Rufinus gestured to his optio and the man nodded, relaying commands to the soldiers, sending them along the line to provide adequate protection to the seventy two wagons full of grain. The private guard that had accompanied the grain all the way from Gaul were men selected by Severus during his tenure there, and could be trusted. They settled in alongside the Urban Cohort for the last two mile stretch into the city centre, the combined force allowing an allocation of two men to each wagon.

The rise crested and then dipped a little between the estate walls of large sub-urban villas owned by the rich and powerful. Here and there they caught sight of the aqueduct at almost ground level and then it began to reappear as the land dipped, marching once more on arches across the ground to the city.

Rufinus braced himself. This last section was the part that might bring trouble. The road began to rise once more to the top of the Janiculum hill. The aqueduct disappeared again and the road began to sprout houses and shops to either side. Then, finally, they crossed the saddle and Rome lay before them.

He sighed at the sight. Rarely had he ever approached Rome from this direction, but the scene was breath-taking enough to make him wish he did. Truly she was the queen of cities. From this vantage point he could see the Transtiberim region marching off down the slope to the river, at the bottom: the bridge they would cross. By dint of accident and natural routing, they would then have to ascend the Aventine and pass right by the Horrea Galbana on the way to their final destination.

Now, people were appearing at doorways and peering out.

The wagons were covered and could, in theory, have contained any kind of goods, but a convoy this long with this level of guard pointed very clearly to the likelihood of long-awaited grain. Breathless awe rippled through the crowds they passed. The people of Rome watched in stunned relief as seventy two wagons bore down on the capital.

Rufinus felt his pulse quicken. All it would take was one man with a little too much bravado and they could be fighting off hungry citizens. Even those floundering at the kerbside, covered in buboes and coughing up their life, lifted their faces in hope. Rufinus was once more struck by guilt at the knowledge of what they had done to the people of Rome, and what they must yet do.

The wagons rolled down the slope, the drivers applying the brake poles with every ounce of muscle to prevent the heavy vehicles racing out of control down the hill. Rufinus' men and the Gallic guards both occasionally leapt to the aid of teamsters to keep their wagons moving at the steady pace required to avoid disaster. After what seemed an age, the aqueduct long gone and the high, strong buildings of central Rome closing in, they neared the river, as any man could confirm by smell alone.

The Pons Aemilianus stood before them, and a small unit of the Urban Cohort who happened to be on patrol moved to clear the bridge of common traffic to allow the wagons past. Rufinus breathed in slowly. As yet no sign of Praetorians. That was unusual. They were often to be seen in the city, if only in pairs. With luck their kind would not encounter the wagon train until it was at least past the Aventine.

Their kind! As if he were not one of them in truth.

Across the river the wagons rolled, now within sight of the Palatine and the Capitol. Rufinus wondered if Cleander perhaps stood on some balcony up there, observing his city and unaware still of the convoy rolling through it that would spell his doom.

As they climbed the Aventine it became clear that they had picked up quite a crowd of citizens. By the time they reached the Horrea Galbana, there was something of a throng in their wake. At the head of the column, Rufinus turned the corner and found Papirius Dionysus standing outside the front of the complex, a dozen of his private guard around him. At the sight of Rufinus, he gave a signal and the doors of the horrea opened.

A second crowd had gathered outside the public warehouses, drawn by the sight of the grain commissioner himself. Now, they gave an awed rumble as four more wagons rolled out of the horrea. Clearly, after days of moving uninteresting goods from here, these four could have contained anything, but the arrival of such a huge caravan to combine with them suggested otherwise.

As the four wagons moved to fall in line with Rufinus' convoy, filtering in among the foreign vehicles, Dionysus strode over to Rufinus, his litter borne aloft behind him, guards staying close.

Rufinus nodded his greeting.

'Prefect.'

Dionysus looked about. The only men close enough to hear anything over the din of the wagons and beasts and the thuds of footsteps were his own guards and Rufinus' soldiers.

'This is it.'

'Yes.'

'When Cleander finds out there is ample food in the granaries, he will explode.'

Rufinus snorted. 'Or when he finds out more grain has arrived from Gaul without him being notified. Or when he discovers that despite his intentions he now owns the Horrea Ummidiana. Or when he discovers that the public are aware of the storage. We're up to our necks in the latrine now, Prefect. All we can do is hope that he doesn't learn of much of this until it's too late.'

Dionysus nodded, and shivered. The dank cellars under the Palatine and the men of a rather specialised Praetorian unit awaited any man who sufficiently aggravated Cleander. All they had to do now was string it out until things had gone too far.

'How will the people find out that Cleander owns the granaries?' Rufinus said quietly.

'I have no idea. I left that in the hands of Severus and his pet frumentarius. But I feel confident that it will happen. Come on.'

They moved ahead once more and Dionysus climbed into his litter, moving like the high-ranking public figure he was, Rufinus stomping alongside. As he marched, Rufinus ran through everything, as he had done night after sleepless night.

Yes, Cleander would explode. And the only thing that would save any man he targeted would be an adequate excuse or no clear culpability.

The granaries they were heading for now belonged to Cleander. The chamberlain couldn't know that or he'd have had the whole thing stopped. And though he'd been unaware of his ownership, somewhere along the line, he had to have put his seal to the documents of ownership without realising it. With the amount of empire building Cleander had achieved in the last few years, claiming stolen property and lands for himself, it had probably been easy enough to slip this one through with a slew of others. While some of his minor administrative staff might suffer for the failure, the end guilt could fall with no one but himself for approving his ownership.

For the public knowledge of his ownership there could be no clear fault. Even Rufinus didn't know how that would be achieved, though all it would take was one whispered comment in the forum and within an hour it would be rumour flying through the city. It would be easy enough and locating the original source of the rumour would be like hunting a specific turd in the Tiber.

The moving of the grain had been done on Cleander's orders and while he might whine that he'd done so on the advice of the prefects of both the grain supply and the Urban Cohorts, the decision had very definitely been his and he would have to shoulder that blame.

The knowledge of the grain being shifted was something different. Dionysus had thus far managed to accede to Cleander's wishes and keep the whole thing quiet. Now, though, the public would know. They would know that the grain had been moved to these private granaries, and they would know just how much there was. All they could do with that was hold up their hands and say that they simply couldn't move grain in the city without drawing public attention. It was such a focus for everyone's mind, it would be near impossible. That might land any of them in trouble, but in the end it would be labelled an unavoidable issue. Still, given how heavily Cleander's hand might come down in response, Rufinus was ready to run and change clothes once more. Better a night flight from the city than an evening with a hot knife in a cellar.

Then came the big one. The arrival of the foreign grain. If and when Cleander learned of that, he would seek someone's head, and only solidarity across the whole conspiracy might save any of them. Rufinus and Pertinax could claim that all they had done was supply an appropriate guard to the wagons, and when asked why they didn't report such important news to Cleander's men, they would have to shrug and say that they had not realised it was their responsibility to do so. They were the Urban Cohort, not the grain dole.

Severus would come under scrutiny, for it was he who had coordinated the ships and the naval grain supply from Arelate in Gaul, through his friend and fellow governor. He would be identified as the source of the grain. Severus would shrug and tell Cleander that he arranged relief for the city. He would escape the worst of trouble, though. Cleander might not baulk at confronting a consul, but Severus was a powerful man and had the support of the emperor. Not only that but when it was made known that Severus had been the source of the food sent to save Rome he would be a public hero. No, Cleander couldn't afford to come down on him.

That left Dionysus. As grain commissioner, he would naturally be the target for blame. Dionysus had done the best he could. He and Nicomedes of the courier service had arranged for several couriers and messages to be recorded as missing. If Cleander accused them of not warning him of the impending grain shipments, they would lay the blame with the missing couriers. It was a poor excuse and not guaranteed to save them, but it was the best they could do.

What they needed was for the city to turn all its hate and anger now against Cleander. Once he was firmly villainised in the eyes of Rome, one demand made of the emperor and the chamberlain's life would be forfeit. It was still a waiting game, after all, but an ever more taut and dangerous one, and now close to the end.

And Rufinus faced a difficult time during that wait, regardless of what happened with Cleander. He had to keep peace in the city, stop riots and destruction, and yet manage somehow to shift any resentment and blame to the chamberlain.

They crossed now the dip between the Aventine and Little Aventine hills and passed the high walls of a villa that had once been a private urban residence of the emperor Hadrian, bearing down on their destination.

The Horrea Ummidiana consisted of an 'L'-shaped complex of three storeys set around a deep courtyard. Only one entrance pierced the exterior into the courtyard, though small shops and offices let out onto the side streets from the lowest storey. Rufinus wondered for a moment why all the shops seemed to be closed up and dark, and then realised that with the ownership of the complex having been somewhat vague over the past decade, those folk who had rented spaces for their stores could no longer do so and had moved out to other locations. As they neared, Rufinus located the set of keys he had been given and gestured to Sura.

'Go ahead and open up the main gate. Take eight men and secure it all, and then another eight inside to check out all the storage and equipment. Should all be in order, but let's be sure before we commit to unloading.'

As the optio saluted and began to give out orders, Rufinus peered at the structure ahead of them. Theoretically the place had been cleared and made ready, but Rufinus was not naïve enough to believe that without checking.'

'How do we do this sir?' the nearest teamster asked, waving at him. It was a fair question. At the Horrea Galbana they would be able to fit all these wagons in the three great courtyards. The Horrea Ummidiana was far smaller, with a correspondingly minor courtyard and only one gate.

'We taken in four wagons at a time. Unload, and while the shipments are being moved into storage, the empty wagons can manoeuvre back out and head for the compound near Mons Testaceus and the next four can move in. If we're efficient enough we can have the granaries full and every vehicle in storage by nightfall.'

The teamster smiled. 'Look at that lot, general. Rather you than me.'

Rufinus followed his angled thumb and felt his nerves rise once more. The crowd they had slowly gathered since they crested the hill across the river was now huge. In fact, if Rufinus were inclined to apply a collective noun to it, that noun would be 'mob'. All they were missing now were a load of broken half-bricks and flickering torches and…

As if the gods were laughing at him, someone on the edge of that crowd produced a stout club of light wood and hefted it.

'Shit.'

The mob were moving ever closer to the wagons, and the men of the Urban Cohorts and the Gallic mercenaries who had accompanied the caravan moved together to hold them back.

'This is going to get messy any moment, sir,' one of his soldiers said close by.

Rufinus nodded. In a way that was good. In a very personal and unpleasant way, it was also really, really bad. Time to capitalise on it. He rushed over to the wagon close by and, to the driver's surprise, launched himself up onto the board seat. There he could see the streets around them, and he swallowed sudden nerves. There were a lot more people here than he had realised. In fact, if this went *really* wrong, by the mere law of numbers, his men stood no chance. He was walking a very fine line between keeping the peace and provoking a dangerous mob. He swallowed, his throat suddenly dry.

'People of Rome...'

It took precious moments for the crowd's unruly rumble to die down and Rufinus realised with irritation that he had chosen the lead cart for his rostrum just as Sura had opened the gates. The next four wagons began to rumbled past him and towards the door of the horrea. Rufinus waited foolishly for them to pass and for the entire column to shift four wagons closer before trying again.

'People of Rome, please remain calm.'

'Fuck calm,' bellowed an unseen orator from the crowd.

'What you see here is not what you think. This is naval supplies and goods for the circus and arena going into private storage.'

An uncertain murmur rippled across the crowd. Rufinus narrowed his eyes. Were they really that credulous? Surely they had already decided all the way across Rome that this was a grain shipment. Rufinus had been trained in oratory and rhetoric as a youth, but even *he* would not have believed this.

'This operation is carried out under the aegis of the Urban Cohorts on the orders of the chamberlain, Marcus Aurelius Cleander.'

It sounded so impressive. It was the Urban Cohorts job, but it was Cleander's fault. The crowd looked a little mollified. Rufinus stared in disbelief. Were they really going to disperse on such a flimsy lie?

'Why's the grain prefect here, then?' someone bellowed, much to Rufinus' relief.

'We have shipped a few supplies from the public warehouses under his control,' Rufinus stated glibly.

The crowd grumbled once more, but Rufinus was pleased to hear a note of suspicion about it. Now was the troublesome moment. He couldn't afford this to erupt into a bloodbath, but the people needed to leave today knowing that Cleander was withholding their grain.

He stood on the wagon and watched. The crowd seemed to tense, in preparation. Rufinus hoped his men were prepared.

Time passed with infinite slowness, every breath of civilian and soldier alike grating on Rufinus' nerves, and the tense wait was broken suddenly as the four carts began to emerge from the horrea once more, now empty and hurrying off into a southern side street, making for the huge mound of discarded broken pots that had become so mountainous that it had taken on a hill name of its own.

Rufinus watched them go and willed the waiting crowd to see what he could so clearly see. He realised they had spotted the sign only when the tone of the constant grumble turned cold and sour. They had spotted it. Chaff and fragments of grain bouncing from the empty carts as they departed. The bags had been nicely sealed on arrival and there was no tell-tale sign on the waiting convoy, but those carts that had been emptied had caught stray grain and were now discarding it as they bounced along the street.

'Oi,' bellowed someone. 'That's grain.'

Well done, Rufinus thought. *A golden wreath to Citizen Brains over there.*

The crowd suddenly surged with discontent. Rufinus looked bac

k along the line. Four more wagons were moving into the horrea and he realised that the drive of the one upon which he was standing was glaring at him, willing him to move so he could get in there, unload, and get gone before he ended up being torn apart by hungry Romans.

The convoy shuffled forward once more to the soundtrack of anger and misery. Sixty four wagons remained waiting to unload, sufficient number that Rufinus could not see more than perhaps halfway along the line, the last ones a distant haze. This was going to take a while, and every moment things became more dangerous.

A few hundred paces away along the line, a small scuffle broke out. Rufinus bellowed for his men to hold position and watched nervously. Some of the braver members of the watching crowd had pushed forward, barging one soldier and one Gallic guard out of the way. While half a dozen of them tried to keep those two busy, others were suddenly up into the wagon and checking the contents.

'Grain,' the man bellowed from the wagon top. The crowd roared.

Rufinus watched the two men defending the caravan struggling not to disappear under the weight of the crowd. This was enough. He'd done what he needed to. The people knew now without a shadow of a doubt that Cleander was hoarding grain in some private granary. And when the rumour began to circulate, quite truthfully in fact, that these granaries were now also owned by the chamberlain, nothing he could do would repair the damage done to his public reputation.

Now, the critical point was not letting this evolve into a full-blown riot.

He dropped from the wagon and hurried along behind the nervous line of guards until he was close to the trouble spot, where his men were pushing and shoving back at the public jostling them, all of them angry, no one yet wounded or wielding a dangerous weapon. Nearby, he climbed another wagon and pulled his way along the side above the seething crowd until he reached the one the angry man who'd found the grain was on. He stopped as the man turned to face him and lifted both hands in a gesture of peace.

'What's your name?' he shouted at the man.

The strangeness of this request in the midst of rising chaos cut into the crowd and those nearby fell silent, watching and listening.

'Corbulo,' the man said suspiciously.

'You a merchant? A family man?'

'Don't threaten me.'

'I'm not,' Rufinus said calmly. 'No threat. I'm Maximus. Centurion Gaius Valerius Maximus.'

'Corbulo. I work for the aqueduct inspection team on the Esquiline.'

'Important work,' Rufinus said. The man glared at him, narrow-eyed, wondering whether he was being sarcastic.

'No, honestly. I know aqueducts, believe me. It *is* important work. Probably more important than mine.'

'Definitely,' snorted the man.

'Family?'

'Two daughters. Five and three.'

'You poor sod. Probably already saving for the dowries, eh?'

The crowd nearby chuckled, and Rufinus took a steadying breath. The mood had shifted. Only slightly and only subtly, but the threat of violence had receded notably.

'Corbulo, you know what's going on here the same as me. All I'm doing is escorting it from one place to another on the orders of the bosses. I have no more say when and where it gets distributed than you do. I can only assume there's a good reason for it, and I'm sure in due course the chamberlain will make his reasons clear and order the dole given out.'

The man nodded, uncertainly and unhappily, but he understood.

'Now the thing is, Corbulo, that we are both just working mules in the machine of state. But if you and the rest of these people take it upon yourselves to try and raid the wagons then it becomes my duty and that of my men to stop you. That's a huge crowd, with some nasty rocks and sticks, and my men have batons. If this goes tits-up, an awful lot of people are going to be wounded, on both sides of the fight. And you know that before any crowd can get away with these sacks, other units of the Cohort and the vigiles will come and join in. Then, gods help us all, the Praetorians might show up, and they won't even bother with sticks. They'll use swords. What we're looking at is bloodbath of epic proportions, and I most certainly don't want that. Do you?'

There was a dangerous pause, but the man shook his head.

'No, of course you don't. Now please help me disperse this crowd before anyone gets hurt and let the administration do its job. No one starves their own people on purpose. Cleander must had a reason. Just wait until we hear what it is.'

Silence. Not just from Corbulo, but across the whole crowd. Everyone was listening carefully now, citizens and soldiers, mercenaries and foreign teamsters.

The man on the wagon with him nodded. 'You speak sense, Centurion.'

A murmur of resigned misery flowed through the crowd. As Corbulo echoed his sentiments to the people and helped him avoid disaster, Rufinus swallowed a knot of tension. All it would have taken was for the very reasonable man on the wagon next to him to be a little less understanding and right now he'd be watching men kill each other. Disaster was coming that close.

And now, with this last very clear move, he had set the final piece of the game in position.

He had averted a riot. He had moved the grain. He had blamed Cleander very publically.

Today was a good day.

Unless the chamberlain found out…

CHAPTER NINETEEN – MEETINGS AND DEPARTURES

Rome, Early May 190 A.D.

Rufinus looked around himself at the somewhat miserable interior of the statio annonae.

'Are you settling in, then?'

Dionysus nodded distractedly as he ran a finger down a long list on the desk. 'Slowly. We're having to work around the damage, but it's not as if there's a huge amount of work to do.'

Rufinus nodded. It made sense in a way. The prefect had moved his central administration back to the smaller office complex near the circus for several reasons. Firstly, the Horrea Galbana had ceased to have any real part in the grain dole for the time being anyway and was now largely a huge conglomeration of empty warehouses and offices. Secondly, while the statio had been the target of arson and had suffered a little damage before extinguishing, so had the horrea, so that made little difference. But thirdly, and perhaps most importantly, the statio was a small complex and therefore considerably easier to defend if the crowds that still periodically gathered outside turned ugly.

Dionysus had doubled the number of his hired guard at his house and now brought half of them with him any time he moved through the city. With that solid force and the two centuries of the Urban Cohorts now assigned to him, he was as safe as he could hope to be in this seething city.

'You wanted to see me?'

Dionysus looked up and then crossed to the door, peering this way and that into the corridor before closing it. 'Yes,' he said quietly. 'We might have a problem.'

'Oh?'

'It seems that the prefect of Aegyptus has done a sterling job whipping his local boys until they gave their all. Word has reached me that a fleet of sixty or so ships of varying sizes is gathering in Alexandria ready to transport enough grain to relieve the current trouble.'

'Shit.'

'Succinctly put. If that shipment arrives then everything we have done is for nothing. And there is just no way to stop it. Even if you were still commanding the fleet you couldn't do much about that. There is now no danger from pirates and even with the best will of Neptune I don't think we can hope for another maritime disaster on the scale of the last one. Our only hope is to bring this to a head before the fleet arrives.'

'How long will that be?' Rufinus asked breathlessly.

'I don't know. Could be ten days, could be two months. Depends how long it takes for them to gather the fleet and load the grain for transport, and also on sailing conditions, of course.'

'It might still be possible. Things here are so close. Rome teeters. I see the dangers every day, and already the chamberlain's name turns sour on the lips of the people. Just pray that fleet doesn't arrive and spoil it all.'

Dionysus nodded. 'I'm doing everything I can. I've spoken to Nicomedes. All reports bound for Ostia and Rome have been diverted to me, so as far as I am aware I am the only official in the whole of Italia who knows of the impending fleet. Rumour will travel, of course, and there's little we can do about that. But without an official report, it will still be considered just rumour.'

'Well...'

Rufinus' words trailed off as they both heard doors slamming back and the tromp of hobnails on marble. The two men shared a worried look and then stepped aside to face the door. Whoever it was could only be here to see the prefect.

The office door opened sharply without even a knock, and Rufinus felt his pulse race at the sight of Praetorian white as the soldiers stepped aside for their master.

Marcus Aurelius Cleander stepped into the grain prefect's office with a face like thunder.

'Can I help you, chamberlain?' managed Dionysus with a calm, innocent and concerned tone.

'I certainly hope so, Dionysus. Have you seen what's happening in the city?'

'Daily, chamberlain.'

'The plebs are drawing comic pictures of me on the walls of the forum. I am depicted with a sword in one hand and a sheaf of wheat in the other, stabbing skeletons. This cannot go on. I had no intention of hoarding the grain in the first place until you...' he paused, noticing Rufinus for the first time with a curled sneering lip, 'and *him*, persuaded me. If this cannot be resolved, then I want that grain back in public sources and your responsibility, Dionysus.'

The prefect spread his arms placatingly. Rufinus wondered what he was going to do. Things were starting to fall apart here, right at the end, and yet Dionysus was playing it so calm.

'Worry not, chamberlain. I am the bearer of good tidings.'

Rufinus frowned, and then felt his pulse leap again as the prefect reached down and produced a recently unfurled document, handing it to Cleander.'

'Just tell me,' spat the chamberlain, thrusting it back at him.

'Tinius Demetrius, the prefect of Aegyptus has managed to gather what he believes will be enough grain to save Rome. He has pulled the new grain fleet such as it is to Alexandria and gathers more vessels even as we speak. As soon as he has all the grain in the port and sufficient ships they will send it to Rome as fast as they can. Relief is on the way. We have only to hold out long enough.'

A number of expressions passed across Cleander's face, the most prominent being suspicion. Finally, he pursed his lips and folded his arms.

'Will it be soon? Things are becoming untenable. Can we not distribute what grain we have in the meantime. And I hear rumours that we had a delivery recently. I had dismissed the notion, but the talk persists. Can you clarify this for me?'

Dionysus shrugged. 'I cannot say how soon the grain will arrive, but I know that everyone involved will be working to bring it to Rome as fast as they can, for everyone knows the situation. Until that time we simply cannot afford to give out what we have, chamberlain. You know why. With the constant threat of unrest and mob violence, we must keep out emergency units fed – the vigiles, the Cohort, the sailors. Might I humbly point out that almost half the grain we do release goes to the Praetorians, who are the only unit not currently on half rations if I hear correctly.'

Cleander flashed him a dangerous glare.

'I will not starve the emperor's bodyguard. And I accept your position, but I do not like it. And what of this rumour of wagons?'

Again, Dionysus shrugged easily. 'We had a small boost from Gaul, courtesy of the fleet grain mills at Arelate, but it is not enough to make a difference. Not enough to feed the people, so it has been put aside with the rest to feed those who need it most.'

Cleander glowered, but his questions had been answered. He huffed for a long moment, and then gave a curt nod. 'I am barked at by a multitude of dogs, Dionysus. Even Consul Vitellius nags me. Severus has thus far been blessedly quiet, though how long it will be before he grumbles at me, I cannot say. I do not wish to be held accountable for grain that should by all rights be your responsibility. I will continue to attempt mollification of the people, but do what you can to speed the Aegyptian fleet along. We need that grain.'

With that he turned, throwing Rufinus a brief angry glare, and stomped out, his Praetorians at his heel. Rufinus waited some time after their departure, listening to the distant, muffled sound of the chamberlain climbing into his litter and leaving, before closing the door and letting out an explosive breath.

'Was it wise to tell him about the shipment? Now he will be expecting it.'

Cleander slumped into his chair. 'His knowing of it makes no real difference, I suppose. It will either come or it will not. He might use it to improve the mood of the crowd, I suppose, but it will still either be in time to save him, or too late to be of use. We will simply have to do what we can in the coming days to exacerbate the situation and further condemn the man.'

Rufinus nodded. This was becoming more difficult by the day. He bade farewell to Dionysus, gathered his men outside and began to march back through the city towards the fortress. It was difficult not to feel nervous at the atmosphere in the city as they moved through it. Months ago the worst fear of the people had been contracting the plague and dying, bleeding out from sores in the gutter. Now people were starving to death before they could die of the disease. Every step hammered guilt into Rufinus for his part in starving his own city.

Malevolent stares followed the men as they travelled and though no one made a move against the forty men of the Cohort marching through the street, Rufinus could feel just how close they were to just such an incident. He had given a standing order that his men maintain silence in the city. One wrong word could start a riot these days.

As they marched, he contemplated that problem. The Urban Cohort were there to keep order and save lives. They were commanded by the honourable Pertinax, who only had the best for Rome in mind. Yet the people saw them only as an extension of the Praetorian Guard, who were Cleander's force, and who everyone knew remained well-fed. There had to be some way to separate the two – to malign Cleander's guardsmen while making the Cohort an ally in the eyes of

Rome. He frowned. How long had he been willing to vilify the Guard to whom he had been proud to belong?

He was grateful to pass through the gate and into the Castra Praetoria, out of the baleful eye of the people of Rome, and he dismissed his men from duty and strode into his quarters with a sigh of relief. He had dumped his helmet and cloak and was contemplating whether to eat or bathe first when he noticed the message on his desk. Some helpful soldier had delivered it during his absence. A simple note, brusque and unfriendly. A summons to the house of Tribune Fulvius.

Rufinus sagged. As if today had not held enough unpleasantness. He was still struggling with the urge to put an end to the murderous cavalryman, but every day he let it pass in the knowledge that it was important right now to rock the boat, and that Cleander had to remain the big fish they sought, not the tribune. Yet every meeting between them brought that inevitable clash closer.

With another sigh, he gathered up his cloak and vine stick and left his rooms once more.

Striding out of the Cohort's barrack area, he crossed a road and made for the centre of the fortress. His mind whirled as he walked. Whatever Fulvius wanted it would not be good. Life these days was simply becoming a matter of prioritising which irritation, misery or disaster to shuffle to the top of the list and deal with first. He was so deep in thought about the tribune, the chamberlain, the grain shipment and Dionysus that he walked straight into the two white-clad figures as he emerged from between two blocks.

Startled, he looked up and his heart skipped a beat.

He had seen neither Mercator nor Icarion, his two oldest friends in the Guard, since that day he'd almost bumped into them near the Palatine, when he'd left that first meeting that started this mess. He'd prayed time and again that they had managed to survive the manoeuvres in the Guard and had not fallen foul of Cleander. And here they were.

In the brief moment he floundered and took it all in, he registered several things. Firstly, his two old friends were leading horses, but not equipped as cavalry, so they had been somewhere distant enough to require riding. They smelled faintly of brine and fish, so they had been at the coast at least, and probably on a ship. And they looked travel worn and tired, their facial hair grown out long beyond their usual neat clipped beards. So they had been on a distant assignment, out of the way of what was happening in the capital. Good for them. But they were back, which was less spectacular, for now they would be forced to submit to Cleander as master or to find some way to run away again,

All this passed in a heartbeat as he panicked and tried to work out what to do about this unexpected and most unfortunate encounter. He could hardly afford for even his old friends to know that he was both alive and working under an assumed name.

For the briefest of moments he almost meekly ducked out of the way and ran past, but even in his panic he realised that that would be out of character and would only draw further attention. They may be Praetorians and he the Urban Cohort, but he was a centurion and they only guardsmen. No centurion of the Cohort would bow and scrape to them.

Adopting a gruff posture he rose to his full height, which was half a head below Mercator and therefore not all that impressive. Even as he spoke he realised that he had subconsciously attempted to affect a Gallic accent and winced inside at his poor inflection. He sounded like a character in an Apuleius comedy.

'Why don't your lot watch where they're going?' he snapped, and pushed his way between them, striding off with his vine stick under his arm, all centurion to the core. As soon as he had his back to them and was marching on, he allowed himself to blink away the sweat that had formed on his brow. He was even quivering. Damn it, but if those two were back in the fortress and he had to keep an eye out for them all the time, things were going to start getting very difficult.

As he reached the far side of the street and made his way into the road onto which the tribunes' houses looked, he paused just long enough to glance over his shoulder. His heart raced once more to see that Mercator and Icarion had not moved. Both men remained where he had bumped into them, watching him intently. Regretting turning to look, he spun once more and marched off out of sight towards Fulvius' quarters.

Somehow he knew they had recognised him. Despite his attempt to cover it all up, he was certain Merc and Icarion knew it was him. What they would do with that information remained a troubling question. At least they were no creatures of Cleander's, so there was little chance of them reporting to him, and they were infantry, so would be unlikely to speak to Fulvius.

Damn it all, but how could this day get any more complicated?

Straightening once more into his best 'haughty centurion' posture, Rufinus rapped twice on the door and waited. The doorman opened up, peered at him suspiciously and stepped back out of the way, jerking inside with a thumb in the most insolent manner imaginable. Ignoring him further, Rufinus strode inside and instead of standing and waiting for the door to close and the slave to escort him, simply marched off in the direction in which he knew the tribune's office to lie. The slave, worried that his master would beat him for failing in his duty, rushed after Rufinus, trying to get in front to lead him. With grim satisfaction, Rufinus made sure to occupy the full corridor and stay ahead of the slave.

He arrived at the door of the office with the slave hopping from foot to foot impotently behind him. Fulvius looked up from his book and chewed his lip for a moment. Rufinus noted that another slave stood in the corner of the room and, unlike the dour and useless doorman, this one bore the network of scars and tattoos that suggested a history in the arena. The man was armed with a sica, a Thracian blade, curved and with a wicked edge, at his belt. Did Fulvius expect trouble, or should Rufinus be on his guard? He had his sword at his side, as well as a pugio dagger and his vine stick. The slave might be an ex gladiator, but he would find he had his work cut out with this centurion. Still, Rufinus attended the tribune with an insolent half-slouch and the ex gladiator firmly locked in his peripheral vision.

'Tribune,' Rufinus said, as his mind made a boxing ring of the room, noting obstructions, weak points, places of egress and potential weapons. The man was on his right side – potential trouble for a legionary being able to draw his sword and parry in a rush, but a centurion wore his blade on the left and could draw it easily. Plus the stout wooden baton he carried would turn most blades.

Fulvius drew a deep breath and settled back into his chair, fingers interlocked.

'I could swear that I gave you an ultimatum to leave or suffer the consequences.'

Rufinus gave his calmest shrug. 'My whole life is a string of consequences. I'm prepared to suffer a few more.'

The tribune's lip twitched. 'I am not the ordinary cavalry trooper I was when we first met, Rufinus, lacking authority and power.'

'And yet I continue to walk free,' Rufinus countered. 'How can that be?'

'Do not test me.'

'You will not sell me to your master, because you know the storm of steel and shit that would bring from my friends. No one wants to piss off a consul, especially one close to the emperor. So don't give me your empty threats, Fulvius. I know you for a coward as well as a murderer.'

The knuckles of the tribune's hands whitened as he clenched.

'I cannot fathom why you are still here, Rufinus. You have managed to kill the others in my unit. Well done.

Congratulations, but you will not get me and, knowing that, why are you still here, masquerading as a centurion?'

Rufinus felt his first moment of discomfort. His true reason for being among the Cohort must not become known to this man, and Fulvius believed it to be no more than an attempt to get close enough to kill him. The young centurion narrowed his eyes.

'I am not done with you yet, Fulvius. I swore an oath on the altar of Apollo to avenge the good man you mutilated in the woodlands. And no man reneges on an oath to the gods – not if he is in his right mind, anyway. I give you my word you will be with your former comrades soon enough.'

'Then I think that perhaps it is time to reiterate my own promises. Your woman eludes me. I know she is somewhere in Sicilia, but it seems that your friend the consul has managed to secrete her away somewhere truly inscrutable. I *will* find her, though, and when I do her cries will make you regret your oath. Moreover, long before she lies on my floor, whimpering and pleading, your father's dismembered corpse will bounce down the bank and into the Tiber like the common pleb he is.'

Rufinus flinched. He knew he'd done so, too, despite being determined to hold himself stoically together. Fulvius had seen it as well.

'Yes. Your father who seeks to be Cleander's slave and wishes you harm. And I can imagine how little love there is lost between the two of you. But family still means something to you sentimental types, doesn't it? Try as hard as you might, you cannot condemn him.'

Rufinus shuffled slightly. 'At the moment I am not ready to deal with you,' Rufinus growled. 'That time is not yet upon me, but I swear now on the spirits of my ancestors that if you touch Senova or my father, your death will be a thing that is used to frighten children into line for all time.'

'Brave words,' Fulvius spat. His hand rose and gestured left to the gladiator in the corner. 'Meet Carnax. He has been a victorious gladiator and a beast hunter. He knows how to skin an animal with precision. Of course, they're usually dead when he begins, but I cannot imagine your father has sufficient strength to put up much of a fight. I give you my word that if we pass the calends of June and you are still in Rome, let alone in my fortress, I will have your father peeled alive and crucified for the birds to feed on.

'Do your worst, but always keep an eye open, even when you sleep, Fulvius. The boatman is coming for you.'

The tribune started to say something, but Rufinus simply turned his back and marched out, that doorman once more hurrying along in his wake, trying to get ahead. Despite the confidence he exuded through the house and the sense of aggrieved strength he portrayed, as he emerged into the open once more and the doorman closed up behind him, he felt distinctly shaky. It was not the threats that had done it, either, or not so much. It had been the sudden realisation that he still cared enough for his father to matter. He might not count for anything to his father, but the reverse was apparently not true.

Before he realised he was doing it, he had passed through the fortress gate once more and was stomping out purposefully into the city. He had made two important decisions. The first was that despite the way he and his father had last parted, he owed the old man and the family name enough to at least warn him against what might come. The second was that the moment he had the opportunity, Fulvius had to die. No slow master plans that found a climax with him standing above the tribune with blade in hand making him beg for mercy and renouncing his crimes. No. Just a quick death at the first opportunity.

That might not be so easy, mind. When Fulvius was in the city he was inevitably accompanied by Praetorian horsemen, and would be hard to get to. In the camp he was almost always escorted by two of his men these days and he had clearly even gone so far as to hire slave guards in his own house. Perhaps he was more worried about Rufinus than he seemed to let on. One thing was sure: he had surrounded himself with steel and muscle and that single opportunity Rufinus now sought might be hard to secure.

Half an hour later he was at the tabularium waiting to see one of the clerks. A quarter hour after that he had an address for his father's new, modest town house.

Less than an hour after leaving Fulvius' quarters he stopped outside a house on the Caelian hill in the shadow of the great Temple of Claudius. He realised now just how low his family had sunk on his father's quest for power. Rather than a sprawling estate in Hispania with a going concern in wine and several impressive wings and gardens, two bath houses and a huge cistern, his father was content to settle for a house that had probably been the home of a small-time merchant whose business had failed and forced him to sell up. It was in need of repair and decoration. Even the two shops built into the front were of poor quality and one lay empty and derelict.

Half tempted to turn and walk away, Rufinus paused and, steadying himself, hammered on the door. There was a long pause and then a strange thumping, shuffling noise. Finally the door opened and Rufinus looked at the man responsible. His father had clearly also been forced to the cut-price slave dealers. The old doorman was venerable enough to remember Aeneas landing. One leg was lame, dragged behind him and accounting for the strange noise he had heard, and the man's filmy grey eyes looked out from a face like parchment stretched over a skeleton.

'I am here to see my father.'

The slave dithered for so long over this information that Rufinus gave up and simply walked past him into the house.

'Father?'

The old man appeared suddenly in a doorway. He looked older than ever, and bitterness fought with sympathy in Rufinus' heart for a moment. Then the old man ruined it as usual.

'What do you want, wretched unwanted offspring?'

'Charming as always, Father.'

'You told me we were done for all time. It was a weight off my heart not to have to consider your foolish, selfish ways any more. Sooner or later my other, true, son will come back. When you've died your traitor's death.'

'I warned you about selling me out to your master.'

'And despite the fact that I *should*, I have not.'

'But you did sell me out to a Praetorian tribune who is now threatening me.'

'He knew about you already. He just came to me and pressed me for more details. What do I care?'

'You should care because he has as scant regard for you as Cleander does. He wishes to hurt me, and to do so he will kill you.'

'Lies.'

'No, they are not. Appius Fulvius has threatened your life if I do not leave Rome. And I have no intention of leaving Rome until both he and the chamberlain are walking hand in hand into Tarterus. So that leaves you in a difficult position. You must leave Rome before they come for you. I know you've sold the villa but we still have relations that might take you in. In Abellinum, they might shelter you.'

'You cannot fool me so easily boy. I am of value.'

'No, you're not. Can you not see just how worthless you are to them? Fulvius will kill you, and soon. *Very* soon. I cannot stop him. He will do it, and he will do it in the most agonising and gruesome manner, purely to make me hurt. So do yourself a favour old man and run.'

His father turned back towards the door. 'Dalo, go out and find the first Praetorian you can in the streets and tell him I've apprehended a traitor.'

'Father…'

'Go,' the old man shouted, rewarded by that shuffle-thump as the doorman made his way to the front door.

'Come on, Father, I could have saved Rome, killed them both and sired a large family before that slave could even reach the end of the street. And how do you intend to hold me? You were never that strong and age and bitterness make you weaker by the day.'

'If you do not leave my house I shall not be responsible for my actions.'

'Last time, Father. Run away. I dislike you intensely, and you are reprehensible as a human being, but you are my father for all your faults and I would not see you crucified. Go today.'

'Get *out*,' screamed the old man in banshee tones

Rufinus drew a deep breath. 'I have done all I can. What you do now seals your own fate. Farewell, Father.'

He could still hear his father ranting and calling him names as he passed the lame doorman and emerged into the street. He could not save his father. Senova was, for now, beyond danger. Cleander's time drew nigh and there was nothing he could do to change any of that now, and Fulvius moved with a ring of steel around him. Soon, though, it would come to a head. Cleander would fall, Fulvius would make a mistake, and Rufinus would be on them both.

They were nearly there.

CHAPTER TWENTY – BOILING POINT

Rome, Late May 190 A.D.

'**M**aximus, you lazy shit, get up!'
Rufinus surfaced from the deeply unpleasant dream he'd been having, in which Cleander had hold of one of his testicles and Fulvius the other while his father kept telling them to pull harder. On some days he might wake blearily, but he had been a soldier for most of his life and he was alert enough that a call to duty could cut through the deepest sleep.

Consequently, even as he sat bolt upright and swung his legs from the bed he knew he wasn't as late for whatever it was as the voice suggested.

He'd heard…

Yes, as Cleander had heaved and his scrotum groaned, he'd heard the first blast from the horn cutting into his dreamscape. Then as his father chided the chamberlain for not pulling hard enough, the second blast had intruded too. Then he'd woken. It had not been more than four heartbeats since the alarm arose, he was sure.

He was up a moment later, smoothing down his tunic and looking around for his subarmalis to go beneath the chain shirt. The figure in the doorway who'd called him was Centurion Priscus, an old fashioned type of officer, risen like Rufinus from the Marcomannic wars and commander of the Sixth Century, barracked across the way.

'What is it?'

'Trouble at the granaries,' the man barked before leaving the room to head back to his own men. 'Whole cohort's been called out,' he shouted over his shoulder.

Rufinus paused for only a moment in the midst of dressing. Did the man mean a cohort of men or the entire unit of the Urban Cohort? The former would mean maybe half a thousand men. If it were the entire force, that might mean two thousand. Rufinus drew a sharp breath. Two thousand men pulled to duty could only mean a complete disaster.

He grabbed the rest of his kit and pulled it on, even as Optio Sura appeared in his door.

'Sir, did you… oh, you're up.'

'Yes. How many of us?'

'Our full cohort. You're the senior officer. Best get out there prompt, sir. I'll fall in the lads.'

Rufinus nodded. No time to argue now. If whatever was happening at the horrea had been enough of an issue for the guard to send an alarm, then what they were facing was proper trouble. He glanced out of the window. It was still true dark.

Once he was fastening the last few straps, he stepped out of the barracks to see his men lining up outside, ready to move.

'What time is it?'

'Less than an hour after midnight, sir,' one man responded. Rufinus nodded and moved on, still fastening his chin strap.

By the time he barrelled out of the barrack street and ran onto the parade ground, three centuries were already assembled and Prefect Pertinax stood on the tribunal as though he had been dressed in his uniform all night. Perhaps he had.

Rufinus strode over to the podium. As senior centurion of the gathered force, it was his place to speak to the prefect.

'Ah, Maximus, good.'

'You will address the troops, sir?'

'No. Not if you are ready to take them out. Optio Pavo of the Third Century, Fourth Cohort commands the guards currently on duty at the Horrea Ummidiana. He sent a runner. He thinks we're about to have a small riot on our hands. I'm committing a whole cohort to keeping things settled. You are in command. As soon as your force is gathered, move there with all haste and deal with the problem. I cannot join you as I am required to attend the Palatine momentarily, though I will come with all haste once that meeting is done. If things escalate out of control send for the rest of the Cohort, but only if you really need them. We could do without committing the entire force and raising a public outcry.'

Rufinus saluted.

A riot. At the granary. He didn't know whether to panic or cheer. The responsibility of quelling the trouble was more than he had ever taken on, yet it was a sign that their goal was tantalisingly close; The pot of the city's emotion was boiling over. Cleander still held all the grain. His would be the cursed name here.

Pertinax hurried off with his adjutant, leaving Rufinus alone on the tribunal. He shivered as his own century formed up, along with the Fifth. A sheepish-looking centurion led out the last unit, and moments later they were all formed up in uniform. An odd thrill ran through Rufinus. He was commanding. Finally, properly, he was commanding. And these were proper soldiers. Better, even, for they were soldiers trained with the extra skills required for peace keeping in the city. If only he could be himself...

'There is trouble at the Horrea Ummidiana,' he announced to the parade ground. 'I realise that our tactics will be defined by what we encounter when we arrive, but I want to be prepared. This could be a full-blown riot, so I want the Sixth Century to take on the pioneer role. There may be damage to the granary, and there is undoubtedly a unit of the vigiles attending. You will liaise with them and help them secure the building.'

A nod from the bull-necked officer of the Sixth.

'Second and Third Centuries, you are on flanking duty. Contain things. One of you up the Vicus Portae Naeviae and come in from the left. The other up the Vicus Portae

Raudusculanae and come in from the right. That way we have them in a vice, and here's the weird one: Fourth Cohort? Get a requisition chit and take five hundred horse from the stables. I don't care if they're Praetorian horses or the Praetorian prefect's own steed. Take them. Lay the blame with me, but mount every man and take them out of the city by the fortress. Bring them in from the rear along the Vicus Dianae. If the gods are with us, the entire crowd will lose the will to fight when they are trapped and pressed from every side. I will bring the First and Fifth centuries by the most direct route and demand they stand down. Are there any questions?'

He'd expected some argument, especially from the men who he'd just told to requisition Praetorian horses, but every man nodded and rumbled their approval. Good. At least they might pull this off if they all believed in what they were doing.

'Alright, you have your orders. Move out. First and Fifth centuries on me.'

Without looking back, he turned and marched down from the tribunal, across the edge of the square and off towards the gate. As they emerged into the city, Rufinus felt the lightest touch of rain in the darkened street and cast a quick prayer to Jupiter Pluvius that this single drop herald a downpour. Should there be another attempt at arson, the rain might play a vital role, and such inclement weather had a tendency to put an end to public unrest. Many a rioter suddenly found their vehemence in question when they discovered they were rioting in a rain storm.

Still, only one drop.

He prayed again as he led one hundred and fifty men along the street, heading for the Horrea Ummidiana on the secondary southern slope known as the Little Aventine. The sound of scores of hobnailed boots on the road drew out late night denizens – drunks, thieves, whores and the homeless, all to watch the Urban Cohort stomp past at speed. This particular class of people were the Cohort's usual prime concern. It was often they who the city's soldiers were policing, arresting or muscling off the street. Yet now the air of discontent and menace they gave off was strangely less pressing than that emanating from the ordinary folk of Rome.

That alone was worrying.

But there were more worrying things yet to come. As they passed the end of the circus and moved towards the area of warehouses and sub-urban estates, Rufinus' heart sank. There was a glow hanging over the region ahead, and it was not the muted golden glow of torches or lamps. This was the glow of fire. Above, in the dark sky, roiling clouds of black.

Damn it. When would people stop being so stupid? If you're starving and you want the grain distributed from the warehouse, what good does it do anyone to set fire to the damn place? People were such idiots.

Praying that the other centuries had travelled fast enough to already be moving into place, he gave the order for double time. Several more spots of rain dinged from his helmet. Would it be enough? In the best of worlds the rain would hold off until they arrived, and then come down like a breaking dam. Then it would be in time to help with rioting and fire, but too late make the stone underfoot slippery for hobnailed boots as they ran.

They passed the barracks of the Fourth Cohort of vigiles, and he was satisfied to note that it seemed to be all-but silent and empty, just a couple of guards left in the place. That meant that the vigiles were out in force, probably all at the nearby scene. Turning at the vigiles' station, they ran on up the Clivus Triarius and now Rufinus received his first view of the trouble.

When they had delivered the first shipments of grain here – that day Rufinus had narrowly avoided a riot – he had seen the large, three-storey storehouse and assumed that was all there was. Subsequent visits had revealed more. The Horrea Ummidiana in fact consisted of three similar complexes, close together with only narrow streets between. An open space stood before the gate of the nearest, where they had stopped their wagons that day, and there was a second square to the south, beside the other two buildings. A boiling black cloud hung over the furthest warehouse, and Rufinus could see the red-gold sparks flitting up into the night over that third structure. While the sight of a burning building put the fear of the gods into him, at least it was the third granary, which was the emptiest of the three.

The nearest square was thronged with people, the noise so loud that it drowned out even the roar of the fire beyond. There was no central focus to the mob, though, which was good. Instead of a rhythmic chant, there was simply a cacophony of conflicting shouts and for that Rufinus gave silent thanks. An unruly mob was a hard enough thing to have to deal with, but if they were organised and purposeful, it could be so much worse.

Still, this was an entirely different situation to that day they had arrived with the grain. That had been an uneasy and discontented crowd. This was already an angry mob. Then he had been able to single out figures who would help convince the crowd. Here there would be no sympathetic voice to join them.

There was, in short, no hope of talking this lot down. The Cohort would have to commit to action, and would have to do it quickly, for if this mob suddenly found the focus they were missing, with one or more leaders making the decisions, then they would change from being an angry crowd into being almost an army.

Reaching down, Rufinus pulled his centurion's whistle out from beneath his scarf and placed it between his lips. For a horrible moment he couldn't remember the call, but years of memory tests that had kept him occupied when bored allowed him to run through the list in the blink of an eye and lock on to the one he needed.

One short blast: Attention
One long blast: Stand down
Two short blasts: Deploy in standard formation
Two long blasts: Pull back
Three short blasts: Line and brace

And then there was the one he needed. Three short blasts and one long. *Engage the crowd with minimum force.*

Blowing that signal, Rufinus prepared himself. As his men brought their shields up defensively in front of them and hefted their nightsticks ready to use, Rufinus drew his stout ash stick with his left hand and gripped his centurion's vine stick in the right. No body shield to protect him. He would just have to be careful. And lucky.

He could hear his fellow centurion behind him echoing the call, and the two centuries fell into formation, filling the street from wall to wall, ten lines deep.

'As we move into the square,' he bellowed at the top of his voice to rise above the din, 'widen the line to fill the space, drawing from the rear ranks.'

Moments later the men performed the manoeuvre admirably as the street opened out into the square containing the crowd. A front of fifteen men became twenty and then twenty five and then thirty. He could hear the distant sounds of other whistle calls ahead now, which came as a great relief. That meant that at least one of the other centuries had come round to the side of the mob or behind them. He glanced over his shoulder. A short distance back he could see the Sixth Century, hurrying to catch up having stopped in at the vigiles barracks and borrowed extra equipment to help with the fire. He turned to his left.

'Force the left side forward hard. We need to break the crowd there so the Sixth can get to the fire to help. Now engage.'

He hated it. He hated every word of a command that set his men in conflict with the ordinary citizens of Rome, but he had been right to do so and he knew it. Even as his men pressed silently and fiercely forward the first missiles started to clatter and thud against their shields. And these were not cabbages and fruit. These were chunks of brick, pieces of timber, carcasses of rats and various animals that had died in the street, and various other pieces of debris. Rufinus felt something solid yet wet hit his shoulder and ricochet off into the men behind and tried not to wonder with horror what it was.

Then they were in.

The crowd met them with the violence of a Germanic tribe, swiping, thumping, kicking and roaring unintelligible imprecations. All along the line, the men of Rufinus' centuries pushed, bracing themselves and heaving with their heavy shields. Minimum force, the command had been, and so the men tried not to actively strike out at the people at first. Instead they pushed and heaved, forcing the public back in an attempt to make a way through for their compatriots to reach the fire. And when they met too solid a resistance and there seemed no hope of pushing further, the well-practiced men of the Cohort simply pulled their shields back a little, allowing the crowd to stumble forward, and then smashed the heavy, curved boards against them once more. Then, the iron bosses at the centre started to break bones and cause pain, and with each fresh push the men heaved the crowd back a little.

Rufinus parried flailing sticks with his own and twice lashed out, catching the side of one man's head and the weapon-arm of another, narrowly avoiding going down to a blow from the crowd.

He had to judge this right. Timing was all. One wrong choice and they would end up either at war and killing citizens, which was to be avoided at all costs, or being forced to capture, bind and arrest the entire crowd, which would be near impossible. No, what he needed to do was disperse them, but they were still too angry. They needed to break. They needed to realise how hopeless it all was.

Bellowing encouragement to his men, he twisted slightly and slammed his armoured shoulder into a thick-set man waving a skillet. The big fellow fell back into the crowd with a cry, but the Cohort were pushing them hard enough that the crowd was compressing tighter and tighter, and there simply wasn't space for the man to fall, so he found himself bounced around and constricted, crushed between his angry fellows.

Rufinus couldn't estimate casualties since he was as tightly-packed in the press as any of them, but he'd seen a few of his men cry out and fall to be dragged back by their friends into the rear of the century and replaced instantly by a fresh face. Irritatingly, they would be taking more casualties than the mob, but that was in the very nature of 'minimal force'.

The lot of the soldiers was improving now, though. With the ever increasing press of the tightening, constricting crowd, fewer and fewer citizens were finding that they had adequate room to lash out at the soldiers heaving them back with painful shields. Moreover, most had run out of missiles to throw, and those that still had them couldn't find an easy target now in the press.

The mood was changing. He could feel it. There was still anger, but the aura of the crowd was losing its violent edge. What had moments earlier been the brutal urge to harm soldiers was gradually dissolving into despair and panic. Still angry, but also desperate and futile.

Soon...

He could hear the calls of other centuries now. He couldn't see any of them, but they were close enough to hear, and that meant the crowd had been contained. They were being pressed tight. The mood was almost right.

Something struck Rufinus in the knee and he yelped, reeling and almost falling, but like the civilians, the soldiers were equally tightly-packed and there was nowhere for him to fall. Pain wracked his left knee and as he put his weight on it once more, it screamed at him. He staggered and someone hit him on the helmet. The bulk of the damage was prevented by the heavy iron, but the ringing in his ears was intense, his skull flashed with pain, and for a moment his eyes blurred.

'Sticks,' he bellowed. He hadn't wanted to, but the crowd was almost there, and Rufinus risked collapsing beneath them. If only he could nudge them over the lip from anger into panic.

The men began to jab and swipe with their nightsticks now, having previously been remarkably restrained. Men and women howled as they took painful blows from the heavy cudgels of the soldiers. Rufinus shook his head and almost fell, wobbly knee shaking beneath him. He felt the change in an instant. The will of the mob to fight on drained shockingly fast. Gritting his teeth, Rufinus took a deep breath.

'Sticks up. Break left and clear the road.'

These men were professionals, trained in such manoeuvers, and yet Rufinus was still impressed with the speed and efficiency of his men as they carried out his orders. In an instant they stopped striking the howling rioters and the entire line of men opened up like a gate, swinging back and left until instead of filling the street, they were lined up along the side, and the mob had a route to freedom.

Panic was flooding through the mob now, and they needed no encouragement. Even as the soldiers were moving aside already the crowd were running, limping, hobbling and crawling away, the mob surging into the open city where they split off and melted into any available side street, desperate to do nothing more than get away from the soldiers and home safe.

As the crowd drained like a pond through a sluice gate, so Rufinus bellowed more orders. His men, who had been pressing hardest at the left since the start, now began to push once more, opening up a path through which the Sixth Century ran, hurrying to help the vigiles with the blaze. As the square emptied, Rufinus heaved a sigh of relief and, lowering his vitis, used it as a walking stick alongside his weak left leg. He took a couple more faltering steps on it. It hurt like Hades, but wasn't broken. He was content that it would recover in time. He limped forward, taking in the scene.

Perhaps a dozen civilian corpses lay unmoving in the square. He viewed them with pity and regret, but neither shame nor guilt. They were back where the press of the crowd had been, not at the edge where they had engaged the Cohort. Unless he missed his guess, his soldiers had managed to cause no fatalities, and these bodies had all fallen amid their own fellow rioters. Of course, one might suggest that the Cohort pushing the crowd into that tight press had caused it in the first place, but the fact remained that they were unfortunate casualties of the situation, and not victims of the soldiers' aggression.

Flames were still rising from the third granary, and it might not be salvageable, but the vigiles had concentrated primarily on soaking the walls and shutters of the adjacent buildings, and tearing down and removing anything flammable nearby, limiting the growth of the conflagration and preventing it from burning the other two granaries with their precious contents.

The men of the Sixth were now at the disaster scene, lending a hand where they could, taking directions from the officers of the vigiles who were already smoke-blackened and tired.

'You alright sir?'

He turned to see his optio, Sura, looking meaningfully at how Rufinus leaned on his vitis for support.

'Some bastard kicked me in the knee, but I'll recover. To be honest it's the headache that's threatening to do for me.'

Sura nodded seriously. 'Some bugger hit you hard, sir. It's left a dent.'

Rufinus made to argue and resist, but swiftly gave up as the optio unfastened his centurion's helmet and carefully lifted it off him. Rufinus immediately felt the blood that had been contained by the wool liner trickle down his scalp and into his ear.

'Gods, that hurts.'

Sura nodded again. 'When we get back you need to have the medicus stitch that, sir.'

Rufinus sighed. 'In the meantime, let's finish up here. Have two centuries create a cordon in every street at a distance of a thousand paces from the fire. Let's make sure the roads are clear. Every other man present can lend their support to the vigiles. Let's see if we can save what's left of that building.'

Sura saluted and hurried off to give the orders, but something else attracted Rufinus' attention and his gaze rose past the optio and the men who were beginning to move out to create the cordon. It fell upon a small mounted party, and his already low spirits plunged into subterranean depths.

Pertinax rode his brown mare with only two guards and a slave tramping alongside, but the Urban Prefect was far from alone. Beside him, Cleander rode a white horse with a dozen Praetorian cavalrymen gathered around, including the familiar and extremely unwelcome figure of Appius Fulvius.

'Oh just fucking wonderful,' he grumbled as he tried to pull himself into a rough approximation of attention, which his knee seemed determined to prevent. He swayed and almost fell, but managed to remain upright and leaned heavily on the stick for support.

'Centurion,' Pertinax greeted him with an incline of the head. Rufinus saluted.

'Prefect. I am pleased to report that the situation is under control.'

Pertinax opened his mouth to reply but Cleander, leaning forward in his saddle, fixed Rufinus with a glare and spoke first.

'This is under *control*?'

'We have dispersed a rioting mob of more than a thousand citizens with minimal casualties all round and little damage to the surroundings. It could have been a great deal worse, sir.'

Cleander snarled. 'This is damn disgrace, Centurion. A granary on fire is not "little damage", and where are your prisoners? Where are those responsible? Examples should be made.'

Rufinus could see Pertinax shaking his head slightly, willing Rufinus to be meek and accepting, but his knee hurt, his head hurt, his ear was filled with blood, and the chamberlain was talking out of his backside. And on top of it all, the rain was starting properly, just when he no longer really needed it. Rufinus was in no mood to take shit from anyone right now.

'Thanks to the solid efforts of the local vigiles, supported by my own men, a fire that had begun before we were summoned to the scene has been contained and prevented from spreading to other buildings. The granary that caught light is, thankfully, almost empty, the bulk of what we are hoarding stored in the nearest one. Very little real damage has been done. I could not arrest ringleaders, because there were none. This was not an organised attack, but an angry mob. Every man and woman present was responsible. Would you crucify a thousand citizens? Would that really help? Would that make the people of Rome calmer and more accepting? And given the situation, Chamberlain, I thought it considerably more important to disperse the crowd and concentrate on containing the fire, which we have done.'

Pertinax nodded slowly, though he wore a pained expression. He agreed, but aggravating Cleander could cause a great deal of trouble.

The chamberlain paused for a moment, wishing to dispute everything that Rufinus reported, angry at being gainsaid and spoken to thus, but also aware that in truth, the centurion with the shaking leg and the bleeding scalp was quite correct. Angrily, Cleander turned on Pertinax.

'This was a mess. Your men need to be on situations like this much faster. They need to be breaking up gangs of protesters before they can put flint and tinder to my granaries.'

Rufinus winced. Cleander had just claimed ownership of the granaries in front of perhaps three dozen men of different units, all of whom would have heard him. That comment would be trotted out more than once in soldier's bars over the next twenty four hours, and Cleander's anger at having his granaries attacked would be the talk of the forum by tomorrow afternoon. The chamberlain was beginning to condemn himself.

'Chamberlain,' Pertinax said patiently, 'the moment the alarm was raised, the Cohort fell in and ran to the scene. If you look over there, I think you'll probably realise that the quick-thinking centurion here even requisitioned a few hundred of your Praetorians' horses to get to the scene fast.'

Cleander's gaze flashed back and his face fought between fury and embarrassment. He would hate that the Urban Cohort had borrowed his horses, but he could hardly argue having just told them they needed to be faster.

'And when you're *on* the scene,' Cleander snapped irritably, 'you need to resolve it faster. Stop trying to mollycoddle the public. Bear blades if you have to, but stop messing about and use sufficient force to put the riot down swiftly.'

'It is the remit of the Cohort,' Pertinax responded, still calm, 'to use the minimum force necessary in all situations. We are, after all, formed for the protection and benefit of the citizens of Rome, not to be their attackers and jailors.'

He had the chamberlain, and they all knew it. Pertinax was only stating the purpose of the Cohort, and it supported the actions they had taken perfectly.

'I don't give a shit what it says on the wall of your office, Pertinax. What I want is order and security in Rome. *That* is your purpose, and you are failing to achieve it. If you cannot react swifter and more decisively, then I will be forced to consider deploying the Praetorian Guard in your place. They will not baulk at doing whatever is required to keep the peace. It will look very poor for your future career, Prefect, if the Guard are called out to do your job for you.'

Without waiting for a response, Cleander shot Rufinus a withering look and wheeled his horse to depart. Tribune Fulvius paused for a long moment, eyes narrowed and brow furrowed as he too looked at Rufinus, then he turned and rode off in the wake of his master, the other cavalry following on.

Rufinus shivered. There was something he didn't like about that look. He feared that perhaps Fulvius had decided Rufinus had other plans now, beyond his own death. If he pondered Rufinus' position in the Cohort and decided that he was somehow scheming against Cleander, things could come apart remarkably quickly, and he might well bring down men like

Severus and Dionysus with him. Soon, though, the sort of thing that had happened here would come to the attention of the emperor. All it would take then was one man to call for Cleander's head, and the whole city would join the chorus.

Despite having just broken up a riot, he found himself hoping that something similar might happen again soon.

'Ignore the poisonous lunatic, Pertinax said with a smile. 'You did well and we all know it. Even him.'

'What if he carries out his threat, sir?' Rufinus asked.

'To deploy the Praetorians on crowd control? I doubt he would do it. The Guard would think it demeaning.' He sighed. 'But if he does, we have difficult choices to make. Standing against the chamberlain is dangerous work, and usually carries a death sentence, but I will not allow him to use the imperial bodyguard to kill citizens. If the worst comes to the worst, we will do what is right, regardless of the consequences, will we not Maximus?'

'Damn right we will, sir,' Rufinus said with fierce pride. If only this man had been in charge of the Guard and not Cleander. What a force they could be, instead of the ignoble thug army of a grasping would-be king.

'The fire is almost out, sir. Permission to dismiss the men back to camp.'

'Granted, Centurion. And you have my thanks.'

Rufinus smiled. Sometimes there were bright points even in the darkest of days.

Chapter Twenty One – Evil deeds

Rome, Early June 190 A.D.

Rufinus stood at the rear corner of the office, wincing but trying hard not to be too conspicuous, not that any of those in the room were likely to pay him any attention anyway with the way things were going.

Cleander stood centrally in the room, gesticulating, his arms flailing angrily with every point he emphasised. Dionysus stood behind his desk, red-faced with an equal temper, fists balled to batter on the wooden surface with his own words. The cavalry tribune Fulvius stood by the door, several of his Praetorians outside eying Rufinus' men of the Cohort with suspicion, and Septimius Severus, consul of Rome, stood opposite Rufinus with a serene face like carved marble.

'Open the fucking granaries, Dionysus,' Cleander said for the third time.

'Why are you making me repeat myself, Chamberlain?' the grain commissioner said with a voice hoarse from shouting.

'Because you persist in denying me. People do not deny me, Dionysus. Bear in mind why.'

'Do not threaten me,' Dionysus snapped. 'I am a prefect of Rome, of a good family, with a distinguished record of service and I am doing everything I do for the good of the empire and the city.'

Rufinus gave the slightest of nods. That last was most certainly true, though not the way Cleander would understand it.

'Open the *granaries*.'

'No!'

Severus waved a hand. 'Far be it from me to interrupt your friendly banter, but might I interject?'

Cleander turned on him, angrily. 'What?'

Dionysus just continued to glare at the chamberlain.

'You argue in circles. Cleander, I understand your frustration, and I am sure the prefect here does, too. Yes, the people are restive and things are becoming dangerous, and I am sure that it irks you that your granaries are the target of so many demonstrations, but the facts Dionysus relates remain true. He has confirmed time and again that there is insufficient grain in store to feed the city. If he opens the horrea now and distributes it, the problems will only escalate. Half the city will be fed, and the other half will still go hungry. Can you imagine the riots you will have on your hands if that happens? And then there will be no grain to feed the soldiers whose duty it is to contain such civil disturbance.'

'You are just repeating him,' spat Cleander.

'Because you are not listening to his reasoning,' Severus said quietly. 'And threatening him will not help.'

'Do not think that your consulate will protect *you* either,' snarled the chamberlain.

Severus' eyes grew flinty. 'I am not Vitellius,' he said flatly, with reference to the former suffect consul who had recently stepped down. 'Your threats will not drive me from the city into hiding as they did him. The emperor...'

'The emperor hides away at Laurentum,' Cleander interrupted. 'There he is out of reach for both of us, listening to the honeyed poison words of his whore. He will not step in to save you if I decide that you have become a burden for Rome, Severus.'

'You small-minded, arrogant prick,' Dionysus shouted. 'How dare you threaten a prefect and a consul and insult the emperor's mistress all in one breath.'

'Watch your tongue, Dionysus, lest I have it pulled out and snipped off.'

Rufinus shivered at the threats and anger on display. This was getting more dangerous by the heartbeat. The only thing that had saved them from Cleander's rage so far was that Severus just might be able to call on the emperor for support, though with every month Commodus spent locked away out of the city that possibility shrank. That and the fact that he yet had need of Dionysus, as a scapegoat if nothing else.

Severus took a deep breath and held out a hand, palm flat towards each of the two other arguers.

'Let us all calm down. I have a proposal.'

All eyes turned to the big, bearded African consul, who pursed his lips. 'We know that relief is coming. The fleet from Alexandria could arrive any day. Let us not in the meantime do anything precipitous that might cause Rome to turn upon itself. Here is my suggestion: With the grain already hoarded and the extra from the Arelate mills that we brought in, there is still not enough grain to cover the dole and still feed the military and other groups.'

'We know all that,' snapped Cleander, who now knew that caravans had arrived with grain, though remained entirely unaware of the scale of that delivery. Not once had he actually demanded to look inside the granaries, thank the gods.

'Yes, but I may have a way to bolster supplies enough to feed the city and the army, at least for a month, which will buy us time to wait for the Alexandria shipment.'

'How?' demanded Dionysus, brow furrowed. Rufinus nodded. He could not see a solution, and moreover could see no reason for trying. They had to keep this up after all.

'There are still private merchants with stores of grain, in Rome and around the peninsula, especially in the ports. They hoard what they have, but the public cannot afford them. Their prices have risen to such an extent that it is cheaper to buy a sword than a measure of grain this summer.'

'I fail to see how that helps,' Cleander grumbled.

'Buy those supplies.'

'What?'

'Buy every modius of grain on the market. If you have to pay that exorbitant price, then so be it. I never said the solution would be cheap. Perhaps, given your power, you can put through a temporary edict that limits the price of grain and then buy it cheaper. Such things are possible. Whatever it takes, though, buy all the grain you can find. Liaise with Dionysus here to have it added to the stores we already have, and then, once there is just enough to cover the dole and all rations for a month, open the granaries. That should tide you over until the Alexandria shipment.'

'Even at ordinary prices it will be costly,' said Cleander, but his expression had already slipped from blind anger to calculation. Severus had him.

'But it is a solution.'

Dionysus was nodding now, and Cleander straightened. 'I shall have my people locate all the grain available on the private market. We shall arrange for it to be purchased and shipped here. You will see to its safe storage, prefect, and will inform me when the quantity is sufficient to release. You will not open the granaries yourself, but will wait for me to do so, for they are my granaries, and the acclaim shall be mine, after all the troubles you have put me through.'

Dionysus flashed him an angry look but nodded again, and Cleander turned his back and strode from the room without a word of farewell. Fulvius glared at them all, lingering for some time on Rufinus, and then followed, shutting the door with a click.

There was a tense pause as the footsteps receded, and then Dionysus let out an explosive breath.

'What did you do?'

'What had to be done,' Severus replied. 'If I had not given him a solution, he would not have left here without the horrea being opened, and we all know that must not happen. We are on a time limit anyway. The moment that grain shipment arrives, all our hard work will have been for naught. We need to bring this to a head now, before that happens. All I have done is put him off. He will now devote his time to finding more supplies instead of watching you. You don't need to tell him when there's enough grain, because we all know there is enough already. String him along.'

Rufinus broke into a sly smile. 'Better still, if the people find out Cleander is not only hoarding grain but is also buying up all the private stocks they cannot afford, his name will be blackened yet further.'

Nods greeted this thought. It was still building. The city festered, and Cleander was already a figure of hate. Slogans were scrawled across the city, and the vigiles had received a palace order to add the removal of such graffiti to their standing daily tasks, as if they didn't have enough to do. A statue of Cleander in the forum was daily pelted with rotting veg, and it was only a matter of time until someone toppled and smashed it. All it would really take now was for someone to demand Cleander's fall of the emperor.

That demand could not come from any of the conspirators, of course. They needed to remain apart from the disaster that they had secretly initiated. Severus had, he'd confided in them, all-but persuaded the former consul Vitellius to take the demand to the emperor. As a friend of Commodus', and a man of impeccable character he would be the perfect figurehead to put forth Rome's demand. Unfortunately, Vitellius had been *so* forthright that he'd first gone to Cleander and demanded he step down else Vitellius would approach the emperor. No one knew what the chamberlain had done, but that very day Vitellius slunk away from Rome with his tail between his legs and disappeared.

Thus the pot of Rome continued to boil, and it would require someone else to trigger the finale.

Rufinus was just wondering whether Severus had someone else in mind when they became aware of shouting. Then there came a chorus of thumps on the office door.

'Come in.'

One of the soldiers of the Cohort stood in the entrance as the door opened. He looked wild-eyed.

'Sir.'

'What is it?'

'A big crowd outside, sir. They was getting angry, but we had them contained and they wasn't armed, but when the chamberlain walked out they went mad.'

Rufinus turned to the others. 'Could this be it?'

'Come on,' Severus said, marching out of the office, Dionysus hurrying to catch up with them.

A century of Cleander's Praetorians were lined up at the far end of the courtyard, and Fulvius and the chamberlain were with them, in the saddle and in deep discussion.

As the three conspirators emerged into the courtyard, Rufinus could already hear the angry mob outside the main gate. The raised voices were a rumble of discontent. He had two centuries of the Urban Cohort outside now, and those men would be protecting the building and its important occupants.

'Better send word to your barracks,' Severus said as they marched out towards the trouble. 'If this gets out of hand you'll need more than two centuries of men.'

Rufinus nodded and gestured to the soldier who'd borne the news. 'Leave by one of the other exits. Head to the nearest vigiles station and get them out and running. We might need them. Then get a horse from the nearest stable and ride back to the fortress and alert them. Call out a full cohort on my authority.'

As the man saluted and ran off, Rufinus glanced at the others. 'Of course that will take time. We might all be in trouble before they get here.'

'Your men are professional soldiers,' Dionysus pointed out. 'That crowd are just civilians. Could they be too dangerous to you?'

Rufinus shrugged as they walked. 'Mine are soldiers with sticks. Our main weapon is intimidation. Let's see how the land lies,' he suggested, as they passed the small Praetorian force and approached the main gate. Peering through the entrance, Rufinus could see that trouble was almost certainly theirs for the having.

Men of the Cohort guarded the doorway, and he could see their armoured forms several rows deep outside. He couldn't see much of the mob, other than the fact that a great press of them were only being held back by the soldiers, but even before he'd arrived to give orders, the soldiers already had their nightsticks out and their shields braced. His men were certainly ready for violence.

Damn it.

But then this might be precisely what they needed. Cleander was here. The crowd had turned ugly at the very sight of him. They were so close to watching him topple now. Just a few more nudges...

He stepped between the men at the gate and stopped at the outer edge, Dionysus and Severus flanking him. The crowd was not huge, but it was big enough. He had only two centuries of men here, a hundred and fifty bodies all told against a crowd of maybe a thousand. Enough to grind his men down, certainly. And he couldn't really trap them and break them as he had last time, for *they* had *him* trapped instead, this time. Half an hour, minimum, until more soldiers arrived, unless there were enough vigiles in the area to make a difference.

In half an hour, Rufinus suspected, he and his men would be little more than a red stain on the stonework. He had to shift them before they initiated true violence, or things would turn bleak.

'People of Rome, there is nothing to gain from violence. You know the situation. Nothing has changed in more than a month. I ask you now to disperse. Go home and wait. Grain will be yours once the Alexandrian fleet arrives. Just a few more days.'

The reaction of the crowd was less than positive, a sour anger rippling through them. Rufinus was trying to decide what to say when Severus stepped in front of him.

'People of Rome, rejoice. The chamberlain has decided to buy up the private grain stocks so that we might have enough grain to fulfil the dole. Your emperor and his men wish you nothing but peace and hope.'

'What in Hades did you tell them that for?' snapped Cleander. Rufinus hadn't noticed the man, along with his tribune and a couple of men, approaching but now they were right behind the three conspirators. Severus turned, his expression blank.

'It is the simple truth, Chamberlain. With the way your reputation is currently suffering, I thought perhaps that I might give your something of a boost. When the food comes, you will be a hero.'

'But for now,' Cleander snarled, 'all they will see is that I am hoarding even *more* grain away from them. You dolt.'

The look of injured innocence that passed across Severus' face was masterful, and Rufinus had to fight down a smile even at this dire stage. In one bright moment the consul had managed to drive another nail into the crucifix of Cleander's reputation while appearing to have been doing it for the best of reasons.

The crowd now spotted Cleander once more in the shadows, and Rufinus was thoroughly impressed at the surge of hatred that suddenly washed across the city outside. The chamberlain's popularity was at an all time low. Had the emperor been currently resident in the city, he could not have missed this, and Cleander's fall would have begun. With him in his coastal villa it was more difficult, but surely soon *someone* of import would petition the emperor.

'Do something,' snapped Cleander. 'I have business to attend to and I cannot lurk around in this shit hole all day. Clear them away.'

Rufinus sighed. 'That is precisely what we are attempting to do, Chamberlain.'

'Not with words, man. With weapons. Clear the street. Put the crowd down.'

Severus turned to him. 'You cannot advocate attacking Roman citizens when they have yet to display a show of violence themselves.'

'They might not have struck me, Consul, but their intent is clear enough. Move them on.'

Now Rufinus shook his head. 'I will not engage them unless I am out of options, Chamberlain. They outnumber us five men to one, and my men are armed only with nightsticks.'

'Then step aside and let *real* soldiers disperse them.'

Rufinus frowned. 'The Praetorian Guard have no jurisdiction in…'

Cleander waved him aside angrily. 'The Praetorian Guard have whatever rights and power I care to bestow upon them. And if the Urban Cohort are not capable of doing their job? Well I've warned you once before. The Guard will be forced to step in and do it for them.'

Severus shook his head. 'They are the emperor's bodyguard. Only he or the two prefects can authorise any such action.'

'I command both the prefects, Severus, or did you forget? I am the *dagger bearer*, ultimate commander of the Guard. Stand aside.'

Rufinus shook his head. 'No. These are citizens, and until someone throws a brick they are *innocent* citizens.'

'Tribune?' Cleander turned to Fulvius. 'Have the men draw their blades and engage the crowd. If anyone gets in the way that is their own bad luck.'

Fulvius saluted and marched back into the courtyard yelling commands to the two centuries of guardsmen therein. Rufinus exchanged looks with both Severus and Dionysus. Their overt expressions were of disbelief, horror and anger, yet each of them had that barely discernible twinkle in their eye that Rufinus was sure he also had. By rights, Rufinus should stop them. He should resist, especially with the authority of a consul present. And the very last thing he wanted to do was let civilians die. But opposing Cleander right now would be a terrible idea. The man's anger was at its peak and here outside the Pomerium his guardsmen were armoured fully and armed with edged weapons. If pushed, he might very well cut a path through nobles and soldiers alike before he even reached the public. And there was always the tantalising possibility that the Guard might be overwhelmed and Cleander torn to pieces by the mob.

'Step aside,' the chamberlain snapped once more, gesturing to the three of them. Rufinus, not wanting to be the man to give the order and condemn the crowd to violence, looked at Severus.

'Consul?'

'We have no choice, Centurion. Stand your men down and step aside.'

Rufinus nodded.

'Men of the Cohort? Fall back in a two-man column through the doorway at double time, presenting a shield wall to the front at all times. Form up in the courtyard as you are relieved.'

Immediately the rear ranks of his men began to pour back through the gate in pairs, hurrying into the courtyard and leaving just enough space for the three conspirators and Cleander in the gap. As they fell back swiftly, the Praetorians began moving to the doorway, preparing to take their place. Rufinus was relieved to note that not one face among them showed any joy at what they had been ordered to do. The Guard may have been corrupted almost beyond repair, but there were still limits to which they seemed unhappy to sink.

Rufinus and the other two stepped back now into the courtyard, as did Cleander. The man was no idiot. When his men set upon the crowd he intended to remain safely at the rear. Rufinus watched, tense, as his men fell in at attention within the courtyard. It seemed the mere blink of an eye passed before the last men arrived, walking swiftly backwards, keeping their shields to the crowd.

'This should be stopped.'

Severus nodded. 'It should, but sometimes sacrifices must be made for the greater good. If you step in their way, they will simply cut you down too. You know that.'

With a heavy heart, Rufinus watched a few of the braver civilians edging into the gateway, following the men of the Cohort. They were greeted a moment later by the rhythmic tramp of nailed boots as the men of the Praetorian Guard, four abreast, marched into the gateway, shields forward and swords drawn. Cries of panic and disbelief arose outside, and Rufinus shuddered. This would be butchery, pure and simple.

It was only moments before a whistle blew a command that Rufinus knew all too well and the screaming started. He bit into his lip. How far the Guard had fallen since the day he'd been proud to be elevated to their august ranks. Now they were commanded by a villain and his two snivelling sycophants and had set to work murdering civilians.

Even as he felt the last shred of respect he had clung to for his former unit fade away and die, he saw Appius Fulvius kick his horse and ride forth to join the fray. Once again, Rufinus vowed vehemently to see the vile tribune die. Serving Cleander was bad enough, and murdering a frumentarius unforgivable, but willingly joining in the wholesale slaughter of innocent civilians condemned him all over again in Rufinus' eyes.

The Praetorian column was twenty men long and four wide as they marched into the gateway, and Rufinus could imagine just what was happening outside, even without the screams. The fact that the column continued to march at speed and without even a sign of slowing spoke unpleasantly of just how little resistance their swords were meeting.

As Cleander flashed them one last disdain-filled look and then walked his horse after his men into the gateway, Rufinus, gorge rising, turned to wave at his optio.

'We all know what's happening out there, but we are not a part of it. Once the Guard have gone, I want you men back out there, but I want your nightsticks tightly sheathed and the only thing you're doing with your shields is using them as stretchers. Capsarii, I want you moving through the victims, identifying those who can be saved and giving aid where you can. Get the wounded either walking or on shields. We're taking them to get assistance. The dead will have to wait.'

'What about the rest, sir?' Sura called.

'I doubt there will be a man out there who's not wounded or dead by the time we get there. Any survivors will have run away. The Praetorian Guard have just shown the Roman people that their proud unit can no longer be trusted or respected. I don't want that reputation clinging to us, too. The Urban Cohort will be remembered today as the men who came to their aid.'

The optio, and Rufinus' fellow centurion further over, saluted with expressions of grim satisfaction. Rufinus had just grown in their estimation, and the Guard had finally plummeted into the depths.

'Where do we take the wounded?' the other centurion asked. 'Can't take them back to the Castra Praetoria, for the love of Mars.'

Rufinus nodded. 'Quite right. The nearest place to here with large scale medical facilities is the Castra Peregrina. Take them there.'

The other officers stared at him. 'We won't get in there, sir, not without passes and a bloody good reason. And we don't know if there's a hospital, anyway.'

Rufinus clenched his fist. 'I'll go ahead and get you in. And there is a hospital there. I've been before.'

Ignoring the burning curiosity among his men, Rufinus turned to Severus and Dionysus. 'This is a dark day.'

Severus nodded. 'There may be darker still, but you did what was both right and prudent. Today has done more to damn Cleander and commend your own men than anything we've achieved over the last year. It has been an awful event, but in the end it will play to the good. It will help end this nightmare.'

'Gods, I hope so.'

They stood in uncomfortable silence for a moment, and Rufinus listened to the sounds outside change. There were no longer screams of panic and a roar of anger. Now it had become wails of bitter lament. It was over; this was the time.

'Men of the Urban Cohort, follow me.'

Tucking his vine stick into his belt to make it clear that he was not intending violence, Rufinus moved into the gate. He was no Cleander. The chamberlain might lurk safely at the rear of his men as he ordered them into murder, but Rufinus would go first as a centurion should, leading his men and facing the crowd outside alone at first.

He stepped through the dark passageway and emerged into the light and fought down the mouthful of sick that came up. The first thing that hit him was the smell. The smell of a battlefield was nothing new to him. He had experienced a fair few in his time, and most recently a few short years ago in Dacia. But he had been back in Rome now for some time and even with the rife plague he had not been prepared to experience it in the city's streets.

Blood, gore and bowels. The smell of the battlefield.

Steadying himself and straightening, he lifted his gaze. In fact, the Guard were not yet entirely gone. At the far side of the square, past the slew of corpses, the last ranks of guardsmen, under the watchful, mounted gaze of Appius Fulvius, were gratuitously slaughtering those few who could not run fast enough. The lead men of the Cohort, along with Dionysus and Severus, emerged behind Rufinus, and he bit off the command that immediately rose to mind – to order his men across the square at the run and bring down Fulvius, beating him to death.

Instead, he glared as the last three standing citizens were put mercilessly to the sword. He watched their bodies fall, heard the screams, and reaffirmed his vow to see that man dead, as the Praetorians finally fully disengaged and marched away. As their crunching footsteps receded, Rufinus looked around himself. In actual fact, the death toll had not been quite as bad as he'd imagined. He'd reckoned there were around a thousand civilians out there before. He estimated the dead and incapacitated at somewhere between two hundred and two hundred and fifty. The walking wounded numbered maybe a hundred more. Of course very likely another hundred wounded had fled home before now, and many of them would likely die of their injuries that night. Still, that meant that maybe half the crowd had managed to flee the scene unharmed.

Never had he been more grateful that Senova was safe in Sicilia.

Around him, the officers and men of the Urban Cohort began to move among the stricken crowd, offering what assistance they could. Rufinus saw out of the corner of his eye a unit of vigiles approach, cautiously and with clubs drawn. One of the men nearby took it upon himself to explain to the newcomers what had happened and within moments the vigiles had sheathed their weapons, dropped their buckets, hoses and hooked poles, and were helping with the wounded.

Had it not been for the fact that supposedly noble soldiers of Rome had caused this in the first place, Rufinus might have felt it heart-warming to see men whose jobs were policing and firefighting instead rushing to the aid of their fellow men.

But there was anger gnawing at him now. He had sworn to bring down Cleander, who had made it personal time and time again, and he had sworn to kill Fulvius, whose own actions labelled him a felon. But this was something else. This was villainy on a grand, unconscionable scale. This was death and violence such as men like Nero had caused. He resolved to end it. The grain fleet was coming, and when it did, Cleander would rise once more. If he could not be brought low by then, Rufinus decided flatly, he would be the man to do the deed. If the grain fleet arrived, Rufinus would march into Tribune Fulvius' house and then march back out with a bloodied blade, leaving only a butchered corpse, executed by a loyal citizen. Then he would find a way to reach Cleander. He would put his blade through that bastard's black heart, and save Rome. Oh, he would then be tortured and would condemn all his friends, and so instead he would drag his knife across his own throat like a noble Roman of old and expire before he could betray anyone. Senova was not officially connected to him, and Publius was in a safe house a thousand miles away. He would die for it, but none of his loved ones would suffer, and he would bring the pair of bastards down first.

Leaving everyone else, he marched away. It was not a long walk from here to the Castra Peregrina. Half a mile at most. Even as he moved away from the grisly scene, already his soldiers were lifting wounded men up on shields or supporting them from the side and helping them move. Bloody footprints littered the road as he walked, and he peered at their huge numbers with a sickened pity. How many had fled clutching wounds only to die in their loved ones' arms tonight?

Here and there, he noted new graffiti, some of it even painted in fresh blood. This was different. There was no edge of dark humour to these new slogans and images. They simply spoke of Cleander, and they called him words that made even Rufinus wince, terms that his father would have beaten him for using, calling him an uncouth barbarian.

They were almost there, now. Cleander had gone from being a grand public figure to being the target of the people's hatred.

Ahead, the Castra Peregrina loomed, home of the transit barracks for all provincial military, but also the home of the frumentarii, one of the most guarded, secretive places in the city.

He would see the wounded to their medicus, and then he would begin the final phase of this plan, ruining Cleander and rousing the populace enough to bring him down.

.

Part Four

The last lap

"Nam qui dabat olim imperium [...] duas tantum res optat, panem et circenses."

(The mob that used to grant power [...] hopes for two things only: bread and circuses)

Juvenal – Satires

Chapter Twenty Two – Confrontation

Rome, June 16th 190 A.D., afternoon

The men of the Urban Cohort worked like beasts of burden, tireless and unceasing. Rufinus, feeling a little guilty that his hands were empty apart from his vine stick and that he hadn't moved in half an hour, glanced across at the other officers.

Prefect Pertinax looked as tense as the rest of them, and that was no small number of officers. Fully two thirds of the entire force was present at the Horrea Ummidiana. Two cohorts. One and a half of those cohorts was engaged in moving the grain shipment and seeing it into the two remaining granaries safely, stored away. It was not the Alexandrian shipment, of course, of which there was blessedly as yet no sign. This latest set of wagons was the stock of a merchant from Puteoli who had been pressed into relinquishing it into imperial hands for a relatively low price.

Cleander was getting impatient, demanding to know when there would be enough grain stored to feed the dole recipients and defuse the ever more dangerous city. In truth there was enough in there to cover the grain dole almost twice over now, but the chamberlain remained blessedly unaware. Rufinus had worried for a time that one of the men of the Urban Cohort would let slip the truth, since they had to know how much grain they had moved, but the Cohort were a loyal bunch. They were never going to let the truth get to the Praetorians who despised them, and therefore not to their master Cleander either. So the small shipments the chamberlain claimed continued to turn up, and the Urban Cohorts continued to liaise with Dionysus and his office over security, transport and storage.

The other half cohort present, who were not lugging grain sacks, were standing in a defensive line around the entire operation, watching the crowd like hawks.

The sad fact was that despite the horror of what had happened nine days ago outside the grain offices, the public had not been cowed. In fact, Cleander's violent attack on the restive mob had had more or less entirely the opposite result. In the wake of murder and maiming, the people of Rome had not slunk away into their homes and hidden from the chamberlain's wrath. Instead, they had begun to rise up angrily. Had it not been for the awful event that had triggered it all, Rufinus might have been rather satisfied with the result. Never since the days of Sejanus had the Praetorian Guard and their master been so reviled by Rome.

Cleander's fruit-pelted statue in the forum had gone. It had simply vanished one night. Wherever his name was found painted or carved had become makeshift urinals for the population of Rome. His name was spoken with hatred, and slogans demanding his death appeared nightly. Had the emperor not been locked away in seclusion, he would have had no choice by now other than to seek the end of his chamberlain. But no ordinary man could get to the emperor on his private estate, and any man of influence who might consider approaching the emperor had been threatened sufficiently by Cleander that they had dropped out of sight.

Demonstrations arose across the city time and again, angry and troublesome, always on the edge of violence if never quite achieving it. The men of the Urban Cohort, their reputation unblemished among the people, quietly and calmly dispersed any gatherings. The Praetorians tried to avoid such places. Once, not so long ago, no citizen would have dared insult a Praetorian. Now they only went out in groups, for a guardsman caught on his own would be pelted with rotten food and shit. It had become so bad that outside the palace gates on the Palatine, the Guard had cleared gatherings by force often enough that the people had stopped gathering there.

Things were at breaking point. Rufinus had spoken to the others several times, desperately hoping for some suggestion as to how they could make the emperor aware of what was happening in the city. Repeatedly he had come away disappointed. Severus maintained that it would happen and they had to let things run their course, now. They had done everything they set out to do, and had made Cleander the most hated man in more than a century. Now they had to step back and let natural events take over. If they were seen to be engineering it, they would fall as badly as the chamberlain. Severus was content that it would all work out now.

Still, daily Rufinus kept an eye on the acta diurna and the emporium, half expecting the Alexandrian fleet to arrive and solve all Cleander's problems. Still, thank the gods, it had not.

Rufinus glanced at the crowd now. They were as restive as ever, but at least he felt no danger or malice emanating from them. Where across the city crowds would threaten violence against the authorities in the form of Cleander's Praetorians, no such hate was now aimed at the Urban Cohort or the vigiles. Their heroism and concern for the people in the wake of the recent slaughter had become the talk of Rome. Still, they remained on edge. The crowd might not wish to rise against the Cohort, but the level of anger and desperation was still reaching a critical point.

The men continued to strain under the weight of the sacks as their fellows on guard stood watch, eying the crowd. Rufinus continued to glance back and forth between them.

'Uh oh,' Optio Sura muttered next to him, and Rufinus turned to see what he was worrying about. His spirits sank. A century of Praetorians was stomping in their direction, which boded ill in every way. Rufinus peered at the group carefully and sighed. At least Cleander and Fulvius were not here. This was an ordinary infantry unit under the command of a centurion, and Rufinus didn't recognise the man's crest.

'I wonder what they're after,' Sura mused.

'I don't know, but with that lot over there,' Rufinus thumbed towards the crowd, 'it won't take much to start trouble.'

Pertinax rode across towards Rufinus now, another senior centurion alongside him. 'We appear to have friends visiting,' the prefect said, his tone dripping with sarcasm.

The Praetorians approached the granary and at a gesture from a centurion, the men of the Urban Cohort closed ranks a little, making space for the new arrivals but coincidentally also forming ready for trouble. The white-clad soldiers came to a crashing halt and turned to face Pertinax, their centurion stepping forward and giving him a still salute.

'Centurion, to what do we owe this honour?'

The Praetorian glared at him. 'Marcus Aurelius Cleander, Chamberlain of the...'

'We know who he is. What does he want?'

The Centurion's eyes narrowed angrily in the shade of his helmet. 'The "dagger bearer" wishes to know the level of fill in the granaries and how close we are to being able to distribute the dole.'

Pertinax turned to Rufinus, who remained the Cohort's chief officer liaising with Dionysus. 'Maximus?'

'I spoke to the Praefectus Annonae just this morning,' Rufinus responded, turning to the Praetorians. 'His latest records put us six thousand modii short for the general populace without considering those groups, like yourselves, who we still have to feed separately. Given the size of the shipment we received this morning, two or three more at that level might see supplies reach an adequate quantity.'

'How long?'

Rufinus shrugged. 'How high is up? It depends on when shipments come in and what size they are, and that is down to your master securing them in the first place..'

'The chamberlain is becoming impatient.'

Rufinus smiled nastily. 'Patience is not a trait I have ever observed in him.'

The Centurion bristled at the insult. 'Watch your tongue, grunt.'

'I'd advise you the same, Centurion,' Rufinus smiled. 'Eighty men will not protect you from a good hiding if a couple of cohorts of real soldiers decide you're being a bit too big for your boots.'

The centurion growled, readying himself to retort, but Pertinax's voice cut through the warm, stinking afternoon air. 'Gentlemen, let's have a little conduct befitting centurions of Rome and less of these childish insults.'

The two centurions stood and glared at one another, though both remained silent. The air became taut and dangerous. Above, a bird of prey took a pigeon in mid-air with avian cries. A few errant feathers drifted down in the lifeless air between Rufinus and the Praetorian. He was trying to decide whether to attempt to calm things further, wind the man up again, or simply turn away, when disaster struck.

Someone in the crowd hurled a piece of brick.

The red, dusty rock slammed into the shoulder plates of a Praetorian and he yelped at the blow, falling forward and then staggering to regain his stance. Rufinus was forgotten in an instant as the centurion turned away, peering at his men and taking in what had happened.

A dozen or so of the Praetorians had turned their heads to look at the gathered citizenry, and one or two were shouting foul oaths at them. The centurion, realising what had happened, began to bellow orders.

'Form up and draw swords.'

The loose lines of Praetorians turned with a unified crunch to face the crowd, tightening into a fighting unit, weapons unsheathing with a loud rasping noise. They stood for a long moment like that. The centurion perhaps felt out of his depth now. He'd only come for an update and to deliver the words of

Cleander and now he was facing an angry crowd and with hostile men of the Urban Cohort close by. There was a pregnant pause.

Rufinus glanced back at his own men. The soldiers of the Cohort had stopped work on the grain sacks. Even as he glanced around he saw that several centurions and optios had taken the initiative and closed the granary gates to secure the contents, returning any errant sacks to the wagons and then gathering men protectively around them. The Cohort was ready for trouble. Pertinax looked pensive.

'Sir, we cannot allow a repeat of that disaster at the Galbana.'

The prefect nodded absently, his eyes locked on the Praetorians.

'Sir…'

'Yes, Maximus, I know. But we are in a dangerous position. If we lock horns with these men we effectively declare war on the Praetorians and therefore on the chamberlain. I am not sure that any of us want that.'

Rufinus nodded but, true as that was, he was more concerned with stopping a second grand slaughter.

'Respectfully, sir, that cannot influence a decision like this.'

Still Pertinax was nodding, and said nothing.

Rufinus turned back just in time to see a second missile pelt another Praetorian. Everything happened in the blur of an instant then. The stricken guardsman, hit in the head by the thrown item, lashed out at the nearest civilian, calling him a 'lawless bastard'. Fortunately, perhaps, he only used the hilt of his sword, but the heavy pommel smacked into the man's head in retaliation, and that citizen went down like a sack of turnips, unconscious before he landed.

The crowd roared, and whatever the guardsmen tried to shout disappeared beneath the din of the mob and a sound like the drumming hooves of a cavalry ala as fists, feet and makeshift cudgels thudded against Praetorian shields.

'Maintain ranks,' bellowed their centurion. Do not strike until I give the order.'

Rufinus shivered. He couldn't quite work out whether that was the officer trying to stop his men attacking the public or more an order trying to make the attack an official, coordinated and concerted one. He had a feeling the centurion himself wasn't sure yet. One or two of the guardsmen lashed out angrily despite their orders, but as yet no one had been cut or stabbed.

'*Prefect*,' Rufinus hissed urgently, not taking his eyes off the scene. Somehow the centurion had managed to bark enough discipline into his men to stop them battering the public, though the crowd continued to lash out at the soldiers' solid wall of shields.

'Desist,' bellowed Pertinax suddenly with such command and force to his considerable voice that the struggling stopped in an instant, soldiers and civilians alike startled by the call.

'Praetorians take one step back. People of Rome, move away from the Guard.'

Pertinax had no authority over the Praetorians, of course, yet they did as he said without question, a gap opening up between them and the hostile crowd. The centurion spun angrily.

'Keep your nose out of this, Prefect.'

Pertinax leaned forward over his horse's neck. 'Perhaps, Centurion, you would care to remember that you are speaking to the prefect of the Guard, a former consul, procurator, governor and general. And when you do, perhaps you might want to reconsider your badly chosen words. The Praetorians are not untouchable, and I have rather a lot of men here at my command. But then, perhaps what I should do is stand back and let the people of Rome rightfully tear your limbs off.' He smiled warmly. 'Hmm?'

The centurion bridled for a moment, and Rufinus thought he might actually argue. Instead, rather bravely, but very foolishly, he said 'I do not answer to men of the Urban Cohort, no matter how distinguished their history.'

The smile never slipped from Pertinax's face as he sat back in the saddle.

'Maximus, have the men fall in, barring two centuries to guard the wagons.'

Rufinus felt his blood pounding at the danger rising in the air as he turned and marched over towards the watching men of the Cohort. They had, of course, heard every word of the prefect's, as had much of the crowd. It took hardly a word of command for Rufinus to have the men fall in, lined up and ready. Despite his time in the Praetorians, Rufinus had to admit that they looked a lot more like proper veteran soldiers than the white-clad Guard in their posh uniforms. Certainly they presented a threat that Rufinus was glad *he* did not have to face.

Pertinax, still wearing that smile, rode out of the way of his men so that the Cohort were staring across a short empty space to the rear of the Praetorians, who were still facing the crowd. The centurion faltered truly for the first time, nerves getting to him, aware that his men were already facing a hostile public, but that he had now put an enemy behind them too.

The air sizzled with hostility, and Rufinus felt a rising worry that the Praetorian officer might just be driven by pride to start something. The public had begun to melt away a little to the periphery of the square, all remaining eyes on the two civil military units, every hand among them on the hilt of a weapon. Both units were armoured. Only the Praetorians bore blades, but being restricted to nightsticks would not necessarily make the Cohort inferior. They did, after all, outnumber the Praetorians here by more than twenty to one. At that number they could be wielding sponges and still be confident of victory.

At a quiet command from the centurion, the Praetorians about-faced and remained in position, now with their backs to the public at some distance and facing the men of the Cohort. He was brave, Rufinus had to give him that. Or perhaps just bloody-minded and foolish.

344

Silence reigned once more.

Finally, Pertinax leaned forward in his saddle again.

'I think the time has come, Centurion, for you to take your men back to their barracks and tuck them in for the night, don't you?'

Rufinus watched the centurion's face. He was struggling. He was well aware of his chances if it came to a fight, but backing down now in front of Pertinax would dent not only his pride, but also his reputation and the authority he wielded over his own men.

'The Praetorian Guard,' Pertinax added, conversationally, 'was founded to protect the emperor. That is the very meaning of their name. They were formed originally as the body guard of a praetor – a general who wielded imperium. Augustus made them officially an imperial guard, and Tiberius created you as you are now. In nearly two centuries your role has never changed. Your duty, no matter how tangled in intrigues it might have become, is still to protect the emperor.'

There was an uncomfortable silence. The centurion probably didn't want to be reminded of that, since no one had seen the emperor for a year, since he had taken his mistress out of the diseased city to his villa at Laurentum. There, a few Praetorians were quartered, bolstered by a force of gladiators selected by Commodus himself. But the bulk of the Guard never saw the emperor, protecting instead a complex of palaces that housed the chamberlain and the imperial staff.

'Policing the city and keeping order in the streets is not the job of the Praetorian Guard any more than it is the job of the virgins of Vesta,' Pertinax smiled. 'The Urban Cohort was formed to perform those tasks. Leave us to our duty and return to your barracks.'

The centurion bridled. We have standing orders from the chamberlain, who speaks for the emperor, to put down riots wherever we find them in the city, since the Urban Cohort have proven themselves to be too womanly to do it themselves.'

Brave. And very, very stupid. Every man of the Cohort changed their stance. The mood among them had slipped from amused threat to very real anger in an instant. They were truly walking a knife edge now, and Rufinus was half inclined to released his men to beat the white-clad bastards to a pulp. He restrained himself with difficulty. That was a stupid notion. Right now the Guard was hated almost as much as the man who called himself 'dagger bearer' and commanded them, while the Urban Cohorts maintained a solid level of respect in the streets. They had to rise above this, else that important distinction might just blur.

'Leaving aside entirely the question of Cleander's level of authority,' Pertinax sighed, 'which I suspect he sees as larger than life, you might want to re-examine the definition of a riot. A thrown pebble and an apple do not a riot make. This was, in fact, a peaceful crowd of citizens until your men stomped into view and started throwing your weight around. There is no riot here to put down, unless you happen to trigger one. Now I will say this only once more, and then I shall stop smiling, and I don't think you want that to happen: this crowd is under control. There is no riot. The Urban Cohort is doing its duty with aplomb and care, and there is no requirement here for the Guard. Take your men back to their barracks now, because even in Praetorian white it's very hard to walk that far with a nightstick jammed up your backside.'

Sniggers broke out among the men of the Cohort, and Rufinus turned, along with other centurions, and silenced them with a look. This was not the time. Rufinus himself would have a good laugh about it, but later on, in a bar with his men. Not now.

The centurion was actually shaking, he was so angry. But he was not as foolish as Rufinus had worried. There was no way this would end well for him if he argued. He straightened.

'The dagger bearer shall hear of this, Prefect.'

'Yes, he will. I shall tell him myself. Goodbye, Centurion.'

Humiliated and angry, the centurion turned sharply and ordered his men back to the Castra Praetoria. They marched away with a shush of mail and the crunch of nailed boots, and the Cohort watched them go with a sense of immense satisfaction.

Rufinus heaved a sigh of relief as Pertinax walked his horse back over.

'D'you know, Maximus, I rather enjoyed myself there.'

'We were damned close to a proper fight, Prefect.'

'I disagree. The centurion had to know we would have given him a good hiding. Anyway, I fear we may have just somewhat ruined what little working relationship we had with Cleander and his thugs. I may have to visit the palace and smooth things over with him.'

He frowned at Rufinus. 'What you said earlier, about the grain quantities, is it true?'

Rufinus nodded. He hated lying to this man, but Pertinax had thus far left all matters of grain to him, and if the prefect found out now that they were hoarding sufficient to feed everyone, Rufinus could not imagine it going down well. 'Yes, sir, according to my reports from Papirius Dionysus.'

He also hated laying any potential blame on his fellow conspirator, but things were about to explode, and he couldn't afford the prefect unpicking a lie here, in case everything unravelled in the process. Muddying the waters of blame would at least buy time. He was uncomfortable with the way Pertinax was looking at him again.

'One day soon, I might take a look at those supplies myself.'

Rufinus swallowed nervously and nodded. 'Any time, sir.'

The prefect pursed his lips, eyes still slitted with suspicion, but there was an odd coy smile there too as he wheeled his horse to face the crowd gathered at the periphery of the square.

'Those of you who were close enough will have heard that entire exchange, and they will therefore be able to tell the rest of you how the grain situation stands. The time of relief and plenty is coming, and it is coming very soon. Let us work here and disperse to your homes. I do not want to risk attracting the attention and the blades of the Praetorian Guard again. Thank you.'

He turned away from the crowd, who were already beginning to move.

Rufinus shook off his worries for now. All he could do was pray that Severus' belief was well founded and that events were now snowballing beyond their control. He watched as the last of the crowd melted away and the soldiers were left alone to finish unloading the grain. Despite his worry, Pertinax made no attempt to enter the granaries or request the records. Instead, after another quarter of an hour of supervision, the prefect sighed and rode off to the Palatine to attempt to mollify the chamberlain who would undoubtedly have heard by now of the near battle in the streets of the Little Aventine.

The Cohort finished work an hour later, secured the horrea and then waited for the next shift. A short while later three centuries of men arrived to take over security detail on the granary complex, and the rest of the tired soldiers set out for the fortress, where every man would stick close with his mates and be sure to stay in the Urban Cohort's region and not stray into Praetorian areas, just in case.

Rufinus intended to spend some time in one of the soldier's bars on the Vicus Longus – one of those favoured by the Cohort and shunned by the Guard, for obvious reasons. But first, after this day all he wanted was a bath. He had yet to bathe in the fortress baths, even though there was a separate, smaller complex set aside for the men of the Urban Cohort. His rather distinctive scars might easily cause his true identity to slip out, he'd reasoned, and so he had begun to use a small private bath house three streets away from the fortress. It was exclusive, and not cheap, but there his anonymity remained intact and he did not have to worry about being discovered by any one of his many potential enemies.

Thus it was that on the way back to the fortress, Rufinus left his men in Sura's charge for the last few hundred paces, and sloped off into a side street, making for his favourite baths. It was a relatively small complex that could only really cater for half a dozen clients at a time, each of whom was granted a good level of privacy. Unlike the great baths where people went for hours at a time to socialise and do business, this sort of balneum dealt with wealthy clients who wanted quiet time to relax, or who perhaps wanted to dally with an acquaintance without their family knowing. For Rufinus the solitude was perfect. The only thing he really missed was being able to swim, for the small pool here allowed for only general floundering.

He greeted the slave at the apodyterium, who showed him to an alcove and brought him towel and clogs, and there undressed before moving through into the warm rooms. He spent half an hour sweating out the day in the laconium, then allowed a pleasant, shapely slave girl to use oil and strigil and scrape away the dirt. He was comfortable these days with his relationship with Senova, but still spending any amount of time in the company of a pretty girl automatically made him feel guilty, no matter that he had no designs on her. From there he moved out into another steam room, where the last trace of oil trickled from his skin with the sweat. On a normal day he would revive himself then with a sharp plunge into the cold pool, waking him instantly and energising every sense. Today, with the hours of strain both physically and mentally, he favoured quiet relaxation instead.

He passed through into the warm bath room, grateful that he was still alone, and sank slowly and gratefully into the warm water with a sigh. There he lay at the edge of the pool, his head leaned back over the edge, body floating and legs idly kicking occasionally.

He had no idea how long he relaxed there, and wasn't entirely sure he hadn't drifted off to sleep a couple of times for just a moment or two, but he was finally managing to relax.

Until he heard the footsteps.

He was on the alert instantly. There were three types of footstep one heard in this place: the clack of wooden clogs or the gentle slap of bare feet from the bathers, and the soft 'shup' of fine calfskin from the attendants.

You did not get hobnailed military boots. And not several of them.

There was no proof, of course, but Rufinus knew instinctively that they were here for him. He didn't know if there were any other customers in the balneum, and they might be in the cold bath or the pool or one of the other chambers, but still he knew this was trouble come looking for him. He mentally ran through the floorplan of the bath house and cursed. From here the only doors led back into the steam rooms, another hot bath or the warm room. And whichever he chose he could get nowhere without passing through the decorative octagonal entrance chamber that lay next to the changing room. The boots were already past that.

He was unarmed and naked.

Damn it, damn it, damn it.

In a trice he was out of the bath, water sloshing, droplets cascading from him, hopping from foot to foot because of the almost torturous heat of the floor. He couldn't put his clogs on. Far too noisy. He would have to dance from foot to foot and suffer the heat. He did grab his towel quickly and fold it round his waist, tucking it tight as he ducked out of the warm baths. He was just disappearing into the steam room as white-clad soldiers emerged into the caldarium where he'd been only a moment earlier.

He could hear them arguing now as they looked down at the floor around the bath, which was soaked with pools of water and wet footprints. And then he was gone, in among the sweating clouds of steam. It was not quite dense enough to truly hide him, just make him hard to spot, and so Rufinus ran on the balls of his feet, almost silent, into the chamber where he'd been scraped down, and then through another steam room.

He could hear the soldiers behind him moving into the white cloud and shouting, searching.

He hurried out into the vestibule, making for the changing room and freedom, and instead ran straight into a mountain of human flesh wearing a white tunic and segmented plate armour.

'Thought so,' said a familiar voice as the huge man in Praetorian white delivered a punch like a mule kick to Rufinus' head. Brains swimming and eyes blurring, Rufinus staggered. He should have been slower, more careful. He'd not had time to plan anything. He tried to swipe at the man, but he was half-conscious at best, and making for unconsciousness rapidly. His ears were ringing and his head hurt. He swung again, and the big man thumped him once more for good measure, driving him down to the floor with a groan.

The last thing he heard before darkness claimed him was the voice of the cavalry tribune Appius Fulvius.

'Bring him.'

CHAPTER TWENTY THREE – CAPTIVITY

Rome, June 16th 190 A.D., evening

Rufinus awoke with a start, though his surroundings were every bit as black as the painful unconsciousness in which he'd wallowed for... how long?

He blinked a few times to be sure his eyes were functioning properly, and then concentrated on the faint shapes and patches of different shade in the black. He was in a room, which he could have guessed anyway, but he could make out all four walls, so it was not a large room. He thought he could identify a door as a faint shape, but he would have to touch it to be truly sure. Turning his head, which hurt like the pits of Tarterus, he found another square. A window, he thought. Shuttered for sure, but since there was not even a hint of a glow around the edge, that confirmed that it was night time. The sun was fully set.

Fulvius. It had been Fulvius and his men who'd tracked Rufinus to the bath house – although he'd never made a secret of using it so they probably knew he'd go there. Fulvius had probably been waiting for him to return to the Castra Praetoria and when he didn't made the assumption that he had gone to his usual baths.

If Fulvius had taken him, then he would have to be somewhere out of the way. The Urban Cohorts and their Prefect Pertinax would take a great deal of offence at having one of their centurions snatched by the Guard. So the bastards would have had to sneak him into the camp. That meant avoiding the eastern area where the Cohort was quartered. They must have taken him through back streets around to the north and brought him in past the Praetorian cavalry barracks, which made sense. They couldn't risk taking him near the centre of the fortress where stray soldiers from the Cohort might be found. So he must still be somewhere in the north of the camp, in the cavalry area.

He tried to focus on the room and pick out more details, but there really were none to identify. The room seemed to be an empty box with one door and a shuttered window. It did not smell equine, so it was nothing to do with the horses. It could be about the right size for a barrack room housing a contubernium of eight men. Or one officer. He wished he'd paid more attention to the cavalry while he'd been in the fortress as a legitimate guardsman. Then he might have more of a clue where he was.

No. He wouldn't be in the barracks, he decided. Fulvius might rely upon his men, but Rufinus doubted he would risk leaving the prisoner among them in a barrack block. And if he wasn't near the horses, but he was in the north, probably fairly close to the gate, then that meant this was either a disused workshop or an empty storeroom. Either way it would be supplied with a good lock, on the shutters too. No quartermaster wanted to risk supplies or tools being swiped by enterprising soldiers. And Fulvius was no idiot. Rufinus would be held somewhere secure and out of the reach of the Cohort, but he would also be somewhere where shouting would go unheard or unnoticed.

Crying out for help would be fruitless. Worse, it would let his captors know he was awake, which might draw more attention than he really wanted.

He sat, still and silent, for a moment, listening carefully. He could hear the very distant sounds of camp life, but only faintly. There was something else, though: a faint susurration. There were no trees in the fortress, yet it was reminiscent of leaves in the breeze. After some thought, he came to the conclusion that it was a person not far beyond the door, changing position and shuffling occasionally, his uniform making those sounds. A dulled, wood-and-leather clonk confirmed it for him, as he knew the sound of a full scabbard knocking against things. A chair, he reckoned, by the sound. So, a guard watching the door, seated, but armed and in uniform.

Now he had determined more or less where he was being held and how he was being held there. Two major questions remained: how long would he be held, and why was he being held in the first place. He had no doubt that it was Fulvius' orders that had brought him here and no one else. Fulvius was the only one who knew who he truly was, after all. But why imprison him? If Fulvius had decided to move against him, why not simply kill him? It would probably have been a simple enough job to have stabbed him and left him in the baths. But instead they had knocked him out and brought him here.

With a true wave of fear, he suddenly realised that there was a very good chance that Fulvius intended to torture him. If the tribune had begun to suspect there was more to Rufinus' plans than simply killing him, perhaps he had decided that it was time to take the nails of Rufinus' *other* hand in order to pry out of him everything he had to tell.

And Rufinus was no fool. Brave men might say they would rather die than talk, but under torture everybody talked sooner or later. And while that Persian who had so ruined him at Lucilla's villa a decade ago was an expert at his job, the best torturers in the world served under a Praetorian centurion called Adrastus. It would not be a difficult job for Fulvius to have one of them brought in.

He rose, slowly, as quietly as he could. He was wearing only the towel from the bath house, so while he was poorly-attired, he was at least quiet. As he reached his full stance, he swayed sickeningly. His head felt as though it were swimming in oil. He bit down on the vomit that rose in his gullet and forced it back down, standing still until the worst of the feeling went.

When he felt a little stronger and more balanced, he began to move slowly around the room, examining things closely and feeling his way carefully where he could.

The room was most definitely empty. The shuttered window was locked down. He could see the fastening as a darker shadow in the gloom. The door would be locked and guarded. There were no other features to the place – not even a bucket to piss in – which suddenly made his bladder ache with the need to do so. Damn it.

Still not wanting to risk alerting the guard to his wakefulness, he moved to the far corner of the room and there very carefully, slowly and with painstaking discomfort, urinated in a tightly controlled dribble for what seemed like an hour. It was difficult and horribly uncomfortable, but he was silent in doing so. The longer they remained convinced he was unconscious, probably the better for him.

As he pissed, he made a fairly important decision. He would not allow himself to be tortured. He knew better than most that he would crack eventually. He would sell out his friends and family under the knife, and then he would die, having been subjected to the most incredible pain first. No, he could not allow that. And he just couldn't face torture again.

It took perhaps half an hour of testing floorboards and timbers in the wall to find a broken piece. It was really little more than a giant splinter that he managed slowly and with pain to tear from the wood. He tested it. It was pointed and relatively sharp. Nowhere near as good as a knife, but with only a few blows, he could open the veins on both wrists adequately to bleed to death before anything much could be done to him.

It was not an ideal plan, but as a fall-back it was better than being tortured to death, for sure.

Before he truly considered that, he needed to formulate a better plan. One of escape.

Stages. An escape would require stages. He began to reason the problems through, partially with an eye to freedom, but also as a temporary mental escape from the black room and thoughts of what was to come.

Firstly, getting out of the room. Locked, shuttered window. Locked door. No other means of egress. Briefly, he wondered whether if he could get the floorboards up he could dig under the outer wall and escape. He would only need to go four or five feet along and a foot and a half deep. That notion was quickly brushed aside. Apart from the lack of anything with which to dig, there was the ground itself fighting back. The lower areas of Rome were soft soil, regularly inundated by the Tiber or rain and sitting atop tufa – things soldiers knew from having had to dig from time to time. But up here on the hills, the bedrock was close to the surface and the soil above had been compacted by a century and a half of military activity in the camp. Even if he could dig, he'd probably have died of old age before he saw light. The door and window were both locked, but this was a storeroom, and not a cell. No, even with a blessing from Cardea, the goddess of hinges, these would be inset into the ground and lintel as were most doors. No luck there. If he couldn't open either and there was no way out, then he would have to get someone to open it somehow.

No one would hear or come to his aid at the window. So that left the door, which led to phase two anyway: getting past the guard. He would have to lure the guard into opening the door somehow. Probably not with the old 'oh I'm so ill' ploy. No one would fall for that these days. Perhaps he could offer the man a deal. After all, very soon the head of the Praetorians was looking at a long fall from grace and those who helped make it happen might be more popular than their peers. That would involve talking to him and trying to gain his confidence. It was a small chance, but that was always better than none.

Then there was getting out of the Castra Praetoria. Somehow, dressed only in a towel and armed with a splinter, he would have to get across the camp and either through the gate, over the wall, or into the Urban Cohort barracks. The latter was clearly the best alternative.

That would leave part four. What to do next. There were several alternatives there. He could run to Severus and then disappear, assume a new identity and hide until this was all over – perhaps even run to Sicilia and hide with Senova. That would, of course, require getting out of the fortress, and he couldn't guarantee that. Or he could go to Pertinax and come clean. Tell the prefect who he truly was and about the tribune, his murderous past and his intentions for Rufinus. He half suspected that Pertinax knew the truth anyway and simply chose not to make it known to others. Or, and this was the most appealing of all, he could arm himself, kit up and march across the camp to put Appius Fulvius to the sword.

He was eager at the thought of that, and had to rein in his excitement. To do that he would have to get to the Urban Cohort's barracks, which would require getting past the guard and out of this room.

But he had his plan. It was, he reasoned, the only possibility. He wasn't getting out of this room unless that guard opened the door.

He paced over to the door and stopped in front of it.

'Guard?'

There was a long pause, and then the sound of someone shifting in a chair.

'I know you're listening. And I'm going to lay out some basic truths for you.'

More silence. Rufinus huffed. 'You are a member of the Praetorian Guard. Your oath is to the emperor, then your standard, then your prefect. Nowhere on that list appears Cleander, and Tribune Fulvius is a lesser officer, not one of the prefects. He might be your direct commander, but he is not part of your oath. I cannot believe that the Praetorian prefects would approve of a centurion of the Urban Cohort being held against his will here, and the emperor would demand an explanation. Furthermore, sooner or later Prefect Pertinax will take exception and begin investigating my disappearance. The bath house is a known haunt and the Cohort is currently a lot more popular than the Guard. It won't take much for the bath attendants to reveal what happened. Then the Prefect will come looking for me among the cavalry. This is your only chance to do the right thing and put yourself in the law-abiding camp when the time comes. Take me to the Praetorian prefects and you'll find that they've not sanctioned Tribune Fulvius' actions.'

He fell silent and listened to the occasional creaks as the guard shifted in his chair. Still the man said nothing.

'I have friends in the Guard. Good ones. I am a friend of one of the current consuls, and a decorated war hero. I am being held here because Fulvius and I have a long-standing feud. I bet you didn't know that, eh? That this is personal and nothing to do with the Guard or the Cohort? Do you want to know a little something about Appius Fulvius?'

The silence seemed somehow interested and expectant now. Had he hooked the man? Now to haul him in.

'The Guard have always been honourable. That's one of the prime requirements of a guardsman. I know that well. So it might interest you to know a little of Fulvius' history. That when the traitor Paternus was in command ten years ago, before the emperor killed him personally, Fulvius was one of Paternus' men. Fulvius and his mates were sent to the traitor Lucilla's villa to kill a frumentarius – one of the emperor's own agents who was investigating the plot. Fulvius and his companions murdered an imperial agent. And I am one of very few people who know about it. That is why I'm here. Fulvius knows I took an oath to see him fall for what he did, and my friends are too important for him to have struck before now. You see what a snake you're working for? Do you really want to be part of his fall? Come on, man. Take me to the Prefect.

There was a different noise now. The sound of a man rising from the chair with associated ligneous and muscular creaks. Then three footsteps and the guard cleared his throat.

'You tell an exciting tale,' said the voice of Appius Fulvius, 'but sadly to the wrong person.'

Rufinus heart sank. It had not occurred to him that it might be the tribune himself sitting outside.

Damn it. His entire plan just folded up and sank into the mire.

'Now that you're awake, I have a gift for you.'

The lock at the door rattled, and Rufinus realised that he was almost getting his first wish, that the door be opened for him, but he also knew Fulvius well enough to know that there would be no opportunity here for the prisoner. Sure enough, before the door was opened, several more footsteps joined in. The portal swung in, and Rufinus blinked in the light, even low as it was, cast by two small oil lamps.

Four shadows coalesced in the orange glow. Fulvius stepped aside and the two armoured Praetorians urged a fourth man inside. Even in the gloom, Rufinus recognised the shape of his father. The old man staggered for a moment.

'Enjoy your reunion,' the tribune sneered. 'I shall return shortly.'

The door was swung shut once more, but not before the feeble light illuminated his father's face. It was bloodied and covered with welts, one eye sealed shut and swollen.

Darkness enfolded them, and footsteps receded. Once silence and black solitude reigned once more, Rufinus sighed.

'Father, this…'

'Shut up, you stupid boy. Traitor. Look at what you've done. The shame and ignominy you've brought on your family. I spit at you. Leave me alone.'

Rufinus listened to his father shuffle off into the corner, catch a whiff of the fresh urine there, and then move to another corner.

Rufinus sagged. That was it, then. His best hope had vanished. He was facing torture and death and there really was no way out. Despite everything, he regretted the old man's involvement, deluded and idiotic though he might be.

He could not rely upon Pertinax or Severus, or any of the other conspirators either. The only real glimmer of remaining hope was Vibius Cestius, though he doubted that even Cestius would currently risk infiltrating the Castra Praetoria. The fact was that he had been compromised. Fulvius knew who he truly was. And there was a very good chance that by now that information had reached Cleander. That being the case there was not a hope in Hades of any of his friends touching him. Anyone seen to be in contact with him would fall alongside him.

He was alone, condemned and doomed.

He subsided into gloomy silence, his only company the ragged breaths of his father, which sounded accusatory. The hours passed, one troubled heartbeat at a time. Rufinus' only clue as to time was when a faint glow appeared at the edges of the window, declaring a new day to be upon them. Rufinus sighed. How ironic it was that this might be the very day that saw the end of Cleander, and yet here he was in prison, with the same to be said of him.

It was starting to become light enough to make out much of the room's Spartan interior when the first new sound arrived. Footsteps. Rufinus steadied himself. It could be someone bringing food and water. Probably not, though.

The door rattled and then creaked open, three figures in the light. As the two cavalrymen stood in the exit, Appius Fulvius strode into the room. Rufinus calculated his chances and was not pleased with the result. Fulvius was in full uniform and armoured. Rufinus had a splinter and two fists. He was good, but probably not good enough for that. Still, he was ready for it. His large splinter held in a tight grip behind his back, he eyed the tribune's neck, the only real place he could strike a killing blow with his feeble weapon. As soon as the man came close enough. Let him be the one to move.

'The chamberlain sends his regards,' Fulvius said quietly. 'He compliments you on your tenacity and chided himself for ever accepting unconfirmed reports of your demise. I'm afraid your captivity is not over, Rufinus. The chamberlain himself wishes to be present when we peel you for every jot of information you have on whatever strange conspiracy you're involved in. Sadly, he has more pressing matters in the meantime.'

'My heart bleeds,' Rufinus said nastily.

'It will. In good time. But while we wait for that, the chamberlain is bending his considerable resources to locating your brother and your woman. He is not in the habit of leaving behind anyone who might consider revenge an option. The slave whore and your brother will die without ever knowing why. But then they should be grateful. At least their death will be quick.'

'No,' moaned the old man from the corner. 'Not my son. He has nothing to do with this traitor.'

'Father, quiet,' Rufinus urged him.

'No,' the old man barked. 'Not Publius. He is loyal. The future of the family. He will serve the throne.'

Rufinus winced, but there was nothing he could do. Fulvius straightened, his head turning. 'Ah yes, the sycophantic old fool. A man who knows less than nothing. I have to admit to a grudging respect for Rufinus, for his tenacity and his sticking to his morals, askew as they might be. You, though, old man, have betrayed and lost everything, and you can blame whoever you like, but it is all your own doing in the end.'

The old man gasped and staggered forward, arms reaching up, though Rufinus couldn't tell whether it was imploring or in intended violence. Either way, the tribune simply lifted his left hand which Rufinus now realised contained a pugio dagger. His father never stood a chance. The dagger came up as he stepped forward and slammed into his neck, at almost the exact point Rufinus had been eyeing up for his own attack.

The old man gasped again, this time in agony as the blade tore through flesh, muscle and sinew. For good measure, as Fulvius pulled it back out he dragged it across the throat, and then leapt back, keeping his pristine white uniform out of the range of the blood spray. With an irritated hiss, he held his dagger out behind him and one of the soldiers in the doorway hurried in and took it.

'Clean that for me.'

With a tut of disapproval, the tribune removed his scarf and began to wipe the blood from his hands. 'The old man had very much outlived what little usefulness he had.' He turned to the other men, one of whom was now diligently cleaning the dagger. 'Hold the prisoner.'

Rufinus, his eyes on his father, who was miraculously still alive, though now on his knees, wheezing and bleeding his last, stepped back. The two cavalry soldiers moved in, one handing a now-clean dagger back to his commander. Both men were armed and armoured, but their swords were sheathed and they carried no shield. Their strong hands came up ready to grab Rufinus. He felt the panic rise, and forced it back down. This was not to be torture, for Fulvius had stated plainly that Cleander wanted to be present for that. Just a little roughing up, then. Rufinus could take that.

For just a moment, he considered trying to take on the two guards. He had his splinter and fists, and they were empty-handed. If he was quick, he might just…

No. By the time he took them down, if he could, Fulvius would have his sword drawn and be moving in for the kill. And Rufinus was not naïve enough to believe there weren't more men waiting outside. Fulvius rarely went anywhere without an escort these days. And these two men might one day be redeemed, despite serving Fulvius. No, it was the tribune Rufinus had to deal with. He couldn't risk losing his only weapon in a futile attempt to fight off his guards. He would either use it to kill Fulvius, if the opportunity arose, or if not, he would keep hold of it for that last chance to see himself to Elysium in peace before men came to break him.

He managed to tuck the shard of wood into the waist of his towel just before the soldiers reached him and grabbed his shoulders, pulling his arms back and holding him in vice-like grips. The scratchy tip of the wooden splinter in the back of his waist repeatedly scraped his flesh but he ignored it, his gaze locked on the tribune.

Fulvius stepped forward. 'I really don't want to do you permanent harm, Rufinus. Cleander would be most disappointed if I damaged you before he could join in. But I feel that my former tent mates will haunt me if I don't at least try to achieve some level of revenge, and I owe you something myself for the numerous difficulties you have caused me over the months. So I am going to strike at you six times. As a former boxer, I gather, I'm sure that while this will hurt, you will be able to weather the blows with fortitude and remain intact for the chamberlain when he wants you.'

Rufinus steadied himself and braced. Fulvius rubbed his fists and then pulled his arm back.

When he punched Rufinus hard in the gut, the younger man could have laughed. The man was no pugilist. His blow was weak, badly-aimed and inexpert. Oh it hurt, but Rufinus would have been so much better at it. Fulvius straightened.

'That was for Glabrio.'

Rufinus coughed noisily for a moment, and then took a deep breath. 'You punch like a little girl, Tribune. Release me and I'll show you how it's *really* done.'

The second blow almost cut off the last word as Fulvius lashed out inexpertly once more, his fist catching Rufinus on the jaw, but only glancing, snapping his head to the side. In truth, the sudden jerk of his neck was more painful than the punch.

'For Arvina.'

Rufinus spat out a gobbet of blood. In fact, he'd done it automatically without thinking or aiming, but to his immense satisfaction the blood-filled saliva landed perfectly centrally on the tribune's pristine white sleeve.

Fulvius looked down at his tunic, and Rufinus chuckled darkly as a twitch crept into the officer's left eye at the sight of his marred uniform.

'Messy. Uncouth and pathetic. This is for Pollius.'

The third blow was much harder. As Rufinus swayed back from the punch, he reflected that its strength was more the result of sudden rage than actual skill. That and luck. Rufinus hung limp for a moment, hacking and coughing, spatters of blood from his mouth spraying his attacker.

'Best have... a bath before you... see you master,' he coughed with a crimson grin.

'For Vedius,' the tribune said, his twitch more prominent now, as he landed a fairly light left hook.

Rufinus shook. 'I can see why you were in the cavalry. You'd not have lasted long in the infantry with a punch like that.'

The fifth strike was more brutal, smashing into the side of Rufinus' head and sending it snapping to the left painfully again.

'And that was for Curtius.'

'Just you left, then,' spat Rufinus with a grisly smile. He coughed and spat a wad of red onto the officer's boot. Well if Fulvius was getting so peeved over his white tunic he'd have to change, he might as well have to have his footwear cleaned as well. In actual fact the officer was a bit of a mess. Rufinus' repeated coughing had coated the man head to waist with a fine red spray anyway.

'My last blow,' Fulvius said with a particularly unpleasant smile as his eyelid jumped up and down, 'is not a punch, but a blow of an entirely different kind.'

Rufinus felt the nerves return now. What had the man planned?'

He watched with a sinking feeling as Fulvius crossed to the now-still body of his father. He watched impotently and with a great deal of distaste as Fulvius stepped gingerly for a moment in all the blood, and then gave up, given how Rufinus had already marred the boots, and crouched over the corpse. There, the tribune spent a grisly few moments using his recently-cleaned dagger to saw through the neck until the head came free.

Rufinus silently reaffirmed his vow to kill this man as Fulvius rose, gripping the old man's staring, horrified head by the hair. 'All he wanted, I think, was to be a mid-level noble of Rome. And because of you, instead he will be remembered as a traitor. His head is bound for the Gemonian Stair, where I shall have it jammed on a spike for the people of Rome to spit at as they pass.'

The prisoner forced himself to remain still and not fight his captors. Whatever he'd done, his father did not deserve the treatment of a traitor. Men like the tyrant Sejanus had gone down those infamous steps. His father was just a misguided fool. Rufinus made another silent, private vow to retrieve his father's remains if at all possible, once he got out of this and it was all over, and see them put to rest honourably.

And he realised with this second vow that he had subconsciously decided that he *was* going to get out of this. Somehow, though he didn't know how yet, he was going to escape. He was fairly sure that the gods as a whole disapproved of the sort of things Fulvius and Cleander were doing. The gods would not let him die here when there was vengeance to be had and such wrongs to right. No, he was going to get away.

He spat more blood and turned an expressionless look on Fulvius as the man brought the dangling head close.

'I shall do the same to you, before this is over,' he said quietly. 'You and your master both. And I shall not do you the courtesy of making sure you're dead first.'

Fulvius' lip pulled back as if he were about to sneer, but perhaps he saw something he didn't like in Rufinus' face – something that frightened him, for he drew back in a flinch and, righting himself, gestured at his men. 'Come, I must prepare for the circus on the morn. Leave him.'

The two cavalrymen let him go, and he dropped to the floor as the three soldiers marched out through the door without a further word and locked it behind them before disappearing.

Once more in the dark, illuminated only by the tiniest cracks around the window shutter's edge, Rufinus sat for a moment in

366

the company of his father's headless body, breathing in the smells of recent death. Not too bad now, especially since the room had smelled of urine for some time anyway. But if they didn't take away the body, within a day the smell would change entirely, especially with the weather of a Roman summer.

'Hear me, gods of Rome,' he said with difficulty around an aching jaw and with a mouth full of bloody saliva. 'Great Jove and cunning Nemesis, staunch Mars and wise Minerva, and most of all bright Apollo, master of oaths. I vow here, this morn, to put up the grandest of altars to you, and to offer a bull annually, if you will allow me vengeance. Deliver me from this carcer and put the neck of Appius Fulvius beneath my sword. This I vow.'

And he lowered himself to the floor, delivering his fate into the hands of the gods.

Vengeance.

CHAPTER TWENTY FOUR – FRIENDS AND ENEMIES

Rome, June 17th 190 A.D., morning

Time seemed confused in the empty prison. Rufinus had known when it was night during his frequent awakenings because of the lack of white lines around the edge of the window shutter. He had caught the blasts of horns announcing the watches in the fortress occasionally, but had slept through some and missed them, and could never be quite sure what was coming next.

The last time he had woken it had been morning, as he'd determined from the pale square on the wall leeching between the wooden boards, and he'd guessed it was quite early from the colour and strength of the light. Then he'd slipped into sleep once more.

Slumber had not come easily, hence the repeated waking in a cold sweat, but he had forced himself to rest as much as he possibly could. There was, he'd reasoned, no chance of escape now. He'd pulled his one trick and it had failed utterly, and try as he might he could see no other way out. The window was barred to him, as was the door, and there was still a cavalryman guard out there. And having executed his little ploy with such spectacularly failed results, Fulvius was hardly going to leave him with a guard susceptible to a repeat performance.

No, there was no way out. But he had commended his future to the gods. There was no earthly way out of this, and so he would have to trust in the divine. But even the gods liked men to help themselves where possible, and so Rufinus slept, for it had to be better that he was well rested when the gods rolled the dice for him.

He had found himself thinking idly in one waking moment of his marine centurion adjutant, Philip, who he hadn't seen since he had laid down the prefecture and 'left' Rome. Philip had been a Christian. Did he have the same sort of belief in the divine? Jesus Christ, he seemed to remember. How could one god possibly be enough? Rufinus had prayed to five for deliverance, yet had added another three into the mix over the next hour as possibilities continued to crop up.

He was in some sort of dream involving Philip when it happened. In the world of Morpheus, he was in the great Flavian amphitheatre with the oddball centurion, each of them on one side of the great arena, each holding one hundred and twenty ropes somehow in their tiny hands and trying desperately to operate the great awning usually handled by two centuries of marines.

Why they were having to do it, and why it was such a nerve-wracking experience he couldn't have explained in his waking mind, yet when he awoke it was with a certain relief. He sat up, groggily, trying to shake the panic of rope-handling out of his head and concentrate on what it was that had woken him.

Just a noise, and not even a loud, intrusive or particularly interesting one. But when one has been in solitude for a length of time any change becomes obvious. It had been a click. That was all. A click. But Rufinus was alert now, the rope dream gone and his eyes and ears open, listening carefully as he sat perfectly still, his breathing shallow.

The next sound was one that only a man who'd been through the sort of things Rufinus had experienced could hope to recognise. It was the muted faint sound of an unresisting man being dragged lightly off his chair and placed somewhere else.

Now Rufinus was totally alert. Someone must have overcome the guard outside. His mind rushed through the possibilities. No, it wouldn't be anything to do with Severus or

Dionysus. Similarly it was not Pertinax or Sura, for they would have challenged the guard openly for what had been done. The only name that floated to mind was that of Vibius Cestius, the frumentarius. He was the only man who might have got wind of what had happened and also had the influence and skills to get to Rufinus.

Whatever the case, this was rescue. The overcoming of the guard could only mean that Rufinus' desperate prayers had been answered. With a wry smile, he remembered that he now owed the gods a magnificent altar and a rather expensive annual sacrifice. Not that it wasn't worth it.

The sounds of the lock being opened seemed to confirm it. Rufinus realised with a strange feeling of embarrassment that tears were tracking down through the grime and crusted blood on his face. Tears of relief. He might have *sounded* strong and determined earlier, but the very notion of being tortured again had sat as a marble boulder of cold fear in the pit of his stomach, and the idea that the worst he might have endured in his captivity was a bit of a battering was almost too much to deal with.

The door opened, and Rufinus' spirits sank to a new low at the sight of two Praetorians.

'Do your worst,' he said, miserably.

'Shut up and get moving, Rufinus, you daft sod.'

He frowned. The two figures moved into the room, and as his eyes began to adjust he blinked in surprise. Mercator and Icarion, his old room-mates, crossed to him and helped him rise.

'I told you it was him in the first place,' Icarion grunted as he helped the heavy younger man up.

Mercator snorted. 'I was waiting for him to trip up or walk into something to be sure.'

Rufinus managed to say something, though he wasn't sure it came out in words. More a sort of grateful, questioning and confused squeak.

'Sorry we took so long,' Merc said sheepishly. 'Firstly we had to be sure. It's not healthy to interfere with the business of these people, and we didn't want to risk everything only to find out you were some German recruit who looked like Rufinus.'

Icarion nodded as they started towards the door. 'But an evening of listening in on conversations in the cavalry's favourite bars told us that interested parties were looking into the location of a woman called Senova. Once we heard her name, we knew you wouldn't be far away. If someone was looking for your girlfriend, then you were involved. Finding out where you were being held was the hardest bit. I hope we've not landed ourselves in the shit when this all falls apart later. We've got just a few moments before we're missed.'

Rufinus shook his head, tears still coming. 'This is Appius Fulvius' doing, and he won't last the day, I can promise you that.'

The other two looked at each other, exchanging worried glances. 'Don't do anything stupid, Rufinus. We've got you out of here, but that's about as far as it goes. We can't help you beyond that door. Find a way out of the fortress and disappear like your girl has. It's the only way.'

Rufinus stopped and turned, and the other two followed his gaze to the headless lump on the floor.

'Who's that?'

'That was my father.'

'Shit,' Merc replied with a heavy tone of sympathy.

'Fulvius is going to die for a number of reasons.'

A distant horn honked the new watch, and the two Praetorians at the doorway straightened. 'Listen, Rufinus, we've got to go. We needed an alibi for this and so we came while we're on duty. We're supposed to be on guard at east turret four and if the next shift gets there and we're absent, we'll be in the shit, and we'll get linked to that guard's bad headache.' He thumbed towards the white heap in the corner of the room beyond.

Rufinus nodded. 'Go. And thanks. I'll pay you back.'

'Damn right you will. Now get to safety.'

With that the two Praetorians hurried from that outer room and into the light, running across the street and into a narrow alley between workshops beyond on their way back to their post.

Rufinus shivered. He was free. Still deeply in danger and in the nest of his enemy, but at least no longer caged. Now he had a fighting chance, thanks to the gods and his old friends. He prayed they got back to their posts before their relief arrived. If they did, and their brief absence had not been noted, then they would never be tied to the release of the prisoner. Besides, shortly Rufinus would make sure that Fulvius and his loathsome master both died a traitor's death, and then he could be himself again and Mercator and Icarion would be exonerated of any wrongdoing.

First, though, he had to get out of here and quickly, before anyone found him. Fulvius might...

No. He remembered the man's parting comment last night, after the beating. He had to prepare for the circus in the morning. Fulvius would be at the circus right now for some reason. That not only bought Rufinus a little more freedom of movement in the fortress, but also gave him an objective. Somehow, before the sun set on this day, Rufinus would be staring down at the tribune's corpse, and the circus would be the place to start.

He hurried over to the outer door and looked this way and that, trying to get his bearings. He was indeed in the stores area of the cavalry section. He didn't know it well, but he could see the tops of towers over the roof to confirm his rough position. There appeared to be no one in the alleyways nearby. For a moment he wondered why, and indeed how Merc and Icarion had managed to get to him so readily and unchallenged in the cavalry section of the busiest fortress in the empire. The answer was simple, though. Fulvius would have given orders to keep the area off-bounds. He could hardly afford for anyone not in his direct control to discover that he was keeping a centurion of the Urban Cohort prisoner. That at least played into Rufinus' hands. It had meant that this friends had been able to get to him to release him, and it meant that he could leave the store room without worrying too much about being immediately observed.

But he could hardly leave in a towel.

His jaw ached, and he could feel the bruises and pulled muscles of his beating last night, but there was no permanent damage, and he could deal with it. It was part and parcel of being a boxer, learning to deal with the effects of a punch.

He moved over and crouched at the form of the unconscious guard. The man had been struck on the back of the head by Rufinus' friends, with the pommel of a sword, he guessed. A quick probe of the man's hair revealed a lump the size of an egg, but no blood. They'd done well.

Aware of the pressing need for speed, he began to remove the man's armour and clothing. The way he was going to get out of the fortress at least was clear. As he worked, constantly keeping an eye on the unconscious guard he undressed, just in case the man suddenly came to, he silently cursed that the man was a different shape. Not a great deal, but sufficient difference that this could be uncomfortable. Taller, he was, but narrower in every other aspect.

Moments later, Rufinus was pulling on the man's white tunic with some difficulty. It was, obviously, longer than his own, and hung to just below the knee. He fretted for only a moment. Many centurions clung to the old fashioned notion that only a child or a slave would have a tunic hanging below the knee, but these days, with the influence of plait-haired Gallic and Germanic troops, longer tunics were much more widely accepted, and some units had already begun to wear breeches, especially on the northern frontiers.

Swiftly he gathered the rest and pulled it all on, tutting irritably with each new piece of clothing. The socks had holes in and were uncomfortable, a piece of loose wool catching between his toes. The boots were too big by far, and his feet would slip back and forth inside as he walked, even with the socks on. The subarmalis was a smidgeon too tight, but at least with lace-up sides he could get it to a comfortable fit without too much difficulty.

The chain shirt was another matter entirely. He struggled with the damn thing longer than the rest of the man's clothing and equipment put together. The man was not especially thin, but Rufinus had a boxer's build. Getting the shirt over his torso was a struggle, and once he was in the thing he found that he was limited to fairly shallow breaths. It was not comfortable, and far from ideal, but it was necessary right now. Strapping on the sword belt, he found that the next difficulty was bending low enough in this shirt to reach the helmet that had been placed carefully on the floor. At least the man had brought it with him. Rufinus was well aware that his face would be bloody and bruised, and the helmet would help hide the damage. As he scooped up the decorative item, he couldn't help but grin. The Praetorian cavalry were always so vain, having to have the best and most decorative of everything, and though it was far from a requirement many of the cavalrymen wore as standard the silvered facemasks usually saved for parades. Their officers allowed it, as it only made them look all the more fierce.

It would be of the greatest use to Rufinus. He pulled the helmet on with the latest in the line of curses. It was very slightly too small. It went on well enough, but bits of it felt tight and oppressive, and the end of his nose touched the steel of the face mask uncomfortably.

He straightened. Even a shield stood leaning against the wall close to the door. An elongated hexagonal board painted blue and gold with the scorpion emblem repeated amid the stars and half-moons. He swept it up. No one could possibly recognise him in this. Through the somewhat limiting eye slits, he peered at the back of the shield and there, sure enough, beneath the painted owl of Minerva for protection, was the name and unit of the owner.

Titus Didius Curio, Third Turma, Second Cohort.

Titus Didius Curio. He would have to remember that name, just in case, but at least he had a handy little reference note with him.

It felt odd to be in Praetorian uniform again, and not just because of the ill-fitting nature of this particular example. He had been proud of the white once upon a time, and in some ways he was looking forward to the day when he could wear it again officially and openly, and yet wearing it now he felt tainted, as though the corruption that had spread throughout the Guard had seeped into the very uniform. It had begun with the treachery of Paternus, and had become exponentially worse since the rise of Cleander. Now, Rufinus suddenly realised that with the Guard as they were, barring odd examples like Mercator and Icarion, he no longer wished to be a part of them.

It was a strange realisation, especially while wearing the uniform once more.

By the time he stepped out into the light, he had managed to adjust the kit with stretching and leaning and rolling of the shoulders to the point where it was merely a little restrictive and uncomfortable, and could walk relatively normally.

He forced himself to move with relative slowness in order to attract the least attention possible. The area around the store rooms was clear of humanity, and he shut the door on his prison and strode away from it, emerging soon onto a small road between there and the nearest cavalry barrack block. He had his bearings properly now. What he would have dearly liked would be to return to the Urban Cohort barracks and change into his own kit. There were, however, a number of downsides to that. First of all there was the danger and difficulty of marching in there dressed as a Praetorian and not having seven shades of shit kicked out of him, given the current climate. Then there was the fact that his room might be under surveillance. But the big issue was that he had been absent without leave for almost a day now. Even if he could persuade Pertinax of the truth of what had happened, he would almost certainly be detained in the Cohort's barracks for the foreseeable, while things were sorted out.

He simply couldn't afford that. Both Fulvius and Cleander were onto him now. They thought they had him contained, and meanwhile the city was at boiling point. Anything could happen at any moment, but whatever occurred, Rufinus had to make sure they were dealt with before they came back for him.

He had to get to the circus, and find Fulvius.

Turning his back on the quarters of his own unit, he marched towards where he knew the cavalry stables to be. A certain amount of stealth was going to be required shortly, but combined with a quantity of bare-faced nerve. Luckily there were few people as arrogant as the Praetorian cavalry.

He was in the populated area now, moving along roads filled with other soldiers. Almost all wore the uniform of the cavalry, though there were infantry guardsmen evident here and there. No one batted an eyelid at the slightly ill-fitted masked cavalryman walking among them, and Rufinus swiftly began to settle into the role. While it would have been nice to be back in his own uniform, if he wanted to get to Fulvius, wearing this kit would make it a great deal easier, he was sure.

He passed the cavalry parade ground and noted with interest a dozen cavalrymen formed up there with their optio checking them over. They were kitted out fully, in the same manner as Rufinus, and were clearly assembling ready to move out somewhere, since a parade or exercise would surely involve a full turma. He smiled behind that expressionless mask. There was his way out of the fortress.

Moments later he was at the stables. He walked around a little, unfamiliar with the place, until he noticed the legends visible on the buildings and realised that the stalls were arranged by cohort and then by turma. It did not take long to find the horses of the Third Turma, Second Cohort, and he took a deep breath, hoping the gods were still with him.

Opening the door at the end of the block he stepped inside, forcing himself not to look around curiously. He was supposed to be familiar with the place, after all. A stable hand came hurrying out of one of the stalls and Rufinus was immensely thankful that it was a slave who'd come to deal with him and not the equisio, who would hold rank and might be suspicious. A slave would surely never refuse a cavalry trooper.

'Titus Didius Curio, Third Turma, Second Cohort. Saddle my horse and bring it out.'

No pleasantries or easiness. He had to sound arrogant and sure of himself. To his immense relief, the slave bowed and scurried off about the task. He waited nervously for a short while until the slave reappeared, leading a grey mare from the stall. With a slight tinge of guilt that he'd not thought of her in so long, Rufinus felt keenly the absence of his own precious Atalanta, who he'd left with Severus' own horse in Lugdunum. It had not occurred to him to ask after her, and he wondered whether she was still in that distant city being cared for by the next governor, or whether she had been moved to Rome alongside Severus' mare. Thoughts of Atalanta inevitably led him to Acheron, who in turn brought him to Senova, and he had to shake his head a little and clear it of such troublesome nostalgia.

Without a word of thanks, he took the reins of the mare from the slave and turned his back with traditional cavalry arrogance, leading the mare from the stables. In the lee of the building, out of the sight of all and sundry, he pulled himself up into the saddle with difficulty and a total lack of finesse. Better to do this out of sight. A cavalryman should look natural mounting his horse, and being seen to struggle might raise questions. He was no stranger to the saddle, of course, and could normally mount with ease, but in such restrictive armour it was an entirely different matter. Still, moments later he was in the saddle and urging the beast along the street with a more expert air. He moved on two streets until he was in view of the parade ground, and was just in time to see the unit of horsemen departing at the far side. Tense, he picked up speed and moved in an arc around two other streets until he reached a position level with them. Holding his breath, he glanced ahead at the gate and then across at the optio leading the patrol.

He waited. Prayed. Controlled his breathing behind the mask. The last man in the patrol walked out from the street that led to the parade ground and, seamlessly, Rufinus walked his horse forth and fell into line at the rear. He realised with relief that the man in front of him, and indeed half the unit, wore similar silvered face masks. Not only did that help him blend in, but it also helped restrict sight and sound and, with the overall drumming of hooves and the jingle, clonk and shush of armour and equipment, the rear-guard of the patrol had not noticed he had picked up a follower.

The optio handed over his orders to the officer at the gate, who perused them for only a moment, and then had his men swing the great timber portal wide. No one counted the number of horsemen as they passed beneath the gateway, and Rufinus heaved a great sigh of relief as he emerged into the city's suburbs from the fortress.

The gods *were* with him. They had sent Merc and Icarion to deliver him from his cell, and they had watched over him all through the Castra Praetoria and out to freedom. The unit had exited the fortress through the north gate and the optio immediately led his men off to the left, heading along a street that Rufinus seemed to remember crossed the Nomentana and connected to the Via Salaria heading north. Wherever they were bound it was out in the northern region of the city, and outside the sacred Pomerium, for they were armed and armoured. Entirely the wrong direction for Rufinus. He waited until they passed out of sight of the gate, the few miserable, plague-ridden citizens in this region cowering out of the way of the despised but deadly Praetorians. Then, as soon as he judged it safe, he turned away, slipping off into a side street on the right and immediately picking up pace, moving away from the mounted patrol.

He was free.

He was in the city, in an excellent disguise and out of the clutches of his enemies.

Now to find his way to the Circus Maximus and confront Fulvius. Keeping his distance from the fortress, riding two streets back just in case, he skirted around the eastern and southern sides and then headed south across the Esquiline. The last thing he wanted to do right now was to attract undue attention to himself, and so he made sure to stay out of the boundary of the Pomerium, within which weapons of war were forbidden by ancient sacred law, and within which the Guard moved in togas rather than armour, except where duty required otherwise.

The Circus Maximus actually lay within the Pomerium, which declared its ancient origin, and that meant that he would theoretically be in breach of ancient law if he entered the area equipped as he was. On the other hand, he reasoned, it was unlikely in the current climate that the Praetorians were going anywhere without being prepared for trouble. The circus was at the very southern edge of the Pomerium and almost certainly if Fulvius was there with his men they would be armed and armoured.

As he rode, he was disheartened by the atmosphere around him. The people cowered at the edges of the streets, fearing the Guard where once they might have respected them. But that fear was also laced with malice, and every gaze Rufinus managed to catch through his restrictive eye slits suggested that if they managed to catch him in an alley without his blade he'd regret wearing the Praetorian white. It was an uncomfortable and unpleasant feeling for Rufinus to be quite so unpopular.

The fact that no one would consider even approaching him meant that he almost leapt out of the saddle when a voice nearby said 'I was wondering when you would show up again.'

He turned, lurching in the saddle, now cursing the restricted view. With difficulty he located the source of the voice and blinked as Vibius Cestius pulled alongside him.

'How...?'

'I'd know you if you sawed off both legs and grew a second head, Rufinus.'

'But where…?'

'I've been watching the Castra Praetoria since late last night when it came to my attention that you had not returned. I missed seeing you bundled in by the tribune's men, of course, but I was sure you'd been taken there. I even gave some thought to getting you out somehow, but I bowed to Severus' wishes. He may not be my commander, but the game we're all playing at the moment is his to control.'

'What?'

During the night I warned Severus that you'd been taken and asked his opinion. He was extremely regretful that you'd been captured – genuinely so, I believe – but he also felt that we simply could not risk landing *everyone* in trouble for the sake of getting you out. Rest assured you would have been freed, or at least allowed a quick death, before Cleander reached the fortress and started asking you questions.'

'You're all heart,' Rufinus noted acidly.

'Come now, Rufinus, you know as well as I how this game works. Sacrifices and deniability. Care must be taken at all times and we will not risk the result this close to the finish line.'

'We *are* close then?' Rufinus murmured.

'Very. I apologise for my recent absence from a variety of important events, but I have been on my own mission, sowing discord and ideas among the mob. I have a number of well-placed puppets in place ready to bring this all to a head. Today is the day, my boy.'

'I am on the way to the circus,' Rufinus said.

'Of course you are, for Fulvius is there and you mean to kill him. But, young Rufinus, Cleander is also there. It is the largest gathering of citizens for almost a year, all in the presence of Cleander and his armed Guard, all hungry and angry, and harbouring men prepared with my own words. Time to witness unfolding that which we spent so long putting in motion.'

'Fulvius…'

'Yes, I know. Fulvius should die, and I fear we should not have imposed restrictions on you so early in the game. Had you killed Fulvius a year ago, these past few days might have been easier, and especially so for you. But I must caution you: do not put Fulvius above Cleander. I know this is personal, and I shall not stand in your way when the time is right, but things are unfolding as they should, and I cannot have you cause a problem because you intend to march murderously into the circus and hack off a tribune's head. I will stop you if I have to, but I hope you will see sense and remain patient.'

Rufinus turned to him. 'I swore to kill him by the end of this day.'

'I am confident that you will have ample opportunity,' Cestius replied, 'just not until I give you the signal.'

Rufinus ruminated for a moment. He was being blinded by loathing, and he knew it. Fulvius *did* have to die, but Cestius – and Severus – were right: Cleander had to be the prime target. Without Cleander Fulvius would be powerless, or near enough. He nodded. 'Once things are moving, though, I deal with the tribune.'

'With my blessing.'

The two men walked their horses on, heading down the southern slope of the Esquiline, making for the circus, and Rufinus felt the stirring of excitement despite everything. All the appalling things they had done to the city and its people in a bid to bring down an untouchable tyrant, all were coming to a head this day. By nightfall it would be over. Cleander would fall, Fulvius would die, the city would be free, the granaries opened, and Rufinus could be himself once more. Or… they would fail somehow.

That didn't bear thinking about.

Rufinus' fingers danced hungrily on the pommel of his sword as they rode on to the circus and the culmination of their plot.

CHAPTER TWENTY FIVE – VOX POPULI

Rome, June 17th 190 A.D., morning

C learly something was wrong – Rufinus could tell that
even from a distance. He had been to the races in the
circus plenty of times over the years he had lived in
Rome in one guise or another, and he knew its sounds, its
smell, its feel. Personally he always favoured the gladiatorial
bouts in the arena – to him they showed more skill – but he
understood the danger of driving a chariot for one of Rome's
four teams, and appreciated it. And that, of course, was what
the crowd usually bayed for: blood and wreckage, death and
disaster. What was the point of a day at the races if there
wasn't a crash, after all? Of course there always was one.

He was used to the noises of an excited crowd, the smell of
horses, blood, sweat and the many unrecognisable grilled meats
purveyed in the stands, the crackle of excitement in the air…

This was not like that.

There were raised voices moving together like a
murmuration of starlings, but not in the waves of enthusiasm
that traditionally accompanied a race. There was no tense
silence as riders came close to disaster, roars and cheers in a
crashing din as they narrowly escaped death, and cries of
dismay as a favourite charioteer joined horses and chariot alike
as a pile of broken detritus by the track side. No, this was a
muted din, more like ripples in a dark pond than crashing
waves in the sea. And it contained no dismay, or excitement, or
joy. It carried only seething anger with an undercurrent of hate.

They rounded a corner and paused, bringing their steeds to a
halt. Vibius Cestius looked over at him. 'Clearly we should not

arrive together. I shall be observing events carefully from the top of the eastern arch, beside the statue. Look there for my signal. Fare you well and see you when the world has changed.'

The frumentarius gave him an encouraging hand-clap on the shoulder and then turned his horse and disappeared into a side street. Rufinus waited a moment longer, looking at the great, arcaded curve of the circus' eastern end and the grand, decorative arch that rose in the centre. There was, as far as he knew, no access to the top of the arch where the great bronze chariot statue stood, but he knew better than to ask Cestius how he intended to get there. The man was ever a mystery.

He breathed as deeply as the constrictive chain shirt allowed, wishing for the hundredth time that his jailor had been a little fatter. This was it. Inside that great venue were the two men he hated most in the world. Today would see them both fall, unless things went wrong, in which case it was unlikely that Rufinus would be around to care.

It was not lost on him that so many of the tumultuous events of his life seemed to happen in Rome's entertainment venues. In the Flavian amphitheatre he had saved the emperor's life and won renown. In Pompey's theatre he had witnessed the fall of Perennis to public outcry. And now, here in Rome's great racing venue, he would witness the end of a tyrant's reign.

The strange, even eerie change from a normal race day was palpable even outside. Usually, the streets around the circus would be thronged with people. There would be the disappointed and hopeful spectators, unable to secure a seat but waiting for one to open up as someone else leaves, all listening to the events they could not witness, guessing which charioteer had just died. Then there were the hawkers, selling everything they could to the crowd, the beggars taking advantage of the good humour, the thieves and thugs plying their unpleasant trades, the whores looking for someone bored of waiting but with a fat purse… humanity in its myriad forms. Not today. Today the streets were empty, more or less. A few desperate beggars sat in the gutters, one or two aimless souls wandered, coughing up their life into their hands. And a few members of the Guard, as though there were any need to keep the peace.

No sign of the Urban Cohort, which surprised him. It was standard practice to have a century on duty around the circus on race days to help keep order and arrest the various criminals caught in the act. And in the current situation, it would have been more sensible to triple the number rather than reduce it. Yet there was no sign of even one soldier from Rufinus' unit. It seemed unlikely to be Pertinax's doing, and Rufinus put it down to the machinations of Cestius. Their absence would not worry Cleander or his Praetorians, for they would be here in force anyway. After all, they were more devoted to protecting the chamberlain than the emperor these days.

Rufinus rode towards the circus and around the southern edge of the curve. He could see a small knot of horses corralled by two Praetorian cavalrymen and a couple of slaves, and quickly changed his mind. He needed to blend in and get inside, but the last thing he wanted right now was to get caught up in the duties of a cavalry unit. Instead, he walked his horse over to one of the archways where a young lad with a filthy face was staring out at the world with an expression of abject misery.

He fished in Curio's purse, hanging from the belt, hoping the man had plenty of loose change, and drew out a brass dupondius, holding it up for the boy. 'Look after my horse until I return and there's another one waiting for you.'

The boy snatched the coin greedily, eyes afire, and took the proffered reins as Rufinus slid from the saddle with some difficulty. It was not a lot of money, and the horse was worth much more, but Rufinus had to hope that a combination of greed and the fear of angering a Praetorian would make the boy do as he was told. Leaving the animal with him, Rufinus strode into the nearest entrance.

The eeriness of the race day was continued inside. Where the alcoves beneath the stands were commonly filled with stalls selling everything from toy chariots to sweetmeats to boots, they were almost all empty. There was something unsettling about moving through the tunnels in such solitude and with only an angry murmur from the stands above rather than the dip and roar of an excited crowd.

Had Cestius gone too far with his preparations?

Rufinus passed a couple of Praetorians on guard, and returned their comradely nods. He passed a spectator with a blank face descending the staircase in search of the latrines. He climbed the steps up to the stands. Once more he shivered at the atmosphere as he emerged into the light.

It was a balmy summer's day with a clear blue sky and the annual aroma of warm dung that filled a Roman June. All four chariot teams were still represented on the sand below, hurtling inexorably at dangerous speed around the track. The hangings below the imperial box and at both ends of the circus identified this as the sixth race, while the bronze eggs and dolphins were almost all tipped, indicating that the penultimate lap was in progress. An impressive number of chariots had survived this long, then.

Every seat was filled. The stands were a riot of colour as the population of Rome watched the race. Neither plague nor tyranny was going to stop the people of Rome enjoying the largesse of their emperor, even if he was never in the city these days to see it himself. If a man was deaf, he might even think this a normal day, though with fewer excited spectators leaping up and down in their seats and pointing.

But the sound changed it all. That rumble of malcontent sat like a seething fog over the entire place. Rufinus' eyes strayed around, his head turning this way and that to allow a better view through the narrow eye slits of the helmet.

Cleander was here. Rufinus could make out the figures in the imperial box across the far side. He couldn't actually make out the man's face at this distance, but he was dark-haired and clad in a purple toga, which would have cost more than most people would ever earn. Only the emperor would have worn a garment of that value, other than this tyrannical would-be ruler of Rome. Besides, the box was empty apart from him and a dozen or more white-clad figures. He was well-protected as always.

It took some time to locate Fulvius, on the other hand. Amid a crowd of a hundred and fifty thousand one man is hard to spot, yet some unnatural affinity gradually drew Rufinus' eye to a figure, in white and with a cloak, which had to be the tribune high up at the top of the stands, perhaps halfway between the imperial box and the curved end with the arch. Rufinus mentally marked the position and then continued on with his perusal. Praetorians were at many of the entrances to the stands, by all the significant locations and even at the starting gates, safely out of the way of the racers. More were spaced periodically along the top arcade, like the tribune, and a cluster stood amid the crowd around the imperial box. It looked worryingly like the chamberlain was containing the crowd within a cordon of white and steel. Rufinus shook his head. The man was being careful. He knew just how unpopular he had become.

His gaze finally reached the arch at the eastern end and rose past the carvings and pillars to the top, where a glorious bronze statue of a quadriga drawn by four horses and manned by a handsome youth crowned the structure. The lone figure standing beside it would go unnoticed by almost everyone, especially since he had positioned himself in the shadow of the statue.

How in Hades had Cestius got up there, and so quickly, too.

He wondered idly, as the frumentarius lifted an arm to scratch his head, what signal the man was going to give him. He'd not thought to clarify it. Hopefully not a scratch of the nose. No, Cestius was far too damned clever for that. Rufinus would know when the time was right. But there was something almost rhythmic about the frumentarius' scratching nonetheless, and he was gazing off in another direction. The distinct suspicion that the man was already giving signals to other people sank into Rufinus. He wondered who else was here. Was Severus seated somewhere in the stands? Was Dionysus? Nicomedes?

An explosive noise drew his attention and he turned and peered back along the track. The remaining white chariot had clearly misread his turn. Rufinus had seen enough races to be able to picture what had happened from the marks in the sand. The lines gouged in the surface marked where the vehicle had overturned, and the many stains showed that it had been there where the driver and at least one of the horses had died. The rest had ended in a broken heap towards the stands. One beast seemed to have survived intact and was struggling to free itself of the wreckage, while another screamed, waiting for someone to rescue it, unaware that its wounds were mortal and the first man who came would kill it as quickly and cleanly as possible.

It was a testament to the level of anger in the crowd that reactions to the crash, which would normally raise a din that could be heard halfway to the coast, were instead limited to a few individuals standing and shouting, not enough to be heard over the general murmur of hatred.

The egg and dolphin on the spina tipped and the last lap began.

Rufinus could feel the tension in the air, like a scorpion bolt-thrower that had been overwound, when the cables had become so tight that at any moment either the bolt would shoot a mile and go through a wall, or the whole thing would explode and kill the team manning it. That very thing had happened several times during the war, once even in front of Rufinus' blinking eyes.

That same tautness filled the air now as the chariots raced round on their final lap.

Something preternatural made Rufinus look to his right, and he spotted the shadowy figure of Vibius Cestius holding an arm out to his side like a flag, gazing off into the crowd somewhere. Things were moving. Right now, he realised, they were *already* moving. Like a microcosm of their entire plot over the past three years, this scene was playing out the same: Rome had drifted on in misery and discontent, unaware of the machinations of a select group who worked to bring about a critical change. Here, too, Rome simmered in anger and gloom, unaware of the signals of a frumentarius to a hand-picked selection of figures among the crowd.

The hair rose on the back of Rufinus' neck.

The race was coming to an end, the chariots racing on, the leaders neck-and-neck, for the finish line. Any other day the crowd would be on their feet now, roaring at their champions. No one was standing.

No, that wasn't true.

Rufinus felt that frisson of energy again. Figures *were* standing. Somewhere across the circus, in the far stands, unnoticed by most, figures had risen and were beginning to move down to the lowest tier of seats. Rufinus swallowed. These must be the recipients of Cestius' subtle gestures.

He strained his eyes to pick them out, ignoring the last moments of the race as the Greens swept to victory. He had to check several times to be sure, but there was no denying it. The figures drifting down to the front were children. Not quite *all* of them, though, for he could see another now, risen and moving. A woman. Tall, willowy, elegant, wearing a cloak despite the heat. What was she up to? What were they *all* up to? What was *Cestius* up to?

He watched in surprise as those who had begun to drift down assembled in one spot, waiting for the woman who followed them. Surely the Praetorians nearby must have seen this beginning. They had to have orders to check this sort of thing and prevent it, even if they didn't quite know what it was yet.

His gaze rose to the stands again, now seeking out the white-clad figures of Cleander's Guard. It was then that he realised the scale of Cestius' scheme. Small incidents had broken out in the stands. Only four of them, with citizens arguing and pushing and shoving. Each of them had attracted the attention of the Praetorians nearby, and would require breaking up, but they were so cleverly positioned. Each argument filled a critical junction in the stands, such that any Praetorian wanting to reach the children and their elegant leader would find it near impossible to pass the incidents.

He smiled coldly. That was now exactly what was happening. Men in white had noted the growing crowd of children and were moving to disperse them, but they simply could not find a way to get to them without crossing the difficult spots. Gods, but Cestius was good.

His gaze dropped once more to the children and his eyes widened. Even as the chariots were making their way back to the carceres, and medics and slaves rushed to the injured and dead riders and horses and the wreckage of chariots, half a dozen more burly men in the crowd were lowering the children down from the stands on to the track itself.

What in the name of all the gods was happening?

The Praetorians were becoming more urgent now, pushing their way through the trouble spots and arresting those responsible, hurrying to the place where the children were dropping to the sand below. More figures moved here and there, seemingly at random, but causing momentary obstacles, slowing down the white soldiers, as the last of the children was helped down, and then the cloaked woman.

By the time the Praetorians arrived, the entire group was on the track itself and moving swiftly towards the spina opposite the imperial box. The soldiers were faced with the choice of leaping down to the sand to follow or waiting in the stands to see what was happening. The men who had helped the children down had melted back into the crowd. There was no one to arrest in the stands, and the soldiers seemed disinclined to follow across the track. What harm could one girl and a bunch of children do after all?

Rufinus' gaze nipped back and forth now, and he almost ripped off the face mask to get a better look before deciding that anonymity was still important. Cestius was still there, and still signalling to people in the stands. Another figure had risen near the imperial box, and Rufinus was sure it was Septimius Severus, even at this distance. In the box, Cleander was on his feet now, shouting angrily at an officer beside him. Praetorians were mobilising. Tribune Fulvius was descending the cavea, gathering his men as he went.

Rufinus' gaze landed finally on the children.

They were particularly humble specimens, yet wearing good clothing and shoes that marked them out as free citizens and not poor slaves. And just as his eyes fell upon the girl, she shrugged off her cloak and seemed to grow in stature to a Titanic figure, an optical illusion surely caused by being surrounded by children.

But it was not her stature that made Rufinus hold his breath.

She was a goddess. From her golden curls to her golden sandals, via the dazzling white stola and palla in between, she was a goddess. And in case anyone present were uncertain, the sheaf of wheat in her left hand and the sickle in her right made it clear to all.

Ceres, the goddess of the harvest, had come to Rome.

Now the crowd were reacting, far more than they had to a mere race. Some were standing in awed, reverential silence, staring at the glorious goddess before them. Others were bellowing prayers and hope at the divinity, for Rome had starved for so long. Her arms rose as in a demand for silence, and that silence fell instantly and utterly among the crowd. Suddenly the only noises were the booted feet of Praetorians gathering and moving, though many of them had stopped too, perhaps fearing the goddess more than even Cleander or the tribune. Those, and the tiny voice of Cleander far away, bellowing orders at the white soldiers.

Rufinus stared. He knew beyond a shadow of a doubt that this was no goddess, but an agent of the frumentarius – perhaps a girl from the theatre? Yet despite having an understanding beyond that of the majority of onlookers, even Rufinus felt divinity shining from the girl. Was it possible that she had somehow become a vessel for the goddess in this important moment?

She had to be connected with the theatre, or at least some choral or musical endeavour, for into the silence of the circus her voice poured like a golden wave. Rufinus was perhaps two to three hundred paces from her, and half the seating stand higher with thousands of people in between, yet he heard her voice as clear as anything. Either she was the most amazing orator, or the goddess was really taking a part in events.

'Marcus Aurelius Cleander,' the girl declared, her voice calm and resonant, no hoarse shout or bellow and yet somehow reaching every ear in the silent circus. 'Chamberlain of Rome, Praetorian commander, companion of the emperor... slave of Phrygia.'

Rufinus couldn't see Cleander's face at this distance, but he had no trouble at all imagining the look on it at those words. His less than humble origins were known far and wide but nobody, be they low-born or high, would ever speak of it so in public, and certainly not in front of the man.

It was a master stroke. In a dozen words, the goddess had taken the most important man in Rome and reduced him to less than nothing in the minds of one hundred and fifty thousand people. For months now they had hated him, but at least he had always been feared. Now, suddenly, he was turned into nothing more than a humble, jumped-up slave in another man's boots for a tenth of Rome's population.

Rufinus actually felt the mood of the place shift. He tensed, fingers gripping his shield. He was dressed as one of Cleander's men. This might not be a good time to be so garbed. Carefully and slowly, eyes still on the girl, he backed into the entrance to the staircase.

'Cleander the granary owner,' the goddess continued, 'who took the horrea that belonged to the imperial family for himself and filled them with grain while the people of Rome starve.'

Rufinus stared. Gods, but it was true. To the very letter it was true, even if not quite to the spirit.

'Cleander who buys all the grain that no one can afford, yet hoards it for himself.'

True. Again *not* true, but still in a very real way also true.

There was an angry roar from the crowd now, like a pride of lions thousands strong.

The imperial box was becoming a hive of activity, Praetorians unsheathing their swords and drawing close to Cleander. What had Cestius done? It had started well, but this had the makings of a major riot, and that would be appalling for the Praetorians clearly now had no qualms about butchering citizens on the word of the chamberlain.

'These are your people, slave-tyrant,' the goddess announced, spreading her arms and encompassing the children around her. 'Each and every one the last in their family, their parents and siblings all dead of starvation while your warehouses burst with grain.'

Another outraged roar from the crowd. Louder now, tipping back into silence as the goddess raised her arms once more. Rufinus could hear people shouting that they'd heard the granaries were full and had been for days. Now where might they have heard *that*, Cestius?

'What monster feeds his trained killers while the innocent starve?'

A scream punctuated the line.

How had she timed that? Or had it been Cestius, or perhaps pure chance. Whatever it was, as her last word drifted away, somewhere near the imperial box, a small fracas that had broken out was ended as three Praetorians butchered a man in front of the mob.

The roar began again. The crowd was moving. Every man was up from his seat and most were surging towards the imperial box. Rufinus held his breath. This was dreadful, or would be soon enough.

Then it happened.

The goddess sang. It was a beautiful, haunting song of hope and growth, of spring and renewal, intoned annually at the

Ambarvalia festival of the crops, sacred to Ceres and known to almost every ear. The surging of the crowd faltered and then failed, every spectator coming to a halt amid the beautiful melody.

Severus was suddenly there. Close to the imperial box, yet surrounded by togate men in a protective ring, the African consul seemed a challenger to the chamberlain as he lifted his arms in oratorical stance.

'People of Rome,' he cried, somehow managing to join with the melody and rhythm rather than fighting it, 'let us not be lawless, for Rome is a land of law and always was. The chamberlain has starved you and succumbed to greed and tyranny, but it is for the *emperor* to condemn him, not us. Take your plea to Commodus, to the living Hercules himself, for you know he is your champion.'

Rufinus lifted his gaze to the figures in the imperial box. Again, he could not see Cleander's face, but his expression would be priceless. Suddenly very publically denounced by the very man who had placed him in this situation, he would be apoplectic with rage.

Sure enough, though the crowd had fallen still, the Praetorians began to move at snarled commands from the chamberlain.

Men started to die beneath Praetorian blades.

Severus suddenly shook off his toga and as well as his tunic beneath he bore a blade, in contravention of the sacred laws of the Pomerium. No one was going to argue with him about it that day, though. Moreover, that ring of toga-clad men around him did the same, revealing blades. Praetorians were moving on them now at Cleander's orders, trying to get to Severus and kill him. But Severus was not just a consul of Rome now. He had denounced Cleander alongside the goddess. He was a champion of the Roman people now, and salesmen and housewives and blacksmiths and fishermen leapt to help, tackling the Praetorians alongside their consul.

There would be no riot, Rufinus realised. All there was was the whole of Rome against Cleander and his Praetorians. His gaze slid up to the imperial box in time to see the shape of Cleander slip through the rear door with a number of his men. It took precious moments to locate Fulvius. The tribune was gathering his dismounted cavalry and gesturing back towards the disappearing chamberlain. They were leaving, both of them.

Rufinus knew the two men, though. They were not *fleeing*. To run would be to admit defeat and lose, and neither of those men would think like that. They would be regrouping somewhere safer and gathering men, probably sending to the Castra Praetoria for the full Guard. More unexpected movement caught Rufinus' eye and he frowned to see the goddess and her children running across the sand again, making for the carceres at the end, whence the chariots emerge before a race. The mob was pouring after her, and Rufinus could not for long moments think what was happening other than pious citizens flocking after a goddess. It came to him in a flash: Severus had told the people to go to the emperor, and that was precisely what they were doing, let by their goddess and her diminutive court.

There would be no need for one influential man to see the emperor now and denounce Cleander, for the whole of Rome seemed to be going.

Rufinus shook his head. Severus, Dionysus, Nicomedes and Cestius. Himself too, he supposed, and Senova perhaps even more... between them they had taken an ordered city ruled with an iron fist by an untouchable tyrant, and they had brought him low in a land of chaos. Now his time could be measured in hours, for since the days of Caesar no sane emperor would dare deny a demand from his whole empire.

Where would Cleander and Fulvius go?

His heart sank. Where else? They had to stop the mob getting to the emperor, or get there first and put their case to Commodus.

Breathing as deeply as possible, he turned and looked up at the top of the great arch.

It was hard to see, but he was certain Vibius Cestius was nodding at him.

Before the crowd began to pay attention to the masked Praetorian in the stairwell, Rufinus turned and descended. He had to get to Fulvius, and help stop Cleander. Cestius had done his part in setting the crowd to riot, and Severus had done his in directing their energy at the emperor. Now it was the turn of men like Rufinus to stop the evil bastards. And while Cleander had to fall by imperial command in order to remove all his influence, Fulvius could die *any* time.

He smiled at the thought, and rounded the corner to the next staircase. His heart skipped a beat. Another Praetorian was running up towards him, three civilians after the man, howling for blood. The soldier had lost his sword and his shield, but was clutching his dagger as a man chased him, threatening him with his own blade. Rufinus had only a moment to think. He was dressed as one of them. He would be every bit as much a target.

Regret weighed heavily. He did not know the guardsman, but it was him or Rufinus, yet still possibly both. Unless...

The Praetorian started to shout something at him, but as he got close Rufinus lifted his shield and punched the man in the face with the iron boss, sending him falling with a cry, sprawling across the stair. The three citizens stopped, confusion replacing their anger for a moment as their enemies attacked one another. Rufinus pulled away his face mask.

'For the emperor,' he said. 'Go to the emperor! Tell him of this.'

These simple words seemed to put him in their camp, and the three men nodded and, ignoring both soldiers further, ran on up the steps. Rufinus looked down at the guardsman. He would most certainly have a broken nose, and possibly worse, but at least he was alive.

Gritting his teeth, Rufinus ran on down the stairs. Somewhere out there Appius Fulvius was marshalling Praetorians to face the crowd and save his loathsome master.

Cleander's time might be measured in hours, but Fulvius' time was counted in mere heartbeats now.

CHAPTER TWENTY SIX – REVOLUTION

Rome, June 17th 190 A.D., morning

By the time Rufinus emerged from vomitoria of the circus, Rome was in chaos. Where the surrounding streets had been filled with only sullen silence before, now they were crammed with bodies moving in every conceivable direction, either with furious intent or in aimless panic. It was a disappointment, but no great surprise, to find both his horse and the boy who'd took it entirely gone. On the other hand, there were still those Praetorian cavalry mounts about two hundred paces away being held by a group of terrified-looking slaves. There was no sign of the soldiers who'd been there when he entered, but he suspected they had already come to a nasty end, given that their horses were still there. The mob might have overwhelmed the cavalry, but they had left the slaves alone and, not sure what to do, those slaves had stayed exactly where they were, still holding the horses.

Rufinus ran along the side arcades of the circus, pausing here and there to avoid people, ducking and dodging. As he ran, half a dozen burly, angry-looking citizens gave a great shout and ran for him. Not liking the odds, Rufinus ducked behind a small group of women who were arguing over something and ran on. Twice he felt something hit him, but they were little more than glancing blows and he didn't stop.

He reached the horses without being consumed by the angry mob and tried to vault onto a horse. The utter failure of the manoeuvre reminded him that the shirt he wore was far too constrictive for such activity. With the aid of one of the slaves he managed to pull himself into the saddle. Once again something bounced off his shoulder without causing real damage, but he grabbed his shield back from a slave and lifted it protectively regardless.

He had to find the Praetorians quickly, and for two reasons. Firstly, if he stayed alone in Praetorian white in this mob, someone would soon succeed in bringing him down and he would be torn to pieces by angry citizens. Secondly, wherever he found the largest group of Praetorian cavalry, he would find Appius Fulvius, and probably Cleander too. The pair had both been at the far side of the circus, to the north, and would have exited through that side. There was precious little chance of him making it round to there without falling to the crowd, though. He had to get somewhere safe for a moment and think.

Where would the tribune go?

His eyes scanned the area as something dinged off his helmet and made him wince. The mob was surging this way and that, but the strongest flow seemed to be south, along the various roads heading across the Aventine or down the shallow valley between the Aventine and the Little Aventine.

Something hit him hard in the back and almost drove him from the saddle, and his head snapped round urgently to see that a man with a broom and jabbed him hard and was drawing it back to swing it in an attempt to push him from the saddle. Hands were grabbing his legs and grasping the horse's bridle now. They were trying to bring him down and the slaves looked disinclined to help him. Time was up. He had to get out of here.

Wheeling the nervous, nickering horse, he urged it forward into the crowd. People were still hanging on to him and to the horse's tack, and the broom caught him a glancing blow on the shield as he pressed forward. The last thing he wanted to do was hurt the citizens of Rome – he was on their side, though they couldn't possibly know it – but there was nothing else for it. He had to harden himself to the fact that if he wanted to survive this, he was going to break heads, however regretfully.

He pushed the horse on, using his shield to batter people out of the way, steering with his knees as his right hand worked constantly, flailing and pushing, slapping and punching, knocking away hands and once or twice pulling them off his reins. Slowly, he started to pick up speed, amid occasional shrieks as rabid citizens disappeared beneath his hooves in the press. He felt the repeated battering of blows upon him, though his shield and helmet and the mail shirt took the worst of it. Still, he would hurt later. They were landing better blows than Fulvius had managed in the storeroom.

Suddenly, he managed to push into an open area and immediately kicked the horse into a run. Two more men came for him, but now he was too fast, those few grasping hands still trying to hold him back and bring him down fell away with cries of anger and disappointment.

He was across the open space now and riding into a side street past the temple of Dis Pater. He jogged right and left then, fleeing the mob, and stopped only when he made it into a quiet street with an archway leading into a livery stable. There he moved into the shadow of the arch, stretching sore muscles, wincing at all new pains and trying to think.

The mob were largely surging south, or at least a significant portion of them were. They would be following Severus' call in the circus, running for the emperor to denounce Cleander. It was a good ten miles at least to the emperor's coastal villa at Laurentum. Even if they ran, it would probably take the lead elements of the crowd a couple of hours to get there. Few would have horses, after all. They would surge through the old Porta Raudusculana, now little more than a gap between the crumbling sections of the ancient, forgotten wall. Then, they would race along the main road towards Ostia and Laurentum.

And if the mob were going that way, then so would Cleander. And if Cleander went that way, then so would Fulvius and his cavalry. The imperial box was closer to the western end of the circus, where the carceres lay and where cavalry could assemble easiest. Cleander and Fulvius would come that way, around the end of the circus and then up the long Clivus Publicius, joining the main road to the Raudusculana Gate. There they could perhaps halt the flow of humanity.

Confident that this would be the Praetorians' plan, he guided his horse back out of the gateway and through a few smaller back streets until he sat in the shadow of the baths of Licinius Sura. People were moving along the main street beyond and heading for the gate just as they were along other streets. It is in the nature of a mob to move like herd creatures, and the Roman people were doing just that – or at least that part of the throng which had decided to head to the emperor's residence. Consequently, the bulk of the mob were moving in groups along the larger main streets, ignoring the small connecting side roads and alleys. No one seemed to notice the mounted Praetorian in the shady side street as they passed.

Rufinus was beginning to wonder whether he had misjudged the situation as he sat there waiting, and started thinking about where to go next when he heard the trouble. It began as a distant roar, but as it came closer it rose in volume and coalesced into distinct sounds. It was horribly familiar to Rufinus after that dreadful day by the horrea. It was the sound of vicious slaughter.

He edged closer to the street and peered out. Another wave of humanity was pouring up the street, but they were running in blind panic and screaming. Behind them, he could see Praetorian horsemen riding them down, blades flashing in the sunlight both steely grey and washed crimson as they rose and fell.

Nausea rose in Rufinus at the sight of Praetorians butchering innocents once more. How his once-noble unit had fallen.

He waited, steeling himself. He would not become involved. He would not kill citizens, yet he had somehow to get to Fulvius. His current Praetorian garb might make it possible to get close enough to the tribune to take him on, but it also put him in danger, making him an enemy of the mob.

Tense, he waited as the mobile slaughter closed. Terrified people rushed past the street end, and a few turned into the entrance, though at the unexpected sight of the white-clad horseman in the shadow, most of them returned to the main street and ran on. A few slipped past him and disappeared into the alleyways.

The mob fled past, and finally Rufinus got a good view of the force chasing them down. Several turmae of cavalry were involved in the butchery, more than a hundred in all, and he could see both Fulvius and Cleander in the heart of the mass, along with several other lesser officers. Silently, he cursed. There was little chance of him getting close enough to Fulvius here, and if he did he would get caught up in the slaughter, forced to kill civilians or fall to fellow Praetorians instead.

Angry and impotent, he watched the Praetorians pass by. Ridiculously, he could hear authoritative voices demanding that the crowd disperse rising above the din even as Praetorian blades hacked them down in their flight.

Ignoring the sickening sight of the strewn and trampled bloody bodies in the wake of the killing, Rufinus walked his horse out into the street and began to follow the white-clad killers at a discreet distance. It made him shiver to think on the men and women dying in front of that white wave sweeping along the street, the evidence of which was strewn across the road before him.

He watched as they chased the screaming population down the sloping street and to the junction with the Vicus that led to the gate. The cavalry continued their butchery into that main thoroughfare and Rufinus moved quietly and carefully down behind them, keeping to the shadow at the side of the street, watching with distaste and waiting for any opportunity to get to Fulvius to arise.

At the sight of the gateway, less than three hundred paces from the junction, the Praetorians changed tack. At bellowed commands from Fulvius, they formed into a tight wedge and swept along the side of the street, past the crowd, still swinging out with their blades as they passed and scything down the terrified population. Rufinus realised with disgust what they were doing. A significant number of men and women had already passed beyond the line of the old walls, but the bulk were still within, and Cleander had no intention of letting them leave.

The Praetorians formed up in the gap between the walls and systematically butchered anyone who came close. The mob ground to a halt, panicked. There were still those among them angry enough to override their fear, and they ran for the gate here and there, either intending to slip past the Praetorians and run for the aid of their emperor, or perhaps attempt to bring those riders down and set upon them.

They were doomed, though, for the bulk of the mass were more intent on staying alive now.

Rufinus watched, nervous, tense. Any time, anything could happen, opening up a path to Fulvius for him. Moreover, now that they had stopped and the bulk of the crowd were in flight along whatever side street they could find, the killing had subsided. Perhaps Rufinus could get in among the riders when it all stopped. That would be his time.

Slowly, he became aware of a new noise, as the sounds of slaughter subsided.

The rhythmic tramp of booted feet. From further away, *beyond* the gate.

He strained to look past the Porta Raudusculana and blinked in surprise as he spotted the source of the noise. A large force of the Urban Cohort were closing on the gate from the suburbs, filling the street. As the unit closed, Rufinus spotted several mounted figures among them, including Prefect Pertinax and the consul Septimius Severus. Both had blades drawn, along with the entire force of soldiery.

A loud murmur arose from the crowd. While they may still respect the Urban Cohort, the sudden convergence of two large armed groups who were well known to hate one another was a worrying development for everyone.

Rufinus' mind raced. There was no way the Urban Cohort could have assembled at the Castra Praetoria and got here this fast, especially by a circuitous enough route to come at the Praetorians from behind. They had to have been deployed close by and waited for a signal. The presence of Severus among them suggested that perhaps their timely arrival was his doing, or more likely another facet of Vibius Cestius' machinations.

The Praetorians had noticed the approaching force now, and the killing stopped as they straightened to Cleander's voice and turned en-masse to face the new threat. The civilians remaining in the street took flight, those last few grasping the opportunity to disappear into alleys and doorways, fleeing the two forces closing in the wide street before the fighting really started. As the last few melted away, Rufinus felt a twinge of irritated impotence once more. Finally the crowd were gone and he could potentially slip in with the Praetorians and kill Fulvius without getting involved in the slaughter, but now instead he was to be thwarted by the arrival of his allies. How could he slip out into the street and get to the tribune now?

There were still a hundred or so white-clad horsemen blocking the gap where the city gate had once stood, but instead of facing unarmed civilians, they were now confronting the Cohort, and the odds had to be at least five to one in favour of the new arrivals.

Rufinus saw Cleander gesticulating as he said something to Fulvius. The man would be plotting now in desperation. His world was collapsing around him, but he still thought he could put it right. Cleander was not a man to give up, as Rufinus knew. He had culled the riot in this region. He had dispersed the crowd with excessive use of force, and Cleander probably did not believe that the men of the Cohort would dare launch an attack on the Praetorians. What he would be wondering now was how to get past the Cohort and after those civilians who had already fled the city and would even now be racing along the road to Laurentum to denounce the chamberlain and turn the emperor against him. He had to stop them if he wanted to come out of this alive. For preference he would have to reach the emperor first and put his side of things. And yet here he was stuck at the Porta Raudusculana, facing off against Severus and Pertinax and a superior force of men who stood in his way.

The chamberlain turned to Fulvius again. Rufinus concentrated, straining to hear. He was close enough to make out only part of what was said, but it was enough. The chamberlain had ordered his tribune to return to the Castra Praetoria and call out the entire Guard. Rufinus shivered. This had the makings of a battle, a brutal conflict between Praetorians and the Cohort. Fulvius saluted and gathered two riders to him. As he made to leave, the chamberlain called him over once more and said something to him, very quietly – almost *secretively*, in fact.

Rufinus narrowed his eyes. What was happening? Whatever it was, his chances of getting to Fulvius were about to improve hugely. The tribune escorted by only two men might just be accessible. Fulvius nodded to his commander and emerged from the rear of the cavalry force with his two men, riding back along the road that would take him through the heart of Rome and to the Castra Praetoria. Instead, though, once they were far enough back to be out of sight of Pertinax and the Cohort, they turned and rode into a side street, heading south, just one turning up from Rufinus.

He frowned. That was a strange direction to take to return to the Castra Praetoria, given that it headed in almost the opposite direction, towards the river. Rufinus twitched. He needed to follow Fulvius, but he also wanted to see what happened here. He decided that he could allow himself a few moments. The street Fulvius had taken he knew well enough.

The Urban Cohorts came to a stop at a command, facing the Praetorians at a distance of only two hundred paces.

'Your career is over, Pertinax,' the chamberlain shouted angrily. 'I will not stand for your policemen defying the Guard. You overstep your boundaries once again, and in the company of the treacherous Severus, too, a man who has worked evil miracles to blacken my name.'

Pertinax stepped his horse forward.

'You condemn yourself, Cleander. Your name is blackened by your deeds most of all. The Urban Cohort serves to protect the people of Rome, even if they have to be protected from the Praetorian Guard.'

Rufinus winced. This was unlikely to end well, unless somehow Pertinax and Severus could appeal to the horsemen and turn them against their commander. It was possible. Either way, whether this ended in bloodless victory or mutual slaughter, Rufinus was out of time. He would have to leave Cleander to the others if he was to finish Fulvius.

Praying that his friends would manage to bring this to a conclusion, Rufinus turned his horse and rode back up the Vicus Publicius. Fulvius had only a short lead on him, and was riding up the Vicus Loreti Maioris. Several side streets connected the two thoroughfares, but Rufinus knew the best cut through to save time.

As he trotted up the street, he pondered on what Fulvius might be doing heading this way. It was unlikely in the extreme that he was heading back to the fortress, else he would have gone entirely the other way. Over the months of patrolling the region with the Urban Cohort, Rufinus had a better grasp of the area's geography than most. The line of the old, disused city wall ran from the gateway he'd just left down to the river, mostly now running through warehouses and residences, long since overgrown by the city. But despite being disused as a defensive circuit, the wall itself remained to a good height in many places, often reused as the side wall of later buildings. As such, it still presented a solid barrier. Rufinus knew well that from the Raudusculana Gate they had just left, the line of the wall remained unbroken until it reached the Porta Trigemina, down by the river and not far from the circus.

Connections were made instantly in his mind. That was the next gate. From there, horsemen could leave the old walled region and move through the network of good modern roads in the sub-urbs. In a quarter of an hour they would be on the road to Ostia and Laurentum, chasing down that mob of civilians. Worse still, since the start of the grain problems, Cleander had taken to stationing a small unit of his Praetorians down near the emporium, and there would be even more of the Guard a little further back, near the circus. Fulvius could probably gather a full turma of cavalry on his way out of the city, and he would then be out in the open, free to dispatch that crowd of citizens without Severus and Pertinax even being aware of their departure. This whole thing could still yet collapse if Cleander managed to stop word reaching the emperor before he could pour his poisoned words into Commodus' ear and turn the tide against the conspirators.

Now, more than ever Rufinus needed to get rid of Fulvius, and quickly. As soon as the man reached the emporium he would have reinforcements and be unreachable once more.

Rufinus kicked up from a trot into a fast canter.

He turned the corner, hurried along the connecting street and then back out onto the Loreti Maioris. He could see the three white horsemen further up the slope. They were moving hastily but not at top speed, which confirmed Rufinus' suspicions. If they were only intending to gather local reinforcements or get back to the fortress, they could gallop and be much faster. That they moved at a steady pace suggested that they had a longer distance to ride and meant to conserve their horses' energy.

Rufinus steadied himself, drawing the blade from the sheath at his side. He urged his horse on now into a gallop, and the beast raced on up the slope. He was closing on them. He had to get rid of the other two who rode side by side behind their master first, and quickly else they stop him bringing down the tribune. He was short on time and had to be fast, and that meant he could do with removing both men at the same time, to avoid becoming embroiled with them while Fulvius fled to safety.

With a touch of regret, Rufinus slung away his shield, letting it fall to the ground as he rode. Freed of the painted board, he drew his pugio dagger with the off-hand. He had to be swift and accurate. He had only one attempt at this without turning it into a troublesome melee.

He was closing on the trio now, and finally they became aware of the hoof beats following them, the drumming speed too rapid to be lost among their own. They turned and looked back. Rufinus flinched, but both men simply nodded and then faced forward again. He was a Praetorian. He was one of them. Probably Cleander had sent them an extra man with a message.

Rufinus grinned viciously.

In a matter of heartbeats he was with them. Instead of slowing, though, he made for the gap between the two men escorting the tribune and, as he did so, pulled back his sword arm. A double attack, striking out separately with both arms, is a difficult thing to do, and something that gladiators learned rather than legionaries, but it was also something any successful boxer trained in.

As he came level with the two men, who now turned once more to look at him, he struck.

The sword that had been pulled back now swept forward. The man on the right at which he struck was an optio or other junior officer, clearly, as he wore a shirt of gleaming bronze fish-scale armour. It was decorative and relatively protective. Unfortunately for the man it also had a low collar-line, while his helmet's neck guard, since his gaze was lowered to his reins, was a little high. The resulting gap was not over-wide, certainly less than a hand-width, and wrapped in a scarf, but for an experienced soldier with plenty of preparation, it was enough.

Even though the cavalry sword was longer than the gladius Rufinus was used to, it handled in much the same way, and the edge was narrower and sharper. The swinging blade bit into the man's neck deep enough to smash the bones in his spine despite the scarf.

His scream masked that of his companion, who shrieked simultaneously as the dagger plunged beneath his right arm with which he gripped the reins, sinking into the unprotected flash and hammering deep into the chest cavity.

Calling on every ounce of strength he had, Rufinus ripped both weapons free and used the fists balled around the hilts to push the dying men outwards. The two escorts, still screaming, fell away, sagging in the saddle, and Rufinus was right behind Fulvius as he turned in shock at the noise.

It took a moment for recognition to sink in, and then the tribune danced his horse ahead a few paces before wheeling her sharply to face his assailant.

Rufinus stopped and the two men sat for a moment, eyes locked upon one another. Fulvius then drew his sword and dagger to match Rufinus – a tribune rarely carried a shield, after all.

'The time has come then.'

'It has.'

Fulvius nodded to himself. 'I should have dealt with you long ago. I let caution get in the way. I did not want to cause trouble for the chamberlain, particularly after everything he has done for me, but I should have bitten down on the strop and done it anyway. I would be fascinated to find out how you got out of your cell, though I don't suppose it matters now.'

'I won't let you murder any more civilians,' Rufinus said in low, menacing tones.

Fulvius laughed. 'Don't be ridiculous, Rufinus. I have no intention of killing *anyone* now. Once I've sent you to meet your father, I intend to find somewhere nice and quiet and wait out events.'

Rufinus frowned. 'What? Your master...?'

A snort. 'Cleander's done for now. I'm well aware of that. Whatever little plot you and your friends have been cooking up with the grain shipments has achieved the impossible. Cleander is going to fall a long way, and I intend to distance myself from today's events. When he falls, the two prefects will fall with him, and the rest of the Guard will get just a stiff talking to, for they were just following their commander's orders. By autumn I will be a prefect of the Guard.'

'No, by sundown you will be a corpse.'

Fulvius snorted again. 'I offer you this only once, in a spirit of goodwill. Go away and leave me alone. Forget about your petty revenge, and I will go about my own business. With luck, both of us will see out the day alive and you can reclaim your name.'

'No.'

'Because if you refuse,' Fulvius said, gripping his blades tight, 'then it will be you lying mouldering in a ditch. I am not some gilded flower of a tribune, granted command by the senate because my dad is of old blood. I fought in Pannonia, in the front lines. I killed while up to my knees in blood and mud and shit, just like you. But *unlike* you I am a cavalry soldier. I know horses well, and mounted combat even better. You are infantry. You will die. Last chance to run away, Rufinus.'

'No.'

Rufinus danced his horse forward, sword rising above his head. As he closed on the tribune, it came down hard, but Fulvius simply slung his own blade in the way and knocked the strike away easily. He was good. He was quick, too. The dagger in the tribune's left hand thrust out and Rufinus had to lean back in the saddle sharply. The dagger whispered past him as he turned his horse once more, meeting Fulvius for a second clash.

The two swords met again with a clang and a spine-tingling shriek of tortured metal as the two edges grated apart. This time Rufinus' dagger slashed out but Fulvius was already moving out of the way. Then the tribune was on him. That sword came round again and again, the dagger punctuating each blow, and Rufinus was forced on the defensive, turning and parrying each blow without time to strike back.

His mind whirled. He had plenty of fight in him yet but despite Rufinus' youth spent in the saddle, Fulvius was right. A man trained to fight on horseback is naturally faster and more flexible with that situation. Part of the difference in their ability might also be put down to the fact that Rufinus was having a little difficulty moving well in his tight, restrictive chain shirt. Either way, unless he found a way to even the odds, he would have to be quite lucky to get the better of Fulvius.

The only way, then, was to turn this to his advantage.

He smiled grimly, remembering that fight a decade ago in the amphitheatre when he had put Phaestor, the commander of Lucilla's private army, down. That man had been superior with a blade, and it had taken a trick – a ruse of foolish nature – to defeat him, falling as though by accident in order to get to a place where he could strike his blow.

This time took little planning. He knew immediately what to do. He continued to parry and dodge Fulvius' blows until the right one came. As Fulvius swiped with his blade, slashing across at neck height, Rufinus fell forward in the saddle, lifting his rear as he did so that he came free of the secure horns of leather that held a rider in his seat. He fell forward, past the horse's neck. It must have looked like a totally graceless and foolish failure, ducking the blow and in the process slipping and falling from the horse.

Rufinus dropped, keeping hold of just his sword and twisting as he fell.

Accompanied by Fulvius' triumphant laugh, he landed on the street. He had turned, though, as he fell, and landed with both heels down, sword still gripped and dagger discarded, almost underneath the tribune's horse.

Before Fulvius could work out what was happening or try to crush Rufinus under the hooves, the younger man got to work. His sword held to the side, he reached up and grasped the girth strap of the tribune's saddle. It was the work of but a moment to unfasten the buckle and step back.

With a cry of alarm, Fulvius fell sideways, his saddle still gripping him tight, but no longer attached to the horse.

He landed badly with a thump, and his blades skittered away across the cobbles with the impact.

By the time the tribune had extricated himself from the troublesome saddle and began to rise, Rufinus was in front of him, sword in hand.

'I'd planned to make you suffer,' Rufinus said as he lifted the sword above the defenceless officer. 'But time is of the essence.' The blade fell, the tip aimed neatly between the shocked, upturned face and the collar edge of his cuirass. As the sword slammed down into him through neck and chest, impaling the heart in the process, Rufinus sighed. 'And in the end, you're not worth the trouble.'

He ripped the sword free and stepped back, watching the gasping tribune clutch at his neck as blood welled up in huge quantities.

Rufinus straightened.

Dis was avenged. The last of the six murderous cavalrymen was gone. He might have felt something more, he thought, perhaps a sense of closure, but all that filled his mind now was an image of Cleander – the man who had kept his brother prisoner, engineered the deaths of people Rufinus respected and cared for, controlled Rome with an iron fist and a black heart, and perhaps even saw himself one day on the throne.

And right now, Cleander was back at the city gate, facing off against Pertinax and Severus. The whole thing could end now, but Cleander had to survive the clash, ridiculously. If his entire web of grimy influence was to collapse with him, Cleander could not become a martyr, killed in a clash with the Urban Cohort. He had to survive long enough for the emperor himself to condemn him. And that depended on what happened at the Porta Raudusculana, and on that small group of brave citizens who had managed to get out of the city and were even now running for the emperor's gate to denounce the traitor.

Swallowing his nerves, Rufinus wiped his sword on his scarf and then discarded it before pulling himself with difficulty back up into the saddle and turning his horse around, heading back down towards the stand-off by the gate.

CHAPTER TWENTY SEVEN – ENEMY OF ROME

Rome, June 17th 190 A.D., morning

S omething had happened at the gate in his absence. What had been more than a hundred mounted Praetorians when he left, sitting defiant in the saddle and with that permanent superior smirk plastered across their faces, now looked like a defensive unit in the worst of battles. There were perhaps thirty or so left, and only half of them were still mounted.

Bodies lay strewn across the wide thoroughfare – armoured figures in both white and madder red. Blood filled the crevices between the cobbles and flags, sitting glistening in the sun, and the smell of blood and death had finally overridden the omnipresent stink of summer-parched dung that hung annually over the city.

The fight that had broken out had been brutal and short, and the Praetorians had clearly made good account of themselves despite everything. The number of dead was roughly even despite the odds of five to one.

Clearly someone had given the order to disengage, though whether it had been the white-clad Guard or the Cohort it was impossible to tell.

The Praetorians were formed up now, filling the gateway with their meagre remaining numbers, battered and bloody shields held forth, crimson blades held forth against the enemy. They were defiant even to the end. Had the Guard not fallen quite so far these past few years, Rufinus might have been proud of his old unit for that. The Urban Cohort was lined up facing them once more across the corpses, their first engagement a qualified success.

'Disperse and return to your fortress before we are forced to finish this,' Pertinax bellowed from his lines.

Rufinus peered that way. Pertinax sat astride his horse with blade visible, though no sign of its use as yet showing. Severus, on the other hand, was already noticeably blood-spattered, and his blade bore stains.

There was no reply from the Praetorians, though they remained defiantly in position.

Something struck Rufinus as wrong, though he couldn't immediately identify what it was. His eyes ripped back and forth between the men of the Cohort, glaring belligerently under the controlled command of the prefect and the consul, and the Praetorians, clearly defeated and outnumbered hopelessly, and yet still standing bold.

Both things struck him at the same time: the reason no one had answered the prefect's demands was almost certainly because no one was commanding the Praetorians. Cleander was not there. Moreover, as his gaze took in the scene as a whole and his mind made that important connection, his eyes also told him that the numbers didn't add up. There had been over a hundred cavalry here and now they numbered maybe thirty, and yet there were only another thirty or so white-clad bodies on the ground. Where were the missing thirty?

Rufinus shivered. Had Cleander raced back to the Castra Praetoria to call out the rest of the Guard? Had he been aware that Fulvius had abandoned him, or just realised that the tribune had failed for some reason?

Gingerly, hoping he wouldn't suddenly find himself dragged into this dreadful stand-off and the bloodbath that it was almost certainly going to result in, Rufinus walked his horse out from the side street. It felt exceedingly odd to ride out into the open out here, where bodies of civilians littered the street behind the line of the Praetorians. He paused in the middle of the street, trying to figure it out.

Cleander had been in a hurry. He was a desperate man. His grip on Rome was slipping and he knew it. The emperor was a god to his people, and even the senate would not refuse his word. No man in the empire had the authority or power to touch Cleander in his Rome... except the emperor Commodus. A word from the living Hercules would see Cleander peeled and crucified. And no matter how much the emperor relied upon the man, no matter how long they had been close Commodus was a man of his people. He loved them and they loved him. And if they had turned on Cleander, so would he.

If the mob got to Commodus and demanded Cleander's head the emperor would oblige, and the chamberlain knew it. But if they never reached the emperor, and instead Cleander arrived at that maritime villa, he could undo it all. Given time to work, he could piece together the events that had brought him to this juncture. He could deflect the blame onto Dionysus and Pertinax, for he was an expert at playing that sort of game. In fact, he would probably have never allowed himself to become so hoodwinked in the first place had he not become cocky, certain that he was untouchable.

A significant number of civilians would be racing for the emperor's villa even now, and they would be moving fast despite the distance, for the future of Rome, its chamberlain, and their own lives might depend upon it.

Given that, there was no way Cleander would risk wasting time calling up his reserves. He had to stop that petition now. That was why he had sent Fulvius, unaware that the tribune intended to betray him at the last. Cleander had not gone back to camp, for that would be admitting defeat and climbing up onto the cross, but still Pertinax and Severus had the Urban Cohort blocking the road to Laurentum.

Rufinus' suspicious eyes swung back up the road whence he'd emerged, up to that rise where Fulvius lay sprawled in a heap and a pool of blood. Fulvius had been running for his life, but that was not what Rufinus had assumed when he first saw him go. He had presumed the tribune was following the lines of the old wall round to the Porta Trigemina to gain access to the sub-urbs and chase down the crowd of civilians.

Rufinus realised with a cold knot of fear what had happened.

While he had been up that western street dealing with Appius Fulvius, and the consul and the Urban Cohorts had been involved in a vicious fracas in the gateway that would have been chaotic and noisy, Cleander had taken one turma of cavalry and slipped away. *Fulvius* might not have been meaning to sneak out of another gate, but Rufinus was fairly certain that Cleander had. And if he'd not gone past Rufinus to the west, nor through this gate, and certainly not back towards the Castra Praetoria in the north, then he had gone east.

'Roma Victrix!' came a sudden loud call, and Rufinus' head snapped round. The Praetorians were marching against the Urban Cohort once more. The last fight here was about to start. Rufinus was half inclined to lend a hand, striking at the white figures from behind, but he shook off the notion. Severus had everything under control here. They might fight hard and to the last, but the outcome was inevitable, given the difference in numbers. And if he got bogged down here he could be of little use elsewhere.

With a deep breath, Rufinus turned his back on the last stand of Cleander's Praetorians and rode across the main street into the narrow road opposite. It was the obvious choice. If Cleander and his riders had slipped away in the fight, they had to have used somewhere close that went in the right direction. Again, with the Cohort Rufinus had patrolled all these streets and knew them well. Two brief doglegs would take a man to the next gate in the ancient wall to the east, the Porta Naevia.

Entering that narrow street, the atmosphere changed. Here there were no bodies. Neither the internecine fighting between Rome's military nor the wanton butchery of her citizens had spread into this street. In fact the only signs of life were only just alive, being the ever-present plague victims floundering by the street's edge and hoping for some sort of relief. Citizens had fled up here from the slaughter, for sure, but had left no trace of their passage.

Rufinus' theory seemed to be proved positive only a short distance up the street. Two separate pieces of evidence supported the notion of Cleander's passage. A large puddle of urine from an overturned public pee amphora – a *Vespasian* as they used to be humorously named – had been trodden in by two horses, the wet hoof prints travelling east as they faded. And a little further up the street a pile of horse dung sealed it. Cleander and his riders had come this way, using the sacrifice of their comrades against the Cohort to buy them sufficient time to slip from the city and chase down those troublesome citizens taking their plea to the emperor.

As Rufinus moved through two junctions, making for the crumbling ruin that had once been the Porta Naevia, he ran through some quick calculations in his head. More than ten miles to the emperor's villa, he reasoned. Thirteen or fourteen, in fact. It sounded a long way to go by foot. Pheidippides once ran twenty six miles with tidings of the victory at Marathon in only three hours. Mind you, he died afterwards. Pheidippides could make the imperial villa then in an hour and a half.

Back home, the gate of Tarraco had been just short of seven miles from the estate of their villa. Rufinus and Lucius had raced that distance time and again and had done it in less than an hour, although they'd been younger and fitter than most of the Roman crowd.

Two hours, he estimated, given the urgency of their flight and the likely knowledge that they would be hunted once the Praetorians got their act together. It had been a little more than a quarter of an hour between the first citizens leaving the circus and Rufinus exiting to find a horse. He'd spent at least another quarter of an hour getting somewhere quiet and waiting for the Praetorians. And then probably *another* quarter of an hour following them over the hill and down towards the gate. In truth, all those moves were probably a little longer than that. Likely an hour had passed between the first man leaving the circus and the two forces facing off at the gate. More than a quarter of an hour had passed since then, too, dealing with Fulvius and then cutting back across the gate and up this way

He chewed his lip. If his calculations were correct, the front runners of the mob heading for the imperial villa might well have had almost an hour's lead on Cleander. They would be well on the way and closing on the estate.

What good Rufinus was going to be able to do against a full turma of thirty cavalrymen he wasn't sure, but if one thing was certain it was that he was not going to sit back and let Cleander have even a chance at pulling his backside back out of the fire.

Gripping the reins so tight that his knuckles whitened, Rufinus turned the last corner and rode out to the gap in the crumbling walls that marked the site of the fallen gate. Here was the first true sign of Cleander's passage.

A small detachment from the Urban Cohort had been stationed at the Porta Naevia – again almost certainly the work of Severus or Cestius, for this was not a regular posting. Five bodies lay in twisted positions around the gate wearing the red tunics of the Cohort, and several Praetorians lay among them. There had been a short and brutal fight, which confirmed something for Rufinus: the Cohort must have been given standing orders to stop the Praetorians exiting this part of the city. What had started as an angry demonstration by a girl in the circus has spiralled out past the status of a riot and into something now approaching civil war, with Rome's two central military units pitted against one another for the future of the city.

Trying to harden his heart against what was happening, Rufinus rode out through the gate. Beyond the crumbling walls that had last been of use centuries ago in the Republican civil wars, the city had grown outwards. Indeed, were it not for the higher parts of wall still jutting up it would have been difficult to tell that the city had even *had* such walls.

Making his way between houses and shop, insulae and warehouses, Rufinus followed the Via Ardeatina for a short distance before veering off into a side street and curving around the outer edge of the sub-urbs, heading for the road the mob would have taken.

It was not long before the connecting streets led him out onto the Via Ostiensis, and there he turned and looked back towards the city. The Urban Cohort was visible from here, now with their back to him as they finished off the last of their Praetorian foe and mopped up the fracas. Before they spotted his white-clad figure and decided he was their next target, Rufinus turned south and raced away from Rome.

He was less than two miles from the city when he found the next evidence of Cleander. A dozen or more citizens lay sprawled in mud and blood at the road side, murdered in flight as was evidenced by the wounds all showing in their backs. They had been ridden down by Cleander's horsemen in their panic. Rufinus' lip twitched. He vowed once more that Cleander would not see the sun set on this day.

Less than a mile later at the junction of the two main roads there was worse to come. Here, it appeared that some of the mob who had fled Rome and who had been too slow to escape the pursuing Praetorians had tried to make a stand. Men had armed themselves with branches and sticks. More than twenty citizens lay dead, wounds inflicted at all angles in the slaughter. One Praetorian lay among them. Their sacrifice might not have been in vain, but could it really have been worth it?

Once more Rufinus felt the bile rise into his gullet at the knowledge that he and his fellow conspirators had engineered this, had willingly allowed this slaughter to come to pass. He was beginning to feel sure they would be cursed for this for all time.

Turning off the Via Ostiensis past the ruined bodies, he began the trek along the Via Laurentina, which led to the seaside villas of the rich and the small town that served to give the area its name. His disgust, misery and self-loathing increased with every pace of that road, for now the slaughter became constant. Here and there, every few hundred paces along the way, lay fresh bodies. Cleander and his Praetorians had moved through the travelling throng like a scythe through wheat, destroying all in their path. All to stop the truth reaching the emperor.

Truth?

Rufinus felt sick. He might never be able to say what the truth was again, for the truth that Cleander so feared and that was carried by the desperate citizens was itself little more than a tissue of lies built up by Rufinus and his friends.

He had been trotting thus far, knowing that he needed to save his horse's energy, for this was no short distance and there may be a fight coming at the end of it. But now, as he began to smell the salt of the sea in the air, Rufinus put heel to flank and urged his horse into greater speed. Time was short, and the citizens and Cleander both could be approaching the imperial villa now.

The eight or nine miles of the Via Laurentina passed in a horrible blur of dry, dusty road and twisted, ruined bodies. Twice more on the journey he found evidence of brave stands made by a few to save their companions and slow the chamberlain, such that their plea might reach the emperor's ear. Both of those violent massacres had claimed another Praetorian. Still, there would be so many remaining with Cleander.

Finally, as the salt tang became noticeably stronger the sea came into view, the small town lying visible on the coast just a mile to the south. The great estates of the rich lay along the seafront north of that and so Rufinus turned, his route marked out with dead Romans in case he ever needed directions, and rode for the emperor's villa.

A dozen or more corpses further along the main road, and he knew he was close. The sound of a distant engagement drifted back in the quiet air: screams and clashes and the thunder of hooves still distant enough to become just one great rumble to anyone who had not lived through it often enough to pick apart the strands.

Time was tight. He was near the great estates and that meant that they had to be close to the emperor now. Had Cleander beaten him to it after all this? But then surely if *he* could hear the racket of combat from here, then so could the residents of the imperial estate?

He spotted the end of the emperor's drive easily. He had never been here, of course, but he had served in Commodus' guard and he knew the glorious emperor's style well enough. The other drives he had passed along the road had been tastefully marked with a fountain of tumbling water over statues, or a marble plaque.

Only here did Hercules stand watch along with some Amazon woman with one breast, both in garishly-painted marble at the entrance of the drive. This was the residence of the emperor, and Rufinus would have known it without the small crenulated shed where a guard would usually sit, or the small pile of civilian corpses lying at the junction like some kind of grisly milepost.

He could hear the fighting now in the driveway and turned the corner in the hot summer sun, between the lines of trees that bordered the drive. The sight that met him pulled his heart into his throat.

The drive was perhaps half a mile long and terminated at a low wall that marked the perimeter of the imperial villa. Trees marched in ordered, well-tended lines along both sides of the dusty gravelled drive, and further along more statues added to the border. But it was not the glory of the imperial driveway that grabbed his attention. It was what was happening in it.

Perhaps a third of the way along the drive, horsemen in white were busy hacking and slaying civilians. Another group of citizens were ahead, strung out and racing for the emperor's gateway. Cleander was at the very brink of disaster, desperately trying to kill off the evidence before they could complain to their emperor. It sounded so stupid thinking that he might try such a thing, but Rufinus knew Cleander. The man could yet talk himself out of anything if there was no strong enough voice in opposition with an ounce of knowledge of what had happened.

If he *did* still manage to butcher the citizens…

Rufinus raced on after them. As he rode, his sword rasped from its scabbard. There were still the better part of thirty Praetorian cavalrymen there. There was a very good chance he would die if he launched an attack, but he had to try and help.

It came to him in that moment. There were the sounds of alarms from the imperial villa. The emperor's guards were coming, and they would not be Praetorians in the pay of Cleander. The emperor and his men were coming, and there was simply no longer time for Cleander to do away with the two hundred or so civilians gathering outside the gate.

Rufinus slowed. This would not be solved with his sword.

Indeed, the action was all now taking place right outside the emperor's gateway. Men were being slaughtered within sight of the villa gates, which were even now opening. Rufinus fought against the urge to move forward. Currently he was the only Praetorian in the entire drive not butchering Roman citizens, sitting astride his horse a hundred paces back from them. Cleander was urging his men to the slaughter like some ancient barbarian lunatic.

The gates opened. Probably Cleander and his riders didn't see it at first as they were too busy with their wholesale murder, but Rufinus' breath caught in his throat. This was it: the culmination of everything they had been doing for the three years. Every citizen who had died by plague or starvation or a gleaming blade for those three years had done so because of what had been planned by five people and their contacts. It had been appalling and unforgivable, but it had all been for what was happening right now.

The people hated Cleander now. Even if he lived, he would be a figure of spite forever to the citizens of Rome, and they had come to tell their emperor that, and of his wrongdoings. He had fought to the very last to try and stop it; was still fighting in fact, killing innocents even as they turned to call to their emperor.

He could no longer argue his way out of it. Cleander was bust condemning himself in the sight of Commodus.

The divine Commodus emerged surrounded by perhaps a dozen gladiators.

Rufinus heard the emperor shout something, though he couldn't quite make out what he said. On a whim, and knowing that the time for making a difference was at hand, Rufinus kicked his horse and began to ride forward to where those white-clad riders were busy hewing at loyal people of Rome. Something was happening. The dynamic was changing and Rufinus could see it, detached from the action as he was.

The mob had stopped running. They had reached their emperor and there was nowhere else to run. Besides, the emperor carried a sword and had brutal gladiators clustered around him, not to mention more of their ilk and Praetorians who had to be trustworthy to their emperor beyond.

Cleander was in a mad fit of trying to kill every last man before he could open his mouth in condemnation, the lunatic.

Rufinus had not heard the emperor's clear baritone voice since the day Perennis died half a decade ago, and yet it was impossible to mistake as it cut through the din.

'FORM RANKS!'

Cleander was ignoring his emperor's order entirely and consequently so were his guardsmen. They hurried to butcher as many as they could, despite the clear indications that it was over. Cleander had lost but he hadn't yet accepted it. He was a man moving pieces around on the board after the killing move had been made, but refusing to quit.

He killed mercilessly alongside his men.

This had to end.

In a far smaller voice than the emperor's glorious tone, Rufinus shouted 'put up your swords. Stop.'

He rode in among the Praetorian cavalry, heedless of the danger. He'd had enough blood on his hands from all this, and would have no more, even among the cavalry. To his right, a horseman lifted his sword ready to plunge it down at a cowering shopkeeper.

Rufinus grabbed the man's wrist. The Praetorian turned to him in angry shock, and Rufinus simply shook his head in answer. As if the gesture broke a spell, the rider looked from Rufinus first to his raised blade, and then down to the unarmed man he'd been about to kill.

The man nodded. His sword came slowly back down.

Somewhere ahead, Cleander was still busy howling and killing, but Rufinus had to ignore him. The bastard was the emperor's to deal with now. Rufinus would instead save lives.

He moved among the throng of horsemen, silencing most with a look and grabbing wrists where he had to. In a dozen heartbeats, he had managed to halt the killing. He realised that the only figure in command here was Cleander, and the chamberlain was busy killing with crazed fury. There were no career officers with a powerful presence to take charge. Some of the soldiers had already responded to the emperor's command, but in the absence of one of their own officers Rufinus' tone of power stopped them. He had been a centurion twice now, among the legions in Dacia and in command of the Urban Cohort, and the sheer power of a centurion shone from his very being. Men stopped when he told them to.

With a fierce glare, he opened his mouth.

'You heard your emperor. Form up.'

It took only moments for the Praetorians to become a solid block of unmoving cavalry, ordered and disciplined. Rufinus sat among them. Perhaps there *was* a future for the Guard, after all? Especially if he were in command of it…

He became aware that the emperor had said something else, addressing the soldiers, and he cursed himself for being too busy to notice. Whatever it was raised a murmur of consent from the cavalry. Concentrating, Rufinus now heard the emperor once more.

'What is the meaning of this?'

A rumble of answers, mostly conflicting, arose from the crowd. Rufinus glanced ahead. Cleander had put up his sword and ridden his horse forward, closer to the emperor.

'What is this, Cleander?' Commodus demanded, his tone carrying the threat of violence.

'Rome seethes with riots. I had word that such a mob was bound for the villa, so we came to protect the imperial person.'

'Horse shit,' shouted someone in the crowd.

The emperor's voice came loud and clear again. 'They are curiously unarmed for a dangerous mob, Cleander.'

'An enraged man can kill with his hands. Think what hundreds can do.'

'He lies, Majesty,' called a voice from the crowd.

'I will have your fucking tongue, maggot, before you are nailed up,' Cleander rasped in reply.

Rufinus could not see past the riders and the crowd clearly enough to see what was happening, and the conversation that followed between the emperor, the chamberlain and the unseen speaker in the crowd evaded him entirely. The growing desperation in Cleander's tone did not. Whatever Commodus said, the speaker in the crowd seemed to be the vox populi, and he spoke now in great clear tones, the conversation becoming all the more clear in the silence as the slaughter stopped.

'This man has turned Rome to revolt, Majesty. To the very brink of a civil war, in fact. Even now, the streets of the city run with blood, for good men will no longer take his oppression and raise blades to defy him, even as he has his Praetorians gut the populace in the forum. As the Praetorian commander he has become overlord of Rome, master of spies and butcher of citizens. He casually murders those who oppose him and takes their lands. As chamberlain he is worse. Rome starves, Majesty, and in such dreadful famine the best of emperors in times past have increased the grain dole, doubled shipments, even diverted the navy to aid in easing the crisis. What does this man do? Hoard what little is left in private horrea and put to the sword any man who tries to feed his family from what should be public grain.'

Rufinus felt the gate of Tarterus open beneath him. This was it: the very moment of accusation.

'Is this true, Cleander?' the emperor asked.

'After a fashion. On the advice of the grain commissioner I began to stockpile the grain against the time of greatest crisis.'

Gods, Rufinus thought, *please don't let this be pinned on Dionysus. Not now, at the very end.*

'You do not feel that starvation in the streets *is* the time of greatest crisis?' Commodus snarled angrily.

'Things can get worse. I was preparing for disaster.'

'You were *causing* disaster,' Commodus snapped. 'What do the consuls have to say on all of this?'

Cleander's eyes narrowed. I could see him thinking his way around the problem, but he was too late. That unseen voice in the crowd answered instead. 'Majesty, Vitellius has fled the city, fearing Praetorian blades in the night, for he has already lost a son and most of his property to Cleander. Severus is one of those lion-hearts in the city who wields a blade in defiance.'

'This man is twisting the truth,' Cleander barked. 'I followed the advice of the grain commissioner. He assured me more supplies were on the way. The Misenum fleet has been dispatched to speed the flow. The consuls should be helping to keep the peace in Rome so that I can do my job...'

'Yet you have driven one consul from the city and turned the other against you as a champion of the starving?'

'No.'

'And these people are such a danger that you thought to bring a turma of cavalry and slay hundreds of Roman citizens in my driveway?'

'No, but...'

'But you could not allow news of your mismanagement and cruelty to reach my ears.'

'No.'

'That would be no, *Majesty*.'

There was a murmur now among the crowd, soldier and civilian alike, and it drowned out the muted conversation that followed. The next words Rufinus heard clearly were those of the emperor.

'You are hereby removed from the Praetorian prefecture and the office of cubicularius. I imagine there are legal hoops through which to jump with the senate, but they will not deny me when I brand you an enemy of Rome.'

Rufinus could imagine Cleander's face. He moved as best he could, but could only just see the chamberlain on his horse as an unreachable figure out front.

'No, Majesty!'

Again, Rufinus did not hear what was said next, but he managed through the throng to see the emperor pass a sword into the crowd of citizens and then turn and walk back to his gate. Around Rufinus, the cavalry were becoming restive, uncertain of what to do, perhaps questioning where their loyalties lay. There was the tell-tale rasp of swords being drawn once more.

'Steady,' he said to the cavalry around him in his best centurion's tones. 'You serve the emperor, not the former chamberlain.'

There was a tense silence, but he felt his words sink into them. He had command of the turma now, in the absence of a proper officer. He smiled. 'Senatus, *et Imperator*, populusque Romanum...'

Somewhere in the crowd, someone shouted 'enemy of Rome,' which gained a roar of approval.

Cleander turned now, and Rufinus saw the desperation in his face. 'Defend me!'

'Stand... your... fucking... ground,' Rufinus growled at his men. 'First man who moves will have to get the medicus to remove my boot from his colon.'

The mob were chanting now.

Enemy of Rome.
Enemy of Rome.
Enemy of Rome.

As the mob bayed for Cleander's death, the emperor returned to his gate and abandoned him. The cavalry at this last moment clearly felt more comfortable with Rufinus' orders than their former commander's. Rufinus held them in position.

Cleander made his last play. Escape.

Trapped between his own cavalry, the crowd and the emperor's walls and guards, the chamberlain tried to jump his horse across one of the statues by the side of the track. Rufinus was horseman enough to know if for a disaster even as the attempt was made. The horse simply refused and stopped. Still baying their 'enemy of Rome' chant, the crowd went for him.

Rufinus saw only enough to know that the deed was done. Hands grasped and clawed at the chamberlain and in moments he was pulled from his horse. Screams and howls spoke all too eloquently of what was happening to the man. By tradition, a traitor was hurled down the Gemonian Stair, where the crowd would tear the body to pieces. There were no steps here, but the crowd were content to make do. Rufinus swore that beneath the roar and the screaming he heard the sickening sounds of a limb torn free.

Twenty heartbeats it lasted, and then suddenly Cleander reappeared... or at least, his head did. Jammed on the top of that sword the emperor had wielded, and trailing blood and sinew, the chamberlain's silent scream was passed around above the crowd.

Rufinus swallowed his disgust.

At last, it was over.

CHAPTER TWENTY EIGHT – EPILOGUE

The Palatine, Rome, June 24th 190 A.D.

Rufinus stood in the vestibule feeling oddly out of place. For years he had worn the uniform of a legionary, and then for a similar period the whites of the Praetorian Guard. He had garbed himself as a Prefect of the Fleet and then a centurion in the Urban Cohort. Now here he was standing in a toga like a civilian and feeling strange. What *was* he now? He could hear the murmur of palace life around him as the Palatine settled down to normality again, with the chamberlain gone and the emperor once more in residence.

The return of Commodus had been a glorious thing and had given Rufinus hope for the future. People had been telling him for years now that Commodus was withdrawing from public life as Tiberius had once done, leaving dubious freedmen, both political and military, to run his empire. Indeed, his recent disappearance to his coastal villa for far too long seemed to support that notion, and yet the Commodus that returned to Rome was every bit that glorious golden Hercules Rufinus remembered from the bath house in Vindobona a decade ago. There was perhaps something unsettling about him these days, maybe a gleam in the eye, or the tight creases of his face as though he had worn a mask so long it had become part of his flesh.

Whatever the case, the emperor was back and was ruling Rome once more. He had thrown open the granaries, making the Horrea Ummidiana a public storehouse under the aegis of the grain commissioner. The people of Rome had glutted on bread at last, and barely had the stores been emptied before the first barges of grain from Alexandria began to arrive up the Tiber, just two days after the death of Cleander, proving to Rufinus that the gods had been with them after all. The people were fed, and the unrest subsided instantly. Moreover, the emperor had announced the commissioning of a new fleet controlled directly by the imperial administration to ship grain and prevent any such disaster occurring again. All was good in Rome.

As for Cleander? His head had returned to Rome on a spear point and had been planted by the Gemonian Stair at the top of the forum, on display for all to see. The rest of his body had disappeared in the wake of what had happened at Laurentum, though Rufinus had been among those present when the crowd dispersed and had seen the fragments of rent flesh and quivering offal. His body had quite literally been torn apart, people taking away pieces as a grisly trophy of their victory.

Rufinus had visited the chamberlain's remains on the stair only an hour after they had been placed there, and had discovered with mixed dismay and relief that his father's head was not on display close by as Fulvius had threatened. Perhaps it was for the best. Rufinus would not be able to bury his father, and without a coin beneath the tongue to pay the ferryman the old fool was doomed to wander the world as a restless spirit, but perhaps that was what he'd deserved in the end. At least his memory would not carry the stain of treason, not having been officially displayed there.

Publius had been sent for, way back in Cemenelum, told he could return to Rome under his own name and without fear, and similarly Senova had been sent a missive telling her to come home. Both letters had told their recipients to bring Acheron to Rome, for in the chaos of the last few years, he had no idea whether his great hound remained in Cemenelum or had been taken to Sicilia. Either way it was time for him to be reunited with his master.

Gnaeus Marcius Rustius Rufinus.

It felt exceedingly weird to be himself again after so long, and with no reason to hide or fear. He owed no one, and had no real enemies left, except perhaps a bitter optio out in Dacia, and Clodius Albinus, his master. He doubted he even registered on their list of important names. He was Rufinus again, and could be proud of being so. He tried not to ponder any longer on what Rufinus actually *was* now, since that subject threatened to bring on a headache whenever he reasoned through it.

Septimius Severus had weathered the plot in grand style as a consul of Rome and a hero of the people, thanked in person by the emperor. His future was as yet unconfirmed beyond this year's consulate, though it could only be bright. Similarly, Pertinax, who had been labelled a *Hero of Rome* by the emperor for his actions in defying Cleander's Praetorians and their butchery had come out of the plot well.

The cleansing of the web of wickedness the chamberlain had spun over the years had begun instantly, and it had started with the Guard. A man called Laetus, who was one of the emperor's own most trusted men, had been given command as prefect, and any officer who had been put in place by Cleander or who had commanded during the butchery of citizens was removed from office. A few were dishonourably discharged, and only a couple executed for their actions. The bulk of the Guard remained. The civil administration in Rome, and on the Palatine in particular, experienced a huge list of proscriptions, important posts becoming empty at a rate of knots.

The only event that marred their otherwise total victory had been the one execution that could not in the end be avoided. Cleander had been blamed for it all, but inevitably a little culpability had leaked out to Papirius Dionysus. The emperor had, with a heavy heart, reminded Dionysus that no matter what Cleander did, the grain supply was Dionysus' sole responsibility. Even had Commodus been minded to be merciful, Cleander had blamed him openly for what happened and the people of Rome would always remember and always associate his name with the disaster. Dionysus had been allowed to take his own life quietly and without fuss, saving his family the ignominy of a trial for treason and allowing his children to inherit.

Rufinus had felt low about that, and had vowed to commemorate the man appropriately. Yet another obligation to add to his list – he really must visit a mason and get that altar made. But they had all known the risks, and the fact that only one of them had fallen had to be considered impressive, all told.

Rome was recovering.

Perhaps better still, almost as though the gods had approved of Cleander's fall and wished to celebrate it, there were signs that the latest outbreak of plague was finally on the decline. The number of deaths reported was falling daily. The mood of the city was jubilant.

Rufinus still had no idea of his place in it. He had no job as far as he could see, held no rank really, had no business and no property. He had spent the last few days living in the townhouse his father had bought, though it was a poor example, especially given the great villa in Hispania he had sold to finance it. And even then, since the old man had left no will, the house would be contested. Rufinus could fight for it and would probably win, but he just didn't feel like it and, having spent a few days in the house, he didn't really want it anyway. He had nothing. *Was* nothing.

He'd left the Cohort barracks immediately. In the aftermath he had told Pertinax the truth. The prefect had not seemed remotely surprised, though he did not admit that he'd known all along either, and Rufinus left it at that. But, being Rufinus once more, he could hardly continue his career as Centurion Maximus. Perhaps he could still start again in the Cohort as himself, though?

So he'd wandered the short corridors of the dismal town house. He'd sent messages to his patron, Severus, seeking to join him, as Severus surely would have some use for him, but in the wake of such great events and being a consul of Rome, Severus was busy constantly.

In the end, Rufinus had decided that the only way he was going to work out what he was doing was to confront his friends and masters. He needed to have purpose and perhaps enough coin to rent a better house before Publius, Senova and Acheron arrived. And so he had been to Severus' town house early this morning. There he had been informed that the consul was in a meeting with the emperor himself at the palace. Rufinus had refused to be put off, and had marched off to the Palatine.

The consul was indeed with the emperor, as apparently were Pertinax and the new Praetorian prefect, Laetus, in his aula regia, and so Rufinus had joined the queue of noble citizens waiting for the palace's morning *salutatio* and the opportunity to approach and petition the emperor.

The murmur beyond the door grew louder and the crowd began to buzz with excitement. It had been more than a year since the emperor had held his morning meetings in the palace, and longer even than that since a man had not had to go through Cleander to get here.

Finally the door opened and two Praetorians stepped out, making way for the men within. Pertinax and Severus walked into the entrance hall together, chatting quietly, and there the lictors filed out to escort them. Rufinus caught a momentary glimpse of golden Commodus through the door, and contemplated remaining in line for an audience, but decided against it. He had other men to see today.

Slipping out of line, he converged on the two togate men. The lictors, twelve of them traditionally assigned to guard a consul, moved to stop him but Severus noticed his approach and waved his men aside, nodding at Rufinus.

As he fell in with the two men, emerging into the light of a warm summer Roman morning, it struck Rufinus that he was in the company of two of the most important and powerful men in Rome, and yet felt at ease and almost their equal. Few men would even dare approach a consul or Urban Prefect. He was waved over, despite being nobody.

'Rufinus,' Severus smiled as they strolled gently down the slope.

'Consul. I've been trying to see you.'

'Yes, I know. Apologies, Rufinus. Nothing personal, but I do not seem to have a moment to myself these days. Rome and her emperor are demanding of a consul.'

'I'm unsure what to do,' Rufinus admitted, considerably more bluntly than he'd intended.

'You are of a good family, Rufinus,' Severus smiled. 'You have my patronage. The world is your mollusc.'

Pertinax frowned. 'Are you not still officially a Praetorian guardsman?'

Rufinus shrugged. 'I am officially deceased on the records of the Guard. I know military administration well enough to know the endless circular headaches it will cause if I want my position back. Besides, I'm not certain the Guard is for me, now. There is still too much corruption, despite the fall of their master. I don't think I would be very popular. There would be many enemies.'

Severus nodded. 'I tend to agree. The new prefect Laetus thinks he can put it right, but I do not believe so. I think the only way the Guard can return to its former glory would be to be completely rebuild it from the bottom up, using trustworthy soldiers from frontline serving units. I put that very notion to the emperor and Laetus this morning, but have been turned down.'

Rufinus sighed. 'I fear you're right. And if the day comes the Guard is rebuilt then perhaps my place is with them, but I'm still not sure about the moment. I wondered if perhaps either of you had a place for me?'

Pertinax shook his head. 'You did well in the Cohort, and I will provide a good reference for anything you do, but I don't think it would sit well with the men if you returned. You have lied to them for a year and pretended to be someone you were not. I can gloss over that since you have left, but bringing you back in would be a bad idea. The Urban Cohort is not for you, Rufinus, at least not while I remain their prefect. Sorry.'

Rufinus nodded. He'd expected as much, but had to ask.

Severus shrugged. 'I have little need for a soldier at the moment. Now that Rome is settled, I rely only upon my twelve lictors. But, the emperor has offered me a post in the new year. Once I lay down my consulate in the winter, I shall be appointed governor of Pannonia which, as you know well, is one of the most powerful positions in the empire. There I shall have great need of men like you. In the meantime, you remain a client of mine. I shall not see you wanting for coin or a roof.'

Rufinus nodded his thanks. He'd hoped for something a little more concrete than a potential future career and to live off the consul's charity, but it was better than nothing, for certain.

'Is Rome safe again?' he asked suddenly, out of the blue.

Severus and Pertinax exchanged a look. 'Safer than it has been for years, certainly,' Pertinax confirmed.

'But remember your time in Dacia,' Severus reminded him. 'Remember what you told me and bear in mind that men are lining up. The emperor has no heir, and his reign cannot last forever. Sometime, and possibly soon, men will be vying for power. Best to align with one of them now, lest you find yourself torn apart when it happens.'

The look he shared with Pertinax was odd, then, and Rufinus narrowed his eyes. Were these two men setting themselves up as Clodius Albinus and Pescennius Niger had been? Pertinax was close to power and in a strong position, for sure. And Severus would soon be an ex consul in probably the most powerful governorship in the empire. He shivered. At least he was in with both of them, though even thinking like that saddened him. He could not bring himself to think of Commodus as failing. That glorious golden Hercules would surely rule Rome forever?

'Someone is waiting to see you,' Severus said conspiratorially, and nudged Rufinus, pointing off to the side of the path. They were passing Titus' grand arch now, at the end of the forum, and leaning against the decorative stonework was Vibius Cestius, watching him.

He slowed, and the two leading men of Rome waved goodbye as they continued on their way. Rufinus instead wandered over to the side of the arch.

'Cestius?'

'You look like a lost sheep.'

'I am.'

The man smiled and nodded, knowingly. 'I wondered if you might now find yourself with free time on your hands.'

'I am Severus' client. He will find me a position in his military in the new year.'

'Perhaps in the meantime you might give some thought to working for me.'

Rufinus frowned. 'What?'

'You know what we do. You are more subtle and capable than most. You could flourish in our camp.'

'A frumentarius?'

'Don't look so surprised. I can make it happen. Few men in our ranks are direct appointments. Most are brought in by men from inside. That way we can be certain that we take on only the best men. Men who are strong and capable, but also wise and subtle, and most of all utterly loyal to the emperor.'

Rufinus felt a tiny thrill of guilt over that conversation he'd just had with the other two, and buried it deep where hopefully even Cestius couldn't see it.

'I am sort of bound to Severus.'

'That needn't be a problem. But I have great need of you, I think. You know what our prime purpose is?'

Rufinus nodded. 'You are said to slip in among other units and root out treachery and crimes. That's what they say, anyway.'

Cestius nodded. 'That is the larger part of what we do. And, you see, the rot may have been halted in the Praetorian Guard, but it is far from removed. The Guard is tainted to the core, and it is our duty to clear it. You were, and perhaps are still, one of them. You could also be one of us. You see?'

Rufinus' lip twitched. To rejoin the Guard? But also to work for the frumentarii while there? It would be dangerous.

It would be interesting.

An unintended smile slipped onto his face.

Cestius caught it and grinned back. 'I thought you might not be able to resist.'

'I couldn't do much as I was, though,' Rufinus said. 'A grunt doesn't have much authority.'

'You don't necessarily need a lot of authority to do our sort of work, but let me speak to Laetus. He has a number of senior positions to fill since the cull. Tribunes, perhaps, and centurions at the very least. And your record speaks for itself.'

Rufinus felt that tiny tug of pride. To be not only a Praetorian again and a centurion at that? Legitimately and under his true name. Of that, perhaps a man could be proud.

'Alright. I'll do it.'

Cestius chuckled. 'I had a feeling you might. I've already set the ball rolling. If you return to the Castra Praetoria, report to the headquarters and you'll find the records of your demise being rewritten as we speak.'

'Sneaky bastard.'

'Said the man who brought down Cleander.' With a laugh, Cestius shook his hand. 'Go get the records straight. I'll be in touch.'

Rufinus shook his head. A quarter of an hour ago he'd been a man with no place and no plan, and suddenly all that had changed. His memory helpfully supplied him with an image of the old general Pompeianus in the aftermath of Lucilla's plot.

Do not relax yourself, my friend. The game has been complicated and tough, and you won it with courage and style, but you know as well as I that it doesn't end there. There are always more games to be played; always more opponents to face.

Indeed there were.

The great game begins again.

THE END.

HISTORICAL NOTE

Praetorian 4 was always going to be something of a messy plot, and I've known that since this entire arc started in book 2. I was drawing in so many threads, you see. The great game was self-contained, but these last three books have wound through a variety of plot strands. Rufinus has adventures left open to him yet, but here I wanted to bring to an end all those dangling threads. There was Cleander, who had to die. There were the six cavalrymen Rufinus had moved against. There was Severus and his new patronage. There was the devolving of the Guard into Cleander's private army. And finally there was Rufinus' own family troubles. All of this I wanted to pull together.

Then there were the two outside influences on the plot. My forthcoming novel Commodus will deal with Marcia and Cleander in some depth and will give a perspective perhaps missing from this tale. To truly appreciate what was at stake here, you might want to read Commodus when it is released in the spring and see how it all interconnects. But also there is the matter of Rufinus' tombstone. You see, the only real extant reference to Rufinus' entire family is his own tombstone, which has been found. He has the most incredible career path, and while I might play around over the series with the order in which they occur, rest assured that among his career highlights are listed:

PRAEFECTO CLASSIS PRAETORIO MISENENSIS
CENTURIO COHORS […] URBANAE

So yes. He held those roles.

From 187 to summer 190 Rome was a terrible place. Beleaguered by famine and plague, it had been abandoned by many, and all that remained were those who had to be there and those who were too poor to leave. The rich (the emperor being a prime example) had moved to private estates. We know that the plague, which had been brought back west by Lucius Verus after he crushed Parthia two decades before this, and come and gone in waves. It was one of the worst disease outbreaks in Roman history, known often as the Antonine Plague. It may or may not have been the cause of the deaths of both Marcus Aurelius and Lucius Verus. Certainly it killed many thousands of Romans every year.

What we know about the grain shortage is less sure. Most of what we read is coincidental. We only hear of it in the context of Cleander's fall. Let me give you our primary sources:

HERODIAN: *Famine gripped the city at the same time. Responsible for it was a Phrygian named Cleander, one of the slaves offered for sale by the public auctioneer for the benefit of the state. As a slave in the imperial household, Cleander grew up with Commodus and eventually was raised to a position of honour and authority: the command of the bodyguard, the stewardship of the imperial bedroom, and the control of the imperial armies were all entrusted to him. Because of his wealth and wantonness, Cleander coveted the empire. He bought up most of the grain supply and put it in storage; he hoped in this way to get control of the people and the army by making a generous distribution of grain at the first sign of a food shortage, anticipating that he would win the support of the people when they were suffering from a scarcity of food.*

CASSIUS DIO: *A famine occurred, sufficiently grievous in itself; but its severity was vastly increased by Papirius Dionysius, the grain commissioner, in order that Cleander, whose thefts would seem chiefly responsible for it, might incur the hatred of the Romans and be destroyed by them.*

The entertaining but unreliable HISTORIA AUGUSTA puts Cleander's death down to something else entirely. *put to death on false charges as a favour to Attalus, whom Arrius had condemned during his proconsulship in Asia, Commodus could not endure the hatred of the enraged people and gave Cleander over to the populace for punishment.* Given how the other two sources agree and the HA is chronologically distant from these events, I have clearly chosen to go with the grain issue.

Given what we know, then, the details of this famine where Cleander stocks up the grain on the advice of Dionysus, I was given free rein to turn it into a conspiracy. Indeed, Dio largely hints at this with the above passage. This is where writing two series of books becomes really interesting. Marcia's involvement here might seem quite minor, limited to the meeting in the warehouse, yet she is a prime mover in the plot. *'Commodus'* will explain and tell her story in more detail. But in *Commodus* much of the detail of the actual plot is glossed over, and it is only here in Praetorian where I have been able to reveal that detail. It is my hope that the two books will complement one another well.

During the research into what was clearly going to be one of the most complex bits of plot creation in my life, I read up extensively on the grain shipments to Rome and the subject of piracy. I needed to recreate the attempts of Calvia Crispinilla, who had apparently tried to starve Rome from Africa during the revolt of Macer, also engineered by her.

The first issue I had was the composition and nature of grain shipments. I had seen many times reference to the 'grain fleets'. I had assumed automatically that the fleets were specifically constructed, maintained and run by the Roman government, especially given that Commodus later built a new fleet in Africa to ensure steady flow of grain. I was wrong. In one of the earliest examples of mass private contracting, grain shipments to Rome were exclusively the province of private traders, retained by Rome on an ad hoc basis and encouraged despite the terrible dangers posed by year-round sea transport due to strong incentives and benefits. Moreover, the ships do not seem to have had any level of escort. The danger was all borne by the ship's owner. I could easily divert some of these vessels, then, by having a better offer put their way. I did this through Senova. It was quite acceptable, incidentally, and surprisingly normal to find women controlling mercantile concerns for their husbands. They were in charge of the finances for the domus, after all. And so Senova undercut the government and bought out ships, reducing the capacity of the grain fleets available. She could only buy some, though, and probably only ones she could access in Rome and Ostia.

So how could I shrink the grain supply, and strangle the rest of the fleet? One possibility was to have the other ships seconded to the military. It seems that such large capacity merchantmen as were used for grain were also used for troop transport when needed, for they could certainly carry a higher number of men than busy triremes. Triremes were already full of oarsmen and clutter, while merchant ships were almost entirely sail-based and had a huge amount of room. Sadly, thanks to Commodus' reign being a remarkably peaceful one in military terms, I couldn't really have that happen. Moreover, the only real event over these years for the military was the revolt of Maternus in Gaul, which would not have had much effect on ships. And weather and sea conditions could always be hard, but then they usually were anyway, so that was not going to make a lot of difference. That left only one obvious direction: pirates.

If I could have pirates threaten and disrupt the rest of the grain fleet, that would create the stranglehold I was looking for. Common wisdom has piracy all but extinct for most of the Roman empire after Pompey's suppression of the Cilician pirates in the 60s B.C. The next real rise is not until late antiquity, when the Roman fleets had largely disintegrated. Between times there was a brief surge of piracy in the mid-1st century on the Judean coast, sporadic trouble with Black Sea pirates in those regions, and ongoing raids by the Chauci up in Germany and Britain. Not much use to me. My saviour was Philip de Souza, who's books on piracy are unsurpassed. In his *Piracy in the Ancient World*, I latched on to '*It has been suggested that piracy became a more serious problem in the early third century A.D. [...] evidence of a rise in the level of piratical activity in the Mediterranean, indicated by extraordinary measures undertaken by the Roman authorities to suppress it. An inscription from Rhodes, dated to the Severan period, perhaps around A.D. 220, honours Aelius Alexander, who was charged with suppressing piracy at this time.*' This extract, along with another from the same text: '*A Classis nova Libyca, apparently founded in the reign of Commodus, might be interpreted as a response to the recently perceived threat of piracy in this area, but this can only be speculation,*' suggest a possible rise in piracy in the eastern end of the Med between perhaps 180 and 220. Furthermore, in Starr's 'Roman Imperial Navy 31 B.C. - A.D. 324' he refers to the attacks on Hispania Baetica in the mid to late Second century by the Mauri, and suggests that they being 'addicted to piracy' was the reason for the creation of the fleet based there at Cherchell. So now I had an implication of piracy in the western Med, as well as the east. It might be tenuous, but it was what I needed.

The fact that all Rufinus' efforts fail to have the desired effect and that in the end it is nature that causes the disaster is, to me, nicely ironic. And it is typical of Rufinus' luck, too.

Incidentally, the fragments I included about the fleet's grain supply from southern Gaul came purely from reading a timely article on the Roman mills at Barbegal, which are now believed to have been only active for part of the year, indicating that they were only in use during times the fleet was active. Having just learned this as I planned the book, it was too interesting to leave out.

I am driven to add a note here about the level of research that goes into some of the detail of books like this. It might pass the reader by that an author spends probably as much time as they do on writing looking up things like whether the Romans had a goddess of locks. He's called Portunus by the way. And on investigating him, I discovered that there was a goddess of hinges, who made it into the book for fun. Some of the research goes on really minor details, yet ones that I like to try and get right. Moments like that lead to an hour of going back and forth on Google Street View in western Rome, trying to get a handle on where the Aqua Traiana would be visible above ground and where not. It's a tiny detail, but now I will smile whenever I read that passage back. Similarly, Rufinus' dream where he and Philip are handling the velarium awning at the Colosseum led to a little investigation into how many ropes would be required. An examination of the amphitheatre's top in detail reveals that each of the eighty arches around the outer arcade sports three corbels which supported the posts to hold the awning ropes. Therefore two hundred and forty ropes. This is the sort of thing I go to sleep at night worrying over…

As a last note, Senova was a little limited in her role by necessity. This could not be her story, though she played an important part for a short time. And Rufinus' faithful hound simply had to stay out of things. After all, how could a man play clandestine roles with such an obvious giveaway as a giant black hound following them around.

Rufinus will be back in Fires of Tarterus, and rest assured that now he no longer has to hide and that Severus has his back, Senova and Acheron will be with him. After all, think of what awaits in the final years of Commodus reign and the chaos that follows.

And on a light note, for those of you who remember my Facebook challenge for the year (https://www.facebook.com/SJATurney/posts/1538235489593

275), feel free to reference that post and look for your words in this book. If some were in Latin look for their English translation as this is a novel, not 'Wheelock's Latin'. Some though were subject to floccinaucinihilipilification and were left out of the text, which is of course Stupendibus.

Simon Turney, December 2018

If you liked this book, why not try other series by S.J.A. Turney

Interregnum (Tales of the Empire 1)

(2009) *

For twenty years civil war has torn the Empire apart; the Imperial line extinguished as the mad Emperor Quintus burned in his palace, betrayed by his greatest general. Against a background of war, decay, poverty and violence, men who once served in the proud Imperial army now fight as mercenaries, hiring themselves to the greediest lords.

On a hopeless battlefield that same general, now a mercenary captain tortured by the events of his past, stumbles across hope in the form of a young man begging for help. Kiva is forced to face more than his dark past as he struggles to put his life and the very Empire back together. The last scion of the Imperial line will change Kiva forever.

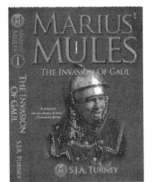

Marius' Mules I: The Invasion of Gaul

(2009) *

It is 58 BC and the mighty Tenth Legion, camped in Northern Italy, prepare for the arrival of the most notorious general in Roman history: Julius   Caesar.
Marcus Falerius Fronto, commander of the Tenth is a career soldier and long-time companion of Caesar's. Despite his desire for the simplicity of the military life, he cannot help but be drawn into intrigue and politics as

Caesar engineers a motive to invade the lands of Gaul. Fronto is about to discover that politics can be as dangerous as battle, that old enemies can be trusted more than new friends, and that standing close to such a shining figure as Caesar, even the most ethical of men risk being burned.

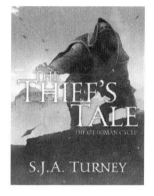

The Thief's Tale (Ottoman Cycle 1)

(2013) *

Istanbul, 1481. The once great city of Constantine that now forms the heart of the Ottoman empire is a strange mix of Christian, Turk and Jew. Despite the benevolent reign of the Sultan Bayezid II, the conquest is still a recent memory, and emotions run high among the inhabitants, with danger never far beneath the surface.

Skiouros and Lykaion, the sons of a Greek country farmer, are conscripted into the ranks of the famous Janissary guards and taken to Istanbul where they will play a pivotal, if unsung, role in the history of the new regime. As Skiouros escapes into the Greek quarter and vanishes among its streets to survive on his wits alone, Lykaion remains with the slave chain to fulfill his destiny and become an Islamic convert and a guard of the Imperial palace. Brothers they remain, though standing to either side of an unimaginable divide.

On a fateful day in late autumn 1490, Skiouros picks the wrong pocket and begins to unravel a plot that reaches to the very highest peaks of Imperial power. He and his brother are about to be left with the most difficult decision faced by a conquered Greek: whether the rule of the Ottoman Sultan is worth saving.

* Sequels in all series also available